EGOFALL

Ego. Paranoia. Murder.

by Tim Kern

EGOFALL
Ego. Paranoia. Murder.

Contents

Introduction

When custodian Tommy Burkett parked his salt-ravaged pickup truck in the far lot at prestigious Lakeview College, he had no idea he would not be driving home at the end of the night shift. He walked out to his truck at two in the morning, lunchtime. It was raining and he couldn't make out the hooded man leaning against the tree. Tommy could see no detail other than the red glow of his cigarette.

The hoarse voice called out, "Hey, kid!" Tommy walked over to him.

Why?

That was all Tommy Burkett could think, as he felt the warm sticky blood pouring out of the jagged slash above his belt. The rain picked up, now torrential. He could barely see. Besides, it was two in the morning -- pitch dark. The man who had attacked him lay face-down on the grass, his hoodie obscuring his face, his cigarette quenched by the driving rain. Tommy had slammed him back against the tree in the momentary struggle, knocking him out.

Why? Who is he? Why did he do that?

But Tommy Burkett had more to worry about than answering questions. He had to get help. His truck was still over a block away, the hospital was on the other side of the river, and the bridge was six miles upstream. Just getting out of the parking lot was a hassle, now that the new security fence and gate system on campus were working. But at the concession barely two hundred feet away, four rowboats nearest the river were unchained.

The river is only a hundred and fifty feet wide, and there are boats right here! I can make it! I can row across!

As he stumbled toward the boats, he asked himself again, *Why? Why would some stranger want to kill me?*

The setup started a year and a half earlier. Here's how things were then...

Chapter 1: Richard Bronner

H. Richard Bronner, president of small but highly-ranked Lakeview College, was heading home from his regular Saturday golf game when his phone rang. "Hi, Richard, this is Jerry Hamilton."

"Well, hello, Jerry. Missed you on the links today. You okay? How's things at the Lakeview PD?"

Lieutenant Hamilton was somber. "Richard, we're friends, or I wouldn't even be involving you in this, but we've had a situation on campus."

Bronner quickly got serious, himself. "Yes? What? What 'situation?' What happened?"

"We had a close call on your campus. A young lady student says she was assaulted, and…"

"Oh, God! Is she okay? What happened?"

"You just asked me that. Calm down a minute, Richard. Let me answer. She's okay, but pretty shaken up. Listen, could you come to the Second Street station? I'm here with the girl and the head of your campus security.

Just a courtesy among friends, but I'd like you to be here. We can fill you in on everything."

"I'll be there in ten minutes, um… Lieutenant. Thank you."

Bronner called his wife. "Hi, Gail… No, I'll be a little late. Can you put dinner in the fridge? I'll warm it up when I get home… No, I don't know when… It's school stuff… Love you!"

"Why don't you ever tell me what's up?" Gail protested.

"Sorry, honey. I'll fill you in on everything when I get home… No! I don't know when that will be." Then, "Sorry, honey. Didn't mean to yell. Just gotta go… Love you, too."

Lt. Jerry Hamilton met Bronner at the police station door. They walked down a hall and into a small room, where a coed was sitting, pale, leaning against a police matron.

“Jill, this is President Bronner. He heard about what happened, and he wanted to come straight here to see you.”

“Hello, Jill. I hear you’ve had a really bad day.” Bronner’s easy manner and middle-aged athletic good looks were attractive and comforting to women of all ages. Jill Schneider, a 20-year-old junior majoring in physical therapy, sobbed a little as she held out her hand to shake his. He was surprised, but took her hand with a firm but unthreatening grip and said in a genuinely caring and soothing voice, “So sorry for you, Jill. Terrible. I’m guessing you’ve already told the police everything. But could you tell me, so I understand?” She nodded, but didn’t look up.

“I was going into the shower, when he just… grabbed me,” she said. Bronner nodded. “He tried to get around behind me, and I screamed and screamed. He yelled at me to shut up, and I just kept screaming ‘Help!’ He let go and backed up and said ‘please,’ even, for me to stop, but by then I was getting mad, and I screamed ‘Help’ louder, then

'Rape! Rape!' and he ran away. Some other girls showed up right then, but… they weren't dressed to chase him outside. You know." She smiled a little, her mouth providing an ironic contrast to her red and teary eyes.

"Have you talked with your parents yet? Can we do anything for you?"

"No. Yes," she said. "I mean, yes I talked with my mom and no, thank you. My parents are in Atlanta. They want me to come home for a few days. They're getting me a plane ticket."

Then she said, "I have exams in two weeks. I'm worried. I'm scared. I don't want to go home, but they really, really want me to. I – I don't need to. All I need is to go somewhere, where I can be safe. But I need to go to class, too. I don't want to go home and mess up the whole semester."

Bronner said, "I assume your arrangement is like all the out of state, on-campus students'. The school says we'll house you on campus and keep track of you, feed you, all that. I have an alternative, if you want to stay here, finish out the semester."

"What's that?" she said, brightening a little as she looked up, catching his eyes for the first time since they shook hands.

"We have a married students' apartment that's empty. If you want to be alone there yet still be in the community, and it's okay with your parents, I could arrange for you to stay there, on campus but not in the dorm, until the end of the semester, or whenever, whenever you feel ready to return to the dorm. Into next year, even. But that's just an option. I'm not telling you what to do. It's between you and your parents."

"Thank you, sir," Jill said, barely audible. "That would be nice."

An officer walked in. "Jill, your father's on the line," and punched the blinking button on the desk phone.

Jill picked up. "Daddy? Hi, Daddy. Yes, I'm all right. I am. I don't need to come home. I don't *want* to come home. Not now, I mean. Finals start in two weeks… No. I don't have to! The school has a place for me to stay, right on campus, but not in the dorm. In married student housing. It's okay – the President said so."

Her father's confused response brought on her first laugh in hours. "No, Daddy, the *college* president! He's right here… Well, okay." Jill turned to Bronner and handed him the phone. "He wants to talk with you."

***

Bronner drove home, where Gail was all questions.

"We had a close call on campus, honey." He explained as much as he knew.

Gail asked, "Why did you get into this? I mean, how did you get into this?"

"Right place, right time, I guess. Jerry was working today and this came in. He thought I'd want to be on top of it. Sorry I was so short with you, honey. It's just – I didn't know anything, and my brain was going a mile a minute."

“It’s okay. I’m… when I don’t know anything either, I get the same way. Sorry I’m always so inquisitive.”

“You’re just a sweet, good, concerned wife. That’s all.” He smiled. “And I forgive you.” They both smiled.

Chapter 2: Perp caught quick

Sunday evening, the day after the incident, Lieutenant Hamilton and one of the detectives gave Bronner some details. Junior Jill Schneider was accosted by a male non-student in the womens' area at the pool complex, between the locker room and the showers. Jill was carrying a towel and shampoo, and was wearing nothing but flip-flops when she rounded the corner and he grabbed her, a detail she hadn't told Bronner.

The detective said, "She has the voice of an opera star and the lungs of a pearl diver. That's what saved her. I mean, she got the creep to practically beg her to stop screaming. Good girl!"

Jill's description helped. He was thin, about five-foot-six, perhaps high-school age, and she didn't recognize him as a student.

Hamilton noted what was obvious to Bronner, "Richard, by the time the end of the year rolls around on a campus the size of Lakeview's, every student recognizes the face of every other student, and Miss Schneider said she had never seen him before.

"We thought right away that we knew the kid she's talking about. We run into him every other month or so, troublesome punk, seventeen years old now, high school dropout, looks in windows sometimes, but I don't think he ever tried anything like this before. When we showed her the boy's mug shot, mixed in with a dozen others, boys with the same general description, she identified him, no question. We picked him up at his parents' house that night."

"And?" Bronner asked.

"He confessed."

Bronner turned in late, couldn't sleep. *This could have been a lot worse! Poor girl, scared half to death.*

Then he got wrapped up in the paranoid 'what if' game. *What if she sues? What if her parents sue? What if this provokes copycats? What if the next rapist succeeds? How could this be my fault?*

He pushed back his sweat-soaked sheets at three in the morning and worked until the sun rose, outlining what he was going to tell the Regents. Then he took a shower, had a slice of toast with his coffee, and got into the car, thinking about the school, where an emergency meeting of the Regents expected him to tell them many things: *What happened? How? Is she all right?*, *Will she sue?* And especially, *What are we doing about it?*

And the big ones for his insecure psyche, *Why didn't you see this coming?* and *What are you doing about it?*

Richard Bronner worried how it was going to be his fault, the next time. How can we prevent this, again? How can I make sure it doesn't land on me?

Chapter 3: Doing something

Gail was up early, but she knew she couldn't interrupt him when he was this intense, working on whatever it was that the Regents were going to see. Bronner got into the car and Gail kissed him. "Good luck today." Bronner just smiled and backed out of the driveway.

***

Most of the Regents were in attendance for the hastily-arranged meeting at lunchtime on Monday. Bronner related the story, adding he had already approved the school's allowing "the young lady" to stay in married student housing with her parents' blessing, and that she was ready to stay through the rest of the year and take her finals on schedule.

"It appears for now that everyone's happy enough with the school. The young lady is staying through. Her parents are satisfied with the living arrangements. They caught the kid. Nobody's calling lawyers.

“So… what do we do, now? We can’t count on being this lucky the next time, and there will be a next time. We all know that. I wrote down some ideas, just off the top of my head. They’re on this handout I’ll be passing around, but I want to hear your ideas, first.”

Lakeview College already had a brick and iron fence surrounding it on three sides. The river provided the fourth and longest barrier. The wall’s one gatehouse was unattended, its iron gate perennially open.

The Regents quickly approved a 24-hour security presence at the gatehouse, and they agreed to convert the other gate to a vehicle-only entrance with card access.

“Fine,” said Bronner. “That will keep this kind of kid out. But it’s for show, not a serious security upgrade. What should we be doing, that’s do-able *and* effective?

“More campus police are about sixty grand each fully loaded, and anything short of an army couldn’t really guarantee campus safety. Five more campus police would allow barely one more person per shift, and would cost

$300,000 per year. And we'd need eight anyway, to cover all shifts, with one floater."

"What's one more cop, on a campus this size?" asked John, a slim engineer from across town and the newest member of the Board, "and what else could we do, so we don't spend an extra twenty-five grand a month, every month, largely for show? Maybe more along the lines of a one-time expense? Video surveillance?"

The only cameras then on campus were in the Communications Department's equipment locker, whence they were shared with the Athletic Department.

John kept up his impulsive talking. "But a camera won't stop anybody. It just makes him easier to find, after the fact," he said. The rest of the attendees were surprised by his brashness and his monopolizing of the conversation. But that didn't slow him down. The other Regents didn't know, but John had quit smoking for good, two days earlier. And he talked some more. "What good, realistically, is even a whole fleet of cameras?"

"Deterrence, John," was the answer from Freida, a wealthy dowager who had been an alumna of Lakeview for nearly sixty years. She dressed in a formal, barely post-Victorian dress, with her huge cloth purse slumped on the table in front of her. She spoke with the natural and hard authority of someone who was the school's largest living donor, the longest-serving Regent. Nobody dared interrupt Frieda, and nobody ever did. She drew her breath. Deep, with an audible wheeze but without difficulty.

"Deterrence. If they think they'll get seen, they won't do it, and if they think they'll get caught, well, that's good, too. And we might actually catch and convict if we have their pictures." She interlocked her fingers and let her hands thump to the table.

Bronner gave the room a moment to absorb Frieda's proclamation, then said, "I was thinking along those same lines. Worked on some rough sketches most of the night. Here's… some ideas," he said, "with a couple options – bare-bones, 'Christmas list,' and something practical, in-between. You'll note that a small system isn't all that much cheaper than a large one. But this is not a proposal – it's an idea that may turn into a proposal. A pro could tell us what we really need. But I wanted to have something for you today."

"How many cameras, and where, and how much would the whole thing cost?" John wanted to know all the details.

Bronner passed out his handouts.

"Remember," Bronner continued, "It's just an idea, covering the building entrances and interiors and as much of the outdoors as seems practical. The cameras won't cover every square foot outside, but they would monitor the high-traffic areas and the building accesses."

Bronner paused, now that everyone was holding their own set of papers. "Take a minute or two to look at the maps and floor plans. Remember, it's just a sketch, just drew it up last night. It's flexible. We might decide to do something else entirely. At any rate, we'd have to consult with real experts to get the final configuration. But I needed to have something realistic to show you, right now. So this is it." Bronner couldn't help repeating himself. He had been up since three a.m.

The engineer spoke up again, as half the room rolled their eyes and sighed. John wasn't shy, or even polite. "Have you priced this out? Does it have, what? two, maybe three monitoring stations? Do we need to hire, like, extra people to watch the screens? Can we record? Are these in color? Will those new sodium vapor lights even show color? What resolution – I mean, if all we get are shadow figures or people so far away they look like dots – does it do any good?"

Freida stopped him again, with an edge on her voice and a steely glance across the table, like an annoyed grandmother. She said, "John, slow down. This is just a design, not even a proposal yet."

Then she looked at Bronner, softening her voice and her look, like a newscaster switching stories. "So, how much for a basic system that would do all this?"

Bronner did his best. "Freida, as you said, this isn't even a proposal yet. But this sketch – thirty cameras, cabling, recorders, screens at three stations – the hardware would be about two hundred thousand dollars. Installation would be another hundred, but we wouldn't need to hire extra security people for every shift – in fact, having one person monitoring these at night would probably be a lot more-effective than having that same one guy wandering around the campus. With these cameras, he could be everywhere at once. We may need a part-time tech, and we'll likely need occasional outside professional help with things."

"So what are we looking at?"

"So, maybe half a million to set up, plus eighty thousand a year for personnel and maintenance. But that's just a back of the envelope calculation. I could be off by thirty, fifty percent, depending on what we find out when it goes out for bid. What we need here is a budget. I mean, if this is what we want to do at all."

John snapped, "Since we in fact have no idea – 'around half a million' is a lot of money, and vague at that – since we don't know, let's see if we can get a formal quote. I say, let's send out an RFP – he looked around the table – a Request for Proposal for… Hell, Richard, we don't have a bill of materials. We'll need to give a spec for coverage, and see what they come up with." John had worn out his welcome, and the looks from around the table reinforced that. John quit talking.

Bronner was more surprised than offended at John's inappropriate manner, but he didn't show it. In fact, Bronner looked like the only one in the room who wasn't ready to strangle John. "Okay, I know this is difficult, and we have several carts in front of our horse. Poor horse, he doesn't even know which cart we want him to push." Everyone laughed. Well, chuckled. "We need to figure out how much we can spend on whatever we plan to do. Can we find half a million dollars somewhere?"

"You know that won't be enough," Freida said, "no matter what we find out. Why so little?"

"Well, if you can find more, that's great," Bronner said, "but half a million would get us in so deep we couldn't quit, and it would be easier to go to the alumni for, say, another two hundred to fund this one-time emergency than it would be to sell them on a seven hundred thousand dollar system, right from the git-go. And we may be able to roll this out in stages."

Frieda pressed. "For instance?"

"For one thing, we could do no hiring for real-time monitoring. We could review the recordings only when we had a suspicion or a complaint. For instance, we could wire the most-vulnerable buildings. We could put cameras in the high-traffic areas, first." He paused, drew a breath. "It really doesn't matter. We simply have to do it. Or do something. And whatever we do, it's gonna cost a lot of money. But no matter what it costs, we can't not do it, we can't not do something significant."

"All right, I get it," said Frieda. "And think -- we don't need to know where the money's coming from at this exact moment. We just know we have to get it, somewhere, and if that means delaying the new dorm for a year, well, that's what we'll need to do. Or maybe something less drastic -- get a little here, a little there, and make up a decent piece of funding, maybe get a loan from an angel. I can't donate a large sum this time, but I can guarantee a loan, if it comes to that.

"But I agree, doing nothing -- that won't get us anywhere. I worry about the safety of our kids. This isn't 1970 any more. Somebody's going to get hurt. And next time, for sure, we'll get sued. Where are we going to get the money for that?"

The Board authorized Bronner to put out an RFP, with an initial budget of half a million dollars. They would deal with the personnel and maintenance later.

***

The Board balked at some of the add-on enhancements he requested as the project took shape, but Bronner was adamant about "doing something" big and obvious, and his influence was matched by his paranoia and ultimately by his influence. The final spec used more cameras, covered more area, required less live monitoring, and cost just under half a million dollars. It was functioning before the fall semester began, and it covered much of the grounds, plus building entrances, stairwells, and hallways.

One frill that Bronner insisted on, to show that "Student security is our top priority," was a monitoring station in his office, where an array of eight screens could cover views all over campus, day and night. From here, he could personally watch most of what went on, all over the campus. Bronner insisted, admitting that the bank of eight screens was more for show, that it wasn't his job, blah, blah, blah. But Richard Bronner didn't want anything to ever expose him to a charge of not caring.

***

Even the locker and shower areas were monitored, which was a bad idea. “I don’t care if that’s where we had the problem,” said John, still craving his tobacco, at the Board meeting following the installation. “It’s not just that it’s probably illegal. It’s just… wrong!” This time, everyone agreed.

Bronner ordered the feed from the lockers and showers disconnected. Since relocating the cameras would cost more than leaving them in place, they left them where they were, “turned on” but disconnected, their little red LEDs brilliant, giving comfort to all.

Security established an automatic camera rotation in their main office, but the locker room and shower cameras were not part of it. They remained powered up, their cabling remained in place, but their feed went nowhere. Across campus, all the cameras were “on” all the time, though only eight could be watched at any time from Bronner’s office.

Students saw the “hot” cameras and complained through the Student Government. The strategy – that the cameras were only powered up, that they weren’t connected to anything -- was explained quietly to the student leaders, who understood and spread the word informally over the campus. Anyone not affiliated with Lakeview College, should they be in the area, might think they were being watched. Thinking they were being watched, even by the kind of person who would watch a locker room, would be a deterrent.

Chapter 4: Finding rest, away

"When can we get away this year, Dick?" asked Gail Bronner of her husband. Only family and his oldest friends called him Dick. That had been his childhood nickname, and Gail had known him since grade school. In his sophomore year of high school, Harold Richard Bronner tired of his nickname, "Harry Dick," and put out the word that henceforth he was to be known as Richard. And so he was. The "H" was never spoken of again, except when he and Gail were planning their childrens' names. And then, to avoid it.

"We can pack any time now, sweetheart." Richard said. "I'll call ahead and make sure the cottage is ready for us. When do you want to go?"

"Dick, I say let's go as soon as it's ready. This weekend? Can we stay a little longer this year?"

"Whatever you like," he said, happy to be getting away from campus, politics, projects, work. "They do want me back before school starts, though." He laughed. "I have three weeks. How much time can you get away?"

"The Foundation said I can take as long as I want." As a key volunteer at the nonprofit, her job was important, but they also knew not to demand too much of a volunteer. They could survive without her, but she couldn't make it without that feeling of being important and needed. Besides, she was a local celebrity, the public face of the Foundation. And she loved it. "Three weeks. Good."

Chapter 5: The Bronners and White Rock

The Bronners had a "cottage," actually a six-bedroom summer home, near White Rock, Michigan, north of Detroit on the shore of Lake Huron. Like many such places in "the thumb of the mitten," it was built as a getaway by an executive of the Ford Motor Company in the 1920s. Back then, South Lakeshore Road was gravel, and the 120-mile trip from Dearborn took the better part of a day.

Today, I-69 and I-94 come within sixty miles, but White Rock itself remains unincorporated and doesn't look much different from how it looked a hundred years earlier. The water for miles up and down the Huron shore is shallow and crystal-clear, making the area wonderful for wading, but not commercial boating. Life in White Rock is quiet.

Way back in October of 1871, White Rock burned to the ground, but few people noticed, because the killer fire at Peshtigo, Wisconsin, raged the same night. "And by the by," some Michiganders would recall, "that was also the night of the Chicago fire. Yup. Same night." White Rock rebuilt, but it never returned to its pre-fire population or vigor.

From the widow's walk atop the Bronners' hundred-year-old cottage, they could see that the "lighthouse house," a modern private home built with a decorative tower to look like a lighthouse, was still shining… in its bright white paint.

A block north was the ANTIQUES barn at the edge of town, its functional hand pump out front still able to draw water, attracting visitors by the… dozens. And White Rock Creek still donated its clear waters to the big lake.

Some modern technology made it clear that the 21st Century, or at least parts of it, had arrived: a satellite dish lived in the Bronners' back yard, a cell tower was near enough that their phones worked most of the time, White Rock Roadside Park was still the "new" public improvement. Frank's Bait & Tackle had wi-fi, and welcomed people to sit on the porch and use it all day, as long as they bought an iced tea or maybe a cigar – and if they bought a cigar, they agreed to smoke it on the lee side of the porch.

White Rock, in short, was a great place to relax, get to know the family again, and… well, that was pretty much it. It was perfect for the Bronners, who learned to unwind there, take a breath of fresh country air, and think little. Or think deeply. There was no middle ground.

Bronner himself was an ardent runner, participating in over half a dozen marathons a year, always using his runs to sponsor good causes. Gail often went with him on his daily route, riding a bicycle and urging him on while carrying extra water and a first aid kit. Only once had they ever used it, when Bronner set his foot crooked in a rut by the side of the road and the ace bandage Gail carried got him to his feet and back to town. "Well, your chronic paranoia has finally paid off," she joked, as she broke out the kit and wrapped his swollen ankle.

Both the Bronners worked out regularly during the school year, Richard at the school before heading home from work, and Gail, in the little gym they built downstairs. They were trim, fit, and attractive. Beyond that, they dressed impeccably and were always perfectly groomed. Except at White Rock, where they felt comfortable just with being clean. "It's a vacation!" Richard had been saying, every summer for over twenty years. And it always was.

The Bronners, sweethearts since high school, had their traditional Catholic faith guide them together over the inevitable rough spots that came up as they raised their two children to adulthood and negotiated Richard's career, from classroom instructor to professor, to dean, and -- going on ten years now -- the presidency of Lakeview College.

"I married you at 23," he was fond of saying to Gail, "because I was too young and too stupid – too stupid to have married you at 21 or 22." Their marriage was one that their friends pointed to, when their inspiration and faith in

Holy Matrimony were tested. Now, twenty-eight years after they walked down the aisle, their union and friendship were unshakable.

Part of the reason for their marital success was the mutual respect and confidence that allowed them to have private space and time, not because they didn't want to be together, but because they each had many interests, and they didn't necessarily share each other's.

Gail didn't invite Richard shoe shopping, Richard didn't insist Gail run with him every morning, and it didn't bother either of them. "Space is fine in a marriage," Gail said, "but not distance."

They each had their little diversions, their private vices. Gail liked small talk, but being conscious of the Bronner image in town, did her discreet talking with the ladies fifty miles away in Glendale, where she got her hair done and did most of her personal shopping. There, she was liked but her social position in Lakeview didn't carry with it any notoriety. In short, the prestige of Lakeview College was unappreciated there, so the magnifying glass under which she lived in Lakeview was didn't exist there.

Chapter 6: Girls

Richard had a secret side, secret even from Gail, who was still stunning at fifty. But Bronner spent so much of his time on campus that his taste in the womanly form had never aged. He would never cheat on Gail – he loved her intensely, plus there was that Catholic thing – but he couldn't control what turned him on. And coeds turned him on.

The surveillance suite installed in his office provided an unforeseen wellspring for his fantasies. He would pick out a sexy girl and follow her on screen as she spent her day on campus. If she should meet her boyfriend in a stairwell, he would take it all in. Sometimes, he would record these moments on his office system and play them back, over and over, after everyone had gone home. He always erased everything every day. The mood passed quickly, and at any rate, he didn't want anyone to find out.

Gail noticed Richard's lowered enthusiasm and performance, but she ascribed it to his longer hours and, dare she think it, age. *After all, he's fifty now*, she'd say to herself, when they had a lackluster evening together.

But lately, it seemed like it was happening all the time. She worried, but more in a selfish way than in a jealous one, for she knew that when he said he was at the office, he was at the office.

She knew, because she checked. "Trust but verify" was her favorite piece of advice, and her husband knew it.

"Honey, of all the things you do that make me crazy," he started, "and there aren't that many of them anyway, this -- calling me at work -- is on the top of the list."

"I worry, dear," Gail said. "When it gets late and I don't hear from you… You're not the only one here who's paranoid, you know." They both laughed. But it was important to her, and he knew it.

"But I always call if I'll be late. When I get into a project, I need to concentrate. That's why I leave a lot of important stuff for later, when everybody's gone home, when nobody will call – so I can get things done, things that require thought."

"But I'm only calling for a minute, just to…"

"Sweetheart, look. Every time you stop my flow of thought for two minutes, it takes me twenty minutes to get back on track again. If you want me home earlier, don't keep interrupting me!"

Those conversations happened every couple weeks for years, but neither Gail nor Richard ever changed their habits.

***

Richard Bronner now found another reason for staying after hours: coeds he caught on camera.

He developed a less-risky system for providing background graphics for his self-amusement. Instead of watching a video, with the risk of being discovered or surprised by a visitor, Bronner would print selected stills. He kept some, but used most of the others just once, and shredded them.

But familiarity soon wears out its original effect, and Bronner, now into a habit, yearned for greater stimulation.

When one of his screens lost its signal one day and the IT guy came in to fix it, Bronner remarked on the swarm of cables in the bottom of the console. Most of them weren't hooked up. They were just lying there.

"What are all those 'extras' doing?" Bronner asked.

"There's a cable from every camera on campus in here, but we only hooked up eight of them," was the reply. "I mean, how many can you watch at one time? And you're the President. Not your job, right?"

"You mean every camera on campus is sending a signal right here, and nobody's watching it?"

"Right. Well, you're not, anyway. It doesn't hurt anything, and, like today, when something goes wrong and you want all the screens to be showing something, we can hook up a different one, pronto." He demonstrated by plugging one of the cables into the back of a dark TV.

The dead screen lit up – with a view of the womens' shower room. The tech recognized what had happened, quickly unplugged that cable, and the screen went dark again. "Oops." He grabbed another cable at random and hooked it up, and Bronner had a lovely view of the entrance to a parking lot. The tech turned to Bronner, who was holding back a laugh.

"So, they're all still working, I guess," the president said.

"Umm, yes," the red-faced tech replied. "But we never hook them up. They're just there because it's a pain to disconnect them and pull all the cable. Besides, if somebody thinks they're on, the cameras 're doing their job, right? So we leave them powered up. But they're always disconnected."

"For the best," Bronner said. The tech closed the panel, packed up his tools, and excused himself.

Bronner said, "Thank you."

Chapter 7: The pres as techie

There were forty-four cameras on campus, including the ones in the locker room. Cables from all the cameras were routed to Bronner's console. Bronner agreed with his Chief of Security that he, as President, did not need even the eight screens they installed in a console in his office. But it was deemed important, for appearance's sake.

Bronner always turned off the lower row of screens, using the controller in his desk drawer. “Too distracting,” he said to anyone who asked. “They work fine, but I don’t need that much going on, and people can still understand that I care, with four screens.” Everyone was accustomed to seeing them dark.

***

One day, Richard Bronner, tired of his limited views, brought a screwdriver and pliers to work with him. After the Administration Building was empty except for himself, he flopped the panel down and turned on the second-last screen in the bottom row. It worked perfectly, showing a picture of the swimming pool. He tried another. Now the monitor showed one end of the running track. Bronner disconnected the cable, then hooked up cable after cable, just to see what camera was on the other end. The ninth cable was one he was looking for. It went to the womens' showers.

He left it plugged in, but didn't tighten the connection. *Cable number thirty-three*, he noted to himself. As he closed the panel, the screen went dark. The cable had fallen off. He was surprised, but *Perfect!* he thought, as he opened the panel, re-plugged cable thirty-three, and carefully, so gently, closed the panel. He figured if someone else opened the panel without taking super-special care doing so, the cable would again fall off the monitor, and no one would know it had ever been connected.

***

Bronner returned to his desk and accessed the console. He turned on the bottom row of screens, and noticed that the pool was empty. But *Bingo!* The showers were full. He stopped at a random moment and ordered a print. His printer buzzed a little. He turned off the bottom row of screens and crossed the room to the printer, where there it was -- his first shower-room print! He repeated the process twice more, with improving results. One picture was definitely a "keeper." He put the test shots in the bottom desk drawer, behind the divider, where they wouldn't be noticed. Then he went to his locking filing cabinet and went through his old stash of stills from the stairwells and here and there. He dropped all but a handful of favorites through the shredder.

Bronner spent the next half hour building his "library," replacing his recently-shredded pictures with new ones from the shower. *Marvelous lighting, too! These are going to be good.*

Gail had a surprise that night, as well, for as soon as Richard walked into the bedroom, and even though they were alone in the house, he closed the door behind him. They were both surprised how early the alarm went off the next morning, and both went to work wearing a look of contentment.

Chapter 8: Bronner's setback

Richard Bronner had a new source of images. He had been content to watch the coeds go through their daily routines and their occasional make-out sessions, but he had just as soon tired of the limited vicarious pleasures that afforded him. With his new views from the "always disconnected" cameras in the girls' locker and shower rooms, he could upgrade his library and then reconnect a random cable to his favorite screen, knowing now that he could switch back at will. He kept the lower row of screens dark, though, to keep everyone used to the idea.

Meanwhile, he had a new stash of "inspiration" in his filing cabinet to keep him going during those boring teleconferences and his frequent phone calls. Gail, who for a while had thought he was "back," soon recognized her familiar old Dick again, boring and flaccid as usual.

Autumn turned to Winter, and then to Spring, and the Bronners' humdrum pattern continued, with the president and his wife used to each other, in love in their way, always mutually supportive, even as the bedroom fire turned to embers. The summer in White Rock, away from campus and the cameras, had brought back some life to the bedroom, but then they were back in Lakeview, back at work, back to their old selves. Especially Richard.

Some nights, he would build his library and come home reasonably early, and he and Gail would have good times. Other nights, when he stayed at the office long enough to go through the library and retire an image or two, he got home "tired."

They were "happy enough," people guessed, but back home the spark was unpredictable. Gail thought it was just the onset of the golden years.

***

Then, on October 9, H. Richard Bronner, 53, was arrested and charged with last year's murder of 29-year-old Thomas Burkett.

While in custody awaiting trial, Bronner was also charged with two counts of voyeurism, the result of files' being found in his office under a search warrant issued as a result of an envelope found in Tommy Burkett's apartment during the investigation following the discovery of his body.

***

"Mrs. Bronner, did your husband do it?" shouted the local TV news lady who accosted her on the Bronners' front lawn.

"Of course not!" Gail shot back, terse, irritated by their uninvited presence. She clutched her dry cleaning under her arm, wound her way past the camera crew and into the car, and left.

Chapter 9: Tommy Burkett

The day Detective Mack Trout called Richard Bronner into the station, all the gumshoe knew was that the body the girls found was Tommy Burkett, a custodian at Lakeview College where he had worked in the maintenance department for six years.

Trout soon learned that Burkett was unmarried, lived alone, had no children. Unremarkable in appearance and accomplishment, he was a quiet but reliable employee who, to acquaintances and co-workers, was content with his life and career. He occasionally had girlfriends, but did not maintain relationships for long.

***

Bronner, neat and methodical to the point of friends' chiding him about being OCD, was in a hurry to get home and so hadn't made his customary circuit of the office that night. In a filing cabinet, in a dark alcove behind an old-fashioned coat tree next to the door, a file drawer hung open.

Burkett came in to clean the office as usual, and he gave the top drawer a push, but a folder was sticking up and the drawer jammed, necessitating additional attention.

***

What Trout didn't know was that shortly after midnight on a Thursday night in late April that year, Burkett was performing routine housekeeping in the office of President Bronner, who worked very late and left the office only after what Burkett described to himself as a "long, muffled" telephone conversation.

What Burkett saw in that folder as he started to rearrange its contents so he could close the drawer – low-contrast color photos of naked coeds – prompted him to make a few mental notes (and two copies) before he rearranged the drawer's contents and locked it up.

When Burkett took his lunch break about 2:00 a.m., he sat in his truck and wrote a note on the back of the previous night's credit card receipt from the gas station where he had filled up on the way to work.

April 20. Found these, others in Pres. Bronner ofc. Top drw file cab. Girls locker room. Don't know the girls.

Burkett drove home just before sunup and put the photos and the note into a brown envelope. It was obvious that the girls didn't know they were being photographed while showering by the women's locker room. A couple times, he pulled the pictures out for a better look. *Cute*, he thought to himself, and pushed them back in.

He dropped the envelope into the top drawer of his dresser. He didn't know what he was going to do with them, but he felt he had something valuable. But no ideas came to him immediately. He showered and went to bed.

Tommy thought about the pictures now and then, but though he sometimes thought he should do something with them, he never concentrated on that thought long enough to come up with any decent ideas. Sometimes he would look at the pictures and wonder who the girls were. But he never recognized them on campus. Didn't remember the faces.

***

Those were the copies Detective Trout would uncover a year later…

Chapter 10: State secrets, paranoia, murder

Bronner couldn't sleep that night. Not only had he been through a stressful day, he hadn't exercised since the weekend, and his body was off its rhythm. As he lay in bed, awake at 3 a.m., another worry crept into his OCD psyche: he had left the office without performing his usual routine, and he had left the filing cabinet open.

Maybe. No, probably. No, for certain – Bronner was looking at some of the pictures while he was talking to a particular grant writer whom he had developed a bad habit of calling late at night.

The grant writer was a recent graduate. She wasn't in any of Bronner's pictures, but she would talk to him, and listen to him as he sorted through his files, looking for just the right picture of a girl to associate with the conversation he was having, as his imagination blended voice, photo, and fantasy together.

Damn! he thought. I'm 100% sure I didn't close that drawer. Then he slept, on and off, for three hours.

When Bronner arrived early in his office, he was exhausted, but he went immediately to the filing cabinet… and it was locked, the drawer in perfect order. Someone put everything away. Bronner was distracted all day, and spent too much time questioning his memory. He knew he had not closed that drawer, yet his strongest hope was that he had. *But I know I didn't. For sure*. Then, *No big deal. Whoever did close the drawer probably didn't look at anything. There's nothing to worry about.* But his mind fed paranoia back on itself in an endless loop. *But what if somebody did look?*

The night he left the drawer open was one of his nights of library-building, and Bronner had hooked two of the "always disconnected" cameras back up, using the cables already in the spaghetti bowl at the bottom of the console in his office, where he supposedly monitored the busiest campus locations on his screens… except at night, when he would review the day's images from his two special cameras.

He wasn't interested in who the girls in the pictures were. He just wanted new, fresh pictures to amuse himself as he made his after-hours phone calls and indulged himself.

The few ladies whose phone calls provided the sound track for his photographic affairs were unaware of his perversion and so were as trustworthy as they were sexually uninteresting, but the photos allowed him to imagine he was talking with someone new and pretty.

***

After another near-sleepless night, Bronner brought his screwdriver with him from home, opened the console, and made certain he had disconnected his special cameras. All the cables were in a jumble behind the console in his office. He just disconnected the #7 and #8 monitors, and hooked up two loose cables that were there from two other random cameras, possibly unwatched since the original install.

By 6:45, he had gathered his photos from the filing cabinet and put them in his briefcase. By 7:00, that briefcase was in his car. He forgot those earliest photos from that first night, still in the bottom desk drawer, behind the divider and abandoned, forgotten once he developed his current filing system, pictures that the police were to find.

***

Bronner knew, he knew the custodian had shut his drawer. *He's the only one who would be there in the middle of the night! But which custodian?* He had no clue. They were all the same.

***

A week passed, and Bronner was again working late. Tommy Burkett walked into Bronner's office, wondering why the light had been left on. "Oh – excuse me, President Bronner. I was just gonna clean your office. I didn't know you're here," and he started to back out. "I can come back later."

"No, come on in. I'm nearly finished, anyway. I've seen you around here before. You're the one who usually cleans this office, aren't you? What's your name?"

"Yes, sir. Every night for almost a year. Tommy Burkett," he said, as he rolled his cart into the office. Tommy instinctively started to the left, his usual routine. He stopped abruptly at the file cabinet. The drawer was open. "Would you like me to close this, sir?"

Bronner looked up and momentarily went wide-eyed. If Tommy caught it, he didn't let on.

"No, not yet. I'm still working on something. I'll get it. Thanks."

"Sure." Tommy laughed. "Just don't leave any state secrets out when you go home."

Bronner didn't look up. He just grumbled, "I'll take care of it." He paused. Then he looked up and said, "Hey, um, Tommy, just skip this office tonight. I'll be here a while longer."

"Yes, sir. Good night." Tommy pulled his cart into the hall and went to the next office, continuing his usual rounds.

He's the one! Bronner thought. *He has to be! What's that garbage about 'state secrets,' anyway? The kid's taunting me!*

Okay, Richard, calm down. He didn't say anything, really. Could have been a joke.

Bronner finished his work after another half-hour. He methodically made the rounds of his office, especially noting that he closed and locked the file drawer.

He got into his car and thought about other things on the way home. But in bed, as he tried to fall asleep, he kept going over Burkett's line. *'State secrets?' What's he talking about? He must know. Why didn't he say something?*

Tommy Burkett didn't have to say anything. Burkett had confirmed himself as the custodian on Bronner's regular office detail. He made a point, despite whether he wanted to, or even whether he was conscious of making it.

Blackmail! That's it. The damn kid's going to blackmail me! But when? For what – what does a kid like that want?

Bronner's paranoia was building, feeding on itself. *When is he coming back to make his demands? What demands? How can I make sure nothing happens? I can get him fired, but what'll that look like? Would anybody look? HR, maybe? Get a grip, Richard. It's nothing. So what if he talks – who'd believe the kid over me?*

***

Bronner mulled over a number of strategies. He had no criminal experience, and he didn't know any criminals, or how to think like a criminal. He didn't even watch crime shows on television, but he knew he was headed down a criminal path. Where would it lead, and how he would get there? He didn't know that, either, but he knew that he was about to go… somewhere, down an unknown, dark lane. And Tommy Burkett was hitchhiking on it.

***

The college president stayed late and watched the janotir's routine for a few nights. Burkett was methodical, his movements routine. He crossed from the administration building to the physical sciences building, across a tree-bordered open area, between 2:15 and 2:20 each morning, and then sat in his truck and ate his lunch.

***

Bronner's neighborhood was pleasant, with neighbors' helping neighbors. The Bronners, like most of their neighbors, maintained a cordial and open relationship in the community.

Women neighbors typically did the old-fashioned homemaker stuff, watching each others' kids and working in volunteer positions, which gave them flexibility as they improved the city and those institutions they helped.

Friends routinely loaned each other tools – and returned them. Howie, down the street, had a pickup truck that select friends routinely used for those small hauling jobs that were too big for their SUVs. Howie didn't mind, as long as the truck was back in his driveway by seven in the morning, with a full tank of gas. And so once or twice a month Howie would be happily surprised by a full tank, even a freshly-washed truck, courtesy of some neighbor he trusted enough to tell them where the key was.

***

The night that Bronner returned Howie's pickup truck in the pitch blackness of the early May rainstorm, he forgot he had taken the unnecessary precaution of leaving the truck's tailgate down. The rain prevented the surveillance cameras from making out the license plate, anyway. He had a lot on his mind that night.

Earlier, Bronner parked Howie's truck in the C Lot on campus. That was at five minutes past two. He waited in the truck, disguised in a hoodie, holding a lit cigarette at the cracked-open window, in case he were spotted. Bronner didn't smoke.

He got out and walked to a tree, using the sidewalk. *How do people keep these things lit in the rain, anyway?*

When Burkett started across the open area and passed into one of the "camera-blind" areas, Bronner was there, leaning against a tree. He called out to the janitor.

"Hey, kid!"

***

Burkett saw the man, a shadowy shape in the dark, the glow of the cigarette doing nothing to light the face in the hoodie's shadow. He shielded his cigarette from the rain by pulling his hood farther forward. Tommy approached the stealthy figure…

Burkett was stronger than Bronner had anticipated. During the downpour and outside the camera's rain-speckled view, the president's knife found its target early in the five-second struggle, but in an instinctive move, the wounded Burkett managed to shove the president back against the tree, leaving no marks on the hooded character, but knocking him unconscious.

Then the bleeding custodian staggered down the shallow slope to the river's edge. Though the nearest bridge was six miles upstream, the hospital was lit up, a beacon of salvation, appearing within his near-delirious grasp on the opposite shore.

Adjoining the property closest to the college was a mom-and-pop rowboat rental that predated the school's latest expansion. Students rented the small boats by the hour as a way to find solitude or, more-often, romance.

Burkett, bleeding inside and out from an amateurish slash to his left kidney, dragged an unchained boat into the water. He hadn't counted on the fast current that the night's rain had brought, nor had he grasped the severity of his injury. *Only a short way,* he thought, perhaps his last thought, as the life drained from his body.

***

They found him, two days later and two miles downstream, in a rowboat obscured by bushes and snagged in a thicket of shoreline brush. One of the oars was missing.

The stab wound was clumsy, amateurish, but it had done its work. The Medical Examiner estimated it took Tommy Burkett about twenty minutes to bleed to death.

Chapter 11: Reality

In these earliest hours, Richard Bronner was dreaming, thinking how calm everything is when the rain is falling. *Gentle. Peaceful. Roll away from the sound...*

Shit! Where is he? Richard Bronner lurched into consciousness, aware of a throbbing pain at the back of his head and the wet grass against his face, the turf turning to mud. He fumbled and slipped getting up, fell back to the ground. He felt something hard and... *Keys! It's his key ring!* Bronner picked up the large ring with its forty-three keys, put it in his pocket. He pulled the wet hood well up, covering all but a small triangle of his face. *Where is he? Shit!*

But Richard Bronner knew he needed to get away, and Tommy was gone. *Where did he go?* Bronner headed for the parking lot, but he didn't know what Tommy drove. *That old Ford pickup! That's got to be it!* But that wasn't it, or at least Tommy wasn't in it.

I've got to get out of here. Richard Bronner got into Howie's pickup and drove to his friend's house, concentrating on driving at a normal speed, a little – but not too much – over the speed limit. He pulled into Howie's driveway where he left the key atop the left rear tire, as usual. He walked the half a block home and slipped into his own garage, hid his wet clothes and changed into fresh, lest he be discovered crossing the dark house to the bathroom where he took a shower. Then he got dressed for real, went to the kitchen, and started making breakfast.

***

"G' morning, honey," said Gail Bronner from the cover of her terrycloth robe. Her hair was fresh from the shower, styled by the towel it was mostly wrapped in. She wasn't wearing any makeup, and Richard didn't care.

"You're looking delicious this morning, honey," he said. Richard's sweetheart since high school, she was to him still the prom queen runner-up where he graduated as valedictorian and a track star, two years before she did.

"Up so early? Something special going on at school?"

He leaned toward her, still fiddling with the sizzling bacon on the stove, and gave her a little kiss on the lips. "Just getting ready to wind up the year," he laughed. "I somehow think if I get to the office a little early, we can wrap up exams early. No matter how many springtimes I try, though, it's always the same. But I can't change."

"No, you can't. I just don't understand how you can be so lighthearted about the most serious part of the school year, early in the morning, when you're usually so OCD and paranoid about everything else. But don't change. Just make mine over easy."

***

When dawn arrived, no one noticed that Tommy Burkett's truck was in the parking lot, but his boss on the college's custodial team saw that Tommy hadn't clocked out that morning. *I'll talk to him tonight*, thought Bill Gunther, and he made a mental note to call Tommy when he started his shift that night.

But at 11:30, when Bill crossed the parking lot on his way to grab lunch, he noticed Tommy's truck, parked in its usual spot. Tommy wasn't due in until eight that night. And Tommy wasn't in it. Bill keyed his campus radio.

"Hank? Hi. Bill. Say, have you seen Tommy Burkett? …Yeah, you know him. Hell, he's been here five or six years. Skinny blond kid. Thirty, maybe, works nights… Yeah, you haven't seen him around this morning, have you? …No. It's just… Well, if you see him, have him call me, okay?"

Bill's day was busy, and, though he wondered why Tommy just up and left, Bill was involved in his work and didn't think about Tommy again until his shift was nearly over. He didn't know if he had to get a fill-in for Tommy. He hadn't heard from him all day. *He's not like that.* So he dialed.

Tommy's truck was still in the lot, and his phone went straight to voicemail.

***

The desk officer at Lakeview's main police station didn't want to argue. It was almost dinnertime. "Look, mister… Gunther, I'm sorry you can't find your employee. But I can't just up and file a missing person report on an adult." He tried to help. "He's not your kin or anything, is he? Does he need medical care? Have a history of mental illness? Anything?"

Bill Gunther just shook his head. "Aren't you even interested?"

"I'm trying to help you here," the officer said, irritated. "If you don't have any evidence of foul play, we really can't do anything. Anything at all."

"Well, good night, officer." And Bill Gunther drove to Tommy's apartment and banged on the door. All was quiet. The door was locked. Tommy Burkett's truck stayed in the campus parking lot for another night while Tommy didn't come to work.

***

And so Bronner finished breakfast with Gail and went to work just like it was a normal day, the morning he stabbed Tommy. He parked his own car in that parking lot and walked slowly toward his office, looking for anything that might be evidence, but not being obvious about it. The rain had washed away the blood, and he couldn't find the soggy cigarette butt. *There's a butt!* He ground it into the mud. His OCD wanted him to pick it up, and his paranoia nagged him. *Maybe that wasn't mine. Maybe there's one here with my DNA all over it. Maybe somebody...*

In the office, he slumped into his chair and remembered he had the custodian's key ring in his pocket. He dropped the keys into the bottom drawer of his desk, slid the drawer closed and laid his head down on his arms which he had crossed in front of him on the desk. Bronner slipped into an exhausted, uneasy sleep as his overloaded brain dismissed the keys.

Chapter 12: It's Tommy

It was the middle of the next day, almost eighteen hours since Bill Gunther banged on Tommy Burkett's apartment door, and some thirty-three hours since Tommy Burkett had stolen the rowboat in his unsuccessful attempt to save his own life.

At the Bronner house, Gail unloaded the washer. She thought she caught just the faintest whiff of stale cigarette, but dismissed that thought and opened the dryer, cleaned its filter, and unloaded it onto the sorting table. *How sweet of Dick to do a load, she thought.* Then, *Hmmm, I don't remember him ever wearing a hoodie.* And she folded everything and put it all away.

***

Along the muddy bank of North Branch River, in an eddy under a canopy of overhanging bushes, Abbi and Shannon, two high school girls on their lunch break, spotted a marooned rowboat through the heavy greenery.

"What's that?" Abbi said, "Is that a boat down there?"

They worked their way down the slick bank to get closer, each relying on the other to keep from sliding into the river. “Oh my God!” Shannon screamed.

“Oh my God!” Abbi echoed, as the horror filled her vision. Then “Shannon!” as she slipped, dragging her friend down to the river as she half-slid, half-tumbled down the slippery bank.

They gasped, whimpering unintelligibly as they scrambled back up, feet ineffectively digging into the mud, their hands frantically grabbing at the tiny roots and saplings that punctuated the steep incline. At the top, the girls collapsed on the tall, thick grass. Both girls were crying. Shannon was hysterical. Abbi managed her phone with a gritty, muddy hand.

"9-1-1. What is your emergency?"

Abbi’s young voice said, in a barely controlled yet very measured cadence, "We're in Shadybend park, and there's a dead body in the river… in a boat."

"Where are you, exactly? And are you sure the person is dead?"

Abbi screamed, “Just come here, now!”

Police arrived at the grisly sight just ten minutes later. The girls were still collapsed on the wet grass, shivering in spite of the day's humid heat, sobbing and comforting each other. They couldn't find the strength for anything but to stay right where they were.

A police matron helped them to their feet and back to a squad car where they told her what they had seen and how they came upon the awful sight.

At the river, the crime scene team secured the boat, took measurements. The fully clothed body of a thin blond man was face-down in the half-swamped boat, bloated, soaking in rainwater-thinned blood. One oar was in its lock.

It was a still, warm afternoon, and the smell was nauseating. Flies swarmed everywhere. They called for a trailer and the Medical Examiner, and they photographed everything. One tech, overcome when they rolled Tommy’s body and saw his face, had to run to the nearby bushes to hurl his lunch.

Half an hour later, the police hauled the boat a hundred feet upstream, to where the bank flattened into a little beach. They dragged the boat from the water and examined and removed the body. The bloated white male had a leather loop on his belt, broken. It was the kind of loop for a large key ring, but the ring and the keys were gone. The man's wallet carried a credit card, some soaked papers, $21.00 in cash, an insurance card, and the driver's license of Thomas Burkett. They put the boat on their trailer, and the body into the ME's van.

***

When police went to Burkett's apartment, they found the envelope containing the shower scenes and the gas station ticket from the previous month. The thermal-print receipt for the tank of gas on April 19 was still legible, with the ink from Tommy's note bleeding through from the back.

Detective Trout identified the pictures' location soon enough. To him, the pictures – and the note mentioning where Tommy found them -- looked like a motive. To the judge, the pictures with Tommy's note looked like enough evidence to issue a search warrant for Bronner's office.

***

Bronner's secretary called him on his cell. "Richard, they're here, and they're going into your office. I tried to stop them, but…"

"Hold on, Lisa, who's here? Who's where?" Bronner had no idea what she was talking about.

"The police. They have a search warrant for your office. They're in there right now."

"Thanks, Lisa," Bronner said. "I'm on my way. Just be nice to them. Coffee if they want it. Stay calm."

The police found the old pictures. They also established that the cables from the locker room cameras were in the console, and, like all the other excess cables, hot.

The "Eureka!" moment in the search came when a latex-gloved hand displayed Burkett's key ring, discovered on the bottom of the desk drawer. “Ka-ching!” said Trout, smiling like a Cheshire cat.

Bronner burst into his office. “What’s going on here?” he asked Detective Trout. Nobody said anything. They just showed him the search warrant and escorted him back out.

Bronner’s mind was spinning. He was worried that they would find his pictures…

***

Another summer passed, the Bronners vacationed again in White Rock. The bedroom, or maybe the air at White Rock was better than at home, Gail reasoned. Of course, Richard didn’t have a “library” in the White Rock house, so he wasn’t chronically “tired.” Gail noticed, and Richard didn’t know she noticed.

This year, Gail’s curiosity about her husband’s up-and-down behavior hit a peak. She dug his hoodie out of the closet and brought it with them to Michigan. She didn't know what she had in mind, just… something. Maybe.

"Here, honey. I was thinking… some mornings when you go running, it's positively chilly, so I brought this for you."

Bronner hadn't given the hoodie a thought for over a year, and was startled at its sudden appearance. He stared at it for a moment, but recovered. "Ahhh, thanks, sweetheart. I love this thing, but I forgot I even had it!" But he never wore it, even on those chilly mornings. And she noticed.

Richard didn't tell her about the search of his office, and they were off to White Rock before the delicately-phrased story appeared on the Lakeview paper's page 4.

***

Over the summer, the prosecution worked on its case. Late in the summer, Hamilton walked in on Detective Trout, whose expression said it all. "Hey, Mackerel," the lieutenant said, "You look like a hen who's trying to hatch a rock. What's up?"

"Jerry, we've got him," Trout said, "but we don't have anything like a perfect case."

Lieutenant Hamilton was angry, disappointed, then angry again at what his friend had done. "We've got to sew this up. He's away on vacation. He knows we're working on this, but he's not going to run. Too much at stake, and he's too self-confident. Probably hasn't even told Gail yet. What, exactly, do we have?"

Mack Trout – he hated "Mackerel," but he let it go this time -- pushed his chair back from the desk that must have been there, under piles and piles of paper.

"Jerry, we have everything we need to convince ourselves, but nothing that'll nail him in court. We have the pictures in Tommy's apartment, but Bronner says he doesn't know what we're talking about, and none of those pictures match the ones we found in his office, and they aren't from any printer we can find on campus.

"We have some surveillance videos that show somebody leaving the parking lot and heading in the direction of the Administration Building, and Tommy coming out at about the same time. Then the guy staggers out of camera range, toward the boat rental."

Hamilton broke in. "But the other guy in the video – not Tommy, the other guy?"

"Not definitive. We're pretty sure that was Bronner arrived in that truck, but we can't ID the truck, and Bronner doesn't have a truck, and he didn't rent a truck. The guy in the truck looks like he's smoking. Bronner doesn't smoke, and we didn't find any useful cigarette butts. And when the guy left in the truck, it was, like, twenty minutes after Tommy walked off. If he's the one who did it, why would he hang around for twenty minutes?"

"Or was his being there just some weird coincidence?" Hamilton offered.

Trout sniffed, "That would be a hell of a coincidence, since we didn't see anybody else anywhere, during that whole time period, or for nearly an hour, either side. But again..."

“What else? The keys?”

“He says he found ‘em and dropped ‘em in his drawer, then just forgot. We know he’s lying, but it’s totally plausible to a jury.”

“Maybe he did forget. I mean, why else would they still be there?” Hamilton asked. Then, “Do we have any other suspects? Or do we have anything that matches Bronner’s habits or methods?”

“Simple answer to that: no,” Mack said. “We don’t have any evidence that anyone else was on that part of campus anywhere near that time. Assuming it is Bronner in the hoodie, of course.”

“And his history?”

“I’ve spent lots of time on that. Our H. Richard Bronner is a stinking Boy Scout. Had a parking ticket about six years ago. Got sent to detention once in high school – a fight he wasn’t even in, after a track meet. Marriage looks solid. His wife’s the only girl he ever kissed, far as we can tell. Not even any rumors that I can dig up. And he's lived around here his whole life."

"Finances?" Hamilton kept looking for angles.

"His house is almost paid for. His car loans are up to date. Can't find any late payments on anything. Always pays his bills on time. Had two insurance claims, but nothing suspicious. And the last one was nine years ago."

"Outside business?"

"This guy lives for his family and the school. He helps Gail now and then on her volunteering – well, he shows up in his tux for the benefit dinners. Always doing little things around town, charity stuff, but not involved to any great degree. Everybody loves the guy."

Hamilton sat down, exasperated. "So, why do we think he did it?"

Trout replied, "Wasn't it Sherlock Holmes who said something like, 'If you've eliminated all other possibilities, whatever remains must be the truth?'"

"Yeah, but that's a fictional guy and, well, Trout, anyway, no offense, but you're not Sherlock Holmes. And I don't know that we've eliminated 'all the other possibilities.' So, opportunity? We'll say sure, why not? Motive?"

"It's got to be something to do with the pictures." Trout got up, refilled his coffee cup. "Or the keys."

"Okay, the pix. I'm not gonna bite on the keys. He could get any keys he'd want, and I believe him when he says he forgot them in his desk. Why would he keep them on purpose? Can we assume the gas receipt – April 19 – was from the day Tommy found the pictures? Otherwise, why would he have stuffed it in the envelope with 'em?"

"Even if we do," Mack replied, "Tommy wasn't killed for another three weeks. What happened, to get him killed? You don't s'pose he tried to blackmail Bronner?"

"Too easy," Hamilton said. "Bronner could just deny. And what do we know of Tommy that would make him think of blackmailing the big boss? And what would take him so long?"

"But," Trout added, "even the pictures don't make sense. They weren't printed on Bronner's printer. Or on any printer on campus. And the fingerprints are old, not readable."

"But the pix are from the same camera. Surely that's something," Hamilton said.

"But what does that *prove?*"

"Proves that either Bronner's the smartest crook in the world, or he's such a lucky dumbass he could get away with it."

"Or that he didn't do it," Trout offered, raising his coffee cup in a mock toast. "Why are you so involved, anyway, Lieutenant?"

"Shut up," Hamilton mumbled. "He's been a friend of mine since my kids were babies." Then, changing gears, "Do we have anything that'd let us get a warrant to search his house?"

"Like what – to see if there's a knife in there, or a hoodie, or a pack of cigarettes with only one gone?" Trout lifted one eyebrow.

"Do we have any idea what kind of knife he used?"

"Nope," Trout answered. "We don't know anything except that the blade was at least two and a half inches long. Like just about every knife on the planet. The wound was so ragged, too. Whoever it was stabbed him, he's either stone cold or a total amateur."

"So, we're not gonna go look at his house?"

"Can't get a warrant."

And Hamilton said, "But maybe we can get in."

***

Next week, the Bronners came home from Michigan. Richard wasn't home. Gail answered the door. "Hello, Jerry," she said to her husband's old friend.

"Hello, Gail," he said. "I'm afraid this is not a social call." He turned to his chubby sidekick. "This is Detective Trout. May we come in?"

Gail offered them a seat, didn't ask, just poured a couple Diet Cokes over ice.

"Gail," Jerry began, "We're on this Tommy Burkett case, and I can't believe it, but things are pointing to Richard's having something to do with it. Can you help us with anything, anything that might clear his name?"

"Jerry, I don't know a thing about it. We don't talk about it, and the papers – we've been gone, and I don't really follow it, anyway. It just gives me the creeps. All I can say is, I know Richard didn't have anything to do with it, and I hope you catch whoever did it."

Trout: "If I may, Missus Bronner?" She nodded. "Does Richard have a pickup truck?"

"No. No, he doesn't," she said. "He almost never needs to haul anything, anyway."

"What does he do, then? Does he rent a truck?"

"No, he usually just borrows Howie's, down the street."

Hamilton gave Trout's foot a little kick.

"Howie who?"

"I don't know, really. He's Richard's friend. I hardly ever see him. Just Howie, down the street. He's about five or six houses that way."

"Okay, thanks." Trout was pretending to be calm. He'd have to wait to learn more about Howie. "And this may sound strange, but… does Richard ever wear a hoodie?"

Gail was taken aback. "No. I mean, y…yes. I mean, he has one, but I've never seen him wear it. Why?"

"Could we see it?" Jerry asked.

Gail went back to the family room, where she hadn't quite finished unpacking all the vacation stuff. She grabbed the hoodie and brought it back into the living room, handed it to Hamilton.

"This? Have you ever seen him wear it? It looks almost new."

"No," she said. "As far as I know, he's never worn it. But I know he must have. I pulled it out of the dryer."

"When?"

“A long time ago. Like spring of last year. I took it with us to Michigan this summer, for…” and she stopped, looked at Lieutenant Hamilton. “You don’t think it means something?”

“Can’t tell, Gail. May we borrow this?”

Gail nodded again, as Detective Trout pulled out an evidence bag from his valise, and put the hoodie in it.

Then she cried a little. “Jerry, did I do the right thing?”

Hamilton said, “Thanks, Gail. I hope it’s nothing, too.” And the police left by the front door.

In the car, Trout said, “Now let’s go find that Howie guy.” Though they looked up and down the street, they didn’t find any nearby pickup truck. Howie was at work.

But that evening, when Howie came home, Trout was watching the street and saw him park the truck and place the key on top of the rear tire. He drove up, blocking the driveway, and took a few photos of Howie’s truck.

Trout walked up to Howie’s door and knocked. “Hi. Detective Mack Trout, Lakeview PD. Got a minute?”

“Sure, officer. C’mon in. What’s up?”

“Detective,” Trout said, grumpy because he hadn’t eaten since breakfast. “Could I ask you a few questions about your truck?”

“Ahhh, sure. Why not? What do you want to know?” And Howie explained the ‘system’ he used with his most-trusted friends, identifying Bronner as one of several.

“Thank you, Mister…”

“Keefe,” he replied.

“Thank you, Mister Keefe. Have a good day.”

Back at the station, Trout asked to see Bronner’s credit card receipts for the days around Tommy’s death, and… there was a gas receipt dated the same day they found the body, for a little over twenty gallons, more than Bronner’s car held. And no time stamp. Still, that was another piece of the puzzle. Maybe.

“Of course, that purchase might not have shown up on his card for a day or two,” Hamilton noted. “But I think we’ve got him.”

The crime lab's analysis of the hoodie came up clean. "Either he washed it more than once, or he never got anything on it in the first place," the tech told Trout. "But there's nothing good on here, not a speck of blood or even a single hair. Doesn't smell like anything. Wonder what kind of detergent she uses. A little organic material, 'dirt,' you'd call it – that's all. Could have been from anywhere around here."

"Even the campus at Lakeview?"

"Yes. Or just about anywhere else within a couple hundred miles."

"Thanks," said Trout. Then, "It didn't smell at all?"

"You smelled it, too. Smelled like… cotton."

***

Hamilton called Gail directly. "Hello, Gail. Can you talk? Personal, this time."

"Sure, okay, Jerry. What can I do for you?"

"I mentioned to my wife how absolutely clean that hoodie was. What kind of laundry detergent do you use?"

“Arm and Hammer unscented. It ought to be clean. I washed it like, four or five times to get the cigarette smell out. Don’t know why it had a scent. Richard doesn’t smoke. Maybe he wore it in somebody’s car.”

“Ya never know. Well, thanks, Gail. Arm and Hammer unscented, right?”

“Right, Jerry. Any time. And say hi to Linda for me. ‘Bye.”

Chapter 13: Bronner's trial and undoing

Bronner's trial began, and the entire community was on his side. Heads of prominent charities lined up to testify to his character. Women of every description testified to his acts of kindness and his willingness to help them start careers.

No one remembered anything incriminating, or even anything negative, about Richard Bronner. There were no "other women." There were no spurned and vindictive business associates. Nobody owed him money, and he didn't owe anybody, either. Richard Bronner had always treated everyone he met with courtesy, friendliness, and professionalism. The whole city considered him helpful and generous. Corporate heads, deans, students – even Jill Schneider, the student who had been grabbed in the shower, walked into the station just to tell the police what a great guy Bronner was. And state and national officials – everyone who knew him, or even dealt with him, knew he was innocent, and everyone wanted him to be.

Bronner's problem, to the extent he had one, wasn't with the police. It was with the Regents and particularly with his wife, though her private doubts were invisible behind her public support.

Of course I'll get fired if I get convicted, Bronner knew, *but I have that beat.* What he worried about was the vague morality clause in his contract. *If the Regents get cold feet, that's all it'd take – I'd be out on my tush. And Gail? – all she needs are enough of her own doubts... and she's asking questions. I've got to convince Gail...*

***

The trial went well for Bronner. He sat quietly through the procedure as his lawyer dismantled the circumstantial case presented by the District Attorney. The evening before they planned to rest the case, Bronner decided to tell Andy, his lawyer and friend for over a decade, his idea.

"Just sit tight. You have this case won," said Bronner's attorney.

"I know I have it won, any way you look at it. It's all circumstantial, and they didn't get anywhere. There are multiple explanations for everything, and all I need is reasonable doubt. You've told me this before."

"Then don't screw it up. Jee-sus, Richard. Just keep your mouth shut and walk out of there a free man. This is a murder case! It's serious."

"Look, Andy, it's not about the murder. They won't hang that on me. They've got nothing. This is my chance to clear my name, in front of all those people who believe in me. But especially in front of the Regents. And more especially for Gail. She just has to believe I'm innocent."

"But she's already told everybody you're innocent."

"Come on, Andy. She has to. In public, she'd say she believed me, even if she watched me do it. What she says in this case means nothing. It's what's in her head that matters. And what's in her heart – and I have to make her truly and absolutely know that I didn't do it. I love her. I love the kids, my little granddaughter."

"But Richard, it's a completely different thing to take the stand in your own defense. First off, you don't need to do it. That alone should be sufficient. But second, it can't help the case…"

"…and it won't hurt it, either," interrupted Bronner, believing in his ability to convince anyone of anything, and the necessity of trying.

"Good God, Richard! You're not going to testify! You can't plead insanity at this point, but that's what I'd have to argue, if you do this! It's out of the question. I won't let you do it."

"I have to, Andy. It's the only way she'll truly believe me. And don't worry. I can handle my thoughts. I can control the testimony I give. I can convince anybody of anything, truth be known. And if you're serious about 'not letting me do it,' you're fired. Clear?"

"Richard, you're winning. This is in the bag. If you do this, you could cast a doubt on your whole case. And if you fire me, you'll have to go through a whole 'nother trial. And you're winning! For God's sake, Richard, sit tight. Don't do this."

"I have to. Don't worry. Just wish me luck."

***

So the last witness for the defense was Richard Bronner. His ego had compelled him to testify and convinced him of his invulnerability.

The gavel fell. Bronner was sworn in, then on the stand. Andy began. "President Bronner, is it your wish to testify at this trial?

Bronner began. "It is."

"Have I advised you against testifying? Have I explained that the State's case is circumstantial? Have I explained that the Fifth Amendment guarantees your right against being forced to testify against yourself? Have I explained to you that court, by its nature, is unpredictable and that you may reveal thoughts you have that may unintentionally enhance the prosecution's case?"

"Yes, and I thank you for that. But it is my decision, and solely my decision, to testify on my own behalf, if the Court will allow it."

The judge raised an eyebrow. Then both, as he looked straight at Andy, who continued. "May I at least ask your reasoning, to clarify your decision to the Court, for the record?"

"I know I am not guilty. But I want to dispel any doubt of my innocence in the minds of the community, the Regents, and especially my wife and family. I believe that my testimony cannot hurt my case, since I am innocent, and I believe that only good, and a total clearing of my good name, can come about by my taking the stand."

Andy turned to the judge. "Will the Court permit my client?"

The judge looked at the prosecutor, who shrugged while unsuccessfully suppressing a shark's smile. "As you wish," declared the judge. "This court is in recess until 10:00 a.m. tomorrow.

***

By 10:15 the next morning, Bronner had been sworn in. It was time for the prosecution's direct examination.

"President Bronner," the prosecution began, "Did you know the deceased, Mr. Burkett?"

"Yes."

"In what way?"

Bronner controlled himself, sticking tightly to the questions. "He cleaned my office."

"When did you last see him?"

"Last spring. April, May a year ago, I think. It was night."

The prosecutor had this guy. He was pumped on adrenaline. "Before he was killed?"

"Uhhh… yes. Before." The courtroom filled with more snickers than the Mars Candy Warehouse. The judge smiled.

"Order," he said. "Proceed." The assistant DA composed himself.

"Where?"

"In my office. He came in to clean it."

"Did you exchange words?"

"Yes, a few."

"About what?"

"About, 'You can skip cleaning tonight,' and 'good night.'"

"That was all?"

"Yes."

"But you saw him after that, didn't you?"

"Objection!" Andy called. "Leading the witness!"

The judge said, "Sustained," and the prosecutor regrouped.

"Is this yours?" he asked, handing the hoodie to Bronner, who turned white but maintained his demeanor. It was on the Exhibit List, but Bronner and Andy hadn't given it a thought, since it seemed irrelevant and had no useful trace evidence on it. He formally entered it into evidence.

"I have one like it. Can't say for sure this one's mine," Bronner affirmed.

"When was the last time you wore a hoodie?"

"Oh, a long time ago. Don't remember."

"Do you wear hoodies as a regular thing?"

"Objection!" cried Andy. "Relevance."

"Let's see where this is going," said the judge. He looked at the prosecutor. "But let's get there soon, counsel. Overruled. Witness, answer the question."

"No, I don't."

"So you would remember a rare occasion when you might have worn one?"

"I already said I didn't remember."

The prosecution played some surveillance tapes from the time Tommy Burkett was killed, time-stamped between two a.m. and twenty minutes later. They showed Tommy leaving the building. They also showed a man in a hoodie leaving a pickup truck and crossing the parking lot. Campus security had confirmed what the police review of the tapes from that night believed: there was no other activity on campus, within half an hour of that time.

The videos showed the hooded man returning to the truck and leaving. They also showed, indistinctly, another man, barely distinguishable but dressed like Tommy, walking erratically in the direction of the boat rental, though both his origin and his destination were not within the cameras' view.

And Bill Gunther's earlier testimony established that the videos did not show Tommy returning to work that morning.

The prosecutor resumed. "President Bronner, do you recognize either of the two people who appeared in these videos?"

"It's dark, they're blurry, it's raining…"

"Just answer the question."

"No, I don't."

"Would you say that this hoodie looks like the one in the video?"

Andy was about to object again, but Bronner stated the obvious. “It’s a hoodie. There’s no way anybody could identify it in those pictures.”

The prosecutor again switched direction, but not his cadence, tone, or delivery. And during that moment, Andy wasn’t paying attention. “So, why did you park the truck in C Lot, when you have a reserved spot?”

Bronner just answered, “It was closer to where I was going.”

Then Andy objected, but it was too late. There was a gasp across the courtroom. Bronner looked ill.

The assistant DA continued as if nothing had happened.

“Why were you on campus that night?”

“I wasn’t on campus that night.”

The DA paused. “Why were you on campus that *morning*?”

Andy stood up. "Your Honor, I object!"

The judge leaned forward. "Your client has volunteered to tell us what happened. Overruled." He turned to the prosecutor. "Proceed."

"Why, Mr. Bronner?"

"Because I wanted to check on my office. I wasn't sure everything was in order."

"Explain."

"It's my OCD. I'm compulsive about making sure the office is perfect every night when I go home. That night, I thought I had left some things out, and I went back to put everything away."

"But the tapes show you never entered the building."

"Is that a question?" Bronner said, going on a feeble offensive.

"Do you agree that the tapes show you never entered the building?"

"I'm not an expert at reading the tapes."

"Mr. Bronner, no one entered the building between two in the morning and six.

“Objection!” yelled Andy. “That hasn’t been established.”

“Sustained,” said the judge.

The prosecutor had made his point, objection or no, and continued. “Where did you go?”

Bronner asked, “What – was I there?”

Andy finally put a stop to that line of questioning, on Fifth Amendment grounds. The prosecutor again changed direction.

"How did you come to have Tommy Burkett's key ring in your desk drawer?"

"I put the keys there, with the intention of giving them to our Maintenance Director."

"Why didn't you?"

"I forgot they were there."

"How did you come into possession of the keys?"

"I found them on the lawn."

"Where?"

"Between Parking Lot C and my office."

"When?"

"In the springtime."

"Was this soon after the night in question, the night of April nineteen-twenty, last year?"

"The morning after. Yes, the same day."

"What time of day?"

"Before work. Early. The keys were wet."

"From dew?"

"Yes. Or rain, maybe. They were wet."

"Why were you walking in that area of campus, when your reserved parking space was in another lot?"

"Just seeing if I wanted to change my parking spot."

"Why would you want to do that?"

"To be more 'of the people.' I was noticing the privilege of my office, and I thought maybe I could give up my old spot to honor some excellent employee. So I tried out other parking lots."

"You never set up that program, though, did you?"

“No. All the other lots would have been really inconvenient, and I realized I really liked my special spot.” Another snicker.

He forgot. He's not pressing. This case is won. Gail will believe me, now. I'll be exonerated, the hero, the victim of a terrible plot concocted by this moron DA's office and staged by this imbecile prosecuting attorney.

But then, "What do you remember of that night, er, early morning?”

On cross, Andy couldn't make Bronner's testimony go away. Bronner couldn't explain his timeline. Summations were scheduled for the following morning.

***

“Andy, they still don't have anything,” Bronner said, hopefully.

“Richard, you made an ass of yourself, but they don't have anything that ties you directly to the killing. They still don't know who, really, was that guy in the hoodie and the pickup truck. You admitted you were there, but they don't have anything that links you to the killing. Let's just hope the jury sees it our way."

Next morning, the lawyers summed up and the judge made a careful charge to the jury, and sent them off to deliberate.

***

"Now that we have a foreman, and I'm her," began Juror Number Four, "let's take a vote, to see if we need to stay here past dinnertime."

Everyone tore a scrap of paper from the notebook that was on the table when they got there, and wrote a single word on the scrap. They passed them to the foreman, and she counted the votes. "Nine 'guilty,' three not. Well, let's get started. Who thinks he's not guilty, and why?"

Juror Number Two raised his hand. "I can't see this guy doing it. He's a respected citizen. Everybody loves him. He's nice to everybody, pays his bills. He's educated, got a great job, and he's good at it. Good family man. He doesn't have so much as a parking ticket."

Juror Number Nine echoed him. "He's just sweet," she said. "You can look at him and know. And his lawyer said there wasn't anything that connected him to the murder."

Number Five rolled his eyes and raised his hand. "With all due respect, he's guilty as sin. Look – nobody else could have done it. Nobody else was on campus. He didn't go to his office. He's there at two in the morning – to rearrange his desk? Come on!"

But Two stopped him. "Nobody saw him do it. There's no knife."

Twelve jumped in. "Look," he said, "I'm old as dirt, but even I can see that he had to be the one. Yeah, nobody else was there, and his alibi is stupid. And did you see him turn white when they showed him that hoodie?"

Five jumped in. "Hold it there, everybody. Let's back up and see what the facts are. Just the facts."

Six, though, interrupted. "The facts have to be considered, and we can't rule against facts. But the facts aren't the only things we need to consider." Five started to interrupt, and Six held up his hand. “But first, let’s list all the facts we do have, and write down everything we actually know.” Five nodded.

Eleven said, “May I speak?” The foreman nodded. “Okay, look. We know… what? We know Tommy Burkett was murdered. We know he went to work late on the nineteenth, and the tapes show he took lunch at two o’clock in the morning of the twentieth.”

Five said, “and he was stabbed outside the building and stumbled down to the river.”

Six said, “We think we saw him. I mean, it’s probably him. But we don’t know for sure.”

Five came back. “We saw his clothes. They matched the clothes Tommy was wearing when he walked out of the building and when they found him, in the pictures in the boat.”

Eight said, “But they only match, light pants, dark top. The tapes were night – you can’t say for sure that the dark top was blue, or red, or dark green, or what.”

Six was taking over the conversation. "Well, right. But nobody else was in the scenes, either. Let's put that down in the 'we're pretty sure' column. I for one don't have any doubt. Anybody else?"

Ten spoke for the first time. "I'd go along with that. I mean, who else? Nobody else is in any of the pictures. We saw Tommy go out of the building at the right time, he didn't come back. Someone of his build, with what could be the exact clothes, went to the shore, where we know Tommy took the rowboat. I mean, do we have any reasonable doubt that the guy in the video is Tommy Burkett?" Nobody had any objections. "Okay, then, we have one fact: Tommy is the guy we see in the video, limping down to the boat at 2:12 in the morning. Everybody okay on that?" The foreman wrote it down.

The foreman said, "While we're on it, can we put Bronner's name down as the other guy on the tape?"

Eight said, "Madam forewoman, I'd like to say that well, we don't have anything that makes him that guy, except the hoodie looks like the one in the video. And we don't have any way to prove one hoodie or another."

Nine said, "Yeah, and he had access to a truck that looks just like the one in the video. And he bought that gas. And -- he said he was the one. There's that."

Ten said, "He also testified that yes, none of his cars holds twenty gallons, but he said he also filled up a five-gallon gas can for his lawn mower. We don't have a time stamp on the purchase, and the cops never even looked to see whether he had such a gas can, or checked the gas in the can they never looked for. I'd chalk up the gas purchase to 'we think,' not anything solid. But I do think he lied, too."

Juror One, who hadn't yet said a thing, spoke up. First, she stood up. "I voted 'not guilty' in the first ballot, but it's clear to me that there were only two people in the area, Tommy and Bronner. And Tommy staggered away, and we have no reason, really, for Bronner to even be there. But he said he was there, so he was there."

Seven spoke up. "Yeah, there's that. I don't think he was lying that time. I say that's all we need, to make Bronner as the other guy in the tape." Nods all around. The foreman wrote it on the whiteboard.

There was a pause. The foreman turned to Juror Number Three. "We haven't heard a thing from you tonight. What are your thoughts?"

Three, a seventy-something grey-haired lady who was hunched over beyond her years, smiled. "Two and two are four," she said. "It's obvious. There's no other possible explanation. These men came together, alive. One staggered away. The other one didn't say anyone else was there, and he certainly could have. For me, it's case closed."

The foreman asked, "Another vote?"

***

Richard Bronner was sentenced to spend the next nineteen years of his life in prison, eighteen as a bachelor, since Gail immediately divorced him. The last two years were a consequence of his subsequent conviction on voyeurism charges.

The public was appalled. Richard Bronner was universally loved. No one believed he could be guilty of such crimes, and no one wanted him to leave the College. But his own testimony had turned public expectations and hopes around.

Justice was done in Tommy Burkett's name, though the people of Lakeview would have preferred to have simply mourned his death, without the disruption to the community. Most of them would rather have continued blaming some unknown assailant.

--- THE END ---

Acknowledgments

This book has taken several turns in its gestation. It was originally to have been a small section of an entirely different book, but thanks to the advice of a number of friends, I broke it out to live on its own.

The original idea came from my neighbor, mentor, and good friend, Tom Newman, who recalled the corruption and paranoia of a university president of his long-ago acquaintance. With Tom and my friend Robyne Highsmith, I wove and embellished a fictional story, and built completely fictitious traits and actions into this warped character's history, finally yielding the completely fictional creepy monster who is here seen as H. Richard Bronner.

I then took the rough work to my Indianapolis-based writers' group, first moderated by Suzanne Harding and populated by Claudia Pfeiffer, Celia Latz, and Lola Berry, who were astoundingly insightful and helpful.

Dear friend Peggy Vore read the final manuscript and, in addition to making numerous prescient suggestions, caught a timeline mistake that could have confused everybody.

Then, my wonderfully overqualified sisters, Rosalie and Theresa, commenced the brutal work of conceptual review and proofreading, respectively.

And so here is "my" first novel.

About the Author

Tim Kern writes for magazines and marketing clients, and is well-known in private aviation as a prolific publicity and feature writer. He holds a Private Pilot certificate.

Kern taught economics for fifteen years, for students from high school through postgraduate levels. His nine-year radio talk show, *Tim Kern, Talking Sense*, was aired on over 200 stations.

He has been a motorcycle racer and still rides regularly; a car racer and race instructor, and a professional mechanic on a championship-winning Can-Am team.

His first book, The Executive Primer, (©1991, 1994) was serialized in *SUCCESS Magazine* over three years.

In corporate life, he has been an international financial analyst, a regional logistics manager, a CFO, and a CEO.

He earned a Bachelor of Music degree at Northern Illinois University, and an MBA from Northwestern University.

He lives near Indianapolis with Moochie and Scraggles, his two formerly-feral calico cats.

This is his first work of fiction.

Also by Tim Kern (nonfiction)

The Executive Primer, 1991

The Manual by Eduardo (pamphlet), 1996

The Americans' Fight to Survive (co-author), 1999

Coming:

The T.R.U.S.T. Device series

Send an email to get notifications, and receive free short stories by Tim Kern!

Connect with the Author

Tim Kern

PO Box 30
Anderson IN 46015-0030
USA
info@timkern.com

Please help the author:
Positive, honest reviews and referrals are always appreciated.

www.ingramcontent.com/pod-product-compliance
Lightning Source LLC
Chambersburg PA
CBHW021024120726
47905CB00009B/3163

William Henry Milburn

Ten Years of Preacher-Life
Chapters from an Autobiography

ISBN/EAN: 9783337073473

Printed in Europe, USA, Canada, Australia, Japan

Cover: Foto ©Raphael Reischuk / pixelio.de

More available books at **www.hansebooks.com**

TEN YEARS OF PREACHER-LIFE:

Chapters from an Autobiography.

BY

WILLIAM HENRY MILBURN,

AUTHOR OF "THE RIFLE, AXE AND SADDLE-BAGS."

"THERE was a time when meadow, grove, and stream,
The earth, and every common sight,
To me did seem
Apparelled in celestial light,
The glory and the freshness of a dream."

NEW YORK:
DERBY & JACKSON, 119 NASSAU STREET
1860.

To One

WHO FOR THIRTEEN YEARS HATH BEEN TO ME AS

A LIGHT SHINING IN A DARK PLACE,

MY WIFE;

THROUGH WHOSE EYES

I HAVE BEEN ENABLED TO ENJOY THE WORLD OF NATURE,

AND WITH WHOSE TONGUE

I HAVE KEPT COMPANY WITH THE GREAT AND GOOD OF ALL AGES,

THIS VOLUME

IS GRATEFULLY AND AFFECTIONATELY INSCRIBED.

PREFACE.

On a starlight night, in the summer of 1854, I was pacing Nahant beach with the poet Longfellow. I could fancy that the smoke from our cigars shaped itself in fantastic wreaths about us. As our talk ran upon the old world and the new, upon the scenes we had visited and the men we had known, "Why do you not write the story of your life?" he said.

The idea had never occurred to me before. Not a week later, Mr. Prescott asked me the same question.

Since then it has been often repeated.

I have sought in this volume to set before the reader a truthful picture of the life of a Methodist preacher, which more than that of almost any other man in this country, is fraught with the experience of vicissitude.

It must be remembered that by reason of my infirmity I have no contact with the printed page, that therefore the ear is my only guide in composition. My intellectual training has been directed to one object—the acquisition of the power and habit of extemporaneous speech; the reader must not be surprised, then, if I have failed with the pen.

Nearly every word of this book has been written with the fingers of the young people of my parish. John Randolph used to exclaim, "No man has such constituents as I have." I may say with equal truth—no man has such friends as I! To the young men and women, therefore, who have used for me the pen of the ready writer, I hereby make my grateful acknowledgments.

BROOKLYN, N. Y., *July 25th.*

CONTENTS.

"It is not now as it hath been of yore;
Turn wheresoe'er I may,
By night or day,
The things which I have seen I now can see no more.

"The rainbow comes and goes,
And lovely is the rose,
The moon doth with delight
Look round her when the heavens are bare
Waters on a starry night
Are beautiful and fair;
The sunshine is a glorious birth,
But yet I know, where'er I go
That there hath passed away a glory from the earth."

"What though the radiance, which was once so bright,
Be now forever taken from my sight—
Though nothing can bring back the hour
Of splendor in the grass, of glory in the flower,
We will grieve not—rather find
Strength in what remains behind—
In the primal sympathy,
Which, having been, must ever be—
In the soothing thoughts that spring
Out of human suffering;
In the faith that looks through death,
In years that bring the philosophic mind."

TEN YEARS OF PREACHER-LIFE.

CHAPTER I.

A DAY OF CLOUDS AND THICK DARKNESS.

WELL do I remember how fair the earth and heavens appeared to me, a child nearly five years old, on a bright summer afternoon, in the year 1828. The sun, fast going down the western sky, threw his slanting beams along the narrow streets and alleys, and over the quaint old houses which met my eye as I stood in one of the oldest portions of the city of Philadelphia.

It was at the end of my father's garden, approached from the house by a long gravel walk, lined on each side by beds of flowers, whispering to the childish ear, even in the heart of a great city, sweet tales of green fields, while over them as sentinels stood two old Lombardy poplars, their tall stately forms almost reaching, as it seemed to me, to the very sky.

Very beautiful to me was that little garden, when over it stretched so bright a sky, and the soft wind rustled through the branches of the trees; and I recollect the hue and aspect of all as vividly as though I had seen it but yesterday. And with good reason do I remember it; for never again was this brave show to appear to me on earth—a single blow blotted out for me the celestial beauty of the outer world.

I was playing with a boy about my own age, when raising his arm, to throw a piece of glass or oyster-shell, and not seeing me behind him, the missile entered my left eye, as he drew his hand back, and laid open the ball just below the pupil. The sharp agony of pain and the sight of dropping blood alarmed me, and I sped like a frightened deer to find my mother. Then followed days and weeks of silence and darkness, wherein a child lay with bandaged eyes upon his little couch, in a chamber without light, and which all entered with stealthy steps and muffled tones. At last there came a morning, when I was led into a room where the bright sunshine lay upon the carpet; and though dimmer than it used to be, never had I been so glad to behold it. But my gladness was suddenly checked when I found several strange gentlemen seated there, among whom was our family physician, a tall, stern, cold man, of whom I had always been afraid. What they were going to do I could not tell; but a shudder of horror ran through me when, seated on my father's knee, my head resting on his shoulder, the doctor opened the wounded eye and he and the other surgeons examined it. They said that the cut had healed, and that all now needed to restore the sight entirely was the removal of the scar with caustic. How fearful was the fiery torture that entered the eye and burnt there for days, I need not attempt to describe! Then came once more the darkened chamber and long imprisonment; until I was led a second time into the light room, and the presence of the same men, who seemed to be my enemies, coming only to torment me. I shrunk from them, and cried aloud to my father to save me. The doctor caught me between his knees, threw my head upon his shoulder, thrust the caustic violently through the eye, and the light went out of it forever!

Matters were now worse than ever. Not only was a live coal placed in the socket of one eye, but it was feared that inflammation would destroy the other. Furiously did the inflammation rage in spite of all that skill and kindness could do. My third imprisonment lasted two years. Living in a little chamber where brooded the blackness of darkness—undergoing bleeding, leeching, cupping, besides swallowing drugs enough to dose a hospital, until the round childish form shrunk to a skeleton, and the craving of appetite was but tantalized with boiled rice, and mush without milk as an alternative—was not this a sad way for a child to spend his life, between the ages of five and seven?

Yet in the midst of all this there was comfort and cause for gratitude. My feeblest cry was never unheard, so light was my mother's sleep; and so constant was her care, through all those weary days and nights, that the bandages about my temples were never suffered to become dry. When the sharpness of the agony had softened down into a numb or gnawing pain, there was a happy time in every day for me; this was when my father, relieved from the cares of business, with a heart tender and pitiful as a woman's, would steal softly into the room, and take me gently on his knee, and break the lapse of the short silence—the cause of which I learned to understand by many a shower of warm drops upon my head and hands—by telling me old stories of the Revolutionary war, in which his father had served from Bunker Hill to Yorktown, and how he when a boy went duck shooting among the celery beds of Elk River, and all the pleasant things that he could think of. Then he would tell me stories from the Bible; and after a while, when we were allowed to have a little light within the room, he and my mother would read to me, the sacred words of that venerable book: and so I came to think upon God as my friend and father, and that thought was as a great light shining in the thick darkness. Ours was a humble home, and there was a stern discipline going on within it for the parents as well as for the child: and yet when the bitterness of the first grief was over, I much question if there were many happier.

My weary confinement, like all other things in this world of change, came to an end; and I stood once more in the breezy air, beneath the sunny sky. True there seemed a shadow on the day. The delicate hues of flowers and foliage, the light of stars, and that diviner light which shines through the human face, had faded into nothingness; but I knew the rapture of liberty. It was like a release from the thraldom of the grave. Frequently afterwards I had to return to the bondage of my prison-house, as a protection from the glare of the summer's sun, and the winter's snow; but never for more than a few weeks at a time.

How much and in what way I could see I never have been able accurately to describe. The left eye was gone altogether! and after the ravages of the inflammation, the right retained the smallest possible transparent spot, not much larger than a pin's point, in the cornea and the pupil, through which the light might enter. To make this fraction of an eye available, it was necessary to use a shade above the eye and place the middle finger of the right hand beneath it; thus forming a sort of artificial pupil, allowing only the due quantity of light to enter. By this means I was enabled to read a little for fifteen or twenty years, in strong daylight, holding the book very close to the eye, and bringing every letter to the precise spot on which the sight was fixed.

Before my hurt I had learned to read, and now as I returned to the world, my school-days recommenced. My infirmity prevented me from sharing the more active and invigorating sports of my fellows, and I was forced to seek a compensation in books and conversation. Miss Jane Porter was among my earliest friends, and Washington Irving's Sketch Book was as familiar as household words by the time that I was eight years of age. I had access to a tolerably well selected library, and slowly spelling out volume after volume of voyages, travels, biography, history and fiction, I was not envious when I heard the shouts and laughter of my schoolmates. "The words of the wise are as apples of gold in pictures of silver," and every author is a wise man to a studious boy. Books open a wonderful world to us, brighter than that on which the sun shines, and to be allowed to dwell and muse at will among its glories makes large amends for being deprived of the loveliness of the dim spot which men call earth, where "the grass withereth and the flower fadeth."

The eye is a haven, at which the treasure fleets that sail through the ocean of light are unladen, and their stores deposited in the vaults of the intellect;

but it is through the whispering gallery of the ear, that man reaches the heart of his fellow man most quickly and surely. Light and knowledge are for the eye, love and music for the ear. Hearing oftentimes seems to me a nobler sense than sight, with richer benedictions attendant on it, with tenderer and holier offices assigned to it. Man's voice, tuned by sympathy, moving to the modulations of intelligence and love, may perform the sweetest and holiest ministry of human life. Do you wonder, then, that with books and with friendly talk I learned to bear my affliction cheerfully?

CHAPTER II.

THE LAND OF THE SETTING SUN.

OUR family story is a common one in this country of financial reverse and disaster. My father, who started in life with nothing but rectitude and business habits, acquired a handsome fortune; but the storm of 1837 overtook him with all sails set, and like many other gallant barks, his was wrecked. When the fierceness of the squall was over, and we looked around to see what was left, we found that it consisted of honor, health, hope and our household furniture. In America to fail in business and to remove to the West are very apt to be cause and effect.

To go from a warm sunny past through a dreary present filled with ruins—to leave behind home, and friends, and church—to break all the old strong ties of a life-time, and journey toward a land of strangers where all is new and untried, has been the heart sickening experience of many who will read these pages. But for the young, hope ever arrays the future with robes of glory; and the Far West is always a land of promise, flowing with milk and honey. The Mississippi was at the time I speak of almost the boundary of emigration, and people of the eastern States were accustomed to look upon Illinois as that part of the civilized globe lying next door to the setting sun. Of course, being so near to the couch of that distinguished luminary, it caught and retained, for the uninitiated fancy, much of the brightness of which he divested himself, on retiring to rest. It would have done your eyes and heart good to see the many beautifully colored and mounted maps of the State, its noble counties, its unnumbered magnificent towns and cities, with classical and musical names, displayed upon the walls of hotels, and at the offices of disinterested and philanthropic gentlemen whose sole object in life seemed to be to help their fellow creatures to find Paradise and Peru combined. How it kindled the eye and warmed the soul to hear these friends of humanity discourse on places whose names were borrowed from memorable spots in the past, apparently with the view to show how much more famous they would become in this second appropriation than they had been in the first. There were Attica, Athens, Sparta, Golconda, Ophir, Cairo, Rome, Bethel, Warsaw, Naples, Vienna, Paris, London, Edinburgh, Florence, Berlin, Petersburg, Pekin, Alexandria, Moscow, Delhi, and scores of others, all giving the eager listener assurance through the persuasive eloquence of the land agents, that however the cities originally bearing them had failed in their mission, their grandeur now mouldering into decay, their faded glory would be more than atoned for by the success and splendor of their namesakes. It was eminently gratifying to observe how the maps bore witness to the public spirit and Christian liberality of the founders and citizens of these august and well named capitals. There were public squares at frequent intervals, whose forest trees shaded beautiful promenades and drives, and in every one of these squares were spots selected where stood, or were to stand, statues of memorable persons, and others from which fountains were to throw their rainbow shafts high in air. Here the Male Academy was placed, and there the Female Seminary, and yonder was the University. The churches were abundant; moreover you were informed that such was the rush of population to the West that the nation would soon have to move its capitol to Cincinnati, and you already began to feel sorry for the poor old deserted eastern States. One fear alone haunted your mind, that—as according to the maps' story the State was covered with towns and cities—there would soon be no farms, and then where would the wheat and corn come from to feed such a population?

I am writing of 1838. In May of that year we took our journey to the far-off country. It required two weeks to go a distance which could now be traversed in two days. At length we reached our destination, Jacksonville, Morgan County, Illinois, twenty miles east of the Illinois River, and a hundred miles northeast of St. Louis.

If the maps and descriptions had wrought us an enchanter's spell, the charm was soon broken. One great capital after another had vanished, and a stage-ride from Naples through Exeter and Geneva to Jacksonville, a distance of twenty-two miles, served to quiet any apprehensions we might have entertained as to the density of population and the multiplicity of the towns preventing the growth of breadstuffs; for the namesakes of the Italian, Swiss, and English cities consisted of about a dozen log-cabins, each with a frame house or two belonging to the great proprietors. But though there were no great towns on the road, there was a country of as quiet, picturesque, and smiling loveliness, as the eye of man ever rested on. We crossed the river bottom, mounted the noble bluff which serves "in the office of a wall," drove through narrow belts of timber, crossed the skirts of rolling prairies, the road passing the summit of an ascending ridge until we gained "the Mound," four miles from our journey's end. From this elevation the land fell off in gentle swells toward the groves on the edge of the horizon. The prospect was divided between cultivated fields, green with the ripening wheat, and the tender shoots of corn, and unfenced prairie, where countless cattle were cropping the sweet wild grass and flowers. Here and there young orchards, near the cabins of the earliest settlers, gave promise by their bloom of rich stores of fruit to come. The air was freighted with the smell of new-mown hay, of prairie flowers, and the blossoms from the distant woods. Sky and earth wore the bright livery of summer, and the air in its balmy incense seemed to offer the New World's first fruits to its maker.

An hour's drive hence brought us to our new home. The pretty village stood in the middle of a high rolling prairie, and already had marks of tasteful embellishment in the trees, shrubbery, and flowers, about almost every house. White lead, however, is the most notable feature in our new towns. Eastern emigrants cannot long brook log houses; and while those unsightly yet necessary and most comfortable abodes, serve the earliest settlers, the saw mill and paint pot are quickly at work to produce the second crop of civilization in the shape of frame houses with very thin walls, covered with clap-boards. I confess to a grateful love of log cabins, and am much inclined to the belief that their humble roofs have sheltered a greater amount of health, content, happiness and virtue than any other style of domestic architecture.

In the centre of the town was the public square

From this proceeded the four principal streets ,which in their continuation kept us in correspondence with the four quarters of the globe; and many a time have I looked upon stages running their several ways and fancied them monster shuttles weaving us into the world's web, and laying our life threads side by side with our fellows in the vast fabric of humanity. The sides of the square were lined with the shanties in which was transacted the business of the place. The occupants of these lowly shops, in which was sold all manner of merchandise—from the ribbon that trimmed the bonnet of the rustic belle, to the plough which broke up her father's acres—were styled merchants, and the occupation of bartering molasses and calico, for beeswax, butter and eggs, was denominated the mercantile. At frequent intervals were located "groceries," most commonly called "doggeries," where "spirits" were sold by "the small" *i. e.* the glass. In the centre of the square stood the court and market houses, the one brick, the other frame. The market was two stories high, the lower story devoted to the sale of meats, and the upper to a newspaper and lawyers' offices, the gallery at the side serving as a rostrum for stump orators. Saturday was a great day, when from many miles around the old and young, male and female, came with every product of the land, by every means of conveyance, to trade. Homespun dames and damsels, making the circuit of the square inquiring at every door: "D'ye buy eggs and butter yer?" and sometimes responding indignantly, as I heard a maiden once when told that eggs were bringing only three cents a dozen: "What, do ye s'pose our hens are gwine to strain theirselves a laying eggs at three cents a dozen? Lay 'em yourself, and see how you'd like the price."

It was a lively scene on a market day; with its crowds of prairie wagons, long, low uncovered boxes placed on wheels, in which the articles sold and bought, to which the generic name of plunder was applied, were conveyed to and from the town; while groups of saddled horses, pawing the earth and neighing their neighborly recognitions to each other, stood fastened at the posts. Here you might descry a piratical cow, boarding a wagon by adroitly raising her fore legs into it, smelling around, while the-trading owner was absent for fruits and vegetables, or even devouring his purchased stock of sugar; and there sweeping along at full gallop, some half drunken jockey, showing off the points of his steed, and with stentorian voice offering to bet any man ten dollars that it was the best piece of horse flesh on the ground. Groups are gathered in front of all the "doggeries," at the street corners, and at the doors of the court-house, discussing politics, or other urgent questions of the time; differences of opinion, stimulated by bald-face whisky, often bringing these conferences to a pugilistic termination. Meanwhile the older ladies, arrayed in dark linsey-woolsey dresses—the lower front adorned by blue check aprons—their heads covered with sun-bonnets, and their feet with yarn stockings and brogan shoes or moccasins, having brought the interesting and complicated operations of trading to a close, stand idly about with folded arms, regaling themselves with fumes of tobacco, inhaled from a corncob or sweet potato pipe. The exercises of the day were usually varied by political speeches, a sheriff's sale, a half dozen free fights, and thrice as many horse swaps. Just before sundown the traders departed, and the town was left to its inhabitants.

The principal denominations of Christians had houses of worship in the village, and the society of the place made up of representatives from all sections of the Union, had a higher intellectual, moral and religious tone than is usual in a new country.

Besides the President and Professors of Illinois College, there was quite a number of men, distinguished in the State by their positions at the bar and in politics; and from all sides the new comers, who deserved it, received cordial welcome and hospitable courtesy.

CHAPTER III.

LIFE IN A HESPERIAN GARDEN.

Our boxes were unpacked, and our household goods arranged, in a little house which was intended to have one room below and a loft above, but the lower room had been skillfully divided by thin board partitions into three. Housekeeping thus began, and as we gradually fitted ourselves to the new order of things, we felt more and more at home.

My father raised a small capital, and taking heart of grace, ventured once more into the uncertainties of business, and I was installed as my mother's assistant in housekeeping, and as my father's in merchandising. In that free and independent country, such things as servants were not—not even help or hired girls—so that the women of the household had their own work to do, their husbands and sons aiding them by attending to the "chores." Therefore this saying passed into a proverb—"It is a good country for men and horses, but it is death on women and oxen."

It devolved upon me to draw the water and cut

the wood; but I cannot boast that, with my best endeavors, I ever acquired much facility in milking a cow. Early rising was the habit of the land, and our family was not second to the foremost; but whether from constitutional indisposition or excess of the discipline, or a failure in it, I cannot tell, yet I fear much that the practice then submitted to from necessity has implanted in me an unconquerable repugnance to Dr. Franklin's adage, and in spite of my better judgment, I feel the tip of my nose suddenly aspiring whenever I hear that wise counsel preached—

> "Early to bed, and early to rise,
> Makes a man healthy, wealthy, and wise."

In winter-time we always breakfasted by candle-light; and, by the way, although I do not believe I should ever have acquired eminence as a tallow-chandler, it is fair to state that I did acquire some skill in the manufacture of "dips and moulds," and also of "soft soap," the kind chiefly in use—I mean the literal, not the metaphorical. It fell to my lot to prepare the early repast. After kindling the fire and putting on the kettle, I ground and made the coffee, laid the table, and then hurried to the store, where another fire was to be lighted, and the premises swept and dusted. Returning, I was in time for the meal, and at its close, my father went to the counter, while I staid to play domestic. These duties ended, I entered upon those of clerk and book-keeper, making small entries, measuring what the natives call—not, I suppose, with the cognizance of Lindley Murray—"them molasses," or weighing out coffee, tea, and sugar.

My old passion for reading had survived, and as I soon became acquainted with almost everybody in the village, books enough were lent me to fill my leisure moments. Nothing came amiss, and with what greediness, nay, rapacity, did I devour every one that fell in my way! There was always a volume at hand, and with my seat at the door in summer time, and by the window in the winter, for the strongest light was needful, every gap in business was appropriated to the beloved page; and even whilst standing behind the counter, counting eggs, weighing butter, or summing up accounts, the rapturous world to which books had introduced me, with its fadeless lights and sounding oracles, its profound truths and majestic ideals, still owned me as a new-born inhabitant, and I was happy. The lowly affairs by which I was employed seemed unreal, and the teachings of the historian or the poet alone appeared to be present and substantial. I have often wondered whether any one ever enjoyed such delight in reading as I did in those days, the opportunities were so spare, and the difficulties so great.

With what rapt and reverential devotion did I muse and ponder upon the writers of books! There was a gentleman in the village who had known Paulding, Longfellow, and Washington Irving. This, together with the fact that he owned several hundred well-assorted volumes, made him a hero and sage to my fond idolatry. Never have I stood in such awe of a human being. Never could I speak to him without stammering and blushing; but I listened to every syllable he uttered, and treasured even the lightest word upon literature that fell from him, as if it had been spoken by an oracle. Little are educated men apt to dream of the lasting benedictions which their conversation may bestow upon the mind and heart of boyhood.

My studies had hitherto been devoted, exclusively, to the English branches, but I began to yearn for an acquaintance with those tongues in which the master-minds of antiquity had spoken, and so my kind father yielded to my persuasion, notwithstanding his fear that persistent study would yet more impair my sight, and brought me home one day a Latin grammar and reader. I wrought away with youthful ardor until I had mastered them; and, at length, as our affairs began to improve, it was arranged that I should have a master for an hour or two a day. The lessons were conned at the store, and recited at the school. Greek was added to

Latin, and in due time I was ready to enter college. Household, mercantile, and collegiate duties bound on me the burden of life's toils and cares, while as an offset, I enjoyed my daily walk of four miles, besides the mirthful chat and frolic of my hearty, romping, yet hard-working classmates. They were noble fellows—our old collegians—among whom a man's worth was determined, not by the clothes he wore, or the money in his pocket, but by his resolution to conquer difficulties, his will for hard work, and his spirit for good fellowship. Not a few of them, to whom eleemosynary aid had been offered, disdained it, and to preserve their independence, and yet acquire an education, cut wood at seventy-five cents a cord, lived on potatoes and corn-meal, paid their own tuition bills, and having hewed their way through college, came out of it with a double education, worth the having. Many of them "boarded themselves," as it was called, and they felt that their knowledge of cookery, thus acquired, was by no means despicable. What feasts we had out of roast potatoes, fried chickens, and roasted turkeys, partridges, prairie-hens, wild geese, and the like, with now and then a haunch of venison; the vegetables being the trophies of the hoe, the winged or four-footed creatures, the trophies of the gun of one or another of the party.

Of course, we had the customary college anecdotes

and songs, the usual amount, no doubt, of sophomoric speech-making; enough of us were addicted to the use of the weed, and all of us incurred the customary charge for repairs, injuring the walls of the rooms by sitting with our chairs thrown back, and our heels placed against the aforesaid walls, at points which would be intersected by horizontal lines running over the tops of our craniums. But we had no society such as I have heard of in some of the Eastern colleges, for the promotion and diffusion of indolence; the first medal offered by which, was awarded to the deserts of a gentleman who nailed his slippers against the mantel-piece, so that when his feet were raised to the level of his head, he should not have the trouble of holding them there.

Our fun was fun alive. In behalf of our alma mater, we can lay claim to a distinction unshared by any other American seat of learning, to wit, that it has never conferred the title of D.D. on any man unworthy to receive it, for in a life-time of five-and-twenty years, it has had the good taste never to confer it on anybody.

Our pecuniary circumstances continued to mend, and I thereby gained more time and greater facilities for study. But the artificial posture which I had to assume in order to read at all, bent almost double, so seriously affected my breast and spine that my health was undermined, and fears were entertained for my life. The physicians peremptorily ordered me to leave college, give up books, mount a horse, and take as much exercise as practicable. This was in February, 1843. A barrier that could not be overleaped was thus placed before me; my road turned off, and I quitted the land of my dreams and hopes; a life of scholastic seclusion and contemplation, for a life of vicissitude and active toil. It cost many an hour of lonely wretchedness and hopeless brooding, to come at last to a surrender, to relinquish desire, expectation, and promise. Not easily nor quickly is the lesson of renunciation learned; yet are we not led, even though it be in a path that we have not known, and stayed by an invisible yet almighty hand? "If any man will come after me, let him deny himself daily, and take up his cross and follow me."

Heavily and painfully, amid the languor of disease and weakness, did the past fade out, and the curtains of the future were slowly withdrawn.

CHAPTER IV.

"THERE WERE GIANTS IN THOSE DAYS."

From my earliest recollection my father's house had been a home for Methodist preachers, and I had grown up with an ardent admiration and vehement affection for the toil-worn veterans of the olden time. The fame of their sufferings and self-sacrifice, of their simple faith and burning zeal, of their persecutions and successes, of their humor and eloquence, was familiar to me. They were noble men, those fathers of American Methodism, and worthy to be held in remembrance,—Asbury, McKendree, George, Roberts, Emory, Merwin, Capers, Hope, Hull, and their associates. Their venerable appearance, set off with straight-breasted coats and vests, and white cravats; their heads surmounted with broad-brimmed white beavers, and their grave dignity, relieved and rendered more effective by rays of humor and pleasant recitals of droll adventures, made a profound and lasting impression upon my childish fancy. It was usual among people of our condition in Philadelphia, to have "evening companies" several times a year, to which the prominent preachers and their families, besides other members of the society, were invited. I heartily wish that Mr. Dickens, whose chief ministerial acquaintances seem to belong to the school of Stiggins and Chadband, could have been present on some of those occasions. He would have seen the representatives of a hearty manhood that must have won his admiring regard, and heard bursts of humor as genial and pathetic as his own.

They were men of a wide and varied acquaintance with life, and an experience of the deep things of God; not lettered to any considerable extent, but reading human nature and its histories at first-hand. The ardor of an early enthusiasm had not been toned down by conventionalism, or chilled by skepticism and unbelief. The hardships, sufferings, and dangers which they had cheerfully undergone, the smallness of their salaries, the self-denying spirit which they were wont to manifest, together with their straightforward, independent bearing, made them dear to the hearts of the people. The relations of pastors and flock were of the most simple, friendly, and even intimate character; and whilst the seriousness of a Christian bearing was never compromised, intercourse was beautified, and adapted to all sorts and classes of persons by an infusion of the most genial human tenderness.

Never, I suppose, will food taste as sweet to me again as did the suppers of those early days at the children's second table. But the relish of the viands was surpassed by the zest with which we youngsters, in the seats allotted to us among our elders, in the parlor, listened to the stories and adventures of these men, who in truth seemed to us prophets of the Lord. They were ever kindly in their regard for children, and were accustomed to speak some comfortable words to each child present. The evening's close was always hallowed by a chapter read from the Bible, a hymn in which the voices of all present joined, and a prayer earnestly commending every one present to the care of Him who careth for all. What a strange fire glowed within the bosom, as I, a tow-headed urchin, stood with my face to the wall, and listened to the harmonious voices swelling the praises of God, and thought of those glorious fathers, who, in all their wanderings and trials, felt that they were hidden beneath the hollow of an Almighty hand. They were the Paladins of my childhood's chivalry; knights, the weapons of whose warfare were not carnal, but mighty through God, to the pulling down of strongholds.

This early veneration and affection went with us to the West, and as soon as we were able to take possession of a house with a spare room, that room was styled the prophet's chamber, and our abode again became the home of the preachers. Making allowance for the differences between an older and a new country, they were men of the same school as those we had before known; for, notwithstanding the play of the most decisive individuality, the strongest family likeness marks all the Methodist preachers I have seen. I knew no greater pleasure than to act the part of ostler on behalf of the horses of our welcome guests, acquiring thereby a knowledge and skill in the use of horseflesh which stood me in good stead years after. The first Sunday after our arrival we attended the Methodist church. It was a bright June morning; the place, the people were all strange, and we felt the keen pang of loneliness more on that first day in our Father's house than at any other time. While sadly brooding over the dear old home far away, and thinking of the contrast between it and this unfamiliar place, our attention was arrested by a strange apparition striding up the aisle. All seemed whispering to their neighbors, "there he goes," and all eyes were riveted upon a man of medium height, thick-set, with enormous bone and muscle, and although his iron-grey hair and wrinkled brow told of the advance of years, his step was still vigorous and firm His face was bronzed by exposure to the weather; he carried a white Quaker hat in his hand, and his upper garment was a furniture calico dressing-gown, without wadding. The truant breeze seemed to seize this garment by its skirt, and lifting it to a level with his arm-pits, disclosed to the gazing congregation a full view of the copperas-colored pantaloons and shirt of the divine—for he was a divine, and one worth a day's journey to see and hear.

He had then been a backwoods preacher for nearly forty years, ranging the country from the Lakes to the Gulf, and from the Alleghanies to the Mississippi. He was inured to every form of hardship, and had looked calmly at peril of every kind—the tomahawk of the Indian, the spring of the panther, the hug of the bear, the sweep of the tornado, the rush of swollen torrents, and the fearful chasm of the earthquake. He had lain in the canebrake, and made his bed upon the snow of the prairie and on the oozy soil of the swamp, and had wandered hunger-bitten amid the solitude of mountains. He had been in jeopardy among robbers, and in danger from desperadoes who had sworn to take his life. He had preached in the cabin of the slave, and in the mansion of the master; to the Indians, and to the men of the border. He had taken his life in his hand, and ridden in the path of whizzing bullets, that he might proclaim peace. He had stood on the outskirts of civilization, and welcomed the first comers to the woods and prairies. At the command of

Him who said, "Go into all the world," he had roamed through the wilderness; as a disciple of the man who said "The world is my parish," his travels had equalled the limits of an empire. All this he had done without hope of fee or reward; not to enrich himself or his posterity, but as a preacher of righteousness in the service of God and of his fellow-men. Everywhere he had confronted wickedness, and rebuked it; every form of vice had shrunk abashed from his irresistible sarcasm and ridicule, or quivered beneath the fiery look of his indignant invective.

In the character of the Christian minister might have been a slightly exaggerated infusion of the frontiersman's traits. The whole line of his conduct may not have been marked by the spirit of meekness, or guided by infallible wisdom; but let those who have been tried as he was, and have overcome, as he has, be the first to throw the stone of censure at him. Many a son of Anak has been levelled in the dust by his sledgelike fist; and when the blind fury of his assailants urged them headlong into personal conflict with him, his agility, strength, and resolution gave them cause for bitter repentance. Another Gideon, he has more than once led a handful of the faithful against the armies of the aliens, who were desecrating the place of worship and threatening to abolish religious services, and put them to inglorious flight. But he only girded on his strength thus, and used the weapons that nature gave him, when necessity and the law of self-defence seemed to admit of no escape. The vocation in which he gloried was that of an itinerant preacher, his congenial sphere that of a pastor in the woods. To breathe the words of hope into the ear of the dying, and to minister solace to the survivors; to take little children up in his arms and bless them; to lead the flock over which the Holy Ghost had made him an overseer, and to warn the ungodly of the error of their ways, entreating them to be reconciled to God by the cross of Christ, was the business of his life. Learning he had none, but the keenest perceptions and the truest instincts enabled him to read human nature as men read a book; a sagacity rarely at fault, a powerful fancy, and a vivid sympathy, that supplied the want of imagination—these, together with the dedication of his whole soul to his work, and a studious and prayerful acquaintance with holy Scripture, made him a workman that needed not to be ashamed.

A voice which, in his prime, was capable of almost every modulation, the earnest force and homely directness of his speech, and his power over the passions of the human heart, made him an orator to win and command the suffrages and sympathies of a western audience. And ever through the discourse, came, and went, and came again, a humor that was resistless, now broadening the features into a merry smile, and then softening the heart until tears stood in the eyes of all. His figures and illustrations were often grand, sometimes fantastical. Like all natives of a new country, he spoke much in metaphors, and his were borrowed from the magnificent realm in which he lived. All forms of nature, save those of the sounding sea, were familiar to him, and were employed with the easy familiarity with which children use their toys. You might hear, in a single discourse, the thunder tread of a frightened herd of buffaloes as they rushed wildly across the prairie, the crash of the windrow as it fell smitten by the breath of the tempest, the piercing scream of the wild cat as it scared the midnight forest, the majestic rhythm of the Mississippi as it harmonized the distant East and West, and united, bore their tributes to the far-off ocean; the silvery flow of a mountain rivulet, the whisper of groves, and the jocund laughter of unnumbered prairie flowers, as they toyed in dalliance with the evening breeze. Thunder and lightning, fire and flood, seemed to be old acquaintances, and he spoke of them with the assured confidence of friendship. Another of the poet's attributes was his —the impulse and power to create his own language; and he was the best lexicon of western words, phrases, idioms, and proverbs, that I have ever met.

Such was the man that now stood before us in the desk; the famous presiding elder of Illinois—the renowned Peter Cartwright. All honor to the brave old man, who still lives after an itinerancy of untold toil, hardship, and sufferings, which reaches nearly to the verge of sixty years, and is to-day as indefatigable, zealous, and faithful as when in the prime of his strength. One feature of his life I must not omit to mention, the fact that he has sold more books than probably any man ever did in a new country. The Methodist economy enjoined it as a duty on the preacher to diffuse a sound literature, and to place good books in the homes of the people. Unwearied here, as in everything else that he believed to be his duty, this minister never travelled, if in a buggy, without a trunk, or if on horseback, without a pair of saddle-bags, crammed with books. These he disposed of with all diligence, and has thus entitled himself to the lasting gratitude of many a youth, who, but for him, might have slumbered on without intelligence or education. I have dwelt upon the character of this man, not only because I love and revere him, but because I know of no one who may more fitly stand as the type of the pioneer preachers of the West—men whose worth, self-sacrifices, and labors, have never had their meed of recognition. Perhaps my sketch may be rendered more complete by the following story; at all events, it illustrates the humorous side of his character: He was brought, some years ago, by business connected with the church, to the city of New York, where a room had been engaged for him at the Irving House. Reaching town late at night, he registered his name, and waited until the sleepy hotel clerk cast a glance at the rather illegible scrawl, and at the farmer-like appearance of the man before him. The servant was directed to show the gentleman to his room, which, toiling up one flight of steps after another, Mr. Cartwright found was the first beneath the leads. The patronizing servant explained to the traveller the use of the various articles in the room, and said, on leaving, pointing to the bell-rope, "If you want anything, you can just pull that, and somebody will come up."

The old gentleman waited until the servant [illegible]d had time to descend, and then gave the rope a furious jerk. Up came the servant, bounding two, three steps at a time, and was amazed at the reply in answer to his "What will you have, sir?"

"How are you all coming on down below? It is such a ways from here to there, that a body can have no notion even of the weather where you are."

The servant assured him that all was going on well, and was dismissed, but had scarcely reached the office before another strenuous pull at the bell was given. The bell in the City Hall had struck a fire alarm, and the firemen, with their apparatus, were hurrying with confused noises along the street.

"What's wanting, sir?" said the irritated servant.

"What's all this hulla-balloo?" said the stranger.

"Only a fire, sir."

"A fire, sir!" shouted the other; "do you want us all to be burned up?" knowing well enough the fire was not on the premises.

The servant assured him of the distance of the conflagration, and that all was safe, and again descended. A third furious pull at the bell, and the almost breathless servant again made his appearance at the door.

"Bring me a hatchet," said the traveller, in a peremptory tone.

"A hatchet, sir!" said the astonished waiter.

"Yes, a hatchet."

"What for, sir?"

"That's none of your business; go and fetch me a hatchet."

The servant descended, and informed the clerk that, in his private opinion, that old chap was crazy, and that he meant to commit suicide, or to kill some one in the house, for that he wanted a hatchet.

The clerk, with some trepidation, ventured to the room beneath the leads, and having presented himself, said in his blandest tone, "I beg your pardon, sir, but what was it you wanted?"

"A hatchet," said the imperious stranger.

"A hatchet, sir, really; but what for?" said the other.

"What for! Why, look here, stranger, you see I'm not accustomed to these big houses, and it's such a journey from this to where you are that I thought I might get lost. Now, it is my custom, when I am in a strange country, to blaze my way; we cut notches in the trees, and call that blazing, and we can then always find our way back again; so I thought if I had a hatchet, I'd just go out and blaze the corners from this to your place, and then I would be able to find my way back."

"I beg your pardon," said the mystified clerk; "but what's your name, sir? I could not read it very well on the book."

"My name," replied the other—"certainly; my debts are all paid, and my will is made. My name is Peter Cartwright, at your service."

"Oh, Mr. Cartwright," responded the other, "I beg you ten thousand pardons; we have a room for you, sir, on the second floor—the best room in the house. This way, sir, if you please."

"All right," said the old gentleman; "that's all I wanted."

CHAPTER V

THE SADDLE-BAGS TAKEN UP.

JUST as the sun was rising on a brilliant December morning, we were starting for a ride from Island Grove across the snow-clad prairie, seated in an open carriage, wrapped in buffalo robes, facing the keen westerly wind, bearing away like mariners, seaward bound, the rearward timber receding until it looked, in truth, like an isle encompassed by the endless reaches of the sea. One could hardly fail to be exhilarated even to the verge of intoxication. Away toward the north and south stretched the billowy land, unvaried by a single hill, unbroken by a solitary tree, until the blue sky stooped from the immeasurable height above our heads to the limit of the horizon, as if to kiss the earth; and the earth, arrayed in vestal whiteness, seemed pure enough for heaven's caress.

As the sun's rays reached the snow, the earth seemed sown with emeralds, sapphires, and diamonds. Before us, toward the west, rose the bare arms of a forest, yet as we drew nearer we saw they were not bare, but robed with raiment whiter than wool; while from every sturdy bough and tender branch were pendent glittering and prismatic stalactites. Even the trunks of trees were covered with ice, and in the morning sunshine the woods seemed one vast palace, almost too dazzling to behold—the work of an enchanter's spell. As we sped along there was no sound to break the solemn and nearly awful stillness, but the clatter of our horses' hoofs, and the monotonous whirl of the wheels.

My companion was a tall, stalwart, weather-beaten man, venerable in aspect, and usually grave in demeanor, almost to the point of constraint. He was a profound thinker, an able theologian, and a powerful preacher of the Word. I loved him much, yet stood in no little awe of him by reason of the elevation and force of his intellect, and the sanctity of his character. I had a presentiment at starting which was oppressive, that he and I were to have a conversation that morning, which should perhaps color and affect all my after life. But the rapid motion, the stinging, yet inspiring air, and the splendid scene had raised me to a kind of ecstasy, when I was at once startled and subdued by the clear, yet commanding voice of my companion, saying, "William, did you ever feel that you were called to preach?" It was a home question, but one I had hardly dared answer to myself. Is it not the teaching of Scripture—is it not the faith of the church that God himself selects, calls, commissions and empowers his servants who are to carry his message to the world? Is it right for any man to make choice of the ministry as a profession, in the same way, and from the same motives that he would adopt law, medicine, or science? Dare any man take upon himself this office and ministry without the monition and sanction of the Holy Ghost? and before he be brave enough to assume the dread responsibility of the care of souls, must he not feel in agony of soul, "woe is me if I preach not the gospel?" If we can be conscious of the warning voice of an inward monitor, if we can be conscious of the living influences of the divine Spirit, can we not be conscious and equally assured of the movement of that same Spirit, summoning us in the serene and prayerful hour of meditation, as in the fierce, hot struggle with self and secular desire, to "go and teach all nations, baptizing them in the name of the Father, and of the Son, and of the Holy Ghost?"

Such, briefly stated, is the theory and belief of our denomination.

I had indeed felt for years that this was to be my duty, to preach the gospel; but I shrank from it with unutterable fear and dread. If an apostle could say "Who is sufficient for these things?" then how much more I; so I stammered out as well as I might, the answer that my venerated friend demanded, and the thoughts that assumed the form of doubts and difficulties to me—youth and inexperience, immaturity of mind, and incompleteness of education, and then want of vision. To all these things, and many more that need not be enumerated, my companion made reply, and urged me at once to adopt the course of obedience and duty. This I could not resolve to do. He said the fields were white unto the harvest, but the laborers few. I said I could not go, at least, until I had graduated.

In less than two months after this, my health was gone—my system seemed a wreck. Books were denied me, and now you will understand why, in the languor of disease and feebleness, I had such hours of lonely wretchedness. It is a solemn ordeal when one ceases to be a youth—when he is to leave the shelter of his father's roof, and the pitiful tenderness of his mother, to take upon him the responsibilities of life, to make or to mar his own character, and in his own, the character of so many others. One instinctively shivers at the prospect of a wide strange world into which he must venture without assurance of what may betide.

Ardent as may be the hope of youth, there is strong likelihood that in this time it will be palsied, and that boding fear will take its place to tell sad tales and to utter sadder prophecies.

On the first of May I was mounted and off for a life of wandering. My horse, excepting his face and feet which were white, was black as a coal. He was a five-year-old, just broken to the saddle, full of fiery spirit and intelligence, frolicksome, but kindly; disposed, like all horses and men, to play pranks and take liberties with those afraid of him, and willing only to submit to a rightful master. His late owner sold him because he had run away with him, and it was predicted that I, an unskillful horseman, whose chief feats had hitherto consisted in riding the preachers' horses to water, would not go far before being landed in the mire, if I escaped with an unbroken neck.

My mother had made every provision that foresight or tenderness could suggest, for the comfort of my wayfaring. A pair of capacious saddle-bags was stuffed with books and clothes; an overcoat, infolding an umbrella, was strapped behind the saddle, and I was attired in a stout suit of blue jeans; my nether extremities were inclosed in leggings; my head was crowned with a skin cap, exchanged in the summer time for a Panama hat. It had been arranged that I was to travel with the license of an exhorter, in company with my venerated friend of the preceding conversation, the Rev. Peter Akers.

Further on, I shall try for the benefit of my uninitiated readers, to explain some of the terminology and practical workings of the Methodist itinerancy, but it is sufficient to state here that Dr. Akers was a presiding elder, and that, as such, he had a sort of episcopal supervision over about a dozen charges, located within a circuit of near five hundred miles. It was his business to visit each of these once in three months, and preside over the conference of official members, to transact the ecclesiastical and financial business, to hear appeal cases argued, to supervise the moral and ministerial character of the preachers, and by his superior weight and spiritual counsel to advance the cause. The elder and abler men were usually selected by the bishop for this responsible office, and among these in Illinois, Dr. Akers for learning, and power as a preacher, stood without a peer. It is true that his interest in his theme and the fervor of his feelings carried him to a length of discourse only equalled by the Covenanters and the Puritans. I there frequently heard him "hold forth" for from three to five hours. But it must be said that the mass of his audience were usually so enchained that they would not have had the sermon a moment shorter. Occasionally, however, he would feel compelled to bestow a reminder upon some impatient hearer, and one night I heard him say to a man in the congregation who pulled out his watch and found the preacher had been speaking about two hours, "Put up your watch, sir, it is not time to go to bed yet." Report said, that at such times he would now and then get a reply which mightily tickled, if it did not edify the audience. I have heard it told, but do not remember on what authority, that once when the services were protracted, an incorrigible sinner whose empty stomach had sounded a dinner-bell in his ears, got up to leave the house, when the preacher shouted out after him, "Stop, sir, I am not through yet." "Go on, sir," said the other, "I am just going to dinner, and will be back long before you are through."

Away we trotted out of the town, and although the roads were heavy, the pace of our horses was good, so that by the time we had reached the edge of a five-mile prairie, I, an unpractised rider, began to be sore from the jolting. By this time it had commenced to rain, so donning my overcoat I tried to raise the umbrella. But my fiery steed seemed to think such an article unworthy of the man that backed him; away he went and away went the umbrella, and I never saw it again, nor did I ever attempt to use one again while riding the circuit. "Let him go," shouted my companion in a roar of laughter. "Good bye." Off we sped in a headlong gallop, and when my charger seemed disposed to slacken his gait, I gave him the whip, nor did we change the break-neck gait until we reached the opposite timber, in a shorter time than men often ride five miles. He never ran away with me again.

This little adventure brought my horse and me to the best possible understanding, and from friendship we grew to intimacy, for he was my companion in all my wayfarings through the West. Many a thousand miles has he borne me, and many a hymn have I sung, and many a sermon have I preached to him. Whenever he heard the sound of my voice at the commencement of such exercises, he would prick up his ears and seem to listen with the most intense attention, and I can say more for him than for some of my human auditors, to wit: that he never went to sleep while I was discoursing. He appeared to appreciate my infirmity, and displayed the power and scope of instinct to an astonishing degree. In a country where bad bridges abounded, where streams had to be forded, where roads degenerated into bridle-paths, or even faint trails, where often there was no road at all, and wood craft and the points of the compass could be the only guides, he bore me by day and night through danger and difficulty, with a constancy of attention, and an unerring sagacity really wonderful. No one of my readers who has ever owned and become attached to a valuable horse, will blame me for this tribute to my faithful charger.

A ride of two days and a half brought us to our first appointment. The quarterly meeting was held at a private house, as was frequently the case, serving on such occasions the two-fold purpose of chapel and hotel. It was a double log cabin, with a door communicating between the two rooms, the women occupying one, the men the other, in both the uses to which the house was put. Seats for the congregation were provided by puncheon slabs resting on four legs. The young people who could not find access to the house, would stand beneath the trees, or loll upon the grass. The congregation would come from fifteen to twenty miles around to enjoy the services. The exercises invariably began on Saturday at eleven o'clock, with a sermon from the presiding elder. In the afternoon the conference of official members was held; in the evening the most available preacher was "put up," in the language of the country, and after this sermon an exhortation was usually delivered by some one else.

At the close of the exercises the benches were carried out and replaced by shuck mattresses, skins, and blankets, the men making their own beds, so that in a little while, as you looked over the sleepy scene, by the ray of an expiring pine knot, you might well conceive it a stratum of compact somnolent humanity. The first cockcrow is the signal for a universal arousing, and while some busy themselves in taking up and packing away the beds, others bring wood, four or eight feet long, to kindle a fire in the capacious fireplace, by which the breakfast may be cooked. Others, with shirt-sleeves rolled up and collars *à la* Byron, in the breaking dawn, trudge to the spring or well, where ablutions are performed. A substantial meal is dispatched, for it may be long before we taste food again. At eight o'clock the Sunday services begin by a love-feast, to which only members of the church are admitted. At eleven o'clock the doors are thrown open and the public enter. The ordinance of baptism precedes the sermon, the communion of the Lord's Supper follows it. On more than one occasion I have known it to be five o'clock before we tasted a mouthful after a sunrise breakfast. In the evening the last sermon of the quarterly meeting proper was delivered, and by daybreak the following morning all were riding off on their several ways.

On the Saturday night in question, after the sermon, the sonorous voice of my chief said, "William, exhort." The will of the presiding elder at these times is absolute, and obedience is one of the lessons enjoined upon young preachers. I had no resource but to stand up, frightened as I was almost to death, behind my split-bottom chair, in lieu of a pulpit, in front of the huge fireplace, and attempt to speak by the light of the smouldering embers and one or two candles fast sinking to their sockets, to the crowd of hunters and farmers filling the cabin, who gaped and stared at a pallid, beardless boy. Of course words were few, and ideas fewer, and on resuming my seat I had the uncomfortable impression, that that congregation had listened to about as poor a discourse as ever was delivered. Such was my first attempt at preaching.

The interval between Monday and Saturday of each week, was generally spent in travelling a daily stage toward the next appointment, and preaching once or twice a day, and visiting the people on the road. Wherever we stopped we were treated with the cordial hospitality for which the West is proverbial. No matter what the time of day, food was produced and we were always urged to eat. This saying has passed into a wise saw, "that yellow-legged chickens (the largest and finest breed), know a Methodist preacher as far as they can see him, and that they no sooner behold one approaching than they squeak with terror, and betake themselves to the timber, knowing that their heads are in danger."

At one of our meetings I met the happiest man, I think, that I have ever known. He was a bachelor, and a shoemaker, who worked half the time to support himself and horse, and attended meeting the other half. I cannot say much for the breadth of his intellect, the extent of his information, or the quality of his taste. His faith seemed to be un clouded, and his soul was ever on the mountain-top. He was passionately fond of singing, and had a repertory of songs and tunes, all his own. I think you might have heard him half a mile off; I have been awakened at all hours of the night by the vociferous strains of this minstrel, and have seen him astride a bench see-sawing to and fro, slapping his hands and pouring forth his stentorian solo. Music seemed to be his meat, drink, and lodging. His favorite verse, self-made, no doubt, was the following:

"I'd rather have religion,
While here on earth I stay,
Than to possess the riches
Of all America.

Chorus.

Crying, victory, victory,
I long to see that day."

The rough and tumble life of the woods, the fare—repulsive at first, but made acceptable by sharp exercise and appetite—of hog, hominy, and corn bread, saleratus biscuit, and fried chicken (none of which I have been able to tolerate since), as the season wore on, began to give me flesh and color.

CHAPTER VI.

"LET NO MAN DESPISE THY YOUTH."

My itinerating life was yet fresh when the two preachers from the Fancy Creek circuit visited one of our quarterly meetings; at its close they besought the presiding elder to lend me to them for a week's round, promising to deliver me safe and sound at his appointment the next Saturday. He assented, and away I trotted with my new-made friends. Our first stopping-place was at a house much like the one before described, where the senior preacher was to solemnize a marriage. We arrived at mid-day, and found a large company assembled—the future man and wife chatting gaily with their friends, as though the knot had been already tied. The ceremony was at once attended to, and the congratulations delivered, when the company was summoned to the most sumptuous banquet that the region could afford. I wish I were versed in the technicalities of feminine attire, that I might favor my lady readers with a description of the dresses worn on this gala day, and a comical one it would be; but, failing in this, I can only commemorate one incident that struck me at the time. A great bowl of boiled custard was placed, with other delicacies, on the groaning board. A gentleman having hurried through with the more substantial part of the repast, seized the bowl and a tablespoon and commenced ingulfing the contents. A bystander, somewhat shocked at this private appropriation of what was designed for the community, remarked to him, "You don't seem to know what that is."

"Know what it is!" responded the other, indignantly, "of course I do; I was brought up on it—it is thickened milk."

As we rode away, the preacher who had united the man and wife said to me, "Billy, what do you suppose that chap gave me for a fee?"

"I don't know," I replied. "Five dollars, I suppose."

"He is a hog without bristles," was the strong metaphorical reply of the other; "he didn't give me narry red."

As we proceeded, he told me I should have to preach that afternoon at four o'clock, and he turned a deaf ear to all my entreaties to be let off. Up to this time I had never taken a text, for all my exercises had been in the shape of exhortations, delivered after some more experienced person had expounded. My first sermon must be preached somewhere, and why not then and there? So it was delivered to half a dozen men in their shirt-sleeves, with the sweat of the plough on their brows, their teams left standing in the fields the while, and to as many women in sun-bonnets, whose knitting and pipes were laid aside when the hymn was given out. The rustle of the green leaves, stirred by the pleasant wind, the song of the birds, and the golden sunshine as it lay upon the puncheon floor on that cheerful summer afternoon, are remembered yet, and also that my first sermon was but fifteen minutes long.

The next day we reached a village consisting of a dozen or twenty houses. In the evening we attended an examination of the school; at the close of the exercises, one of my new friends mounted an empty barrel which stood in the corner of the room, and had been used as a seat, and called out in the old Norman form, "Oyez! Oyez! take notice that Brother William Milburn will preach in the meeting house to-morrow night at early candle-lighting!" No sooner was the last word out of his mouth than the barrel-head gave way and the reverend clerk, falling to the earth, went after the fashion of Regulus, rolling about among the legs of the audience, his desperate exertions to escape only making his plight the sadder and increasing the confusion.

Between the wheat harvest and the time for gathering corn, the farmers had a respite, and this (yclept roasting-ear time) was the season for camp meetings. Those who have attended them only in the neighborhood of large cities or in populous districts, where they are apt to be a rendezvous for the idle, profane, and lewd, can form little notion of their impressive beauty and real usefulness in a new and thinly settled country. A grove of sugar maple or beech, with abundant springs and pasturage near at hand, is selected, and here the tents of canvas, logs, or weatherboards, are erected in the form of a parallelogram, inclosing from one to four acres. Within this area, upon which all the tents open, are arranged the seats, the altar, and the pulpit, or stand as it is called. Spaces for streets are left open at the four corners of the square. In the rear of each tent, a large, permanent table is erected; for the meeting is sacred to the rites of hospitality as well as of devotion. The tenters move into their temporary abodes on Thursday or Friday, and the religious exercises commence at once. A horn is blown about daylight as the signal for getting up; after a while, it sounds for family prayers, and soon you may hear strains of song from every tent, celebrating the praise of Him who hath given the slumber and safety of the night. The blast summons the people to the stand at eight and eleven, A.M., at three P.M., and again at early candle-lighting. The meeting continues from four to six days. It is a grand sight to behold several hundreds—sometimes swelled to thousands—of people gathered beneath the shadow of the green wood, worshipping in the oldest and noblest of cathedrals; its aisles flanked by straight or twisted shafts springing from a verdant floor to a light, waving tracery unapproachable by man's poor art. The scene is one to furnish inspiration to the speaker, and to open for him the surest and swiftest access to the hearers' hearts. But it is at night that the ground wears its most picturesque appearance. From fire stands, placed at short distances over the encampment, heaps of blazing pine knots shed a brilliant light upon the assembly, and strive to illumine the dim, whispering vaults overhead, through which the stars, those candles of the Lord, may be seen blazing in their far distant sockets. Never have I been so moved by music, as when the great congregation have stood up on such a spot, and poured forth a hymn with one heart and voice. Truly was it like the voice of many waters.

No one can fully estimate the beneficent influences of these "feasts of Tabernacles," where the unsophisticated people of a new country are schooled and refined by the offices of hospitality, friendship, and devotion. Not least among the good results, is the acquaintance with sacred poetry here acquired; for introduced and commended by the strains of a lively and heart-stirring music, the best effusions of Montgomery, Heber, Cowper, Watts, and Wesley, win their way to a lasting place in the affectionate remembrance of the motley crowd. It is quite wonderful to see how retentively poetry and Scripture are held in the memory of many of these plain and comparatively uneducated backwoodsmen. I have seen more than one preacher, who had, probably, never enjoyed the advantage of three months' schooling, who, nevertheless, seemed to have at command a large portion of Milton's, Young's, and Cowper's poetical works, besides vast stores from other authors; and the citations from these, though often long, and sometimes not altogether appropriate, were keenly relished by the people.

The stimulating quality of life in this fresh, unhackneyed world, the constant and vivid play of the perceptions, the charm of variety and adventure, a first-hand acquaintance with nature, the action of sensibilities unchilled and almost unconscious, the use of words in their primary and oftentimes their strongest signification, the effectiveness of fancy and imagination, combine to produce a striking, and, sometimes, astonishing style of popular eloquence.

As I went the round of the district, with my venerable guide, philosopher, and friend, riding sometimes for whole days through almost limitless stretches of prairie, much time was spent in asking and answering questions concerning theology and kindred sciences, in which he was profoundly versed. His full and satisfactory explanations in response to my eager queries, together with his exhaustive discourses delivered in public, afforded me a large store of material to digest and assimilate. The intimate association of the elder and younger men, the habit of constantly seeking and imparting instruction, and the urgent need for the immediate use of all information thus acquired, constitute a prominent feature of the mental discipline of the Methodist preachers. I have never known such strong bonds of sympathy and affection to unite men of any class as those which bind these brethren together. The healthful action of the sensibilities is always the best condition of mental growth. Love is the mightiest teacher. You can well fancy that the powers of the mind and heart will not be sluggish or inapt when you have the wide open universe, with the glowing sunshine or the glimmering starlight, the fathomless azure or the embattled clouds joining in the fierce din of the tempest above you, and the land all around arrayed in the luxuriant garb of summer-time; when you have these for a seminary, a teacher by your side whom you both revere and love as a father and a friend, and a theme deep as life and solemn as eternity. Thus did the months glide by from May until September, the latter closing the conference year, when all the preachers gathered themselves together for the transaction of their official business, and to receive at the hand of the bishop their "appointments" for the next twelvemonth.

This is, perhaps, the proper place for me to give some explanation of the machinery and internal working of Methodism, for the benefit of my uninitiated readers.

Persons are admitted to membership on trial in our societies, on profession of a desire "to flee from the wrath to come and to be saved from their sins." Twelve or more persons constitute a "class," one of whom is called a "leader." It is his business to see his members once a week, to inquire into their spiritual state, to counsel, reprove, admonish, or encourage them. At the close of the probation of six months, the candidate, if satisfied with the church, and a good report be made of him, is received into full membership. A person feeling himself moved to take upon himself the office and ministry of a teacher, makes this known to the preacher, who, if satisfied upon consultation with his leader and brethren, gives him a license to "exhort." Having made proof of his gifts, graces, and usefulness, in this capacity, he is called before the quarterly conference, a body composed of the presiding elder as chairman, the preachers on the circuit or station, the stewards (who have charge of the financial affairs connected with the ministry), and the class leaders. He is now to pass an examination as to his education, religious experience, and doctrinal views. If these be satisfactory, and he has given promise of usefulness, he is recommended by the conference to the presiding elder as a proper person to have a license to preach, and that functionary furnishes him with the requisite authority. At the proper time, the same body furnishes the candidate a recommendation to the "Annual Conference," desiring that he may be received on trial as a preacher in the travelling connection.

The Annual Conference is composed of those preachers living within a given region of country, who receive their appointments from the bishop and their support from the church, and who devote themselves exclusively to the ministry. The territory of the conference is divided into districts, the charge of which is given, as before stated, to presiding elders. The districts are subdivided into circuits and stations, the latter being towns or cities where one or more societies require the constant services of one or more pastors. The former are rural districts, composed of from four to thirty or forty neighborhoods, in each of which the minister is to preach as often as circumstances may allow, and they are technically styled in accordance with the frequency with which he is enabled to visit the appointments, one, two, three, four, or six weeks circuits.

The business of the preachers in conference assembled, is to examine the intellectual, moral, and ministerial character of each man, to receive candidates, and to make a report of the sums which they have received for the various benevolent undertakings of the church. At a proper time, the bishop, who is the presiding officer, asks the question: "Who are to be received on trial?" When the presiding elders read the recommendations of the candidates, and make such statements concerning them as their acquaintance and opinions justify, and the men are then received or rejected by a vote of the conference. If he be received, the candidate must enter upon a four years' course of study, and be prepared to stand an examination every year at the conference. This *curriculum* embraces a wide range of literary and theological study, the rigor and effectiveness of the examination, be it said, being dependent on the character and attainments of the examining committee. If he make full proof of his ministry, at the end of two years he is received into full connection—for hitherto he has been on trial—and ordained deacon. At the end of another period of two years, on the same condition, he receives ordination as an elder.

During the session of the conference, the bishop who presides over its deliberations, holds a council every night with the presiding elders, who are called the members of his cabinet. Together they make out the appointments of the preachers for the ensuing year. All the other business having been attended to, the bishop closes the conference with a brief and pertinent address, with singing and prayer, and then by the announcement of the "appointments," of which the preachers generally, until this moment, have remained in ignorance.

Once in four years, the members of the annual conferences elect delegates, according to a fixed ratio, to a "General Conference," which is the legislature and high court of judicature of the church. To this body the bishops, who are elected by it, are amenable for their moral, ministerial, and executive conduct. Thus, then, this quadrennial synod causes the bishops to revolve regularly in their itinerant orbits. These, in turn, keep the thirty or forty annual conferences in regular rotation; the presiding elders turn the quarterly conferences once in three months; the preachers cause the revolution of the leaders and stewards once a month, and these the private members once a week. So that the machinery consists of a wheel within a wheel, and the ideal is that of perpetual motion.

CHAPTER VII.

"BREAKING BREAD FROM HOUSE TO HOUSE, THEY DID EAT THEIR MEAT WITH GLADNESS AND SINGLENESS OF HEART."

At the time of which I speak, the Illinois Conference embraced two-thirds of the State, and was composed of about 110 preachers. It was to sit at Quincy, two days' journey from my home. A party of four rigged out a two-horse wagon, in which we journeyed together. Two of the company were old preachers who had seen much service on the frontier. The third was a junior, a man full of electricity and humor. The way was shortened by the discussion of many grave and knotty points, and by the recital of many a story. One or two of these may shed light upon the primitive state of society on the border, and afford a notion of the varied experiences of the early Methodist itinerants.

One of our old preachers, the Rev. S. H. Thomp son, was travelling a circuit in Tennessee at an early day. He was invited to cross the mountains and visit a settlement where a preacher had never been. The entire population turned out to give him a hearty welcome, and to hear his message. In the midst of his discourse, a man rode up to the edge of the assembly and alighted; whereupon, every man, woman and child in the congregation rushed to the new-comer to ask and hear the news. One of the party, with an encouraging look and gesture to the preacher, saying, "Go on, parson, we'll all be back directly." In due time they returned, and Mr. Thompson proceeded with his sermon. At its close, he called on an exhorter who had accompanied him to the place, to pray. The brother's spirit was willing but his flesh was weak, for he had a great boil on his right knee. The audience beheld his energetic yet ludicrous attempt to put himself in the proper posture; when one of the bystanders, a good-natured giant, touched with compassion, stepped forward and lying flat on his face, said: "Here, brother, kneel on me." The exhorter accepted the living stool, and becoming much excited in the course of his prayer, would often raise himself up and then come down with emphatic force on the back of his prostrate friend. At the close of the lengthy supplication, the latter rose, and shaking himself, exclaimed: "First-rate prayer, weren't it? —a little long, though."

One of our beloved bishops, the Rev. Thomas A. Morris, when a young man, was travelling somewhere in the West, and left an appointment to preach in a neighborhood little frequented by the ministry. Due notice was given, and a large company assembled. The service was to be held in a double log-cabin with a porch in front. The men were gathered in one room, the women in the other, and the boys on the porch. The preacher stood in the door. As he proceeded, a couple of men in the congregation began to whisper, and at length spoke so loud that all the congregation could hear them; the theme of their discourse being a horse-swap. The preacher paused and said, that as it was bad manners for more than one to speak at a time, if it were necessary for them to bring their trade to a conclusion on the spot, he would stop until they had finished. They were silent, and he resumed, when an officious old gentleman came bustling through the crowd with a split-bottomed chair raised high above his head, and placing it in front of the preacher, said: "I forgot you had no pulpit; a man can't preach without a pulpit; here is one." The preacher began again, but was soon interrupted by the noise made by the boys in the porch quarrelling. This was promptly quelled by the old gentleman's striding among the urchins, cuffing and boxing them soundly, and shouting, "Be still, you little savages, or I'll knock your heads off." Order restored, the preacher tried to go on again, but now there came a noise from the female side of the house. A boy four or five years old, who was seated in his mother's lap, was engaged in earnest whispering with her. He said, "Mammy, mammy," and she, "Hush!" At length he seemed to think that endurance had ceased to be a virtue, and bawled out, "I say, mammy, scratch my back." She, in fiery indignation, boxed his ears soundly; whereat, he set up a terrible yell. She rose, and dragging her promising offspring after her, forced her way among the auditors, rushed by the preacher in the door, and at once began the satisfactory operation of trouncing, she shouting "hush!" and he, "I won't—scratch my back!" This last attack was too much for the preacher's equanimity, and the excited state of his risibles obliged him to close the services on the instant.

With abundant store of such reminiscences and anecdotes, we beguiled the tedious way. As the evening of the first day closed upon us, we reached a hamlet where we were hospitably lodged at the house of a brother in the church. Our host was from Connecticut, and began at once to importune our elders for a sermon to the people that evening, promising them a congregation of as many souls as Noah had in the ark. But they declined, pleading fatigue as an excuse, saying, however, "Here are the boys, either of them will preach."

"What, them?" said our landlord, contemptuously; "do you suppose the people in these parts would come out to hear such younkers hold forth?"

"I'll tell you what, Billy, " said my junior friend, as he went to the stable to put up the horses; "that fellow's got no more manners than a bear. It's my opinion that he came to this country peddling tin-ware and wooden nutmegs. I reckon the time will come when they'll be glad to hear us as well as Uncle Peter and Jonathan."

To know what the pleasures of conference are, a man must have been a western Methodist preacher. A life of incessant toil, privation, hardship, and poverty, borne bravely and cheerfully for a single sublime object, breeds a unity of feeling and a warmth of affection not elsewhere equalled. Like the early Christians, they regard themselves as the soldiers of the cross; and the militant sentiment is strengthened by their out-door life, and their frequent exposure to danger. No dragoons are better horsemen, or are more in the saddle. They delight to describe life as a warfare, death as the last conflict wherein the Christian places his foot upon the neck of his last adversary, and with a shout of victory rises to the scene of a triumphant coronation. One of their favorite hymns commences:

"Soldiers of Christ, arise,
And put your armor on,
Strong in the strength which God supplies
Through his eternal Son."

Indeed, there is very much in the sacred lyrics of

Charles Wesley to nourish this martial spirit. The coming together of the preachers at conference is, therefore, much like the gathering of an army after a campaign. Old friendships are strengthened, old associations vivified. Trials and triumphs are recounted, and messages are brought from one and another brother who has died during the year, or, as they are accustomed to say, "fallen in the field with his face Zionward." "Tell my brethren at the conference," said one of these saintly warriors, "that I died at my post." The conference, which lasts about a week, is, in truth, a feast of reason and a flow of soul. The preachers are billeted upon the members of the church and other citizens who are willing to entertain them. And the season is ever one of open-handed hospitality. And outside of business hours, the order of the day is good cheer, story-telling, friendly chat—in a word, the comfort and delight of body and soul. Here they are a band of toil-worn veterans and eager young soldiers, martialling for review, and the enjoyment of the one week's holiday for the year. Their salary is a hundred dollars per annum, and many of them have received not more than one-third or one-half that sum; but from the manner and amount of their offerings to the various benevolent institutions of the church, you would suppose them wealthy men. Let a story be told of a brother having lost his horse, and having no money to buy another, many a man will instantly surrender his last cent to purchase a new one. The widows and orphans of deceased brethren are ever remembered out of the scanty stock. The *esprit de corps* could not be stronger, yet personal independence and self respect are defended as sacred rights.

I must describe one of these men, the Rev. Wilson Pitner, familiarly known among his associates as Wils Pitner. Swarthy as an Indian, he was lithe and strong as one. Born and bred upon the border, he was thoroughly versed in the whole range of woodcraft. He could pick a squirrel's eye with rifle-ball at a hundred yards, or guide you with unerring precision across an untracked prairie. No trapper was more skilled in snaring the muskrat and otter, and his line from the flowery meads, where the bee collected his honied sweets, to the hive in the hollow tree where they were stored, was as true as the insect's own. Books had done little for him, but nature had taught him many a lesson, deep and long. With a powerful voice, capable of almost every modulation, a brilliant eye, a vivid nature, and a soul deeply in earnest, he would sometimes pour forth torrents of fiery eloquence that no human sensibilities could withstand. Let him have "liberty" as it was styled—or to employ its equivalent, let him "swing clear" in a treatment of a subject with which he was familiar, technically called "a sugar stick,"—and not Christmas Evans, the great Welsh orator, could surpass him in the power of his popular appeals. It could not be expected that his expositions would always be as correct as they were independent. He once said, "My brethren, the Apostle Paul declares that faith cometh by hearing, and Mr. Wesley says so too; but I take liberty of differing from both these gentleman. I knew a man once who was so deaf that he could not hear the loudest thunder, and he had more faith than anybody I ever saw. Now, did his faith come by hearing?" He was subject to fits of great depression. On recovering from one of these, a friend asked him how he felt on coming out of the fog and gloom. "Feel!" he exclaimed, "why, as if my soul were running horse-races in the grand prairie of divinity." In preaching, he once said: "I look upon myself as less than the least of all saints; and when I hear the great sermons preached by the presiding elders and bishops, I feel so badly about my own ignorance and weakness that I think I will never open my lips again. But I take courage when I remember what the Bible says: 'Not by might, nor by power, but by my spirit, saith the Lord.' We have this 'treasure in earthen vessels, that the excellency of the power may be of God and not of us.' I have been riding through the woods, before now, and seen a poor little grapevine that had crawled along the earth to the roots of a big tree, and with its feeble tendrils was holding on and trying to climb up the sides of the mighty monarch of the forests. Then I have seen another vine, as big around as a man's arm, and lifting its head far in the light it stood as noble and stately as if it had been a tree itself. But if you look close, you would see that it still leaned for support to the branches of the tree, and that its arms still clung to the mighty giant. It had climbed up as the little one was now trying to do; and strong as it now seemed, if it were to let go only for a moment, it would fall and be snapped in pieces, its strength and protection, like the hope and promise of the little one, is the tree. So," he continued, "frail and weak as I am, I still strive to cling to that tree, on which all the great ones of the earth must rest, and without which they are nothing; a tree whose roots underlie all things—whose trunk is the strength of the universe, its branches are the heavens, its blossoms are the stars; its whispering breath is the joy of souls redeemed, but its shadow is the night of the damned."

Into the companionship of such men was I received as a preacher on trial in the travelling connection of the Methodist Episcopal Church on the day that I completed my twentieth year. Right heartily was the right hand of fellowship given by the brave and hardy band of pioneer preachers whose confidence and esteem I coveted more than that of generals and kings.

The last scene of the conference is one peculiarly touching and solemn. A hundred men, many of them married, have surrendered their right of choice, and placed their lives and fortunes, under God, at the disposal of a single man—the bishop. He, with the wisdom of an overseer, with the simplicity and sincerity that spring from the abiding consciousness that his motives and decisions are ever in the great Taskmaster's eye, and with all a father's tenderness for the preachers and the people intrusted to him—he has considered the claims of the men and of the work, and is now to read the weighty decision. At his word they are to go forth to their fields of duty and of danger, accepting his arbitrament as the interpretation of providence. Whither they are to go they know not, nor what shall betide them; only of this are they persuaded, that a life of voluntary poverty and hardship awaits them, and, probably, a home in some pestilential river bottom, or in a region where fever stalks as a strong man armed. Nevertheless, "the love of Christ constraineth them," and they count not their lives dear unto themselves so that they may finish their course with joy, and the ministry which they have received of the Lord Jesus, to testify the gospel of the grace of God. Most of them, are vigorous, robust, and athletic, yet it is almost certain that they will all never look upon each other's faces again until they stand upon Mount Zion in the general assembly and church of the first-born, which are written in heaven. The prayer has been offered which commends them and their families to God and to the word of his grace, which is able to build them up and to give them "an inheritance among all them which are sanctified;" and in the midst of a profound silence the bishop reads out the appointments. A new year has begun, the week's holiday is over. Hands are shaken, farewell is said, and ere an hour has passed most of the men are on the road to their new posts.

CHAPTER VIII.

BRUSH COLLEGE.

As he was reading, the bishop had announced "Winchester circuit—Norman Allen, William H. Milburn." "The work" embraced Scott county, lying on the eastern side of the Illinois River sixty or seventy miles above its mouth. There were about thirty preaching places; a few of them chapels, more log schoolhouses, but the greater number were private dwellings. It required four weeks to make the round, a ride of nearly three hundred miles, and demanding on an average a sermon a day. After the public duties of the ministry are performed, it is expected that the preacher shall meet the members of the society in private, and converse with each one on his spiritual concerns. In his twelve or thirteen rounds during the year, if he be a man of active and enterprising habits, he will almost inevitably make the acquaintance of every man, woman and child in the county, and break bread at the tables of the great majority of the hospitable householders. The school of human nature thus opened to him, the constant free and easy intercourse with all classes and conditions of persons will teach the man of open mind many a lesson of invaluable knowledge and wisdom: so that while his opportunity for the study of books may be small, a rich compensation is afforded him in this first-hand acquaintance with men and life. A new country demands courage, decision, self-reliance, habits of keen and sleepless observation, a fertility of resources and a versatile employment of various powers to suit changing occasions, and the various well defined characters you meet. You must have eyes and ears, hands and feet, an unshaken fortitude, and a will to turn your hand to anything that is honest and of good report. The terms of tuition in Brush College and Swamp University are high, the course of study hard, the examinations frequent and severe, but the schooling is capital.

I shall never forget a word of wholesome counsel given me by an old preacher, as I was starting in my new career: "Billy, my son, never miss an appointment. Ride all day in any storm, or all night if necessary, ford creeks, swim rivers, run the risk of breaking your neck, or getting drowned, but never miss an appointment, and never be behind the time."

This same veteran had rather an odd way of mak

ing the young preacher at home in his house. "Now brother," he would say, "yonder are the stable and corn-crib for your horse; here is a room and a plate for yourself; but if I ever catch you making sheeps' eyes at my girls, remember there's the door, and never enter it again. One woman in a family is enough for the wife of a Methodist preacher. It is hard for us, but a heap harder for them."

Among Mr. Wesley's characteristic rules for the government of the young preachers are the following; and to these, as far as practicable, it was expected we should yield unswerving obedience:

1. Be diligent. Never be unemployed a moment; never be triflingly employed. Never while away time; neither spend any more time at any place than is strictly necessary.

2. Be serious. Let your motto be, holiness to the Lord. Avoid all lightness, jesting and foolish talking.

3. Converse sparingly and cautiously with women, particularly with young women, in private.

4. Take no step toward marriage, without first acquainting us with your design.

5. Believe evil of no one; unless you see it done, take heed how you credit it. Put the best construction upon everything; you know the judge is always supposed to be on the prisoner's side.

6. Speak evil of no one; else your word, especially, would eat as doth a canker. Keep your thoughts within your own breast, till you come to the person concerned.

7. Tell every one what you think wrong in him, and that plainly, and as soon as may be, else it will fester in your heart. Make all haste to cast the fire out of your bosom.

8. Do not affect the gentleman. You have no more to do with this character than with that of a dancing-master. A preacher of the gospel is the servant of all.

9. Be ashamed of nothing but sin; not of fetching wood (if time permit), or of drawing water; not of cleaning your own shoes, or your neighbor's.

10. Be punctual. Do everything exactly at the time; and in general do not mend our rules, but keep them; not for wrath, but for conscience' sake.

11. You have nothing to do but to save souls. Therefore spend and be spent in this work. And go always not only to those who want you, but to those who want you most.

12. Act in all things not according to your own will, but as a son in the gospel. As such it is your part to employ your time in the manner which we direct; partly in preaching and visiting the flock from house to house; partly in reading, meditation and prayer. Above all, if you labor with us in our

Lord's vineyard, it is needful that you should do that part of the work which we advise, at those times and places which we judge most for his glory.

Minding these things, and walking by these rules, the frontier preacher, however arduous and manifold his toils, could redeem a portion of every day, for the study of good books; and as it was one of his duties to carry his saddle-bags full of them, that he might dispose of them to his parishioners, he ever had a library near at hand. Hunger is the best sauce for food. Crowded dainties and groaning boards seldom yield the most satisfying repast. A hearty appetite will make homely fare more agreeable, delicious, and serviceable than all that French cookery can do for the palate of the dyspeptic gourmand. To most men the multitudinous array of a great library is like the surfeit of a feast, and excessive reading for reading's sake alone will as surely produce an overloaded or paralyzed memory and mental indigestion, as a continued indulgence in the pleasures of the table, will issue in plethora and gout. Books yield the most exquisite enjoyment to him who rises early and sits up late, and eagerly snatches every instant that can be taken from more pressing affairs for increasing his acquaintance with them. The delight of a traveller in the wilderness as he reaches the cooling shade and refreshing spring, is only equalled by the joy of the earnest student who redeems brief intervals from daily toil for communion with his beloved oracle.

That reading is most valuable which is pursued with a definite object; and knowledge is beneficial as it can be assimilated. The mind grows by use; and its finest powers are called into play by the demand for public speaking at once premeditated and yet improvised. The effort of the mind to project and crystallize thought in language, if faithfully performed, must tend to increase the force and clearness of the mind itself. A man's culture is broader and better when sought not for himself alone, but also for the benefit of others; with their wants as well as his own in his eye. The truth by which a man converts his fellow, acquires new lustre and glory for the man himself. The preaching of Christ crucified, though it be to the Jews a stumbling-block, and to the Greeks foolishness, is to them that believe, the power of God and the wisdom of God. The pulpit, for the man who occupies it, may be the noblest seminary ever erected. The sublimity of its themes, their awful yet beautiful relations, the majesty with which they invest every human soul and the grandeur which they attach to the issues of life, cannot fail, if truly believed, to impart a masculine vigor to the intellect as well as a divine benediction to the heart. It is a theatre where scope is found for every faculty, and use for every endowment. It is an altar where memory may heap its treasured offerings, and the divinely kindled imagination may consume them with its lambent flame of radiance and the odor of a sweet incense. Well might the simple platform on which an Athanasius, a Basil, an Ambrose, or an Augustine stood, expand itself into the bright consummate flower of human art. What are those most triumphant exhibitions of genius, the cathedrals wrought by the devout builders and masons of the middle ages, those piles whose

> "High embowered roof,
> With antique pillars massy proof,
> And storied windows richly dight,
> Casting a dim religious light"—

What are they but becoming shrines for the pulpits, where a Saint Bernard of Clairvaux, or a Saint Francis might stand to stir the hearts of the people as with the sound of a trumpet? When such men as the golden-mouthed John of Antioch, and George Whitefield occupy it, what throne of earth can equal the pulpit in ascendency over the thoughts and affections of mankind? When the people look up and listen to such men as Robert Hall and William Archer Butler, it is with them as with Hermon, on which the dew descended, refreshing every living plant, and reviving them that were ready to perish. Human nature assumes its finest prerogative when engaged in earnest manly speech reproving the wrong-doer, inciting the indolent, encouraging the faint-hearted, and soothing the weary and broken in spirit; it reaches its loftiest height of dignity when it stands as an ambassador for Christ.

My first round upon the circuit began in that most gorgeous season of the year, the Indian summer. The rich, mellowed sunshine stole lazily through the softening haze that filled the atmosphere, crowning corn-fields and orchards and prairies with a golden glory unparalleled at any other time. The groves girt with the brave pomp of the changing leaf, seemed to have borrowed the splendor of the rainbow to wear it as a scarf. The warm dreamy days were followed by chill lengthening nights, which were illumined by magnificent spectacles, visible only in the wild West. When the hand of the frost has done its first work in the fall of the year, scathing and blasting the long grass of the prairies, rendering it dry and combustible as tinder, the settlers, following the example of the Indians, are accustomed to fire it, not so much now for the sake of the game, as from the notion that the conflagration will enrich the next summer's crop of grass. As your road skirts the edge of the timber, amid the deepening shades of the twilight, you see a single fiery column rising, far out in the sea of blighted verdure. From a column it changes to a pyramid of flame. The wind rises, the pyramid is transformed into a legion of fiery serpents, that writhe, and leap, and dart onward, their heads high in air, waving and bending forward, then tossing themselves erect as if preparing for a new and more desperate spring. An embattled host of dragons, panoplied with a mail almost too bright to look upon, bannered with wreathed folds of smoke like breathings of the pit, their errand seems to be the destruction of the world. They are swift as the fleetest horse, and their sound is like the sweep of the tempest. The dragons disappear, and in their place stands a wall of fire, stretching across the plain from one verge of the horizon to the other, a wall whose presence is the touch of death to every living thing. The next day, your way lies by the side of a waste, apparently boundless as the ocean, black as the waters of Acheron, and canopied with clouds of smoke.

Usually I had the escort of a friend from one appointment to the next, that my horse and I, between us, might learn the way. Rising early in the morning, breakfasting for six or seven months in the year by candlelight or the blaze of "pine-knots," the meal having always been preceded by reading or reciting a chapter from the Bible, singing and prayer, we were prepared to enter upon the duties of the day with the rising of the sun. My noble "Charley" was always attended to, fed, curried and brushed, with scrupulous care. From one to three hours were then passed in study, and then to horse for the preaching place of the day. A ride of from five to twenty miles brought me to this by noon. In busy seasons of the year, when the people were engaged in ploughing, planting, harvesting, or gathering corn fodder, a week-day congregation would sometimes consist of three or four aged sisters. Trotting gaily along toward the end of his ride, the young preacher would overtake two or three of these matrons engaged in quiet discourse, knitting and smoking as they walked on their way to the meeting. Springing to the ground, there is a cordial shaking of hands all round, and followed by the horse, he trudges along with them to the log cabin, where the services are to take place. The weather, the health of their families, each member being asked after by name, the news of the neighborhood, the state or prospect of the crops, and the condition of the church are all discussed, until they reach their destination.

The preacher hastens to the stable to "put up" his horse, and then with saddlebags on arm approaches the house, where the good wife stands in the door to greet him. There is another shaking of hands and another dish of chat, until the hour appointed, when he withdraws from the spacious fireplace and after a brief meditation commences the service. Hymns, prayers and sermon are gone through as faithfully as if the congregation were composed of a thousand. His morning study and ride have furnished him material and opportunity for reflection. He has thrown his thoughts into the best order-he could and now interprets them as he is best able. With the floor for a rostrum and his chair for a desk, he may draw as close to his auditors as he pleases; and in the urgent warmth of his appeals he will sometimes find himself gesticulating just under their spectacles and noses. If he has succeeded to their satisfaction, he may hear his motherly auditors, as they take their pipes from the chimney-corner at the close of the exercises, saying to one another: "Our young preacher is a powerful piert.' "Little fellow, isn't he?" This translated into the polite phraseology of the city means "eloquent sermon!" "profound discourse!" "able and masterly argument!"

While dinner is preparing at the hearth by which they are seated, the good dame brings out from underneath the bedstead, her only cupboard, a tin-cup full of nicely frosted persimmons or some other delicacy, and presents them to her young favorite. The dinner of "hog, hominy and pone," or of fried chicken and saleratus biscuit, to which is added a cup of "seed-tick" coffee, is disposed of: and the remainder of the day is passed in study, and in visits to the neighbors. At night-fall, all hands gather home from their work; and after a substantial meal, a general talk, and evening prayers, all get ready for bed. Mattresses are spread upon the floor and eight, ten, or twenty people, old and young, male and female, stow themselves away under cover in one room; how, I never could precisely tell. Sometimes there is a kind of loft, where amid all sorts of odds and ends, broken tools, strings of onions, piles of potatoes—a bed is made for the young divine. I think, however, that I preferred the sleeping down stairs; for in the upper apartment I have often been covered by the snow, or drenched by the rain, which descended upon me through openings in the roof. The sermon studied and preached to-day, is tried again to-morrow, and repeated the third day; and thus one well-prepared discourse is ready for Sunday, when the congregations are much larger. The other three working-days of the week, will furnish the preacher with a second sermon. Language is the test of thought. What you really know you can tell; and there is no better training for a young minister, than daily preaching in log-cabins and school-houses.

A prominent divine of another denomination, meaning to be slightly sarcastic, once said to my old friend Mr. Cartwright: "How is it that you have no doctors of divinity in your denomination?" "Our divinity is not sick and don't need doctoring," said the sturdy backwoodsman. Assuming a graver tone, he then said: "Tell me how it is, that you take so many men from the plough-tail, the forge and the carpenter's shop, and in a few years make excellent preachers of them, without sending them to college or theological seminary?"—"We old ones tell the young ones all we know, and they try to tell the people and keep on trying till they can; that's our college course," was the answer.

Sunday's work was the hardest of the week, for it was frequently necessary to preach three times, to lead three classes, and to ride from thirty-five to forty miles.

There was work enough of all sorts to be done. The voice to be drilled to an easy obedience, and the development of all its tones. Large portions of the Bible and hymn-book must be committed to memory, for all my reading in public had to be done by rote. Fresh stores of knowledge for daily use had to be added daily. I had to learn all the roads and near cuts, the landmarks, bridges, and fords, as well as the names of all the men, women and children in the circuit; and besides, not the least difficult of the lessons, was to learn to eat anything, everything, and sometimes to do without eating at all; to learn to sleep in any place and every place, with or without beds and covering; and to ride all day wet to the skin, and then get up in the evening and preach without changing my clothes.

To my other labors were added those of a chorister; for it often happens that there is not a man or woman in the congregation that can or will start a tune. It is not pleasant to be reduced to the strait of an old parson, that I once heard of, who in giving out his hymn said: "I would thank some brother present to raise the tune, and then *tote* it." A dead silence ensued. It was at length broken by a member of the congregation, saying: "I reckon you'll be dreadful sharp, if you trap anybody here in that way." I therefore armed myself with three tunes—a long, short and common metre; and when there threatened to be a "flash in the pan," from the musical inability of my audience, I would fire away with one of these. But unfortunately, sometimes I would pull a trigger and the wrong barrel would go off, and great was my confusion time and again at hitching a long metre tune to short metre words.

Sometimes days were passed in a solitude as deep and unbroken as that of the African deserts. Under such conditions, a man must be on prodigiously good terms with himself, or have a vast deal to think about and observe, or he will occasionally be tired of his own company. For such times, however, I usually had an unfailing resource in my Bible and hymn-book; checking my horse until I had spelled out a verse, I started again and trotted along until this was firmly fixed in the memory. This operation, repeated for hours together, week after week, will be likely to cultivate a man's powers of recollection, and furnish him with an ample store of sacred and lyrical language; when the mind wearied of this, new occupation was found in exploding the radical sounds of speech, or, "barking" as college-boys call it. This was followed up by practising the articulation of the most difficult words in the language. Then all the faculties would be summoned, for the composition and delivery of a discourse, in the hearing of my faithful charger, who listened with unflagging interest. My lonely wayfarings were now and then cheered by the companionship of an older and more experienced preacher friend; who would come to take a week or two's round and to preach with me "time about." One of these in whom I greatly delighted and who afforded me endless entertainment, by the variety of his knowledge, as well as by the singularity of his expressions, must have, if not a description, at least a passing mention. From his youth he had been a voracious reader and was thoroughly booked in all the standards, especially of theology and poetry. It was evident that in his early life, his study of Johnson had only been equalled by his admiration of him. His style had been moulded by that of the great lexicographer; and I suppose that the Johnsonian manner has never been carried to a higher pitch, than by my friend. His sermons were most elaborately prepared, and delivered with the greatest fluency and unction. He poured forth his sonorous periods with the most weighty seriousness; yet I confess that I have not always been able to repress a smile when I have heard him utter a periphrase of this kind: "The small particle of the aqueous fluid which trickles from the visual organ over the lineaments of the countenance, betokening grief." Riding into his yard once, in company with a friend, intending to breakfast with him, we were thus hospitably saluted: "Brethren, how are you? Alight, and allow me to conduct your quadruped through the orifice, erected for ingress and egress into the stabulatory department, in order that he may obtain somewhat of the herbiferous and graniferous wherewith to sustain his strength; while ye yourselves shall tarry until ye have partaken of aliment furnished by the females in the domicil, and having attended to sanctimonious exercises go on your way rejoicing." The meal having been prepared, it was announced in this wise: "Come, friends, bites are about to be distributed."

The following is attributed to him, but with what correctness I cannot state; it is certainly characteristic of his merry moods: An old man engaged in emitting dense volumes of tobacco smoke from an old pipe, until the atmosphere of the apartment became oppressive and sickening, was thus politely and humorously addressed: "Venerable sir, the affumegation arising from the deleterious effluvia emanating from your tobaccoistic reservoir, so overshadows the organistic power of our ocular, and so abflustrates our atmospheric validity that our apparat must shortly be obtuned, unless through the abundant suavity of your eminent politeness you will disembogue the aluminous tube of the stimulating and sternutatory ingredient that replenishes its concavity."

A man of quenchless zeal and indefatigable industry, he abounded in labors, preaching constantly while he supported himself by his farm.

From the communings of these friendly journeys, we derived not only profit and pleasure, but also scraps of intelligence concerning our brethren in distant quarters. One of these was as follows: A young man in my position, as a helper in his first year, was complained of at his quarterly conference; to the effect first, that he could not preach; second, that he was attentive to all the girls around the circuit; and third, that he was constantly engaged in swopping horses. In defending himself he stated first, that he knew as well as any of them that he could not preach, and he was sure it did not trouble them as much as it did him; second, that they need not be alarmed about his attention to the girls, for he would not think of marrying the daughter of any man present; and third, as to trading horses what else was he to do? they paid him nothing, and he had no other way of making money enough to buy his clothes.

I received my salary regularly every three months, and at the end of the year was paid my hundred dollars in full, besides presents of various yarn stockings, woollen shirts and other useful articles.

Within the year I preached nearly four hundred times and rode over three thousand miles, chiefly on horseback; but during the summer, when the Illinois bottom was under water for nearly a month, I reached my appointments by canoe over a lake nine miles wide, ten feet above the road along which I had been accustomed to trot.

The experiences gained in that year's campaign, I would not exchange for those of any other year of my life. It was a scene of constant adventure, or hair-breadth escapes; for notwithstanding the sagacity of my horse, my piece of an eye was a poor substitute for the two good ones that had fallen to the share of my contemporaries; and in this wild, roving sort of life, it could not be but that I should be especially exposed to peril. Nevertheless, it was a life full of hearty enjoyment, and of toil that inspired, while it tasked one's powers.

CHAPTER IX.

WALKING THE HOSPITAL.

I MANAGED to pass my examination at the ensuing conference without much difficulty. That it was not very formidable, may be gathered from this: A young man who had been hard at work on the first part of Watson's Institutes, one of our text-books, said to the chairman of the examining committee, "I confess that, notwithstanding my best exertions, I have been unable to master Mr. Watson's argument on the evidences of Christianity, and I should be obliged to you for some explanations."

"Now look yer," said the venerable chairman, "I want you to understand, that I come here to ask questions, not to answer them."

As my eye was growing rapidly worse, I visited St. Louis in the autumn of 1844, to get medical advice and treatment. A number of physicians in consultation agreed to undertake the case, hoping that if they could not benefit the eye, at least to keep it from getting worse; offering, moreover a free ticket to attend the lectures delivered in their medical school.

Thinking that no kind of knowledge should come amiss to a Methodist preacher, I determined to accept the proposal.

Acting on this suggestion, an old brother in a neighboring conference had made himself acquainted with the Thompsonian theory of physic, and took great delight in practising it on his circuits. Some of his brethren, not liking his theory or course, complained of him, when his name was called in the annual examination of character. In maintaining his right, he said: "Now, Mr. Bishop, you know that we are commanded to do good to the bodies as well as the souls of men. If I were travelling in a region where doctors were scarce, and were to find a man in a bad spell of bilious fever, ye know I would throw him into a sweat, and then give him a dose of lobelia or thoroughwort"—

"No, sir," interrupted the bishop rather haughtily; "no, brother, I do not know, and what is more, I do not care, what you would do."

"Very well, sir, very well," retorted the other, "you have as good a right to live and die a fool as any other man."

Notwithstanding I had decided to attend the lectures and adopt the treatment, how I was to support myself meanwhile was not so clear. I had just fifteen dollars in my pocket, and that paid my board for a month and a week. As I sat in my chill and bare apartment, gloomily ruminating upon the prospect of parting with my last dollar, and wondering what was to come next, I received an invitation to take tea with the family of a distinguished lawyer of the city. The warm, cheerful glow of the house, the sunny hospitality of the family stood out in bright relief against the dark background of my dreary and lonely lodgings. Many a stormy night during my five weeks' stay, had I wandered out in the rain and darkness, while the gusty wind was sweeping along the streets, and the clouds pouring out their torrents, and seen broad beams of light falling through the windows of pleasant houses, through which issued, too, strains of merry music, the sound of laughter and of pleasant voices, and felt the wretchedness of solitude in the midst of a peopled city. Unable to read at night, with scarce an acquaintance in town, my condition had been dismal and lonely enough. My evening by this friendly fireside, had therefore been one of the pleasantest of my life. My host was not only learned in the law, but deeply read in polite letters. Accomplished in manners as he was engaging in conversation, he fascinated me no less by his graceful attentions than by his charming and varied talk. As I arose to take my leave, his generous wife said with true Virginia warmth of tone, "Whither are you going?" "To my lodgings," I replied. "These are your lodgings," she answered; and her husband taking both my hands in his said, "This house is your home, sir, as long as you will stay in it; yonder is your room, and your trunk is already there." How this came to pass I never knew, for the major could not have been aware that I was on my last dollar.

The next nine months were passed beneath this friendly roof. In the society of my gifted and eloquent friend, I made the acquaintance of the great English essayists, and of some of the great English poets, especially of Shakspeare. Cupping, leeching, physicking, and attendance upon anatomical lectures were alternated by readings from the masters of style and song. I went from the skeleton in the museum, or the corpse in the dissecting-room, to the pervasive and ethereal soul that shines through the verse of the bard. The darkness that fell upon me after some painful operation on the eye, was lit and illumined by

> "The light that never was on land or sea,
> The consecration and the poet's dream."

It was a pleasant thing to go from the smell and taste of nauseous drugs, to breathe the air of the ideal world, and to exchange a wreath of leeches and a necklace of cups, for a sprig of amaranth that blooms in the immortal fields of poetry. My friend was the finest reader as well as talker I had ever listened to, and his exquisite appreciation afforded me a rare interpretation and insight of the achievements of sceptered monarchs in the realms of thought.

Ambrosial nights were those in which the major, returning from his office or the courts, would render for me the glorious voices of the past.

Then there were other friends to minister to my delight and instruction. One of these was a marvellously gifted woman of society, the widow of a late distinguished member of the Senate of the United States. She charmed me with stories of her long life in Washington, with sketches of the eminent personages she had met there, with analyses and descriptions of their oratory, with anecdotes of the private life and manners of the capital. I came to know Clay, Webster, Calhoun, McDuffie, Preston, Mangum, Wright, Forsythe, Benton and Jackson, almost as vividly as if I had seen and heard them. Another of my friends was a young Methodist preacher, about my own age, stationed at one of the churches in town, and now in a city for the first time. Starting upon his first tour of pastoral visitation, he reached the door of one of his flock, and seeing the silver handle of the bell-pull, and underneath it a foot-scraper on the marble step, and supposing that the knob was to hold on by while he cleaned his feet, used it accordingly, and then began hammering on the door with his fist to gain admittance. When the servant came, he inquired rather tartly, "Why did you not pull the bell?" "Bell!" said my friend, roused from his dream of admiration at the munificent spirit of the householder, in providing the silver companion to the iron scraper, "there is no bell here; what is the use of a bell when a body's got a fist?"

The region in which I now dwelt was historic ground,——for two or three centuries formed the historic horizon of our continent. Although our past is only as yesterday, its weird visions have a spell for the imagination of those who have never looked face to face upon the hoary antiquity of the old world. Here underneath the limestone bluff, where now rose the proud babel of the West, lay the mouldering ashes of the greatest of the Indian sachems and warriors, the renowned Ottawa, Pontiac, whose gigantic scheme for the extirpation of the Anglo-Saxon colonists west of the Alleghanies, less than a century ago, filled the people on the seaboard with dismay, and bathed the border in blood. Here he sleeps the long sleep of death, undisturbed by the busy tread, and unburdened by the increasing industrial and mercantile trophies of the race which in life he so abhorred. A metropolis of the white man is the mausoleum of the Indian. In the whir of its spindles, and the scream of its steam-whistle, civilization chants the death-song of the red man.

On the bosom of that mighty river whose tawny current now washes the levee of merchandise and traffic where hundreds of steamboats lie moored, the saintly Marquette and his companion, Joliet, the first Europeans whose keel ever furrowed its waves, floated in their bark canoe, from the mouth of the Wisconsin, a thousand miles or more past wooded and unpeopled banks. A century and a half before the knight De Soto had gained it five hundred miles below this point, and amazed at its breadth and volume, had instinctively named it, the Rio Grande. The French in Canada had heard of it as "the great river," but now the pious Jesuit, his grateful heart filled with love toward the virgin mother of Bethlehem and her divine Son, calls it reverently the river of the Conception.

The indomitable voyageur, La Salle, leaving his fort of the Broken Heart, had entered it through the Illinois, and found a rapture in sweeping along a torrent as impetuous as his own passionate spirit. First he called it the Colbert, in honor of the great minister of Louis XIV.; but afterwards, thinking it worthy of *le grand monarque* himself, called it the St. Louis, and all the countries that it washed, Louisiana.

Beyond the river which has now reclaimed its aboriginal name of the Mississippi, stretches the great American Bottom, seven or eight miles in width by forty or fifty in length. Here at Kaskaskia and Cahokia were the earliest French settlements of the far West. On these alluvial lands, which had once been the bottom of a lake, whose tumultuous waters had poured themselves over a precipice more dread and awful than Niagara's, these simple-hearted people had reared their humble cabins, and lived on such friendly terms with the aborigines; so contentedly, lovingly, and piously with each other, that their story forms the idyl of American history. With boundless expense and pains, their governors had reared, more than a century ago, on the bank of the great river, the impregnable Fort Chartres, as a sure defence against the encroachments of the Spaniards and the English. But now the river's changing stream has undermined the bastions, and tall trees are springing from the parade-ground. In this region, the Spaniards, French, English and American settlers had intrigued and wrestled with each other, and with the Indians, for supremacy. Here, under the direction of the great George Rogers Clark, "the Washington of the West," had been accomplished some of the most brilliant feats of the American Revolution. By his sagacity and indomitable valor, and the conquests which they gained for him, his native State, "the Old Dominion," had won her title to the great northwestern territory, which she ceded to the Federal Government twenty years later.

My life moreover had the diversity afforded by frequent "pulpit sweats," and of short journeyings to neighboring places, to give many people who were comparatively destitute such ministrations as I could. For these were not forbidden, when taken in moderation, by my medical advisers. My life was by no means monotonous, and I have rarely been busier than during those ten months spent under the doctors' hands. As has generally happened to me, however, I quitted them not much the better for their skill and pains. My angular pin's-point of transparent eye was not one whit clearer or stronger, and I went to the conference in September, 1845, to report myself as effective, more nearly blind than ever.

CHAPTER X.

"CRY ALOUD AND SPARE NOT."

The conference sat at Springfield, the capital of the State; and having passed my two years of probation, I received ordination at the hands of Bishop Morris as a deacon.

At that time we had under our care McKendree College, and it was considered desirable to erect a Female Seminary of high grade; but considerable sums of money were necessary for both. It was then customary for the West to call upon the East for material aid in all such enterprises. After the selection of a site for the future seat of learning, and making out an estimate of the sum that would be necessary to put it into operation—all this being kindly and gratuitously performed by a board of trustees—the next step was, to select some man as an agent, who should be intrusted with full powers to lay the pressing claims of education in the West before the enlightened, Christian communities of the older Eastern States; and by his eloquence or skill, to raise and bring back all the money he could get. To persuade men to part with their gold for the benefit of some distant region, particularly when it is shrewdly suspected that the people in that region are, or ought to be, able to help themselves, I have found to my cost is a delicate and difficult operation. Moreover, if you would make your plea successful you must be able to read the faces of men, and to explore their temperament and sensibilities through their eyes. I therefore think that a blunder was committed when I was appointed by the conference as an agent to travel in the Eastern States for the pecuniary advantage of its institutions. Nevertheless, this was my appointment for the ensuing year. An old and valued friend offered to accompany me as a travelling companion. We reached Cincinnati without adventure, and began our work in this new department. I found my ministerial brethren very willing that I should preach as often as I could; but I discovered that whilst my sermons were listened to by the people with patience, the appeals in behalf of my cause were not responded to. There appeared to be a difference of opinion between us; for their estimate of the importance of a Male and Female College in Illinois was not nearly as high as mine—at least, they seemed to conclude that if the two institutions were so indispensable, the people in Illinois might build them. I preached incessantly for three weeks, and found that I had my pains for my reward. My old friend and I were disposed to shake off the dust of the Queen City from our feet, and to take our journey to some more promising place, at least to some place were promises would be more productive. We started for Wheeling, and it was to the last degree important, that something in the way of getting funds should be done there; for my fare upon the steamboat took the last cent I had. Of course the trustees of a college in sending out an agent, would esteem it gross folly to furnish him with money—let him do as Cortes did, burn his ships —that is, go without funds, and then he will have to raise them, and fight his way through from sheer desperation.

We left Cincinnati on the steamer Hibernia early on Friday morning, the captain promising to land us at Wheeling by Saturday night. The boat was very much crowded, and among the passengers was a considerable number of Congressmen, members of both houses, on their way to the capital to take their seats. As several of them were men known to fame, whose names I had been familiar with for years, I took great interest in observing them, and in listening to their conversation; when, as is often their manner in such environment, they talked for the benefit of the company. I cannot say how much I was shocked nor how indignant I became at discovering that not a few of these representatives of the sovereign people of the United States, swore outrageously, played cards day and night, and drank villainous whisky to excess. I expressed my surprise and chagrin to my friend; but the only comfort that I received was, that this was the fashion in which many of our politicians acted.

The river was low—fogs came on. Sunday morning arrived, we were yet eighty miles below Wheeling and there was no place where we could land to spend the Sabbath. At breakfast time a committee of the passengers waited upon me to know if I would preach to them. Never did I say yes more gladly; for never had I been so anxious to speak my mind. A congregation of nearly three hundred persons assembled at half-past ten o'clock, and I took my stand between the ladies' and gentlemen's cabins; seated in the places of honor upon my right and left hand, were most of my late objects of interest—the members of Congress. I had never before spoken under such circumstances, but nevertheless, preached as well as I could, which is not saying much. At the close of the discourse proper, however, I could not resist the impulse to speak a straightforward word to the men on my right and left; turning to them, therefore, I said something to the following effect: "I understand that you are members of the

Congress of the United States, and as such you are or should be the representatives not only of the political opinions, but also of the intellectual, moral and religious condition of the people of this country. As I had rarely seen men of your class, I felt on coming aboard this boat a natural interest to hear your conversation and to observe your habits. If I am to judge the nation by you, I can come to no other conclusion than, that it is composed of profane swearers, card-players and drunkards. Suppose there should be an intelligent foreigner on this boat, travelling through the country with the intent of forming a well-considered and unbiased opinion, as to the practical working of our free institutions—seeing you and learning your position, what would be his conclusion?—inevitably, that our experiment is a failure, and our country is hastening to destruction. Consider the influence of your example upon the young men of the nation—what a school of vice are you establishing! If you insist upon the right of ruining yourselves, do not by your example corrupt and debauch those who are the hope of the land. I must tell you, that as an American citizen I feel disgraced by your behavior; as a preacher of the Gospel I am commissioned to tell you, that unless you renounce your evil courses, repent of your sins, and believe upon the Lord Jesus Christ with hearts unto righteousness, you will certainly be damned."

At the close of the services, I retired to my stateroom to consider my impromptu address word by word, and whether, if I were called to a reckoning for it, I should be willing to abide by it and its consequences. Plain speaking and stern acting are common things among the men of the West and the Southwest, and whosoever starts to run a race of this kind should be prepared to go unflinchingly to the goal. I came to the conclusion that nothing had been said of which I ought to be ashamed, and that I would stand by every word of it, let the issue be what it might. While cogitating, there was a tap at the door. A gentleman entered, who said: "I have been requested to wait upon you by the members of Congress on board, who have had a meeting since the close of the religious exercises. They desire me to present you with this purse of money"—handing me between fifty and a hundred dollars—"as a token of their appreciation of your sincerity and fearlessness in reproving them for their misconduct; they have also desired me to ask, if you will allow your name to be used at the coming election of chaplain for Congress. If you will consent to this, they are ready to assure you an honorable election." Quite stunned with this double message, I asked time for quiet reflection and for consulting with my friend. He warmly urged my acceptance of the offer. As the boat neared Wheeling my decision was asked. I assented to their proposal. They went forward to the capital; I tarried in Wheeling to preach. But the sermon on the boat was far more remunerative than all the labors at Cincinnati and Wheeling united. By the agency of my new friends, I was in due time elected. Their money paid my expenses to Washington, and so I entered upon my duties as chaplain to Congress.

CHAPTER XI.

A REED SHAKEN BY THE WIND.

Called thus unexpectedly to fill a novel and responsible position, I found myself sorely perplexed as to the course I should pursue in preaching. I was to occupy the desk which had been filled by many of the most eminent divines in the country, and to address an audience familiar with the eloquence of our greatest statesmen and orators. I was twenty-two years of age, with small discipline as a speaker, and with little experience of life, and a stranger in the land. Hitherto my preaching had been the result of as careful and thorough a premeditation as I had been able to bestow, digesting and arranging the truths and facts to be uttered, but trusting for the words and illustrations, and the living presentation of the subject, to the impulse and power of the occasion. I suppose this to be what is meant by the term "extempore speaking." In order to success in it, the mind should work as naturally and serenely in the presence of a multitude as if pursuing its processes in the quiet of a cloister. Fear of the audience, and every other form of self-consciousness, must be overcome, or the result will be mannerism, constraint, failure.

In oratory, as in every other noble path, self-forgetfulness is the condition of the highest success. I remember a favorite clause in the prayers of some of the backwoods preachers which, by a vivid metaphor, illustrates the true secret of successful preaching: "Lord, help me to get behind the cross." Let self and the audience alike be hidden, let the infinite pity and tenderness of Christ quicken every sensibility and swallow every other concern, let the intellect and the heart be pervaded with the thought of his compassionate love, and a man will be eloquent in spite of every difficulty. But how shall a shy, sensitive boy do all this? Moreover, it is to be considered, that as one virtually blind, I occupy the most unfortunate conceivable position before an audience. This is not said in the way of whining complaint, for I have ever been grateful for the modicum of vision that has fallen to my share; but I may as well, once for all, attempt to interpret the peculiarity of my attitude as a public speaker. Who has not felt the matchless power of the human eye? Was there ever an animated and soul-stirring conversation, where the understanding, memory, invention and fancy performed their choicest offices, carried forward in the dark? Should the gas which brilliantly illumines a crowded theatre or church be suddenly extinguished, would it not be every man's instinctive act to place his hand upon his pocket-book, thereby declaring his fear of his neighbors? No sagacious man will ever trust another who refuses him the tribute of a responsive glance, while they are talking, but ever turns his head away, and fixes his eye upon vacancy. What orator could electrify an audience, speaking to them behind a screen? What would Whitefield have done if he had been blindfolded before ascending the pulpit? Men not only see with their eyes, but hear; for the beaming eye and expressive face speak a language that articulate sounds can never express—a language more moving, soft, and irresistible than ever entered the soul through the galleries of the ear. Through the eye, the speaker enters into sympathy with his audience, by it he perceives their capacity, reads their wants, appreciates their condition; by it they are persuaded of his simplicity, earnestness and faith. Unless his eye bears witness to his truth, his words will only be sounding brass or tinkling cymbal, so true is it, here at least, "that seeing is believing." Does his theme quicken his pulse and inflame his heart, his glance will kindle every eye in the audience, "as in water face answereth to face, so the heart of man to man." If the truth be spoken truly, it will be reflected from the souls of the hearers through their faces.

With every new convert a man's own confidence in his teaching is assured, while the answering looks of a multitude not only reveal it to the speaker, but make himself more deeply known unto himself. The secret of eloquence is to be found in the eye of the audience, and through it the orator gains his highest inspiration—through it they lend him attention, interest, sympathy—their best thoughts and passions. He is reinforced by their strength, and his powers are enriched by the unrestrained gift of their sensibilities.

Thus, then, as it seems to me, the true power of the speaking man consists in the balanced and serene movement of his intellect, and his near and living connection with his hearers through the eye. Unfurnished with knowledge, unpractised by use, how was my slender intellect to bear the burden of a great and imposing congregation, in a hall where the most brilliant and gifted of the land had stirred the hearts of a nation, and yet work on with harmonious ease and undisturbed composure? Separated from my congregation by the impassable gulf of darkness, across which no lightning flash of intelligence and kindness could send its message of comfort and cheer; how should I, destitute of excellency of speech and wisdom, gain access to their hearts? So far as the intellect was concerned, true I might acquire a certain amount of easy and self-possessed activity on condition of composing my discourses beforehand, word by word, committing them to memory, and delivering them by rote. In this way, at least, I might be able to speak with less discredit to myself and friends, and possibly produce something worth the hearing; but, after all, is not this the substitution of a vigorous recollection for a vigorous mind—the cultivation of one power at the expense of many? Most of my time must be consumed in this preparation, and little be left for liberal study and general improvement. Was not this becoming a mere maker of sermons, when the first and last of all duties is to become a man, rounded, complete and full? Here, in the Congressional Library lay about me the vast fields of knowledge, in which, as one travelled farther and farther in any direction, the azure veils of the horizon lifted themselves and receded, while the delights of the way and the rewards of the journey daily enticed the traveller to go farther. Here, in the society now opened to me, were men and women, whose acquaintance with the world, whose knowledge of life and character, whose manners, conversation and culture might be invaluable as spurs, encouragements and auxiliaries. Would not this memoriter style of preparation for the pulpit, by engrossing most of my time, and narrowing my efforts to a single point, deprive me of many of these advantages which I coveted? By rendering myself dependent on it, should I not mortgage my future and bind myself as the slave of a bad habit? Thus it seemed, and after much fear and bewilderment I resolved to adhere, come what might, to the old style of preparation. True, I was laying up in store for myself many an hour of bitter mortification and chagrin, when, crushed by the weight of gathered crowds, I stood before them almost as a paralyzed imbecile. Well might it have been asked of them, "What went ye out for to see?" and most appropriate would have been the answer, "A reed shaken by the wind." There is one comfort, however, to every conscientious workman, let him toil wheresoever he will, that his labor shall not return unto him void. If humbly yet firmly trusting in the spiritual laws that undergird and prop the universe, a man bend himself with dogged and unconquerable resolution to his task, whatever it is, his reward shall come in due time. I had given two years toward acquiring the use of my voice, and learning to speak in such a way as not only not to injure throat and lungs, but to conserve the welfare of a fragile and delicate frame: Could I not afford to pay four years, if necessary, of discomfort, annoyance and failure to insure a natural connection between the tongue and the brain, and to gain for the brain itself the healthful and natural play of its faculties when the body was erected upon its legs in the midst of an assembly however large, or upon an occasion however momentous? Most things in this life have their price, and he who is willing to pay the full worth of an article can generally have it. "What will you have? quoth God. Pay for it and take it," saith the proverb. I was a preacher for six years before I gained the power and habit of extempore speech. Great as are my losses in the worlds of nature and of art from imperfect vision, I feel now, as I have ever felt, that incomparably my greatest loss is as a speaker. Could I only look into the face of my brother man as we talk together, gladly would I welcome darkness at all other times—the light of the human face divine would reconcile me to the loss of the Sun. Thus, though I be debarred from the use of that noblest power with which God has gifted man, the power of spoken eloquence; though I be hedged and hampered by the constraint of an ever-during gloom, why grieve or be heavy of heart. "Though no chastening for the present seemeth to be joyous but grievous: nevertheless, afterward it yieldeth the peaceable fruits of righteousness unto all them that are exercised thereby."

"God hath many aims to compass, many messages to send,
And his instruments are fitted each to its distinctive end;
Earth is filled with groaning spirits, hearts that wear a galling chain,
Minds designed for noble uses, bondaged to the lust of gain—
Souls once beautiful in whiteness, crimsoned with corruption's stain.

"Through earth's wrong, and woe, and evil, sometimes seeing, sometimes blind,
Ever must the homeward pathway of the humble Christian wind;
Stooping over sin and sorrow, bending by the couch of pain,
Holy promises outpouring, grateful as the summer's rain
To the heart whose hope had withered, never to revive again.

* * * * * * * *

"Thus are God's ways vindicated, and at length we slowly gain,
As our needs dispel our blindness, some faint glimpses of the chain
Which connects the earth with heaven—right with wrong, and good with ill,
Links in one harmonious movement, slowly learn we to fulfill
Our appointed march in concert, with his manifested will."

* * * * * * * *

They also serve who only stand and wait.

CHAPTER XII.

CONGRESS AND TWO OF ITS YOUNG MEN.

The duties of the chaplaincy were simple enough. To open the two Houses of Congress with prayer daily, to preach in the Hall of Representatives on Sunday morning; and as there were two of us to perform these offices, there was abundant leisure to follow our bent. Of course, my fancy had pictured the Capitol as an Olympian summit, where the greater and lesser gods held their festivals and dispensed their favors. The debates of the two houses were to furnish me an endless fund of entertainment and instruction. What was Hebe's nectar to that which I should imbibe from the glittering chalice of Congressional discussion? I had heard a great deal of speaking—good, bad, and indifferent—from the stumps and pulpits of prairie land; but here, with the flower of the nation in council, I should enjoy a repast whose delicacies could never cloy, and whose abundance could never fail. But our ideals fade away into thin air when brought to the touchstone of experience, and disappointment is the common lot.

The first effect of life in Washington for a young enthusiast is that of disenchantment; and he must become familiarized with the routine of business and inured to the commonplaces and platitudes of speeches for "Buncombe," before he is thoroughly prepared to enjoy the gladiatorship of the Capitol. It was mortifying enough to see an honorable representative or senator speaking to "a beggarly account of empty boxes," while even such of his colleagues as were present seemed to treat him and his discourse with utter contempt, engaged as they were in writing, reading newspapers, chatting jovially, or even lunching. Few speeches in Congress have any effect upon Congress itself; nevertheless, there is scarcely one delivered which is not productive of good results. A nation that has assumed the awful responsibility of self-government needs abundant instruction. The abstract doctrines of political science can have little interest or weight with the masses of the people. They have neither the education nor the powers of reflection to appreciate or apply them.

They must be addressed on their own level, and while their plane should be an ever ascending one, the politicians must meet them on the common ground of their capacities. If the majority of the nation are fitly represented by the inhabitants of Buncombe County, North Carolina, of necessity the greater part of our political eloquence must be of the Buncombe order. I fancy that the reason why our public speaking has assumed a lower range of discussion, and a less finished style, is that the audience in the Republic has become wider and less select. In the days of Hamilton, Jay, and Jefferson, public opinion was created by a few men, and Congress represented an oligarchy. But now the multitude claims its rights. We have become a nation of newspaper readers. Every man affects to be informed upon the questions of the day; and every Congressional speech delivered to an inattentive and listless house is nevertheless read by some thousands of the speaker's constituents and political adherents. The fitness of their audience might compensate the fathers of the Republic for its smallness; its ample size must satisfy our contemporaries for its want of quality. Congress must be for some time to come less and less a theatre of high debate: more and more a kind of lyceum for the delivery of lectures on current topics usually addressed to hundreds, sometimes to millions of listeners. As we have fewer Titans in the Senate, we may yet congratulate ourselves that the average of intelligence, truth and ability is constantly increasing. I firmly believe that in the proportion of members there is far less of drunkenness, gambling, duelling, and all the grosser sins, and more of uprightness, honor, and patriotism in Congress to-day than there has ever been. No single name is now such a tower of strength as the names of Clay, Calhoun and Webster once were; but Congress has not lost its significance for all that. Above the Vice-President's chair is a narrow gallery, traversed by a line of desks, where sit the reporters. That is the whispering-gallery, through which the faintest tone uttered in the chamber travels to the extremes of the Continent. The intellect of our forum now has the lightning harnessed as its post-horse; and the symbol of the age is a saucy, dirty newsboy astride of a telegraph wire, shouting, "*Tribune*, *Herald* and *Times*."

After John Quincy Adams and a few other veterans the two members of the House in whom I became most interested were young men who had entered the national service side by side, from distant quarters of the Union two years before,—one from Georgia, the other from Illinois. As two of the most significant men of the country, it may be allowed me to sketch them.

Alexander Hamilton Stephens is the most powerful orator in Congress, and that with all the odds against him. When standing he is a man of medium height, but when seated he looks like a boy, for his trunk is remarkably short, and his face exceeding youthful. Careless of his personal appearance, his hair, falling in masses over his fine brow, his black, brown, or any other colored cravat, he seems to know not which, tied in a sailor's knot, his clothes fitting well, if he has been fortunate in his tailor (rarely the case), an immense gold chain terminated by a heavy seal falling from his watch-fob, he presents an unpromising, not to say an *outré* appearance. When in repose, his face does not promise much more; pale, with a slightly sallow tinge, sometimes with a hectic flush upon his cheek, it seems to belong to a beardless boy. His arms and legs are very long, and his whole frame, not compactly knit, appears loose and awkward, and the victim of lifelong disease. How nearly disease and genius may be associated is a question which I leave for physiologists and psychologists to settle. But I feel sure that sleepless nights and days of pain and fever have had much to do with the brilliant intellect of this remarkable man. His voice, too, in common talk, gives as little token of his power as his other features, for it is thin, high-pitched, and inclining to the falsetto. Trained as a lawyer at the Georgia bar, a wonderful school for the development of popular eloquence (for the jury system is there pushed to its remotest limit), he early displayed those gifts which have made his name so famous; a sharp, incisive intellect, broad in its comprehension, firm in its grasp, as keen in its perceptions, coupled with an emotional nature, delicate as it is strong, giving him an invincible hold upon the interest and sympathy of his hearers. Returned to the House of Representatives when scarcely thirty years of age, he had by the time I first saw him already gained the undivided ear of the House. When he stood up to speak, there was no lunching, chatting, or apathy in the Hall, which seemed divided between the silence and his voice. The almost feminine squeak of his opening soon became a consistent, ringing tone, penetrating every corner of the spacious apartment; and judging from his effect upon the ear, I can well believe, what I have so often heard, that the impression of his presence upon the eye almost amounted to a transformation. In defence of his position he is at once logical and persuasive, setting his argument before you in a clear light and striking attitude, insomuch that the remark of Mr. Horace Greeley is justified, "that you forget you are listening to the most eloquent man in Washington, and only feel that he is right." His manner is rapid, sometimes vehement, always collected. Having in an instant gained your absorbed attention, he wins your confidence by his apparent fairness of reasoning, until at length you submit yourself to his control without compunction, or the dread of his being overcome. The most brilliant, albeit not the most satisfying, part of his oratory is seen when he turns upon his opponents. His powers of satire, ridicule, sarcasm, and invective are fearful; and yet the man of good breeding never forgets himself, nor is hurried away into truculent abuse. Many a man has smarted or even withered under Mr. Stephens' irony or denunciation, but I question if any has ever had cause to say that he was not a gentleman.

I fancy that there are several points of apparent resemblance between Mr. Stephens and John Randolph of Roanoke, but there must be more of real difference. Both have been the victims of disease, whose origin dates far back in life, and each has consequently been the owner of a body, which, however exquisitely it may have been strung, has been perilously sensitive. Both have exercised almost unequalled sway upon the floor of Congress; and both have been noted as masters in the art of offensive parliamentary war. Both have been admitted to be unimpeachably honest and fearless statesmen, shunning no danger and braving every peril in the maintenance of their peculiar and cherished convictions. But Mr. Randolph had scarcely a friend; Mr. Stephens has hardly an enemy. Bodily infirmity, if it did not master Mr. Randolph's will, soured his temper, and gave to his perfect diction the poison of wormwood, and to his spirit the gall of bitterness that verged upon misanthropy. Mr. Stephens has conquered suffering, and keeps himself strong and noble by entering heartily into the sweet charities of life. Proud of his lineage and his birthplace, an intolerant aristocrat, with varied and finished culture, refined taste, a high sense of honor, a mind disposed to prey upon itself, and a contempt for those who did not share his advantages, the Virginian, nevertheless, presented a curious spectacle, as the unflinching advocate of extreme Demo cratic doctrines, whilst at the same time he was unable to free himself from the tyrannous sentiment of exclusiveness and caste. With an air of stately haughtiness he entered the lists of congressional debate, like some solitary champion, with visor up, that all might recognize him, wearing the colors of a fair lady, whose place upon the throne of his affections never knew a rival, and in the honor of his own Virginia defiantly threw his gage of battle to all comers. He challenged your admiration and demanded your submission; he disdained your sympathy and scorned your weakness. If you were not a gentleman by the four descents he would hurl at you all the fiery darts of his jeering ridicule; and if you were not born in the "Old Dominion," nothing could expiate your offence, and as a Pariah you must bear the insult of his complacent or scoffing pity. Any provincialism of pronunciation or phrase upon the part of a man whom he thought worthy to be considered as an antagonist, was chastised in the summary fashion of a pedagogue, and more than one distinguished member of our national council has been taught English by the great Virginian, insomuch *that in his day* he deserved the appellation of the schoolmaster of Congress. The Georgian, on the other hand, is as simple and genial in his manners as a child; considerate and kind to all, his friendliness begets for him friendship. He rarely speaks except upon an occasion which demands all his powers, and then, after mature deliberation, and a careful survey of his own position and of that occupied by those opposed to him; so that he is like a great general leading disciplined and well-concentrated forces to the attack, and so admirable are at once his instinctive and reflective powers, that he seldom makes a mistake or suffers a defeat. He is a born leader of men, because his comprehensive intellectual nature is seconded and animated by his yet finer social nature; and whether Mr. Stephens continue in the House, which I presume he would prefer as the great popular body, or be removed to the Senate, I think that the country will one day adjudge him the finest orator and ablest statesman in either. The idol of Mr. Randolph's political worship was State sovereignty; the coördinate rights of the State in harmony with the unity and ascendency of the Federal Government is the platform of Mr. Stephens. Mr. Randolph was a Virginian; Mr. Stephens is a patriot.

The other member of the House to whom I allude is Stephen Arnold Douglas. The first time I saw him was in June, 1838, standing on the gallery of the Market House, which some of my readers may recol lect as situate in the middle of the square of Jackson ville. He and Colonel John J. Hardin were engaged in canvassing Morgan County for Congress. He was upon the threshold of that great world in which he has since played so prominent a part, and was engaged in making one of his earliest stump-speeches. I stood and listened to him, surrounded by a motley crowd of backwood farmers and hunters, dressed in homespun or deerskin, my boyish breast glowing with exultant joy, as he, only ten years my senior, battled so bravely for the doctrines of his party with the veteran and accomplished Hardin. True, I had been educated in political sentiments opposite to his own, but there was something captivating in his manly straightforwardness and uncompromising statement of his political principles. He even then showed signs of that dexterity in debate, and vehement, impressive declamation, of which he has since become such a master. He gave the crowd the color of his own mood as he interpreted their thoughts and directed their sensibilities. His first-hand knowledge of the people, and his power to speak to them in their own language, employing arguments suited to their comprehension, sometimes clinching a series of reasons by a frontier metaphor which refused to be forgotten, and his determined courage, which never shrank from any form of difficulty or danger, made him one of the most effective stump-orators I have ever heard.

Less than four years before, he had walked into the town of Winchester, sixteen miles southwest of Jacksonville, an entire stranger, with thirty-seven and a half cents in his pocket, his all of earthly fortune. His first employment was as clerk of a "Vandu," as the natives call a sheriff's sale. He then seized the birch of the pedagogue, and sought by its aid and by patient drilling, to initiate a handful of half-wild boys into the sublime mysteries of Lindley Murray. His evenings were divided between reading newspapers, studying Blackstone, and talking politics. It is a droll sight to see a crowd of men and boys gathered in one of the primary conventions of squatter sovereigns, at a village store on the public square, after night. It is a Rialto for the merchants, a news-room for the quidnuncs, a mixture of the town-hall and caucus-room for the politicians, and a theatre and circus united for the huge entertainment of the boys. The establishment is closed for business, but the door is open for all comers, and in winter time a cheery fire is kept blazing for the common weal. The "counter-hopper," as the clerk is familiarly called, is on duty as sentry, the counters, boxes, bales, barrels, are used as seats by the potent assembly, while every one is solacing himself with a quid of tobacco laid away in his cheek, or a rank cigar, poetically styled a cabbage-leaf. The principal speakers are expected tc surround the stove, each with his back toward it, his hands occupied in keeping the tails of his coat as far asunder as possible. The members of the society address each other by the diminutive of their Christian names, as Pete, Jim, Bill, or Steve, and the grand doctrines of liberty, equality and fraternity are realized on the common level of story-telling, smoke, tobacco-spit, and boisterous declamation. Such are the debating clubs wherein I imagine most of our western orators, legal and political, have first spread their unfledged wings and tried to soar toward distinction; doubtless it was in just such a school that Mr. Douglas took his first lesson in oratory. He, before long, by virtue of his indomitable energy, acquired enough of legal lore to pass an examination, and "to stick up his shingle," as they call putting up a lawyer's sign. And now began a series of official employments, by which he has mounted, within five and twenty years, from the obscurity of a village pedagogue on the borders of civilization, to his present illustrious and commanding position. First, he was elected the State's Attorney for the judicial district in which he lived, and next, to a seat in the Legislature. He then ran for Congress, but was defeated by five votes, and was afterward appointed Register of the Land Office in Springfield. Resigning this, he was chosen to be Secretary of State, and while he filled the office, was elected Judge of the Supreme Court of the State. His next step was into Congress, and in 1846 or '47 he was elected to the Senate, in which he will soon enter upon his third term of six years. Thus, in the twelve or thirteen years that had elapsed from the time of his entering the State, a friendless, penniless youth; he had served his fellow-citizens in almost every official capacity, and entered the highest position within their power to confer.

No man, since the days of Andrew Jackson, has gained a stronger hold upon the confidence and attachment of his adherents, or exercised a more dominating authority over the masses of his party than Judge Douglas. Whether upon the stump, in the caucus, or the Senate, his power and success in debate are prodigious. His instincts stand him in the stead of imagination, and amount to genius.

Notwithstanding the busy and boisterous political life which he has led, with all its engrossing cares and occupations, Mr. Douglas has, nevertheless, by his invincible perseverance, managed to redeem much time for self-improvement. For one in his situation, he has been a wide and studious reader of history and its kindred branches. Contact with affairs has enlarged his understanding and strengthened his judgment. Thus, with his unerring sagacity, his matured and decisive character, with a courage which sometimes appears to be audacity, but which is in reality tempered by prudence, a will that never submits to an obstacle, however vast, and a knowledge of the people, together with a power to lead them, incomparable in this generation; he may be accepted as a practical statesman of the highest order.

It must be confessed that there was formerly a dash of the rowdy in Mr. Douglas, and that even now the blaze of the old Berserker fire will show itself at times. But it must be recollected that his is a vivid and electric nature, of redundant animal life and nervous energy; that he was bred, not in scholastic seclusion, nor amid the conventional routine of a settled population, but that his character has taken shape and color from that of the bold men of the border, where pluck was the highest virtue, and "back-bone," to use a phrase of the country, compensated for many a deficiency in elegance. His organization is exuberant, but not coarse. Like the prairies of his adopted State, which in their wildness yield a luxuriant bounty of long grass and countless flowers, but return to culture unmeasured harvests of wheat and corn; so his youth may have known the flush and pride of rude health, yet his manhood turns up, under the ploughshare of experience, a loam fit to mature the glorious plants of wisdom, power, virtue and patriotism.

In society, few men are more agreeable, provided you are willing to make allowance (which most peo ple in this country are bound to do) for the defects of early breeding, which can never be entirely hidden. He is singularly magnetic in conversation, full of humor, spirit and information, and charms while he instructs. Of course, he has one habit which constitutes a Masonic bond of brotherhood among all western men—I mean that of chewing tobacco.

I cannot refrain from telling a story, which, though somewhat at the expense of Judge Douglas, tells at least half the truth in regard to his competency for a seat on the Supreme Bench, and moreover illustrates the power of repartee produced by "stumping it," as the political canvass is styled. In his last exciting contest for the Senate, the judge began the campaign by a speech in Chicago. Among those seated on the platform behind him was his competitor, familiarly called Abe (instead of Abram) Lincoln. In the course of his argument, Mr. Douglas said, that the attempt of the Republican party to appeal from the decision of the Supreme Court, in the Dred Scott case, to the people, reminded him of a remark made once by Mr. Butterfield, a late member of the Chicago bar, in relation to the Supreme Court of Illinois, for whose ability and learning, or rather want of them, he had a profound contempt. Mr B. said that he presumed the judicial system of

Illinois stood without a rival in the civilized world; that it was as near perfection as a human institution could be, and that there was only one amendment of it which he could suggest, namely, that an appeal from its decisions might be taken to any two justices of the peace. Of course the hit was evident, and the crowd burst into a loud laugh, at the expense of the judge's opponents. But high over the sound of the boisterous merriment, rose the sharp, peculiar laugh of Mr. Lincoln; and when the noise had sufficiently abated, for his voice to be heard throughout the assembly, he retorted, "But, Judge, that was when you were on the bench." The judge had nothing for it but to "acknowledge the corn."

CHAPTER XIII.

THE SENATE.

It is impossible for an American to enter the Senate chamber, without feelings of respect and veneration. The time-honored memories which enshrine the place, the traditions of illustrious men that have occupied these seats, the grand words of statesmanship and patriotism uttered within these walls and which still seem to linger in the air, and the august assembly now gathered for high deliberative purposes, combine to impress the imagination and to awaken something like a solemn delight. Here have stood Macon, of North Carolina; John Taylor of Caroline; Randolph, Barbour and Giles of Virginia; Pinkney of Maryland; Porter of Louisiana; Rufus King and Silas Wright of New York; Benton and Linn of Missouri; Grundy and White of Tennessee; and a host of other men who, together with Clay, Calhoun, and Webster, by their conspicuous abilities and virtues, constitute the parliamentary glory of our brief history. I doubt not that by the purity of the motives of its members, their incorruptible patriotic integrity, their eminent endowments coupled with large experience, and by their powers of oratory and debate, we may boldly challenge a comparison between the Senate and any body of lawgivers ever convened.

I may be pardoned for refreshing the recollection of my readers with brief mention of some of the men whose names seem sacred to the spot.

Probably no man has ever filled a chair in the Senate, whose personal influence was so weighty, whose character was so revered, as Mr. Macon of North Carolina. A sturdy patriot even from boyhood, relinquishing college-life to take part as a private in the Revolutionary war, serving with Greene in his arduous campaign against Cornwallis, he had won the respect and confidence of the citizens of his native county, before attaining his majority, and despite his youth, was elected by them to a seat in the General Assembly of the State. Receiving the Governor's requisition, while Greene's forces were protected from the superior power of Cornwallis only by the swollen torrent of the Yadkin, he determined to disregard the summons and to abide the perils of the camp with his fellow-soldiers. The wise commander, hearing it, sent for him and demanded if the story were true. The young private quietly answered, "Yes." "Why, then, do you remain in the camp, while the halls of the State-House await you?" "Because," said the energetic yourg soldier, "I have often seen the faces of the British, and for once I want to see their backs." Greene showed him how, as a member of the Assembly, he could be of far more service to the country, and especially to its army, by representing their distressed and forlorn condition and pressing the vote of supplies, than as a private soldier, and induced him to proceed to the capital. Such was Mr. Macon's entrance upon the noble legislative career, which the earnest desire of his constituents induced him to pursue, for fifty years. Identified with the founders of the Republic; some will read these pages who remember "the noblest Roman of them all," as he quitted the Senate a little more than thirty years ago. A planter of moderate means, accustomed to work in the field in company with "his hands;" living in frugal but hospitable style, raising his own wheat, corn and bacon; his two or three hogsheads of tobacco, shipped annually, serving to procure him all the luxuries he ever knew; he always appeared in Washington, in a suit of navy blue, in the cut of Revolutionary times, in immaculate linen, his head surmounted by a broad-brimmed Quaker-hat, and his hand grasping a massive gold-headed cane. As to the Constitution, he was a strict constructionist. He was the confidential friend and adviser of Mr. Jefferson and the next two Presidents, as well as of all the first statesmen of the time. "Nathaniel Macon was the austerest of advocates for public economy and simplicity. A late President of the United States informs us, that while in office, he and several members of his cabinet paid a visit to the North Carolina patriarch. He was quartered on his plantation, in half a dozen log-houses, one of which served for kitchen, another for dining-room, and so on. Fine linen, old wine, silver and cut glass, however, profusely abounded. The first day wore off briskly. Early the next morning, the President and his secretaries were invited to a horseback ride over the grounds. When they stepped out to mount, our informant was struck with dismay. There stood a dozen grooms stripping the requisite number of race-horses, whose fiery eyes, dilated nostrils, impatient champing, and light, sinewy forms, apparently capable of mounting into the air, augured anything but a quiet morning's airing to sedate, middle-aged gentlemen who had never ridden a steeple-chase or made experiments in flying. Macon insisted, the well-broke horse was as kind as he was spirited, and all took a parting look of the ground and mounted. The animals vindicated their master's eulogium, and no accidents occurred. As they swept along in the exhilarating morning air, with the sensation of being poised on aërial springs, the patriarch 'held forth' on his horses. One was an 'Archy,' another a 'Wildair,' another something else; but each had a pedigree as long and aristocratic as a German baron of sixteen quarterings. Their exploits, and their ancestors' exploits were proudly recounted. Each, in his opinion, was worth a plantation. Mr. Macon's amused guests were 'almost persuaded' before their return to become horse fanciers."*

Although a consistent member of "the Baptist persuasion," as he called it, the great Senator could not resist the taste for horseflesh, so predominant among gentlemen south of the Potomac. Another illustration of the same passion is connected with one of my earliest recollections. The only time I ever saw Andrew Jackson was early on a bright summer morning, when he came into my father's yard to look at some blooded animals that had just been imported from England. And well do I remember how the patriarch's face glowed and his eye shone, as he gazed upon the noble creatures,† and spoke in excited tones of the exquisite blending of beauty and strength in their mold. Never shall I forget the impressive appearance, the tall spare figure, the glittering eye and the commanding presence of the erect old man.

Returning to Mr. Macon; . . . when he had reached his seventieth year, which according to the Psalmist is the due limit of human life, he resigned his seat in the Senate in 1828, to spend the residue of his days in serene preparation for the last silence; leaving behind

* Randall's Life of Jefferson, p. 665, vol. ii.

† By the way, "Creetur" is almost the universal name for horse in many of the rural parts of our country.

him an almost unequalled reputation for firmness guided by wisdom, and integrity softened by goodness. At his death, some years after, he desired that his body might be buried in a stony ridge, and that his only monument should be a cairn of flint rock.

The transition is a natural one, from the unimpeachable rectitude and primitive simplicity of Nathaniel Macon, to the equally stainless honor, coupled with universal culture and preëminent powers, of William Pinkney. It is true that his fame is more especially identified with the chamber underneath the Senate, the Supreme Court room; but in both these, as well as in the House, for learning, genius and eloquence, he was like a star, and dwelt apart; and although dying *in his very prime*, he has left a reputation which can never pale, so long as the verdict of such men as Randolph, Wirt, Gilmer, Jefferson, Benton, Tazewell, and Webster, has worth. He was the pride and Colossus of our bar; the Gamaliel at whose feet most of our jurists that have attained distinction since the last war, sat with grateful docility. Gifted with genius which might almost have disdained labor, he yet felt that labor was the all of genius, and at length by the severity of his application, forfeited his life. Doomed to a youth of poverty, in consequence of his father's adhesion to the loyalist cause in Revolutionary times, he nevertheless managed to gain enough of academic lore and legal erudition to place him at the bar of Maryland, by the time he was twenty-five years of age.

He advanced with rapid strides to a front rank in his profession, was immediately enlisted in the diplomatic service of his country, and sent abroad to perform the delicate and responsible duties of commissioner to adjudge private claims, growing out of the Revolutionary war, under the treaty with England.

He resided much in London, prosecuting his legal studies, occupying all his leisure in scrupulous attendance upon the courts of Westminster and in the best society of the world's metropolis. He was subsequently a minister to several of the first-class European courts, never for a moment relaxing his studies nor his attempts to improve himself as an orator. He, more than any other man, introduced into the highest courts of the country the most impressive style of argumentative eloquence, enriched with all the graces of varied and exact learning outside his own profession. As Attorney-General under Mr. Madison, as member of the House of Representatives and of the Senate, he surpassed competition. On his entrance into the House, he was called upon to deliver a speech upon the treaty-making power. As a full lawyer and experienced diplomatist, he exhausted the subject and could not but seem to instruct the House. Mr. Randolph, who thought that a new member should pass a novitiate before attempting to teach, administered to him one of those subtle yet significant reproofs which he, better than any other man, knew how to give. Rising to reply to Mr. Pinkney, he said, "Mr. Speaker—the gentleman from Maryland"—and then pausing as if in doubt, he added, "I believe he is from Maryland," and then proceeded. The hit was palpable, and no one relished it more than the man at whom it was aimed, who coming round to Mr. Randolph's seat at the close of the speech, requested permission to dissipate his doubt, and to assure him that he was from Maryland. An intimacy at once sprung up between them which lasted until Mr. Pinkney's death. No announcement of a similar event has probably ever produced such a sensation in Congress, as that of Mr. Pinkney's death, by Mr. Randolph. Rising in the midst of a stormy sectional debate, growing out of the Missouri Compromise question, he said in his slow, impressive way, "For this one day at least, let us say, as our first mother said to our first father:

> 'While yet we live, scarce one short hour perhaps,
> Between us two let there be peace.'

I rise to announce to the House the most unlooked-for death of a man who filled the first place in the public estimation, in the first profession, in that estimation, in this or any other country. We have been talking of General Jackson, and a greater than he, is, not here, but gone forever. I allude, sir, to the boast of Maryland and the pride of the United States—the pride of all of us, but more particularly the pride and ornament of the profession of which you, Mr. Speaker (Mr. Philip P. Barbour), are a member, and an eminent one."

"Mr. Pinkney was kind and affable in his temper, free from every taint of envy or jealousy, conscious of his powers, and relying upon them alone for success. He was a model to all young men in his habits of study and application, and at more than sixty years of age, was still a severe student. In politics he classed democratically, and was one of the few of our eminent public men who never seemed to think of the Presidency. Oratory was his glory, the law his profession, the bar his theatre, and his service in Congress was only a brief episode, dazzling each House, for he was a momentary member of each, with a single and splendid speech."

But it is time that I had turned from the Senate of the elder days, to the body as it was composed when I first stood in the Vice-President's place, to open its deliberations with prayer. The solemn hush that pervaded the room, betokened the grave decorum of the fifty men who stood with their grey heads bowed reverently, as a beardless boy commended them to the care and guidance of the God of nations.

Among those who have filled a prominent place

in the nation's eye, there were Messrs. Dix and Dickinson of New York, John M. Clayton of Delaware, Reverdy Johnson of Maryland, Willie P. Mangum of N. Carolina, McDuffie of S. Carolina, Berrien of Georgia, Dixon H. Lewis of Alabama, Crittenden of Kentucky, Corwin of Ohio, Hannegan and Bright of Indiana, Atchison and Benton of Missouri, and Cass of Michigan. To these were added during the session, from the new State, Texas, Gen. Houston and Mr. Rusk.

The President's chair was filled by the urbane and courtly George M. Dallas, whose abundant hair, white as wool, a beautiful crown to his graceful person, and whose dignified, high-bred manner, seemed to qualify him peculiarly for his place. I shall never forget one example of his good breeding. The State of Arkansas was represented at that time by Messrs Ashley and Sevier, who were in the habit of pronouncing its name differently—Arkansas and Arkansàw. In recognizing them upon the floor, Mr. Dallas never failed to say, "The Senator from Arkansas" or "the Senator from Arkansàw," according to each man's use of the accent. But, high over all their colleagues, in authoritative influence, power, and the general estimation, towered Daniel Webster and John C. Calhoun, two of the immortal triumvirate of the Senate. Mr. Clay had resigned his seat in 1842, disgusted at the ingratitude of the

Whig party, as manifested by the chicanery of its leaders in the nomination of Gen. Harrison for the Presidency in 1840, and subsequently by the defection of Mr. Tyler from the Whig ranks after attempting by every means in his power to deprive Mr. Clay of the leadership of the party. The high-souled Kentuckian had become wearied out by the turmoil, strife and unsatisfactoriness of political life. And well he might have been, as let the following unrecorded fact attest. On Gen. Harrison's election to the Presidency, he paid a visit to Ashland to ask Mr. Clay if there were anything in the gift of the government he would accept, and to take counsel with him as to the policy to be pursued by his administration. Mr. Clay declined all offers, whether of foreign ministries or cabinet appointments, and declared his intention to remain in the Senate.

The President then said, you must allow me to consider you my most honored and confidential adviser, and I trust you will ever feel free to give me your best and constant counsel. At his instance, Mr. Clay named the men he thought fit for the head-ship of the different departments, all of whom, I believe, were offered seats in the Cabinet. But the new administration had not been mounted two weeks, before the evil reports of talebearers had so soured the mind of the President toward his most able and magnanimous friend, that he sent Mr. Clay a note requesting him, if he had advice to give, to be good enough to submit it in writing.

Few speeches have ever been delivered in the Senate, which have so stirred and softened, not only the members within, but the nation without, as Mr. Clay's leave-taking of the Senate in 1842.

His seat was now filled by Mr. Crittenden, one of the ablest statesmen as well as most accomplished debaters of the body. It was always pleasant to hear the tones of his silvery voice and his steady flow of good sense, mingled with good humor, in diction sometimes of classical purity. Mr. McDuffie, stricken in the prime of his brilliant career by the bullet from a duellist's pistol, and in consequence of which his system shrivelled and shrank, went tottering about the chamber, leaning upon a long staff, a frightful monument of the fiendish effects of the "code of honor." Mr. Hannegan, whose fine nature and admirable powers were even then being undermined by a passion for strong drink, stood forth as the avowed champion of the "54 40′ or fight" doctrine, as it was called; for this, as so many other sessions of Congress, before and since, was disgraced by an attempt, on the part of a number of prominent politicians of the bullying and badgering school, to get up a war with England. A few years previous to this time, the Webster and Ashburton treaty, by its settlement of our northeastern boundary line, had effaced a cause of trouble between the two countries.

Another was now brought up in the unsettled northwestern boundary, which some of the hot-blooded western men insisted should be run along the parallel—fifty-four degrees, forty minutes. The President, before his election, had committed himself to this line, but on coming into office, found it opposed by the facts of history and the dictates of honor; and, together with his Cabinet, he was endeavoring to recede from a position to which he had been unwittingly hurried by the vehemence of partisan politics, and to assume a stand justified by right and the national conscience. This course was branded by the war party, of which Mr. Hannegan was the spokesman, as an attempt to "craw-fish," and the President was obliged to have recourse to an alliance between a minority of his own party in the Senate, composed of its more wise and pacific men, and his political antagonists the Whigs, to save his administration from a disgrace, and the country from a dishonorable and bloody war. The speechifying, caucusing, and manœuvering, which grew out of this attempt, formed a droll, and, I confess, very humiliating spectacle, to an ardent young patriot just emerged from the woods, and who was disposed to look upon affairs through a rose-colored medium.

Colonel Benton was a striking figure, see him where

you would, whether sauntering through the capital, his hat stuck slightly on one side of his head, or standing in his place delivering himself a good deal in "Sir Oracle" style of speeches, not agreeable from a graceful manner and pleasing elocution, but impressive and convincing from their sturdy independence, cogent arguments, and the immense stores of digested learning which they displayed. Notwithstanding his strong partisan bias, his view of a subject was still comprehensive, and his support of it, by an array of facts, dates and figures, almost irresistible.

Mr. Calhoun was much given to pacing the corridor back of the President's chair, in conversation with a friend, or buried in rumination. Careless of his appearance, slouching in his gait, his tall, spare figure bent, there was little about him to arrest the casual glance as he passed you, one hand behind his back, the other grasping and sometimes flourishing an immense East India handkerchief. But as you looked more narrowly at him, at the not very large head covered with a mass of rather wiry, iron-grey hair, the wrinkled brow and attenuated face, wherein both nose and mouth told of uncompromising decision, and from which the eyes, in moods of excitement, shone like live coals of fire, you felt yourself to be in the presence of a king of men. His manner of articulation, in conversation as well as in public speech, was abrupt, rapid, and almost crabbed; his average was one hundred and eighty words to a minute, his style was sententious, dogmatic and authoritative; sometimes negligent of grammatical structure and elegant pronunciation, it nevertheless at once arrested, and then riveted you by its clear, cogent reasoning, its directness and sincerity. His speeches were delivered standing in one of the narrow aisles of the Senate Chamber, bracing himself by grasping the desk on either side of him, while his right hand occasionally flourished his bandana: they were totally destitute of the graces of manner peculiar to Mr. Clay's, and of the elaborate finish of composition characterizing Mr. Webster's. For an hour (he hardly delivered a speech which lasted longer) he poured forth a vehement stream of logic, free from personal asperity, in homely, and for the most part, idiomatic English. He seemed to be the logical understanding embodied; he claimed no suffrage from your sympathy, he levied no tribute upon your admiration, he convinced you, or demanded that you should answer him by arguments as convincing, and by logic as passionless as his own. There was little of the orator, and nothing of the poet about him; his intellect was eminently metaphysical; and yet his frank and generous spirit, the unsullied purity and ingenuous nobleness of his character, attached men to him as with links of steel. He delighted in debate, and like most politicians, in vaticination.

That instinct of our nature apparent in all women and most men, for predicting the future and foretelling its dread secrets, and self-felicitatingly, in the one time out of fifty that it is correct, expressing itself in the well known phrase, "I told you it would be so," but taking no notice of its forty-nine mistakes, finds its culmination among our politicians. You cannot spend a week in the capital without hearing at least a hundred prophesies, nor hear an oration from a distinguished member or senator without being reminded that in the horoscope of the nation which he drew in his speech on such a day, in such a year, he foretold the occurrence of the events which they now discuss; and you at length come to believe that a knowledge of astrology is necessary to the practice of statesmanship.

Mr. Calhoun's mind was incisive rather than comprehensive; more the disciple of Aristotle than of Plato or Bacon, preferring deduction to induction; holding both you and himself to his irresistibly reasoned conclusions from his accepted premises. It grew more from contact with men and affairs, than by the study of books; more by the athletic exercise of conversation, than by a familiar acquaintance with the sages of the past. He delighted in young men, as indeed did both his illustrious rivals, Clay and Webster, and by impressing himself in full, free, fascinating talk upon their receptive minds and kindled sensibilities, he created a self-perpetuating influence which cannot soon decay.

The eye of a discerning visitor, in its first rapid sweep of the chamber, would make its first pause, and then fix its steady and oft-repeated gaze upon a figure seated almost on a line with the Vice-President, and half way between the secretary's desk and the door. The head, which seemed to belong to Jupiter, with its immense domelike brow beetling over the cavernous depths, from which, like diamonds, glowed his eyes, the noble contour of the face, and shoulders broad enough for Atlas, satisfied you that this was Mr. Webster, or the immortal "Black Dan," as he was sometimes loosely called in Washington. There was something about him to inspire awe, and your self-confidence had a trick of deserting you, as you addressed him. A singular illustration of the power of his bodily presence to awaken the imagination and create an illusion in regard to himself, is the fact, that everybody thought him a very large and heavy man; whereas, for many years of his life, his weight was 148 pounds. But as the reserve (which, by the way, characterizes the northern and eastern men in Washington as elsewhere, differencing them from the men of the South and West) wore off, you found him to be a most delightful companion, abounding in glee, sportive anecdote, and a love of merriment. His talk was full of wisdom, learning, wit and humor. I think I have never known another man with a memory so stored with historical, agricultural, geographical, topographical, legal and personal information. He had an eye for fine oxen, and an ear for old psalms and tunes. He could repeat poetry by the hour, seemed to know the Bible by heart, and was an unfailing story-teller; his fund of knowledge was exhaustless and his use of it was as accurate as it was profound; his style of speaking was grave and measured, and so exquisite was his taste in words, that he would often pause until the hesitation became embarrassing to every one but himself, to call up the proper one, for none other would he use. Sometimes he would remodel his sentence, refusing to proceed until the precise phrase to convey the very shade of thought came obedient to his will; as witness the following examples: "We want," said he, speaking of the necessity of a national bank, "an institution that shall—an institution that has—an odor of nationality about it;" and the applause that followed attested the force and the felicity of the figure. Making a speech on the great Wheeling Bridge case, before the Supreme Court of the United States, he said: "Now, your honors, we want the bank to come out—to show its hand—to render up—to give forth—to disgorge!" and the last word was given with such emphasis that it seemed to weigh about twelve pounds. I have seen him stand in the Supreme Court room, engaged in an argument, halting for a word, with his hands inserted into the mouth of his trowsers-pockets, and as the right expression began to dawn upon him, his relief was betokened by the gradual slipping of his hands deeper in; but when it came, they went down with such a force that you felt the sewing must be good or the muslin strong that could resist the shock. It may be a fact worth knowing, that Mr. Webster's immense head continued to grow sensibly throughout his life, insomuch that it was necessary for him to wear a hat one size larger, every four or five years. There is no need, however, that I should attempt an analysis of his colossal intellect or a description of its public working: that task has been and will be performed by abler hands than mine. Clay, Webster and Calhoun, entering the theatre of affairs almost side by side, their lives and influence mark an era in our national history. The previous race of our statesmen had conceived and expressed their ideal of a national organization, but as yet, it was little else than an ideal. They had shown a most penetrative insight into the constitution of man and the wants of society; they had shown a transcendent wisdom; but still it was by the force of abstract intellect, grasping the great cardinal doctrines of humanity, and interpreting their present import in the signs of the times, that they had erected the magnificent fabric of American Liberty. It was the task of succeeding men to apply these new sentiments, to devise measures to meet the exigencies of the country, to correct the errors of speculative intelligence, and to embody generalities in the safe form of practical adaptation. Men cannot foresee the changes of society. The laws of circumstance are not disclosed to mortal eyes. It is a province of thought and action that God reserves to his personal supremacy, and from which, he is ever sending forth, in varying intervals of years and centuries, the reforming or revolutionizing powers of the world. A few simple and permanent principles are all that a government can safely pledge itself to uphold, and consequently it will not fail to provide a certain degree of elasticity, by which the machinery of political operation may be so modified as to suit the necessary mutations of all earthly interests. It is in this department of statesmanship, that skill finds its most onerous burdens and heaviest responsibilities, and it was here that the great minds, so lately taken from us, were called to the service of their country. A vast field for private ambition and patriotic effort was here opened before them, and without exaggeration, it may be said that it afforded opportunities for impressing the genius of the age, and imparting an impulse to the progress of society, which have scarcely been surpassed in the annals of our race. Let any man review the events of the last fifty years, and he will have an idea of the magnitude of those difficulties which taxed the ingenuity and patience of our second generation of statesmen. Who could have anticipated these wonderful movements? Who could have divined the sources whence they sprang, the lateral connections they would form, or the direction which they would take? Who could have foretold the effects on England of her East India possessions—the results of Napoleon's wars—or appreciated the sudden growth of Russia and the convulsions of South America? Who could have estimated the consequences of Whitney's invention of the Cotton-gin, or Fulton's application of steam to navigation? And lastly, who could have imagined, that within so narrow a compass, all the educational and benevolent enterprises of our time, would have been urged forward with such mighty zeal to issues so stupendous! Amid these exciting scenes, when incidents were converted into events, and the energies of men everywhere were receiving an almost supernatural enhancement, our young country was to take her place among the ruling powers of the earth—to insure respect and honor by the demonstration of her capabilities—to govern herself, both in relation to her citizens at home and communities abroad—to call out her strength and yet discipline it to the work before her—and above all, to set an example of moral dignity that should immortalize the virtues of republican character. Could statesmanship have been more severely tasked? All experience had failed—all history had been belied—all "the foundations of the earth were out of course;" and yet in the presence of such difficulties, in the full recognition of their amazing vastness, and in the calm trust of their own faculties, these men conducted our country through her dangers and exacted from the world a tribute to her grandeur.

The highest order of statesmanship was demanded in this era of our national history. To conceive a great and good system of government can scarcely fail to be considered the noblest exercise of the human mind. All the records of our race confirm this assertion. The fortunes of government are suspended on legislative wisdom and administrative integrity; and it is in this connection, that the services of Calhoun, Clay, and Webster are worthy of the most liberal commendation. They were trained among the people. Whenever they represented the people, it was a representation in fact, as well as in form. They cherished its spirit, spoke its language, and obeyed its will. The sacredness of the people's homes and altars was never forgotten, and to its authenticated rights, they were never insensible. The influence of the people was then direct and immediate, for newspapers had not as yet established themselves as a secondary power between representatives and constituents. Such a state of circumstances enabled the statesmen to act personally and freely upon the mind of the country, whose public opinion was then under their control; editors and contributors had not then invaded their dominion, hence the full power of their position devolved upon them. The necessary results of this relation may be easily apprehended. Men in political life were formed to independent thought, and measures were adopted on their own merits. The numerous agencies that now exert themselves through the press, could contribute neither their wisdom nor folly, in any considerable degree, to the legislative intellect of the country, and personal responsibility in the halls of the nation was compelled to feel the magnitude of its trust. The various elements of political and social life were never more favorably combined for the development of great character. Talents were adequately appreciated. Wisdom was revered. Patriotism was a hallowed name. Everything gave value to mental endowments and virtuous services. The profound thinker, the far-sighted politician, the philosophic statesman, were then in the ascendant, and their superiority was acknowledged. Genius and worth had no temptation to stand in the market-place and court popularity. Demagogism had not learned its modern arts. Shufflers and tricksters had not ventured on their political caricatures. The word "Humbug" was not known, and pantomime was confined to theatrical boards. The whole country leaned upon its strong men, and confessed its obligations to them, for confidence in systems had not yet betrayed it into indifference to personal endowments. The magic of machinery had not imposed upon its senses, nor had the lapse of time begotten a sort of superstitious belief, that the government could take care of itself. Popular knowledge had not been diffused, the masses of the people had not been educated; every schoolboy was not then a politician, and debating societies did not settle tariff questions. Women's Rights conventions had not threatened their parliamentary authority over rebellious husbands, nor issued their edicts against St. Paul and other weak apostles. Brains, in that day, were not bought or sold; encyclopedias had not become substitutes for study. Europe was not our next-door neighbor; railroads, belting the land, and telegraphs, spanning the air, had not been invented; men had not then realized their strength. Self-consciousness had not become a disease, nor self-reliance a fanatical extravagance. The transition period had just commenced, and American Mind was preparing for its new installation. The thoughtful intellects of the country began to see that there was more involved in the struggle for independence than they had imagined, and ere they were aware, they found themselves in a partnership with the mightiest forces of the universe in behalf of eternal truth and divine right. A towering mountain summit had been gained; could the dizzy elevation be maintained? could the rarefied air be breathed? could Freedom dwell on such a heavenward height? and around its youthful form could it fold the clouds in which the fierce lightning hid its fire, or the wild tornado held its fury? Such were the questions which the statesmanship of that time had to answer, and answer, too, out of its own mind and heart. Whatever virtue is in circumstances, our departed statesmen were accessible to its complete influence. Whatever endowments Nature had bestowed upon them, there was ample room for their exertion and display. They were secure in their position, for the seal of the age was upon them. Accepted by their countrymen as the leading spirits of their nation, and marked by Providence for a great work, what remained for them, but to receive their anointing, and consecrate their royalty of mind to the cause of humanity?

There is one other fact that gives a most impressive interest to their personal and political position. The moral of our Revolution was the character of its MEN. Our strength lay in kind, not in degree. Compute it by arithmetic, and it seems feeble and impotent, but measure it by intellectual and impassioned sentiments, and the number swells into an "exceeding great army." Providence has often illustrated this principle; Greece was a small country, so was Judea, and yet, what vast power went forth from their narrow limit! Science may well take pleasure in the insignificant. The coral insect may justly be magnified as the builder of continents, and the humble bee, acknowledged as the first of architects. But if we wish the most significant example of this law, we must turn to the providential connections of man: a great truth enlarges his personality, everything receives his overflowing life, the winds and waves help him, all nature takes sides with him, the very angels do his bidding. Our early struggle was the struggle of true and strong-hearted men; men who perilled all for principle; who valued their cause more than themselves, and invoked the martyr-spirit to baptize them for their work. Is it, then, strange, that the public opinion of the country attached such importance to men? The history of Washington was before it. Any one of its pages was sufficient to redeem the name of Man, to establish confidence in his noble capacities. Our best lesson was learned from him. It was not the mere fact of his greatness, but the peculiar type of that greatness which instituted the heraldry of our land. If, then, our statesmen would be honored and loved, such are the associations they must covet, in that constellation they must fix their star. Standing beside them in their opening career, we may easily imagine the animated sentiments and fervent aspirations that quickened the intellects and warmed the hearts of our illustrious Trio. That portion of their biography is already written. Every man has done it for himself. Shall the sequel realize the glowing fancy? The conditions of greatness are a severe tax on our wisdom and fortitude; the sternest laws have to be implicitly and devoutly obeyed; the hands must never weary, nor the feet ever falter; our country must be our better self, and Heaven infuse energy into every generous thought and heroic action.

CHAPTER XIV.

SOCIAL LIFE IN WASHINGTON, AND SOME OF ITS TRADITIONS.

To one whose enjoyment of society is not impaired by a conventional bondage of fashionable routine, and whose taste is not vitiated by the spirit of exclusiveness, Washington offers greater attractions than any other city of the country. Around the great officers of State, are gathered persons from every part of the Republic, representing all professions and types of character. Nearly every man in Congress has made himself noteworthy at home by some gift or accomplishment; he can play the fiddle well, tell a good story, manage a caucus, make an effective speech, indite striking paragraphs, laugh loud and long, listen complaisantly while others talk, talk fluently and copiously himself, or has a pretty and clever wife. These gifts and graces are, of course, brought to the Federal Capital, and invested in the joint stock company of social life. The small salaries paid to American officials, and the drain of politics on the pocket, used to keep the mass of our statesmen in moderate, not to say humble circum stances. The new comer was therefore struck by the unpretending plainness of the houses and furniture, and the simplicity of the *ménage* of our lawgivers. The noble public edifices, some of them yet in course of erection, formed as striking a contrast with the private residences of Washington, as did those of Rome before the time of Cæsar. The White House itself, except for an occasional gorgeous carpet, by its meagre and almost bare appearance, would have satisfied the requirements of the austerest democrat; nevertheless the doors of hospitality stood open to all, and while the fare was, for the most part, frugal, it was rendered acceptable by open-handed kindness. A President's *levée* is probably the most curious and characteristic expression of our individual, social and national peculiarities, to be seen in any single spectacle throughout the country. No cards of invitation are issued, but notice is given through the newspapers, that on a stated evening of every alternate week, the Chief Magistrate will receive his fellow citizens. The first and last of the season are usually the most interesting. At eight o'clock the pedestrians begin to arrive, and by nine the carriages are depositing their loads at the main entrance of the executive mansion. The President stands in a little reception room, with the ladies of his household on his right, and on his left the Marshal of the District of Columbia, who, in a very unostentatious way, performs the duty of grand chamberlain, announcing to his excellency the names of such parties as he may know. The President, generally, his left hand gloved and his right hand bared, spends two hours shaking hands with an uncounted crowd, in such a way as to make the impression on each person, that *he*, the President, is particularly delighted to see *him*, and that if he had only a little more time, he would vastly enjoy a *tête-à-tête*. The procession files past the President into the great east-room, where promenading is the order of the evening, until the press renders it impossible. Here are officers of the army and navy in uniform; foreign ministers with their stars and ribbons, public functionaries of every grade; merchants, shopkeepers, mechanics; sometimes a group of backwoods hunters or Indian chiefs; and women of every age and condition, in magnificent toilets or rustic gear, yet all good-humored and polite. I fancy that it must the most extraordinary social medley to be witnessed anywhere. All seem to feel that the occasion has equalized them, there is neither obsequious suppleness on the one hand, or haughty condescension on the other, and I have never known a deviation from the rules of good behavior. The band of the marine corps discourses good music from a distant part of the building, and the time for dispersion is indicated by the performance of "Sweet Home," or "Yankee Doodle."

President Polk's coachman, a colored man named Gee, used to interest me very much at these times. He officiated in the gentlemen's dressing-room, receiving and returning hats, coats, canes, etc. A party of a dozen would enter together and pass over to him their exterior habiliments, and almost before he had time to deposit these, another group would be waiting for him; yet, such was his power of individualization, that I never knew him fail to hand to every person his appropriate belongings, and that on the instant. His was the most remarkable power of memory I have ever met.

The asperities of debate, and the sharpness of sectional views, are very apt to be modified and softened by the free and easy dinner parties and the evening reunions of the capital; and these assemblages are often more potent for the shaping and success of measures, than is the committee-room or even the Legislative Hall. It is rarely the case that the partisan contests of Congress interfere with the private social relations of the members. When Washington society, as well as the two houses, is divided into northern and southern cliques, we may expect the dissolution of the Union; but so long as the member from Maine dines in the evening with the member from Louisiana, whose speech he demolished in the morning; or the senators from Massachusetts and Alabama go home arm in arm from a pleasant little supper, notwithstanding they railed at each other in the forenoon's debate; the patriot has little reason to fear the exhibitions of our wordy gladiators. Cold and austere indeed must be the nature which does not relax and soften under the influence of hospitable cheer and good company, and the failure of many an honorable member to fulfill the pledges made to his constituents in the canvass, is to be attributed to the charm and magnetic power of the dinner-table. I am satisfied that the stigma of *doughface-ism*, imputed to political cowardice, is, for the most part, the natural and almost inevitable result of good victual and drink, dispensed and received with genial courtesy and graceful cordiality; and that what is often stigmatized as treachery to a man's party, is nothing more or less than a testimony to the strength of his own refined social nature. Nowhere are fine conversational powers and engaging manners more effective than in the capital: many a man who is almost dumb in the halls of Congress, and of whom the newspaper-reading community hears little or nothing, nevertheless wields immense power, and succeeds in carrying or thwarting many a scheme, in virtue of these accomplishments.

The power of women in political affairs is not a recognized fact in our republican metropolis, as in the French court before the revolution, and yet the spell of bright eyes and sweet voices is not only mighty in deciding the fate of private bills, the appointment and confirmation of friends to office, but often affects the entire policy of the government. The library of Congress, a magnificent room on the west side of the capitol, is not so much a cloister for book-worms and plodding students, as a superb drawing-room, where fashion and beauty hold daily court, and where honorable members may seek occasional relief from the platitudes of debate, in proffering delicate attentions to their fair countrywomen. I have observed, that while women are very apt to tire of their seats in the galleries, and to yawn over the public disquisitions of their friends on the floor below, their interest at once grows profound and unflagging when the oratory is exchanged for conversation, and she becomes, instead of one in a thousand, the sole listener. Many of the ablest forensic efforts that have graced the capitol were never chronicled in the "*Congressional Globe*," but are treasured alone in the single heart to which they were addressed.

One hears many anecdotes of our public men from the lips of their coëvals, and I may be allowed to mention some of them in this place. John Randolph, of Roanoke, is the hero of many a racy story. After the last war with Great Britain, the House was engaged in the discussion of the currency question. Mr. Calhoun, one of the youngest but foremost members, toward whom Mr. Randolph entertained the strongest feelings of antipathy, was making an elaborate speech, in which he declared that no statute of the country required the tender of gold or silver for revenue. Mr. Randolph, who sat near Mr. Webster, leaned toward him and inquired if this were so; the latter replied that he thought not, and calling a page, desired him to bring a certain volume of the Statutes at Large, in which he found a law requiring the payment of postage in gold and silver. He handed the volume to Randolph, who glanced at the statute and returned it to the page, that it might be replaced on the shelves behind the speaker's chair. Slowly rising, he interrupted Mr. Calhoun, and desired to know through the speaker, whether the gentleman from South Carolina felt positive as to the accuracy of his assertion. Mr. Calhoun replied that he did. Mr. Randolph responded, in that irritating tone which none better than he knew how and when to use, that he had doubts as to the honorable member's correctness. Mr. Calhoun, much chafed, retorted with asperity—that he considered the interruption undignified and contemptible—that he had examined all the statutes and knew his position to be impregnable. Mr. Randolph then summoned the page to bring him the desired volume, and opening it, as if by accident, at the very leaf, sent it to

Mr. Calhoun, with the request that he should read it to the House. The latter was so much disconcerted that he took his seat, covered with confusion.

The great Virginian, a lifelong victim to sore disease, was at the same time subject to great depression of spirits, at which times he was in hourly expectation of death. Imperious in his friendship as in his disdain, he would require the attendance of his friends at his bedside, that they might see him breathe his last. On one of these occasions, his servants went flying through the town, bearing messages to various persons for whom he felt esteem, desiring them to hasten to him immediately, if they would see him die. Most of them were dressed or dressing for parties; but, obedient to the mandate, came in hot haste to his lodgings. The emaciated invalid, apparently at the last pulse, surveyed his guests, and saw officers of both arms of the service in full uniform, and a group of gentlemen, old and young, in full evening dress. Scanning them narrowly, he asked, in a faint, husky whisper, "are there any but Virginians here?" Some one answering, No; he said, "turn the key in the door, I wish none but my compatriots to see me die." "Gentlemen," he continued, "I want you to promise me, that as soon as the breath leaves my body, you will carry me across the Potomac, into the old Dominion. Bury me like a gentleman, at my own expense, and not like pauper Dawson," a member of

Congress who had died a few days before and had been buried, after congressional usage, at the public cost. The excitement attendant upon the delivery of these remarks seemed to give him strength, and he proceeded—"I find that I have a few minutes more to live, and I should like to spend them in asking you some questions." Addressing an officer of the army who stood near him: "Colonel T——, where were you educated?" "At Yale College, sir." "At Yale College," he repeated in contemptuous tones, "among the Yankees? Was your father such a fool, sir, as to suppose that the Yankees could teach a gentleman anything?" Turning to another he said, "And where were you educated, Mr. P——?" "At South Carolina College, sir." "In South Carolina;" and then with increasing warmth and deepening scorn, "and your father sent you to the State which produced John C. Calhoun, and that for an education." As he continued his questioning, he found that every man present had been educated out of Virginia, and at last became so furious, that springing from his bed, he determined not to die at that time, and so dismissed those who had come to be mourners at a funeral.

I cannot forbear to insert here the following incident related by Mr. Benton. On one occasion he wanted some gold; that coin not being then in circulation, and only to be obtained by favor or purchase, he sent his faithful man Johnny to the United States Branch Bank to get a few pieces, American being the kind asked for. Johnny returned without the gold, delivering the excuse that the bank had none. Instantly, Mr. Randolph's clear silver-toned voice was heard above its natural pitch, exclaiming, "their name is legion, and they are liars from the beginning. Johnny, bring me my horse." His own saddle-horse was brought him, for he never rode Johnny's nor Johnny his, though both, and all his hundred horses, were of the finest English blood, and he rode off to the bank, now Corcoran & Rigg's, down Pennsylvania Avenue, Johnny following, as always, forty paces behind. Arriving at the bank, this scene took place. "Mr. Randolph asked for the state of his account, was shown it, and found it to be some four thousand dollars in his favor. He demanded the sum. The teller took up packages of bills and civilly asked in what sized notes he would have it. 'I want *money*,' said Mr. Randolph, emphasizing the word—and at that time it required a bold man to intimate that United States Bank notes were not money. The teller, beginning to understand him, said inquiringly, 'You want silver?' 'I want my money,' was the reply. Then the teller, lifting boxes to the counter, said politely, 'Have you a cart, Mr. Randolph, to put it in?' 'That is my business, sir,' said he. By this time, the attention of the cashier was attracted to what was going on; he came up, and understanding the question and its cause, told Mr. Randolph there was a mistake in the answer given to his servant; that they had gold, and he should have what he wanted.

"In fact, he had only applied for a few pieces for a special purpose. A compromise was effected, the pieces of gold were received, the cart and the silver dispensed with; but the account with this bank was closed, and a check taken for the amount on New York."

The following story of General Jackson has never before, to my knowledge, seen the light. When he demanded of Louis Philippe indemnity for the spoliation of our commerce, the commercial interest was panic-struck in apprehension of certain war, and our land was filled with the invectives hurled by the newspaper organs of the moneyed classes against the great President and his policy. It was said that he was either a blockhead or a ruffian; either unable to count the cost of war, or regardless of the waste of blood and treasure; determined to pursue his narrow and ignorant schemes, whatever the risk to the nation. One of the justices of the Federal Supreme Court was about this period taking the great eastern cities en route from his western home to the capital, spending some time in Boston, New York, Philadelphia and Baltimore. As he was known to be intimate with the President, he was waited upon by many bankers and merchants of these places, who urged him to remonstrate with the General against the folly and wickedness of his course; representing that our commerce would be crushed and that all our interests would be ruined in the unequal nay hopeless contest with the great monarchy. They knew, they said, the belligerent disposition of the French king, and that his people were not only prepared, but eager for war, and the judge was implored in the most moving tones, to use his best powers, as a patriot, in averting the threatened collision, and to secure the fadeless wreath of the peacemaker.

Reaching Washington, just before the commencement of the session, when the war message was to be sent to Congress, the judge called to pay his respects to the President, and before long the topic of the day was introduced. "Well, Judge," said the old chieftain, "what do they think of my war policy in the great cities?" The judge, who had really been very much impressed by what he had heard, stated in concise but strong terms, the remonstrance with which he had been charged. The President, laughing long and heartily, said, "What fools they are!" Opening his desk, he produced a map of France and a couple of letters. The map showed at a glance the departments which produced wine and silk, and on its margin was a tabular statement, showing the number of the deputies in the chamber, sent from these, as compared with the other departments of the kingdom, by which it appeared that they had a strong majority in the legislative branch of the government. One of the letters was from Mr. Livingston, the President's minister in Paris, announcing that he had the honor to forward with the accompanying map and annexed information, prepared by himself and the French minister of foreign affairs, an autograph letter from Louis Philippe. In this the king of the French stated explicitly that he felt the justice of the American President's claim for indemnity, and was desirous to satisfy it, but that he was prevented from so doing by the impracticable temper of his chamber of deputies; that as the President would see from the map, its majority was composed of members from those departments whose industry would be ruined by a war with the United States, yet that these were the very men who refused to vote the supplies to pay the debt. His majesty therefore urged the President to threaten immediate war unless the debt were paid, with the assurance that this measure would have the desired effect of alarming the intractable deputies into more equitable dispositions.

The judge therefore joined the President's hearty laugh, and felt how groundless were the fears and how undeserved the bitter denunciations, poured out upon the head of the noble Tennesseean.

Shortly after the battle of New Orleans, a conference of Methodist preachers was being held in Nashville, Tennessee. My old friend Peter Cartwright was appointed to preach in one of the churches on Sunday evening. As he rose to announce his text, there was a stir in the crowded congregation; he paused until the excitement should subside. The pastor of the church took advantage of the opportunity to pull the skirt of the preacher's coat and admonish him in a whisper, "Brother Cartwright, you must be careful how you preach to-night, General Jackson has just come in." In a loud tone, Cartwright replied, "what do you suppose I care for General Jackson; if he don't repent of his sins and believe on the Lord Jesus Christ, he will die and be damned like any other sinner," and then proceeded with his sermon. The next morning (both rose with the lark), as the preacher passed the general's quarters in his morning stroll, a servant ran after him with the message that General Jackson wished to speak with him. Turning, his hand was grasped by the hero, who shook it heartily, saying, "Sir, you are a man after my own heart; if I had a regiment of men as brave as you, and you for the chaplain, I'd agree to conquer any country on earth." A strong friendship sprang up between these men, in whom were many points of resemblance. Mr. Cartwright happened to travel a circuit near the Hermitage and was often the general's guest. One Sunday, the preacher had gone home from church, with his friend and a number of visitors, to dine. Among other persons at table, was a young Nashville lawyer, who desired to exhibit his wit at the expense of the backwoods preacher. Addressing him across the table, he said: "Mr. Cartwright, do you really believe in any such place as Hell? I know you preach a great deal about it, and that's all very well, but I want your private opinion; you are certainly too intelligent a man to believe anything of the kind." The lake of fire and brimstone was a prominent article in the preacher's creed. As he paused an instant to consider how best to answer a fool according to his folly, General Jackson, impetuously thumping the table with his knife, broke in, "Mr. Jones, I believe in a hell." "You, General Jackson," said the startled fledgling, "what possible use can you have for any such place?" "To put such infernal fools as you in, sir," thundered the infuriated host.

Notwithstanding the footing of easy familiarity on which social intercourse in Washington is conducted, there are certain points of etiquette rigorously adhered to. The principal of these is the rank of the different functionaries of government, about which the feeling is as strong as in the army, and especially among the wives of the parties concerned. For many years it was an open question in theory, whether foreign ministers, supreme judges, or senators should take precedence. It was, however, practically resolved by the overmastering influence of one man, Henry Clay, who contended that the representatives of the sovereign States of the Union occupied a position second only to that of the President, and so long as he lived, his social power maintained the superiority of the Senate; but since his death, the ambassadors and judges have carried their point, and the wives of senators must now therefore leave the first cards.

I can give no better illustration of Mr. Clay's ascendency in social life, than the following incident, which took place during the session of Congress in the winter of 1840–41. The Whigs had elected General Harrison by an overwhelming vote, and toward the end of the session, which was to be closed by his inauguration, a meeting of the leaders of the party was held, to form a programme for the new administration, and especially to determine whether an extra session of Congress should be called. The caucus was held at a famous restaurant, and was composed of twenty-three gentlemen, Whig chieftains from every section of the Republic. Mr. Clay was resolved to have the extra session; Colonel Wm. C. Preston, of South Carolina, felt that to call it would be hazardous in the extreme, and might be ruinous to the party, which in truth it was. Knowing Mr Clay's immense power over men, Colonel Preston had visited every gentleman invited to the meeting, exchanged views with them, and found that his opinion in regard to the bad policy of the proposed measure was confirmed by every one of them except the great Kentuckian. Still, dreading Mr. Clay's authority, he pledged them to a manly support of these views in the forthcoming council. The meeting was initiated by an ample repast. When supper was announced, Mr. Clay led the way and took the head of the table, presiding with his accustomed grace and dignity, charming every one at table by his fine spirits and admirable talk. After the servants had retired and the doors were locked, he called the meeting to order, announced the purpose for which they were assembled, and in his masterly way unfolded his views upon the necessity of a called session. He then asked the opinions of the various gentlemen at the table, calling them, one after another, by name, not in the order of their seats, but of their attachment to himself and their known submission to his leadership, so that Mr. Preston came last; this gentleman had entered the room the file-leader of twenty-two men bound to uphold his views, and now found himself in a minority of one, for every man of them had deserted him.

On another occasion, Mr. Clay felt called upon to

define his position on the subject of Slavery, and having carefully prepared his argument, he read it to Colonel Preston, at the same time asking his opinion of it; "I quite agree with you in your views, Mr. Clay," replied the latter, "but I think it would be better for you to leave out such and such parts; the expression of such opinions, I fear, will injure your prospects for the Presidency in my part of the country." "Am I right sir?" said Mr. Clay. "I think you are, sir," replied the other. "Then, sir," with that generous pride and kindling ardor which made him so grand a nature to all who ever knew him, "I shall say every word of it and compromise not one jot or tittle. I would rather be right than be President."

If any of my readers were ever fortunate enough to hear Mr. Clay tell the following story, they can never forget the inimitable grace and humor with which it was done. "While I was abroad, laboring to arrange the terms of the Treaty of Ghent, there appeared a report of the negotiations or letters relative thereto, and several quotations from my remarks or letters, touching certain stipulations in the treaty, reached Kentucky and were read by my constituents. Among them, was an old fellow who went by the nickname of 'Old Sandusky.' He was reading one of these letters, one evening at a near resort, to a small collection of the neighbors. As he read on, he came across the sentence 'This must be deemed a *sine quâ non.*' 'What's a *sine quâ non?*' said a half dozen by-standers. 'Old Sandusky' was a little bothered at first, but his good sense and natural shrewdness was fully equal to a mastery of the Latin. 'Sine—qua—non?' said Old Sandusky, repeating the question very slowly; 'why, sine qua non is three islands in Passamaquoddy Bay, and Harry Clay is the last man to give them up! No sine qua non, no treaty, he says; and he'll stick to it!'" You should have seen the laughing eye, the change in the speaker's voice and manner, to understand the electric effect the story had upon his hearers.

But of all the illustrious men whose presence has rendered the society of Washington so justly celebrated, no one has exercised a mightier fascination over the select circle he admitted to his intimacy, than Mr. Webster. You could scarce have thought, as you looked with an admiration that approached to awe, upon his colossal figure fitly overarched by his dome-like head, in the Senate or the Court Room, that he, so grave and venerable in dignity, so grand in port and speech, could yet be the most delightful and mirthful of companions. By the wealth of his memory, his fondness of story-telling, his enjoyment of a joke, and his keen sympathy, he shone as much at the table, as in the forum. No man could more completely unbend, without forfeiting your respect, or excite greater pleasure, yet plant no thorn of regret. He talked of fat cattle and green fields, of fishing and shooting, of old hymns and divines of the colonial times, and of the curious experiences he had picked up in out-of-the-way places of life. Few men had seen more of society, its low places and high, than he, and no one ever enjoyed the varieties of a wide observation with a keener relish. Unspoiled by the world's applause, he retained his early simple tastes and habits to the last. Rising an hour before the Sun, in winter, with all his faculties refreshed—for, as he said, he had a genius for sleep—the first application of his new-born powers was to kindle all the fires about the house, for which task he thought himself to possess as great genius, as for sleep. Then, basket on arm, he sallied forth to provide the larder for the day, and to enjoy a friendly chat with the butcher and market women. Regular, for the most part, in his habits, he found early bed-time necessary to his early rising, and usually required seven, eight, or even nine hours of sleep. Nevertheless, he would sometimes work twenty-four or even thirty-six hours continuously. His customary bed-time was between nine and ten, and tired nature would often assert her claims, despite the usurpations of society; for he has been seen to fall asleep upon his feet in a crowded drawing-room, and stand nid-nid-nodding, while those not familiar with him, shocked at the sight, would go out and say that they had seen Mr. Webster drunk; yet in all likelihood, he had not tasted a glass of wine during the day. He never gambled, yet his purse was almost always low, notwithstanding his immense fees. He must have got rid of as much money as did Charles James Fox, although by entirely different methods. He was liberal to prodigality and charitable to a fault. When, upon one occasion, he had gained an important suit for a poor man, the client called upon Mr. Webster's associate to ask what the fee would be, remarking, at the same time, that he had only two hundred and fifty dollars to divide between them. The lawyer replied, that they had expected to receive five hundred apiece, but that he would call upon Mr. Webster and learn what he was willing to take. Listening to the poor man's plight, Mr. Webster said with inimitable naïveté, "I supposed I should get five hundred, and I need the money; but I'll take the hundred and twenty-five, for to a man always as hard up as I am, a few hundred dollars more or less is neither here nor there. He was standing one day at the Capitol gate, engaged in earnest discourse with a brother senator, when he was interrupted by a poor woman, who began the recital of a pitiful tale. He cut her short by pulling a bank-note out of his pocket, thrust it into her hand, and proceeded with his animated talk. His colleague,

—chairman of the Committee on Finance, and therefore considered to be acute on money questions—had observed the operation and noted the denomination of the bill. Checking his interlocutor, he said: "Webster, do you know what you gave that beggar?" "No," said the other, a little chafed by the interruption; "five dollars, I suppose." "It was a hundred," said his friend. "It is no matter" replied the other, "she needed it more than I did."

The following conversation occurred at the dinner table where Mr. Webster for the first time met Col. Preston, then a new senator from South Carolina. "Col. Preston," said the great Massachusetts lawyer in his stateliest manner, "I am happy to greet you as a member of the body to which it is my pride and honor to belong, but I regret to see that southern gentlemen so often stand aloof from me." Mr. Preston answered in polite and deferential terms, when the other continued; "the truth is, I am far more a southern than a northern man, and I think that I should be treated as 'hail-fellow' by all my southern colleagues." "May I beg to know, said the other, the grounds upon which you make this claim." "Certainly," replied Mr. Webster. "In the first place, I am very fond of a horse-race, and I believe the turf is a southern institution. Secondly, I have in my cellar a hundred dozen of the best wine, unpaid for, and that I understand to be a trait of southern life.

Thirdly, before daylight, I shall be under the table, and I suppose you are willing to admit this to be characteristic of southerners." "Enough," shouted the other, laughing, "you have vindicated your claim to be my compatriot."

Some of my readers will recollect the exquisite manner in which Mr. Webster used to relate the following. One night, before railroads were built, he was forced to make a journey by private conveyance from Baltimore to Washington. The man who drove the wagon was such an ill-looking fellow and told so many stories of robberies and murders, that before they had gone far, Mr. Webster was somewhat alarmed. At last the wagon stopped in the midst of a dense wood, when the man, turning suddenly round to his passenger, exclaimed fiercely; "Now sir, tell me who you are." Mr. Webster replied in a faltering voice, and ready to spring from the vehicle, "I am Daniel Webster, member of Congress from Massachusetts." "What!" rejoined the driver, grasping him warmly by the hand, "are you Webster? Thank God! thank God! You were such an ugly chap that I took you for a highwayman."

But it is time that I should turn my back upon the capital and resume my pilgrim staff.

CHAPTER XV.

A WEDDING TRIP.

CONGRESS adjourned 10th of August, 1846. Three days afterward I was married in Baltimore, taking Philadelphia, New York, Boston, Niagara Falls and Chicago, by way of the Great Lakes, en route to Paris, the seat of the Illinois Conference. The first time I visited Chicago was in July, 1841, when it was a miserable little village of log-cabins and frame-houses, standing by the lake on ground almost low enough to be a marsh. The ague and bilious fever seemed to stalk the streets as lords paramount, and a sorrier set of squatters than formed its population, one could not wish to see. And yet during the speculating mania, a few years before, town lots in this prospective centre of an empire, encompassed by hundreds of thousands of acres of unfenced, flat, wet prairie, were assessed at prices which would have been esteemed enormous for eligible sites in London or Paris. The revulsion, however, had brought Chicago to its lowest ebb, and you might almost have bought the town site for a thousand dollars. On my second visit, it seemed to be, as they called it, "a smart chunk of a town," with a few piers thrust into the lake, at which lay noble steamers, while numerous sloops and schooners were moored along the shore; a few brick houses relieved the monotony of log and white frame, and the townspeople thought that when the canal connecting the Illinois River with Lake Michigan should be finished, it would be "a right sharp place." I was there again in 1855: it had grown, in 14 years, from a village of three thousand inhabitants, to be a city with a population from one hundred and thirty, to forty thousand; the terminus of countless railroads, one of them then the longest on the earth. I suppose that its tax list embraced the names of the keenest, most adventurous and reckless land-jobbers and speculators in the world, out of California and Australia, and that a more pestilential atmosphere for the intellect and morals never canopied a civilized place. Colossal fortunes had been acquired in a trice, and every form of vicious extravagance had to be created, as a mill-tail to relieve the pond of redundant prosperity. Broad avenues, lined with marble and brown-stone fronts, stretched away toward the retreating prairie, and splendid equipages flashed along the streets, which had just been raised four feet out of the mud. Scarce a man had time to stop and chat with you, and even the old-fashioned western lawyers, the jolliest crew that ever cracked jokes in a log bar-room, were transformed into quick-witted money-changers. All the talk you heard on the street, in offices and stores, was of cent per cent, corner lots, shaving paper, land warrants, preëmption claims, new locations and a chance to make a fortune. And if you happened to sit down by a cozy fireside, hoping to have a rational talk with some old friend, you were astonished into silence by his persistent demonstration that in ten years Chicago would be ahead of New York, in wealth, population and power, and by the prophecy that in so many other years, it would leave London far behind. In truth, I never saw so many crazy or intoxicated people huddled together in one bedlam or drinking shop—which it was, I never could make out. The tone of its population formed the most sadly impressive commentary upon making haste to be rich. Everywhere men and women were rioting in ostentation or stimulated to frenzied energy, racking their brains with schemes of sudden fortune, or if rich, then wasting thousands in senseless, tasteless show; accounting man's life to consist in the abundance which he possesseth, and wasting breath to clutch the unsubstantial shadow of a dream.

After a quiet Sabbath, spent with an old friend, we started, bright and early, in a stage coach with eleven passengers—(in those days, Chicago had no rail roads)—for Peru, the head of navigation on the

Illinois River. The distance was a hundred miles, and we accomplished it in about twenty-four hours. The Illinois was very low, and only the smallest boats could navigate it. A sort of mud shallop, dignified by the appellation of a stern-wheel steamer, awaited our arrival at Peru, and according to the fashion of western boatmen, several hours after everything was in readiness for our departure, the captain rang the bell and we started. Our fare at dinner was, of course, the never eaten roast beef, roast pig and sole-leather pudding; and for breakfast and tea, a dark colored witch's broth, that reminded one of Mr. Randolph's retort upon a waiter, in hearing of the proprietor of a Richmond hotel. "Boy," said the beardless lord of Roanoake, "change my cup." "Will you have coffee or tea, Mr. Randolph?" "If this is coffee, bring me tea; and if this is tea, bring me coffee—I want a change."

An experience of twenty-four hours upon the wretched little craft, made us glad to exchange sailing for staging, at Peoria. Bidding adieu to our travelling companions, my wife and I started, sole occupants of a coach, for a long ride across the State from west to east. Eleven miles out of town, we were informed that we must leave the stage, with its four horses, and take a wagon with two, as "they only kept the stage for grandeur, to run into 'Peory.'" But we were young and light-hearted, and as the weather was fine, thought we could put up with rough accommodations. Placing a trunk in the rear of the wagon—which, by the way, had only wooden springs—to make a more comfortable seat than the rough unplaned board, we jolted off. At the house where we stopped to dine, my wife was for the first time, introduced to all the mysteries of a western kitchen. The chickens were killed, picked and cleaned, cooked and served before our eyes, and the leaden biscuits and half raw corn bread were kneaded and baked under our inspection. Mine was a hearty meal, but hers was very slender. I had the advantage of her in being accustomed to such fare, and withal, as she averred after starting for our afternoon's ride, in the fact that I couldn't see what I was eating. Eyes, she thought, were very much in the *way* of people who proposed to travel "out West." Indeed, one of the precepts of the country is, "Shut your eyes and go it blind," and it may have sprung from the amount of dirt intermixed with some man's dinner. Toward sundown, we were approaching the town of Bloomington, where we were to lie over until two the next morning, in order to make connection with another stage line. I inquired of our driver, what sort of accommodations we should find at the hotel in town. He assured us that we should get nothing fit to eat, and that if we attempted to sleep, the bedbugs would eat us up. Not disposed to run this gauntlet, I asked him to drive me to the door of the

Methodist that lived in the largest and most comfortable house. As we stopped at the gate, the clatter of knives, forks and plates within, and the sound of merry voices, announced that the family were at supper. "Halloo the house!" cried I. "Halloo yourself; what do you want?" was the reply. "I am travelling with my wife, and learning that the quarters at the hotel are bad, have come to get some supper and spend a part of the night with you." As I said this, I was making the word good by getting out of the wagon. The man of the house came striding toward the gate, saying in an angry tone, "Look here, stranger, we don't keep a tavern, and if you're a traveller, you must put up with traveller's fare and go to the hotel." "Don't be so savage," said I, "have you never heard the saying, be not forgetful to entertain strangers, for some have thereby entertained angels unawares." "Oh, ho," said he, "that sounds like preaching, you ain't a preacher, are you?" I intimated that I was, and mentioned my name. Eying me from head to foot, he exclaimed: "Well, I never! Who would have taken such a poor little dried up specimen as you for that man; why we've thought of trying to get you here as our preacher."

Of course we received a hearty welcome, and ere long were seated at a bountiful board. But we had not finished supper, when a messenger came in hot haste, with the request that I should go to visit a dying man and administer the last offices of religion to him. I spent a couple of hours by his bed-side, and in attempting to console his heart-broken wife, then by ten o'clock, was fast asleep. At two, we were roused by the elemental strife, by the horn and shouts of our stage driver. We were soon seated in our miserable wagon, with no protection from the driving rain but a tow linen cover, through which the water dripped in showers. We had been overtaken by a furious equinoctial storm, which began about midnight, and our plight was pitiable enough. The temperature had fallen about forty degrees; the night was pitchy dark, only relieved by frequent flashes of lightning, most vivid and sometimes appalling, instantly followed by sharp and stunning reports of thunder; but the flashes helped to light our driver on his way, or would have done so, had they not showed the whole prairie, a pool of water. After a time, we reached a little belt of timber, indicating our approach to a creek. As we crossed the bridge, we heard the now swollen torrent rushing through a deep ravine, when the broad glare revealed our position.

"By Jove!" shouted the driver with glee; "Weren't that lucky? a half minute more and we'd have been all smashed. I never was so near goin over a bridge; half an inch more, and we'd been over, and then salt wouldn't have saved us."

To the rather timid question of my wife, as to whether there were any more bad bridges to cross before daylight, he replied; "Oh yes, severals; but you mustn't be skeered; we must all die sometime, you know."

At length, day broke and revealed the dismal picture of a cold, leaden sky, from which torrents still poured upon the low prairie, that appeared a lake. It seemed as if chaos had come again, and that the waters under the firmament were united to the waters above the firmament, and the dry land had disappeared. We floundered on through the water, until, several hours behind time, we reached the breakfast-house. It was a log cabin of a single room, and the only habitation within many miles. The front door was nailed up, and entering by the back one, we found the entire family stretched out upon beds and shake downs. "What's the matter?" I said. "Oh," answered a saffron colored, shrivelled old woman, at the same time crawling out of her bed, "we've all got the ager, bilious and congestive." "Have any died?" I said. "Yes, two or three," she answered, "and I reckon the rest of us'll be dead soon, for there ain't one well enough to wait upon another." "I suppose there's no chance for breakfast then." "If you're willing to take what you can ketch, we wouldn't like to see you starvin." She gave us the best her larder afforded, and offering a prayer with the miserable people, we pursued our weary way, and late in the afternoon, reached a place, called Mount Pleasant, evidently to show how great is the difference between names and things. It was a wretched hamlet, consisting of a tavern, a groggery and a blacksmith shop, squatted upon the edge of a low prairie. Here we had to lie over again for another stage connection, and I advised my wife to improve the interval by seeking needed repose. She stretched herself upon the bed and I took the floor; but scarcely were we composed, before a great rat, who had probably been enjoying a siesta, started from the neighborhood of her pillow and springing over her head, landed near me. Of course, sleep refused to visit her eyelids in that house. Toward nightfall a carriage stopped at the door, and we found ourselves joined by a New England gentleman, his wife, and several children, who, we were not long in discovering, were on their way to the neighborhood of Peoria, as missionaries. I confess to the wickedness of rather enjoying their lugubrious estate.

In common with my brother Methodist preachers on the frontier, I had become prejudiced against a very worthy class of orthodox New England evangelists, who are accustomed to enter the new countries, and before doing any real service, or facing many of the hardships and privations of border life, hasten back to their native land, to tell long and gloomy stories concerning the destitution and heathenism of the great West, and to raise collections for sending the Gospel to those pagan parts. They seemed to think that because they had failed to stay and do their duty, there were no ministers or church in prairie land; while *we* had been there from the earliest settlements; had preached to the Indians and the first squatters, had borne the heat and burden of the day, and thought, according to the course of nature, that these sprigs of theological seminaries had no right to represent us, though inferior to them in the matter of Hebrew and Greek roots, as little better than the wicked. Yielding to the impulse, I was not sorry to find the new comer very much depressed, nor was I very much disposed to help him toward a more cheerful frame of mind, but thought, as he had left his native land to be a missionary, his heroic purpose should have the benefit of a thorough test. He related the doleful way he had come, how the roads were almost impassable, and the people, in every house, sick and dying; how he had heard that a man, seized by a congestive chill, would sometimes die in an hour, and that the victims never survived a third attack. I told him that, so far as I knew, this was true, and in reply to his eager questions as to the condition of the country through which I had come, could only assure him that it was quite as bad as that through which he had travelled, and if possible, worse. While he and his wife were holding an anxious consultation, as to whether they should not, with the morrow's dawn, turn their backs upon this region of horrors, our stage drove up and we embarked, for judging from the rain-covered earth, you might almost as well say that it was sailing, as riding. Our conveyance to-night, was an improvement upon the last, but it was not much to boast of; only an old, broken-down coach, with both the windows out, and a mass of wet mail bags piled upon the front seat. Nevertheless, we made ourselves comfortable as might be, my wife taking possession of the back seat, while I, doubled up in as small compass as possible, lay upon some hay on the floor. Plunging through mud and mire, sometimes stalling in a particularly bad place, and at the best getting forward only at a snail's pace, I was suddenly roused from a fitful nap, by the sound of a man's voice, in angry conversation with the driver. Our lamps disclosed a man in his shirt-sleeves, riding a horse and leading another. His mouth was filled with blasphemous oaths, and he was the very impersonation of unbridled rage. He proved to be the driver of a coach coming from the opposite direction. His team had mired some distance back, and he had no alternative but to unharness and go a dozen miles for help, leaving his stage and the mails in the slough. An hour afterward we reached the foundered coach, and by way of giving myself something to do, I shouted at the top of my voice, "Halloo! the stage!" When, to my surprise, for I had not dreamed that a human being save ourselves was near, there came forth the reply in a cheery tone—"halloo, yourself, and tell me how you like it." "Who are you?" I asked, "and what are you doing there?" "Only a passenger, and taking it comfortably," he answered. His composure was as imperturbable as the driver's wrath had been boisterous. Toward daylight, we suddenly drew up again, and the driver shouted, "Out! out! for your lives! I am on a bad bridge, and I reckon we'll go through!" I opened the door, sprang out in the darkness, and found myself performing a series of somersaults down an inclined plane of mud, and landed in a swamp. "You don't expect my wife to get out here, I hope," I said, as soon as I could get breath. "Do you want her neck broke?" he asked. "Not exactly, for I am just married; you lubberly fellow, why don't you get down and carry her to the bridge? It will hold her, if it won't the team;" "Hold the horses, then," said he; and I managed to crawl to their heads, keeping them steady, while he deposited my wife on the shaking timbers, drenched by the falling rain, while the swollen torrent rushed and roared through the black chasm beneath our feet. There we stood for an hour, while he backed his team down, and drove off to find a ford across the swollen current. At length he returned, and we, chilled to the bone, wet to the skin, capital subjects for congestive fever, made our way back to our places, thankful to be alive, with whole bones. Another dreary day came at last, and an early dinner-time found us established before a blazing fire in the hotel of Danville. Having partaken of the bacon and greens, my wife thought she would try to take a nap, while I went out to look for a conveyance to Paris, distant about forty miles, for the stage route terminated here. It was not long however, before my search for carriage and horses was arrested by a hurried message, requesting that I should visit a brother preacher, who lay dying with congestive fever. He was a noble fellow, thoroughly enlisted in his work, had joined the conference, at the same time I did, and was now ceasing at once to work and to live. He was collected and peaceful, for the sting of death was gone. As I bade him farewell, he said, "you will see the brethren to-morrow, but I shall never see them again until we meet before the throne. Tell the conference that I died at my post." A little while after, he entered his rest.

It took me two full hours to arrange for our start, procuring a horse from one man, a second from another, a set of harness from a third, another set from a fourth, a carry-all from a fifth, and after much diffi culty I succeeded in persuading a blacksmith to act as driver. All things being in readiness, I drove up to the hotel for my wife, supposing that I should find her refreshed by a good nap, but she had hardly lain down when two-thirds of the ceiling of the room fell with a crash, barely missing her head.

After that, sleep was of course out of the question. The night came down upon us still twenty miles from Paris, and in front of a rather good-looking house, which our driver assured us was the only one fit to stop at on the whole road. I requested him, therefore, to inquire if they could accommodate us with supper and bed. They answered, "No, they could not take strange travellers." The driver said that it was impossible to go on to Paris, that he did not know the road, and we should be sure to get lost, for the night was going to be pitchy dark. I was not disposed to endure hunger and cold and darkness for twelve mortal hours, to gratify the inhospitable churls; so, alighting, I bade the driver take off the luggage, and started for the house, but was met, before reaching the door, by its master.

"Didn't I send you word you couldn't stay here." He began. "Of course you did," I answered, "but I am going to stay all the same. Are you savage enough to make a woman spend the night on the prairie, and you sleeping with a house over your head? the Indians ain't as mean as that." "Well, I reckon you'll have to stop; you're a right determined little creeter. Once in the house, they made us comfortable. When bedtime arrived, I said, "I am a Methodist preacher." "You!" interrupted our host, "who'd ha' thought such a lookin' little thing as you was a preacher!" "Yes I am a Methodist preacher," I continued, "and it is my custom to have prayers with the families in which I stay, if there be no objection." "I'm agreeable, fire away," said the landlord. Our devotions over, we prepared to retire. There were two sleeping apartments; one belonging to the family, consisting of a dozen grown people besides sundry children; the other, through which, by the way, the entire brigade had to pass on their way to and from bed, was assigned to us. There happened to be a young woman visiting the family, and she was shown to a second bed in our room. She and my wife had gone in to undress, when the latter, feeling sympathy for a girl in such delicate circumstances, said in a commiserating tone, "I am sorry you are obliged to sleep in this way." "Yes, replied the other, feeling the bed-clothes, "it is kinder uncomfortable when a body's been used to sleeping between blankets, to have to lay on a sheet." Bright and early next morning we were roused by the heavy-shod platoon marching by us on their way to their day's work. Prayers and breakfast over, we were ready for the road, when I said to mine host, "what's your bill?" "The damage, you mean? Will you pay me what I ask?" "Certainly, if I can." "Well, if you ever come within ten miles of us again, give us a call and stay all night; I'll be consarned if I don't like seech a chap as you are."

High noon found us in Paris. This was Saturday; we had left Chicago on Monday. You can now leave it by rail, after a comfortable breakfast, and take a late dinner the same afternoon in Paris. Conference had been in session since Wednesday, and you can well fancy that the meeting with old friends after a year's separation was a joyous one.

The bishop presiding was the victim of a heart-disease. Over his head the sword of Damocles hung ever suspended by a hair, the death's head was never absent from his banquet, and the dread of sudden death had discolored all his ideas of life. He was the morbid and sworn foe to everything like gaiety, and while not sour or sullen, yet his piety was weighty and lugubrious. It may well be imagined that such a chairman had trouble to keep in order a man like Peter Cartwright, with whom humor and drollery are as natural as to breathe. Brother Cartwright had the floor one day, and by his irresistible fun, set the Conference in a roar. "Stop, Brother Cartwright," said the bishop; "I cannot allow such sin to be committed among Methodist preachers when I have the charge of them. I read in the Bible, be angry and sin not, but I nowhere see, laugh and sin not. Let us bow down and confess our offence. Brother Cartwright, lead in prayer." The backwoods preacher kneeled and repeated the Lord's prayer, and then rising, said, "Look here, Mr. Bishop, when I dig potatoes, I dig potatoes; when I hoe corn, I hoe corn; when I pray, I pray; and when I attend to business, I want to attend to business—I wish you did too, and I don't want you to take such snap judgment on me again."

"Brother," said the bishop, in a monitory tone, "do you think you are growing in grace?" "Yes, bishop, I think I am—in spots." It is hardly necessary to add that the bishop gave him up as incorrigible.

One of my cronies, Billy Rutledge, as we called him, as genial, warm-hearted and lovable a Methodist preacher as ever carried a pair of saddle-bags, had brought a carriage to Paris to take us to my father's home, a three days' drive. The first evening, we reached the edge of the grand prairie, where stood a single cabin, consisting of two rooms. About twenty-five preachers were in our company, and this was the only house at which we could put up. The people received us gladly, notwithstanding the disparity between our numbers and their accommodations, and said they would do their best for us. The horses were cared for, and active preparations made for supper. One party filed in to the supper table as another left it, in due time we all ate and were filled; then, gathering around the huge fireplace in the other room, our venerable friend Dr. Akers, occupying the seat of Gamaliel, expounded such knotty points in divinity as were proposed by the juniors. It was a picturesque scene, as the ruddy glare of the pine-knots, shining from the chimney corner, lit up the eager, generous faces of a score of devoted itinerants, to whom hardship and privations were as nothing, and unrewarded toil a pleasure. It would have done your heart good, in the pauses of graver discourse, to listen to their good stories, followed by the peals of hearty laughter; then as bed-time drew near, and the lesson had been read, to hear their full voices join in the evening hymn, followed by fervent responses to the prayer which commended them and all they loved to the care of Him who never slumbers. There was one bedstead in the room, for my wife and myself, she being the only woman of the party; while shuck-mattresses and buffalo skins were laid upon the floor for the men, some of the juniors repairing to the hay-mow, no unusual chamber for a circuit rider. These arrangements completed, the room was vacated to afford my wife an opportunity of undressing. The pine-knots were then extinguished, and every man found his couch as best he might in the dark

Our next halting-place was to be on the other side of the grand prairie. We were up at three o'clock, and not a bit too soon, for my wife was hardly out of bed, before a heavy shower poured through the roof, upon the very spot where we had lain.

Our hospitable entertainers furnished an ample breakfast and abundant provision for our lunch, but refused to receive a picayune, saying they would expect their house to be struck by lightning if they took pay for feeding Methodist preachers and their horses. A hard day's drive, without seeing a habitation, or the least sign, except the road, to tell that man had ever been on this boundless prairie, brought us, by nightfall, to a stopping-place much like the last. Next morning, about ten o'clock, we drew up for breakfast before a house which I had been accustomed to visit when travelling the district with the presiding elder. The old people were from home, but a rosy cheeked, bouncing damsel, calling her brothers to her aid, soon prepared a bountiful repast. That breakfast lives in our grateful recollection until this day, for the house in which it was prepared, the vessels in which it was cooked, the table on which it was served, and the bright-eyed, cherry-lipped damsel, were all clean, and cleanliness at that day was something for a traveller in the West to take note of and be thankful for.

That night, after a year's absence, I sat by my

father's fireside; it was the first time I had ever been long away from home. Greetings exchanged with father, mother and brother, I hurried to the stable to see my dear old Charlie. He knew my voice, rubbed his nose against my cheek and breast, laid his head affectionately over my shoulder, and I—can you wonder at it?—threw my arms around his neck while the tears were in my eyes.

CHAPTER XVI.

LIFE ON WHEELS.

AFTER a month's sojourn at my father's, we set forth upon our travels, for I had been reappointed agent by the Conference. My wife established herself in Baltimore, her old home, which, of course, became the centre of my operations for the year. She rented a small house, and procuring some furniture, transformed our narrow premises into the dearest of all places upon earth—a home. We sat beneath our own vine and fig-tree, but whence the means to water the one and prune the other were coming, was only known to Providence. My only income was the agency, which meant simply ten per cent. of all the funds I collected for my western colleges. I declined an invitation from many of my late parishioners, to become their chaplain again, in order that I might the more fully test my capacity as a beggar. Much time was spent from home, visiting the principal seaboard cities: trying by every legitimate method, in public and in private, to bring the object of my mission before the money-making and money-giving public. One incident may serve as a specimen of the trials an agent has to encounter. Entering the store of a great merchant in Philadelphia, who belonged to the Society of Friends, and who was said to do a large western trade, which it was considered gave me some claim upon him, I began the statement of my case. He interrupted me by saying, "Does thee call thyself a Methodist minister?" I replied that I was known as such. "Then thee is an hireling." I intimated that they that preach the Gospel should live by the Gospel. He answered, "I wish to have nothing to do with thee, I would not give thee a cent; thee is an hireling; thy children can get no milk of the word, and thy old men no strong meat from thee—there is my door, get thee out of it at once. I cannot abide hirelings." Conference year, which terminated my labors as agent, closed in September 1847.

I had now been "in the work" four years, and during that period had preached 1,500 times, and travelled 60,000 miles. The preaching had been done in the open air, and in houses of every imaginable description: from barns, log cabins, and school-houses, up to the noblest and most spacious edifices in the land; and addressed to congregations ranging from two or three persons up to uncounted thousands.

The travelling had been accomplished by almost every mode of conveyance known to us, except the balloon and wheel-barrow. Meanwhile my health, which had never been robust since its failure in college, had suffered, and my physician prescribed a winter in the South. It became necessary to conclude our six-months' experiment at housekeeping, and my wife was placed in Carlisle, Pennsylvania, that she might enjoy the society and care of some old friends, and study German, so as to assist me in the pursuit of that language and literature. In those days we were obliged to cross the Alleghanies by stages from Chambersburg to Pittsburg. As we were arranging in the former place to take our seats for the forty hours' ride, it appeared that eight passengers had been allotted to our stage. An old colored woman was anxious to be the ninth, but objection had been raised. She declared, with tears in her eyes, that she had been waiting for several days to get a seat, that although she had her ticket, they had been unable to carry her, the stages having been crowded with through passengers; that now her money was spent, and she must get home to her daughter. A stout Missourian, who was to be of our company, swore roundly that he "wouldn't ride with a nigger, and that she shouldn't go." Touched by the old woman's condition, I said to him quietly, "My friend, what right have you to interfere. Her ticket is as good as yours, and she has as much right to a seat as you have." "No," he said, "she is a nigger, and I am white, and I'll whip any man that says she has as good a right to a seat as I have, or insists upon taking her along." "Then," said I, "you can whip me, for I say she shall go." The idea of a giant whipping a pigmy, was too preposterous. It raised a laugh against him, and he submitted, because ridicule was more potent than reason. "Well," he said, "I suppose, if it must be so, it must; but, as we are to be shut up in the stage with her, in the name of noses let us strengthen our stomachs with some bald-faced whisky. I declined his amicable and æsthetic proposal. I tried to take good care of my protégée, giving her money to provide food at our various halts, and in every way sought to promote her comfort. As we went rattling down the streets of Pittsburg, late in the second night, I threw open the curtain on my side of the coach, and sat looking out into the night, through which the street lamps struggled with their feeble rays, my thoughts divided between the indefinable curiosity and awe one always experiences in entering a strange city, late at night, and the prospect of a good bed and a quiet hotel, when I was suddenly roused from my reverie by a violent blow on my side, delivered by my old dame, as she screamed in anger, "Lean up! lean up! what you takin' all de winder for? Don't you suppose pussons ob culler hab dere rites as well as you good-for-nothing whites? I wants to see de scenery too." I believe it was the verdict of my fellow-passengers, that I received what I deserved.

Pittsburgh, whose ever-driving canopy of smoke reminds one of Birmingham or Manchester, stands almost at the foot of the Alleghany Mountains, at the entrance of a broad plain, unmatched among the valleys of the earth, embracing its millions of square miles, almost every rood of which is fertile as the Delta of the Nile. This city used to be the gate of the West, and over it was inscribed as a grateful tribute, the imperishable name of that noble Commoner of England, by whose policy the vast region of the Ohio was wrested from the French during the old seven years' war.

The blaze of countless forges and the din of the hammer chorus, which almost blinds and deafens one in Pittsburgh, form a fit introduction to the battles and conquests by which coal and iron, in the cunning hand of instructed labor, have been vanquishing idleness and sterility—triumphs by which the desert is made to blossom as the rose, and the wilderness and solitary places are gladdened.

One can hardly stand in such a place, and think of the changes which a century has wrought, since the rising star of Anglo-American civilization was clouded by Braddock's inglorious defeat, without recalling the language of the Prophet:

"It shall blossom abundantly, and rejoice even with joy and singing: the glory of Lebanon shall be given unto it, the excellency of Carmel and Sharon. And the parched ground shall become a pool, and the thirsty land springs of water: in the habitation of dragons, where each lay, shall be grass with reeds and rushes.

"And an highway shall be there, and a way and it shall be called the way of holiness; the unclean shall not pass over it; but it shall be for those; the wayfaring men, though fools, shall not err therein.

"No lion shall be there, nor any ravenous beast shall go up thereon, it shall not be found there; but the redeemed shall walk there.

"And the ransomed of the Lord shall return, and come to Zion with songs and everlasting joy upon their heads: they shall obtain joy and gladness, and sorrow and sighing shall flee away."

In moving upon the bosom of our western waters, in the canoe, the broad-horn, or the steamer, where human genius, organed with machinery, invades the solitude of nature, there is a spell whose charm stirs me to ecstasy. You float on the placid bosom of the Ohio, La Belle Rivière of the early voyageurs, whose sources are in the ice-fed springs close by the eagle's eyrie, on the tops of the Alleghanies; or on the equally tranquil Illinois, skirted by its boundless undulating flower-clad prairies; or are driven among the eddies by the wild impetuous current between the sliding banks of the Missouri. You are borne by the majestic flood of the Mississippi from the wild rice lakes of the frozen North to where its tawny waves are lost in the blue bosom of the summer gulf, emerging from regions where moss and lichens only grow, and the frost king holds almost perpetual court, to gardens of orange and pomegranate, where the Magnolia sheds her perfume, while the deep silences are broken only by the paddle's dip, the crack of the rifle, the scream of the steam whistle, and the buffet of the engine's fleshless arms, beating the stream to foam. Primeval woods overshadow the skirts of savannas undulating out of sight. Wood-crowned bluffs stand forth where the savage lay in wait for the emigrants' flat boat, and their verdure crimsons in the memory of many a fight between the white and the red man. Then pictures of this land, when time and labor shall have wrought those changes which imagination summons, combine to weave a spell of weird enchantment, heightened rather than diminished by your consciousness of danger from sawyers, snags, fire, collisions and explosions.

Since the opening of commerce by the settlement of the country, the navigation of these water-courses has developed a type of character peculiar and remarkable as the rivers themselves. When the long and deadly wrestle between the aborigines and the invading whites terminated by the triumph of the latter, many a scout and Indian fighter found himself without occupation. Like the Indian and his buffalo, a life of wild freedom and adventure was necessary to them; they could not, like the farmer and his patient ox, bend their necks to the yoke of systematic, drudging toil. Some repairing to the Rocky Mountains, became hunters for the fur companies; others found outlet for their energies in a new vocation which the rising trade of new countries developed. The fabrics of civilization could be introduced into the great West only by trains of loaded mules across the Alleghanies or by keel-boats ascending the river from New Orleans. Now, the labor of urging a freighted barge against a rapid current fifteen hundred or two thousand miles, exposed to all vicissitudes of weather, subject to every species of privation and hardship, required, it well may be supposed, a brood of giants. In describing them, I will draw from the graphic pen of my friend Col. T. B. Thorpe, to whom the public is indebted for many of the most truthful and lifelike pictures of western habits, character, and humor ever published:

"The keel-boat was long and narrow, sharp at the bow and stern, and of light draft. From fifteen to twenty 'hands' were required to propel it. The crew, divided equally on each side, took their places upon the walking-boards extending along the whole length of the craft, and, setting one end of their pole in the bottom of the river, the other was brought to the shoulder, and with the body bent forward, they walked the boat against the formidable current.

"It is not strange that the keel-boatmen, always exercising in the open air, without an idea of the dependence of the laborer in their minds, armed constantly with the deadly rifle, and feeling assured that their strong arms and sure aim would anywhere gain them a livelihood, should have become physically the most powerful of men, and that their minds, often naturally of the highest order, should have elaborated ideas singularly characteristic of the extraordinary scenes and associations with which they were surrounded. Their professional pride lay in ascending 'rapids;' this effort of human strength to overcome natural obstacles was considered by them worthy of their prowess. The slightest error exposed the craft to be thrown across the current, or to be brought sidewise in contact with rocks or other obstructions, which would inevitably destroy it. The hero vaunted that his boat never swung in the swift current, and never backed from a 'shute!'

"Their chief amusements were 'rough frolics,' dancing, fiddling and fist fights. The incredible strength of their pectoral muscles, growing out of their peculiar labor and manner of life, made fights with them a direful necessity—it was an appetite, and, like pressing hunger, had to be appeased. The keel-boatman who boasted that he had never been whipped, stood upon a dangerous eminence, for every aspirant for fame was bound to dispute his claim to such distinction. Occasionally, at some temporary landing-place, a number accidentally came together for a night. From the extreme labors of the day, possibly quietness reigned in the camp; when, unexpectedly, the repose would be disturbed by some restless fellow crowing forth a defiance in the manner of a game-cock; then, springing into some conspicuous place, and rolling up his sleeves, he would utter his challenge as follows:

"'I'm from the Lightning Forks of Roaring River. I'm *all* man, save what is wild cat and extra lightning. I'm as hard to run against as a cypress snag. I never back water. Look at me—a small specimen, harmless as an angle worm—a remote circumstance, a mere yearling. Cock-a-doodle-doo. I did hold down a buffalo bull and tar off his scalp with my teeth; but I can't do it now—I'm too powerful weak, *I am.*'

"By this time those within hearing would spring to their feet, and like the war-horse that smells the battle afar off, inflate their nostrils with expectation. The challenger goes on:

"I'm the man that, single handed, towed the broad horn over a sand-bar? the identical infant who girdled a hickory by smiling at the bark, and if any one denies it, let him make his will, and pay the expenses of a funeral. I'm the genuine article, tough as bull's hide, keen as a rifle. I can out-swim, out-swar, out-jump, out-drink, and keep soberer than any man at Catfish Bend. I'm painfully ferochus, I'm spiling for some one to whip me—if there's a creeter in this diggin' that wants to be disappointed in trying to do it, let him yell—whoop hurra!'

"Rifle shooting they brought to perfection—their deadly aim told terribly at the battle of New Orleans. As hunters, the weapon had been their companion, and they never parted with it in their new vocation. While working at the oar or pole, it was always within reach, and if a deer unexpectedly appeared on the banks, or a migratory bear breasted the waves, it was stricken down with unerring aim.

"By an imperative law among themselves, they were idlers on shore, where their chief amusement was shooting at a mark, or playing severe practical jokes upon each other. They would with the rifle ball, and at long distances, cut the pipe out of the hat-band of a fellow boatman, or unexpectedly upset a cup of whisky that might, at 'lunch-time' be for the moment resting on some one's knee. A negro, exciting the ire of one of these men, he at the dis tance of a hundred yards, with a rifle-ball, cut the offender's heel, and did this without a thought that the object of his indignation could be more seriously damaged by an unsteady aim.

"Taking off a wild turkey's head with a rifle-ball at a hundred yards' distance while the bird was in full flight, was not looked upon as an extraordinary feat. At nightfall they would snuff candles at fifty paces, and do it without extinguishing the light. Many of these extraordinary men became so expert and cool, that in the heat of battle they would announce the place on their enemy they intended to hit, and subsequent examination would prove the certainty of their aim. Driving the nail, however, was their favorite amusement. This consisted in sinking a nail, two-thirds of its length, in the centre of a target, and then at forty paces, with a rifle ball, driving it home to the head. If they quarrelled among themselves, and then made friends, the test that they bore no malice, was to shoot a small object from each other's heads. Mike Fink, the best shot of all keelboatmen, lost his life in one of these strange trials of friendship. He had had a difficulty with one of his companions, made friends and agreed to the usual ceremony to show that he bore no ill-will. The man put an apple upon his head, placed himself at the proper distance—Mike fired, and hit, apparently not the inanimate object, but the man, who fell to the ground apparently dead. Standing by was a brother of this victim either of treachery or hazard, and in an instant of anger, he shot Mike through the heart. In a few moments the supposed dead man, without a wound, recovered his feet. Mike had evidently, from mere wantonness, displaced the apple, by shooting between it and the skull, in the same way, that he would have barked a squirrel from the limb of a tree. The joke, unfortunately, cost the renowned Mike his life." False indeed, would be the supposition that these men, lawless as they were, possessed a single trait of character in common with the law-defying wretches of our crowded cities. They committed, it is true, great excesses in villages where their voyages terminated, and when large numbers of them were assembled together. If they defied the law it was not because it was irksome, but because they never felt its restraints. They had their own laws which they implicitly obeyed. With them fair play was a jewel. If the crew of a rival boat was to be attacked, only an equal number was detached for the service; if the intruders were worsted, no one interfered for their relief. Whatever was placed in their care for transportation was sacred, and would be defended from harm, if necessary, at the sacrifice of their life. They would, from mere recklessness, pilfer the out-buildings of a farm-house, yet they could be intrusted with uncounted sums of money, and if anything in their possession became damaged or lost, they made restitution to the last farthing. In difficulties between others, they invariably espoused the cause of the weaker party and took up the quarrels of the aged, whether in the right or wrong.

"As an illustration of their rude code of honor, is remembered the story of 'Bill M'Coy.' He was a master-spirit, and had successfully disputed for championship upon almost every famous sand-bar visible at low water. In a terrible row, where blood had been spilled, and a dark crime committed, Bill was involved. Momentarily off his guard, he fell into the clutches of the law. The community was excited—a victim was demanded to appease the oft-insulted majesty of justice. Brought before one of the courts 'holding' at Natchez, then just closing its session for the summer vacation, he was fully committed, and nothing but the procurement of enormous bail would keep him from sweltering through the long months of summer in durance vile. It was apparently useless for him to expect any one to go bail for him; he appealed, however, to those present, dwelt upon the horrors, to him more especially, of a long imprisonment, and solemnly asseverated that he would present himself at the time appointed for trial.

"At the last, Col. W.——, a wealthy, and on the

whole rather a cautious citizen, came to the rescue and agreed to pay ten thousand dollars if M'Coy did not present himself to stand his trial. It was in vain that the colonel's friends tried to persuade him not to take the responsibility; even the court's suggestion to let the matter alone was unheeded. M'Coy was released—shouldering his rifle, and threading his way through the Indian nation, in due time he reached his home in 'Old Kaintuck.'

"Months rolled on, and the time of trial approached. As a matter of course, the probabilities of M'Coy's return were discussed. The public had doubts. The colonel had not heard from him since his departure. The morning of the appointed day arrived, but the prisoner did not present himself. The attending crowd and the people of the town became excited—all except the colonel despaired—evening was coming on apace—the court was on the point of adjourning, when a distant huzza was heard; it was borne on the wings of the wind, and echoed along, each moment growing louder and louder. Finally, the exulting cry was caught up by the hangers-on about the seat of justice. Another moment, and M'Coy—his beard long and matted, his hands torn to pieces, his eyes haggard and face sun-burnt to a degree that was painful to behold—rushed into the court-room, and from sheer exhaustion fell prostrate upon the floor.

"Old Col. W. embraced him as he would have done

a long-lost brother, and eyes unused to tears filled to overflowing when M'Coy related his simple tale. Starting from Louisville as a 'hand on a boat,' he found in a few days that, owing to the low stage of water in the river and the other unexpected delays, it was impossible for him to reach Natchez at the appointed time by such a mode of conveyance. No other ordinary conveyance, in those early days, presented itself. Not to be thwarted, he abandoned the flat, and, with his own hands, shaped a canoe out of the trunk of a fallen tree. He had rowed and paddled, almost without cessation, *thirteen hundred* miles, and had thus redeemed his promise almost at the expense of life. His trial in its progress became a mere form; his chivalrous conduct and the want of any positive testimony won for him a verdict of not guilty, even before it was announced by the jury or affirmed by the judge.

"A few years ago, the Mississippi, from an unusual drought, shrunk within its banks to a comparatively small stream, and, as a consequence, under the protection of a high bank, nearly opposite the town of Baton Rouge, there was exposed the wreck of a small boat, the timbers of which, as far as could be ascertained, were in a good state of preservation. Few particularly noticed the object, because such evidences of destruction form one of the most familiar features of the passing scenery; yet, there was really an interest connected with those blackened but still enduring ribs, for they were the remains of the first steamer that ever dashed its wheels into the waters of the Great West, and awakened new echoes along the then silent shores of the 'Father of Waters.' This boat was built at Pittsburg by Messrs. Fulton and Livingston. It was launched in the month of March, 1812, and landed at Natchez the following year, where she loaded with passengers, and proceeded to New Orleans. After running some time in this newly-established trade and meeting with a variety of misfortunes, she finally snagged and sunk into the half-exposed grave we have designated."

When steam had been successfully applied to the vast inland navigation of the West, it was feared that the keel-boatman's occupation was gone, but no sooner had fire and water taken the laboring oar, than these men appeared as the natural officers of the new marine. It is not then surprising that moving accidents by flood were of such common occurrence, or that the recklessness of these captains and pilots have hurled thousands of passengers into eternity without a moment's warning.

In the good old times, the trip from New Orleans to Pittsburg needed a hundred and twenty-five days, now it is accomplished in ten or twelve.

Voyaging upon these waters, and all the circumstances of Western life, impart to the people a tone of exaggeration either repulsive or ludicrous to the more quiet and methodical residents of the eastern States. The following "splurge" may be taken as a specimen of an educated western man's "norating" in the social hall of a western steamboat. "Gentlemen, what is poetry, but the truth exaggerated? Here, it can never arrive at any perfection. What chance is there for exaggeration in the Great West, where the reality is incomprehensible? A territory as large as classic Greece annually caves into the Mississippi, and who notices it? Things, to be poetical, must be got up on a small scale. The Tiber, the Seine, the Thames, appear well in poetry, but such streams are overlooked in the West, they don't afford water enough to keep up an expansive duck-pond—would be mere drains to a squatter's preëmption. I have heard of frontiersmen who were poets, because their minds expanded beyond the surrounding physical grandeur. Books are not yet large enough to contain their ideas—steam is not strong enough to impress them on the historic page. These men have no definite sense of limitation, know of no locality—they sleep not on a couch, but upon the 'government lands'—they live upon the spontaneous productions of the earth, and make a drinking-cup of the mighty Mississippi. Settlements within fifty miles of them vitiate the air: life for them means spontaneity and untramelled liberty of personal movement in space and time. Their harmony with the Nature that engendered them, annihilates the most formidable local barriers. The first pennon of blue smoke that daily arises from the chimney of a new settlement admonishes them to penetrate more deeply into the forest. They have an instinctive dread of crowds—with them, civilization means law and calomel."

Greater varieties of human character can nowhere be met than in a week's trip on the Mississippi, and the student of human nature who enjoys intercourse with all sorts of people, can here observe the most curiously original types of mankind. The luggage stowed on the boiler deck, affords a significant clue to the pursuits of your fellow passengers: a large box of playing cards supports a package of Bibles, a bowie knife is tied to a life-preserver, and a package of garden seeds rejoices in the same address with a neighboring keg of powder. There is an old black trunk, soiled with the mud of the Lower Nile, and a new carpet bag direct from Upper California; a collapsed valise of new shirts and antique sermons is jostled by another, plethoric with anti-bilious pills and cholera medicines; an elaborate dress, direct from Paris, brushes a trapper's Rocky Mountain costume; a gun-case rests upon a bandbox, and a well preserved rifle is half enveloped by the folds of an umbrella. The volume of a strange, eventful, and ever changing life is before you, on the pages of which are impressed phases of original character such as no other country produces, no other sphere assembles.

The crowd of passengers presents a mosaic of our cosmopolite population. On the deck are to be seen emigrants from every European nation; in the cabin are strangely mingled all the aspects of social life—the aristocratic English lord is intruded upon by the ultra socialist; the conservative bishop accepts a favor from the graceless gambler; the wealthy planter is heartily amused at the simplicities of a "northern fanatic;" the farmer from about the arctic regions of Lake Superior, exchanges ideas and discovers consanguinity with a heretofore unknown person from the everglades of Florida; the frank, open hearted men of the West are charmed with the business thrift of a party from "down East;" politicians of every stripe and religionists of all creeds, for the time, drop their wranglings in the admiration of lovely woman, or find a neutral ground of sympathy in the attractions of a gorgeous sunset.

The following may be taken as a specimen of the droll encounters which often occur on board, affording infinite mirth to the bystanders. A sorry-looking owner of the human face divine, whose fortunate position as agent of the Rothschilds in New Orleans, made amends in the eyes of Mammon worshippers for his almost deformed appearance, took his seat with ostentatious complacency at the breakfast-table, the morning after the boat had started. The captain, informed of the high-standing and long purse of his distinguished passenger, had instructed one of the colored waiters to show him every mark of attention. The negro asked, in the most courteous tone, what he would have for breakfast. "Some venishun," replied the man of money, but in an accent not intelligible to the thick ears of Cuffie, who, supposing that a nice piece of broiled ham was the daintiest morsel, and not aware of the Mosaic prohibition of hog meat, presently reappeared with a slice of bacon, whose tempting odor might have seduced a Mohammedan. As it was placed on the table with a flourish, the nose of the Israelite appreciated the nature of the article, and with offended dignity, he said, "Dat ish ham! Take it away. I want venishun." There sat opposite an old Kentuckian, who embarrassed in his pecuniary affairs, had been making an unsuccessful attempt to negotiate a loan, and who found a solace to his irritated feelings in the uncomfortable plight of the millionaire. For him, there was no delicacy comparable with broiled ham, and sharing the vulgar prejudices against the Jews, he exclaimed with indignant scorn, as the servant removed the dish, pointing his knife at his neighbor, "No, sir, you darsn't eat ham. Your people crucified the Saviour, and God has cussed you by not allowing you to touch pork. Heavens!" he continued, with awful solemnity, turning to a friend, "can you think of anything more dreadful than not being allowed to eat bacon? And yet, I reckon, the sins of the Jews makes it only just."

CHAPTER XVII.

THE THUNDERER OF THE BAR AND THE STUMP.

LEAVING winter on the Ohio, I found in New Orleans, flowers and the bland atmosphere of summer. Seated in the pilothouse, with the steersman for my interpreter, I had been overjoyed by my vision of the novel and picturesque scenery on the river banks. It may seem paradoxical to my readers that one so nearly blind as I, should have a keen relish for the varieties and beauties of landscape, and yet I fancy that few persons enjoy them more. It must be recollected, that up to the age of five years I had perfect sight and had been accustomed throughout childhood to spend the summers in the country, surrounded by every form of glorious scenery. Memory has vividly preserved the outlines and colors of nature, and if I am fortunate enough to have a kind hearted companion at hand to sketch the view even roughly, imagination, with the ample material which remembrance furnishes, fills out the picture. Whether the objective reality, or the subjective impression, predominate in my portfolio, whether by virtue of necessity, fancy colors my canvas after the school of Millais or of Raphael, I suppose matters little, so only that the outer world becomes to me a presence of blessing and of power.

All the conditions of a first trip on the Lower Mississippi combine to render it a memorable journey. Your monster boat quivers in every part with each stroke of her engine, and the sensitiveness of your nerves is increased by the hoarse voices of the "scape pipes" as they perform their horrible antiphony throughout the voyage. The din of machinery, however, is softened by the chorus of the negro firemen, as they ply their scorching labors before furnaces that might have answered as forges for Vulcan. If you succeed in winning the favor of captain and pilots, and thus gain a seat by the wheel when you please; you can hear stories of fire and flood, of races, collisions, snaggings and explosions, enough to haunt your dreams for months. Almost every snag and sawyer has its own catastrophe; each sand bar and bend of the river has witnessed some frightful accident in which scores, perhaps hundreds, of human lives changed worlds. Your narrator details these casualities with all the relish with which a soldier speaks of battles, or a surgeon of operations. The monotonous scenery on either side the river does not help to enliven you, the banks are leveed at infinite cost, and stand eight or ten feet above the surface of the country, to save the plantations from annual inundation. For several hundred miles above New Orleans, swamps that run parallel to the Mississippi on both sides, approach within a mile and often nearer. Groves of cottonwood and of cypress, wreathed with the Spanish moss which floats in pendulous silvery veils along the green walls and is significantly styled the curtain of death, fringe the interminable morass. The scene however brightens at times as you near a town, which may have the good luck to be perched upon a bluff or "round to," or at some well ordered plantation, whose noble mansion, with its lawn and gardens, is flanked by rows of white-washed cottages called the "people's quarters." Before long, you become accustomed to your new life with its attendant sights and sounds and enter into its excitement with zest; the boding thought of danger is forgotten, and after a night or two, you will sleep as soundly as if at home, over the roaring furnace and seething boilers, lulled to deeper slumbers by the lately frightful blasts of the steampipes. If another boat heave in sight, you find yourself becoming anxious that she shall not pass you. If she gain upon your craft, all your fears about the dangers of racing are laid aside and with your fellow passengers, male and female, you are urging the captain to do his best. Of course he answers that he never races!—I never knew a

Mississippi captain that did. He just wanted a little fun, "to see how the old thing would go with a full head on." You run first to the deck to incite the firemen, and then to the hurricane deck to note the speed. The interest deepens, the first shot is fired, the battle has opened, and men and even women are no longer cowards. Every sense is strained, and yet the mind and nerves are wonderfully calm. Side by side the boats go thundering along, and so completely has the thought of victory taken possession of you, that you would almost as soon be blown up as beaten.

The standard daily recreation of steamboat life is "wooding." As the boat nears the wood-yard, the captain shouts, "What kind of wood is that?" The reply comes back, "Cord-wood." The captain, still in pursuit of information under difficulties, and desirous of learning if the fuel be dry and fit for his purpose, bawls out, "How long has it been cut?" "Four feet," is the prompt response. The captain, exceedingly vexed, next inquires, "What do you sell for?" "Cash," returns the chopper, replacing the corn-cob pipe in his mouth, and smiling benignly "on the pile."

Wood yards are apparently infested with mosquitoes—I say apparently infested—such is the impres sion of all accidental sojourners; but it is a strange delusion, for though one may think that they fill the air, inflame the face and hands, and if of the Arkansas species, penetrate the flesh through the thickest boots; still upon inquiring of any permanent resident, if mosquitoes are numerous, the invariable answer is, "Mosquitoes—no! not about here; but a little way down the river they are awful—thar they torment alligators to death, and sting mules right through their hoofs."

On a first-class steamer, there may be sixty hands engaged in the exciting physical contest of wooding. The passengers extend themselves along the guards as spectators, and present a brilliant array. The performance consists in piling on the boat one hundred cords of wood in the shortest possible time. The steam-boilers seem to sympathize at the sight of the fuel, and occasionally breathe forth immense sighs of admiration—the pilot increases the noise by unearthly screams on the "alarm whistle." The mate of the boat, for want of something better to do, divides his time between exhortations of "Oh, bring them shavings along!" "Don't go to sleep at this frolic," and by swearing, of such monstrous proportions, that even good men are puzzled to decide whether he is really profane or simply ridiculous. The laborers pursue their calling with the precision of clockwork. Upon the shoulders of each are piled up innumerable sticks of wood, which are thus carried from the land into the capacious bowels of the steamer. The "last loads," are shouldered—the last effort to carry "the largest pile" is indulged in. "Zephyr Sam," amidst the united cheers of the admiring spectators, propels his load, and for the thousandth time, wins the palm of being a "model darkie," "the prince of deck hands."

At length you gain the "Coast," as the country on both sides the river for one or two hundred miles above New Orleans is called, and you exchange the region of cotton, for the sugar country. Nothing can be fairer than these green fields in which the genius of the summer seems to have taken up his abode, and the palatial residences, with their out-buildings and neat negro villages, are worthy of their surroundings. The delicate hue of the orange-blossom contrasts with the stately pride of the magnolia, and the corn-fields are relieved by gardens of roses. But sweeping round the sharp horn of a crescent, the centre of southwestern trade is soon at your feet, literally at your feet; for as from the deck of the steamer, you look down upon its streets, the broad river flows at a level so high as to be above the head of any man walking them, and the floods are only kept in check by a broad, strong levee that fronts the town.

The St. Charles Hotel was the wonder and centre of the town. All strangers stopped at it and all citizens frequented it. On its ground floor was its bar-room, and at ten o'clock at night you beheld it in its glory. At least a thousand men, speaking all languages, habited in all costumes, representing all nationalities, were engaged in laughing, talking, betting, quarrelling, chewing, smoking and drinking.

A sketch of two of the habitués of this place, will represent the poles of this strange world of life. The first was a man with an idiosyncrasy. He followed wood-cutting as a profession and wrought with exemplary zeal the six working days, hoarding every cent not required to furnish him the most frugal fare. As his "pile" increased, he invested it in gold ornaments: watch-chain of massive links, shirt and sleeve buttons, shoe buckles, then buttons for vest and coat, a hat-band of the precious metal, a heavy gold-headed cane, and in short, wherever an ounce of it could be bestowed upon his person, in or out of taste, it was done. The glory of his life, his one ambition, was to don this curious attire—which was deposited for safe-keeping during the week in one of the banks—on Sunday morning, and then spend the day, "the observed of all observers," lounging about the office, or the bar-room of the St. Charles. He never drank and rarely spoke. Mystery seemed to envelop him. No one knew whence he came, or the origin of his innocent whim. Old citizens assured you, that year after year, his narrow savings were measured by the increase of his ornaments, until at length, the value of the anomalous garments came to be estimated by thousands of dollars. By ten o'clock, Sunday night, the exhibition was closed, his one day of self-gratification enjoyed, his costly wardrobe was returned to the bank-vault, and he sank back into the obscurity of a wood-chopper.

The other, as different from the fore-mentioned as genius from stupidity, was Seargent S. Prentiss, the renowned lawyer and orator. He was a compound of contradictions. With a noble bust and superb head, he was yet short of stature, and was deformed by a shrivelled leg. The master of nearly all manly accomplishments, a fearless rider and bold hunter, he yet halted painfully in his gait; with exuberant animal spirits and matchless powers of conversation, (which made him the delight and soul of every social circle) he would sometimes, in solitude, locking himself in for whole days, shed scalding tears, goaded almost to madness by morbid self-torture. Gifted with every power to win the admiration, confidence and love of women, he shrank from their society, dreading lest his one drawback should excite unsympathetic remark, and this, when his genius had already dazzled the first minds of the country. Born and bred a Puritan, he was the representative man of southwestern life. Pacific in disposition, and remarkable for sweetness of temper, he was famous as a duellist. With virtues of character that won for him the lasting regard of all good men that ever knew him, it is nevertheless computed that he lost hundreds of thousands of dollars by gambling; possessed of a fancy as gentle and sportive as Herbert's or Cowper's, I suppose that the eloquence of invective has produced nothing since the days of Demosthenes, equal to his thunders against Mississippi repudiation. The most effective man on the stump in the country, he at the same time shone conspicuously in its highest courts. Cogent in argument, copious in imagination, he pleased while he persuaded, convinced while he charmed. With a memory whose wax-like retentiveness held not only the thoughts and images, but even words, of ancient and modern poetry, there was coupled a wit as fertile as it was brilliant and an understanding robust as it was comprehensive and original. The Bible, Shakspeare, and Milton were his hand-books and it is said that he knew them from lid to lid. His pathos was as extraordinary as his scorn. At first you might have fancied him a mere rhetorician, but he had not proceeded far before you found him a consummate orator. He was master of all the passions of the human soul, and moved them as the expert musician draws from his instrument a concord of sweet sounds. He gave in bounty what might have been the ransom of princes, yet toward the proud he showed the pride of Lucifer. He would stand before a crowd of repudiating Mississippi voters, hurling at them taunts, ridicule, sarcasm, defiance, until their faces grew pale and their lips livid with rage. And then when the pestilence walked the streets of the city, and in almost every house there was found one dead; without a thought of personal danger, he would devote weeks to the bed-sides of the poor and the stranger, with all the watchful tenderness and untired patience of a woman. He was the idol of children and no less of Indian warriors. He is said to have delivered the greatest speech ever made in the Halls of Congress, and yet the people of the backwoods grew almost delirious under the spell of his eloquence. Before the pistol of an antagonist at ten paces, his mien was calm, his nerves firm as steel; but if introduced to a lady, his knees trembled, and his embarrassment would have been ludicrous had it not been so painful. Take him for all in all, he seems to me the most wonderful man that our country has produced. And yet he has left little to justify this remark to the world, if I except the unparalled impression upon all who ever knew or heard him.

Leaving Maine, his native State, when 19 years of age, he made his way to Cincinnati and thence to Natchez. His object was, by teaching, to provide the means of preparing himself for the bar. "I left Cincinnati," he said, "because everything was so tame, everything so cheap. I couldn't spend a ninepence. I was haunted too, by the ghosts of slaughtered swine. I arrived at Natchez with one five dollar bill in my pocket. I knew that it was not a capital to trade upon, and I spent it in the purchase of confidence. So soon as I reached the threshold of mine host, the Boniface of the hotel, I ordered a bottle of wine with cigars, and called the landlord, as the only guest, to join me. He drank, and I told him who I was, what I wanted, and what he had to expect in the way of pay for my fare, beyond what was before us. He looked at my face, said he would trust it, gave me his hand, and without a word more did trust me for board and lodging till I got a school. I kept school and cleared ground enough, of birchen rods with which I taught the young idea how to shoot, to entitle me to a preëmption right of public land." He brought letters of introduction to a wealthy merchant of Natchez, from whom he borrowed fifteen dollars with the promise to return it as soon as he was able; at the close of his first quarter's tuition, he came into town with a proud heart to fulfill his pledge, but was shocked by a severe reproof which the strict man of debt and credit administered for his delay and the trouble it had given. Some years afterward, Prentiss gained a suit for this old friend, which saved him the bulk of his fortune, and the generous friend of the old time counted out a five dollar bill as the fee, which the lawyer had left to his honor.

Removing to Vicksburg, notwithstanding his youth and that he was a Yankee, he at once took the foremost position at the bar, and was ere long drawn into the maelstrom of politics, as every man of decided character in the South soon will be. Although he defended many a man charged with murder, and no doubt often robbed the gallows of its due, he never, except in two instances, prosecuted men charged with capital offences. One of these was a desperado named Phelps, who after a series of high crimes and misdemeanors, setting the officers of the law at defiance, had killed an unoffending citizen in cold blood. He had borne himself throughout the trial with the insolence of a bravo, treating all persons in the court with disdain. When Mr. Prentiss rose as the assistant of the prosecuting attorney, to deliver his speech, the ruffian glared fiercely at him, like a wild beast ready to spring upon a victim; but as the lawyer proceeded to rehearse his crimes and portrayed them in the dark colors of their guilt, the culprit quailed, his head sank upon his breast, and he sat abashed and overwhelmed, not daring to lift his eyes again until after sentence of death had been pronounced. While in the jail awaiting his execution, he sent for the man who had sealed his fate, and the heart which had long been chilled and defiled in the breast of guilt, softened and bared itself to the prosecutor. He told the story of his life to Mr. Prentiss and then mentioned that he had formed the purpose of escaping during the trial. His plan was twofold; first to leap upon his prosecutor, who aside from his lameness, had the look of a mere boy; to kill him, and then amidst the confusion, secure his own flight. He was deterred from attempting to execute this fine scheme, by reading in the eye and bearing of the youthful orator unmistakable signs that such an attempt would prove an ignominious failure. When he had disclosed his plans, Mr. Prentiss quietly remarked, "I saw it all, but I was prepared for you." His main object, in soliciting the interview, was to unbosom himself by making known the particulars of his private history.

In those days, the law of honor was the *higher law* religiously obeyed in Mississippi. Street fights and duels were of daily occurrence, and every professional and political man was expected to take a hand with rifle, pistol, or bowie knife, as often as convenient. Such was the general delight in these encounters, that as soon as the sound of shots was heard, the entire community flocked to the scene to witness the exhibition. It is related that as two gentlemen were engaged in target practice at each other, in one of the villages of Mississippi, some twenty years ago, an overgrown lad, the down upon whose chin scarce required a razor, rushed up and down the street along which the bullets were whizzing, wringing his hands and shrieking convulsively, while tears dropped from his eyes—"A gun! a gun! will nobody lend me a gun? I understand it's a free fight and I'm dying to have a crack."

It was a matter of course that so conspicuous a person as Mr. Prentiss should take his share in these honorable encounters, which were of almost daily occurrence in Vicksburg. It is stated, on what seems good authority, that an enterprising capitalist built a steam ferryboat to ply between this thriving city, and the opposite bank of the river where the formal interviews usually took place, for the express accommodation of the duellists, their friends and an interested public. It is added that the returns from the investment were large—the fare charged was twenty-five cents each way. Mr. P. had scarcely made his brilliant debut at the Vicksburg bar before a plan was set on foot to get him out of the way. It was arranged that a person who, having been born and educated a gentleman; had thrown himself away and was fast becoming a sot, but who was withal a capital marksman, should perform this service for the community. His second bore the challenge. Prentiss quietly read it and stated that he would answer it at his own time and in his own way. Selecting one of his best shirts, he dispatched it by his body-servant with the following note:

"SIR: I accept your challenge, but with one proviso—that you appear on the ground in the accompanying piece of raiment, as it is impossible for me to fight any one who does not observe the externals of a gentleman."

The gentleman withdrew the challenge, but kept the shirt. Mr. Prentiss had two duels with General Foote, which, by the way, were the only times he ever fought, for the various little episodes with fists and canes are not to be taken into the account. At their second meeting, a large crowd was assembled to witness the scene. One shot had been fired, Foote's ball flying wide of his antagonist, while Prentiss' had missed fire. The parties were placed at ten paces for the second round, pistol in hand, only waiting the word. The intense interest of the spectators had drawn them in two long lines close to the combatants, leaving only a narrow lane for the passage of the balls. An urchin, who had small chance to see, in the crowd, had taken a tree in the rear of Mr. P., and by alert climbing was rapidly gaining the branches, where from a comfortable seat he might witness the transaction. Prentiss observed him and said in his kindest tone, "My son, you had better look out; I am afraid you will be hit. General Foote is shooting very wild to-day." The remark and the manner of its delivery called forth a round of three cheers from the bystanders, when, order being restored, the fight proceeded.

As he was about to retire one morning toward three o'clock, there was a violent rap at the door; opening it, he encountered a mechanic known to him by sight, who was evidently under the influence of liquor, and demanded immediate satisfaction for some fancied insult he had received at Mr. P.'s hands. Prentiss reasoned with him, suggesting that he should go home and sleep on the matter, and if, after cool reflection, he desired to appease his honor, he should be satisfied; but the fellow was immovably set upon fighting then and there. Always disposed to oblige his friends, Mr. P. called up his body-servant Burr, and good-humoredly requested him to bring his case of duelling pistols, and then proceeded with great deliberation to load them. Giving the choice to the aspirant for duelling distinction, he took the other, and it was arranged that the parties should take their stands on the piazza in rear of the office, at eight paces. Burr, greatly elated at the thought of his important post, was to hold the candles, so that the light, falling through the windows, should be thrown directly upon the combatants. When all things were in readiness, he was to count, in a loud, clear voice from one to five; the firing to take place at discretion, anywhere between the first and the last number. Pistol in hand, the men took their stand, their eyes glancing along the barrels; waiting only the dreadful word, one! . . . when the mechanic, flinging his pistol to the ground, cried, "Prentiss, do you suppose I'm such a fool as to be fighting you at three o'clock in the morning, with nobody but a nigger by? I thought I was as brave a man as you are, but I ain't; so let's shake hands and be friends."

Riding the circuit in Mississippi a quarter of a century ago was no child's play. Bench and bar, mounted on horseback, with briefs and records stuffed into saddle-bags, had to make long journeys over roads which were sometimes knee-deep in mud and which sometimes dwindled to a bridle-path or even to a faint trace; fording and swimming streams frequently out of their banks, flooding the country for miles on either side, and crossing swamps where miring was a common occurrence, and where it was no uncommon thing for a quicksand to swallow the horse and put the rider up to all he knew to save his own life. The taverns were log cabins, so were the court-houses and jails. The recreations of the sprigs of the law—after a hard day's journey, or the yet more arduous duties of the court-room—were story-telling, whisky punch or whisky reverend (as the unmixed is styled), and a game of "seven-up" or "poker," in which judge, jurors, sheriff, clerk, witnesses, clients and lawyers united.

I cannot refrain from inserting here the account of one of Mr. Prentiss' journeys, from the pen of Col. Baillie Peyton, as characteristic of the man and the times.

"On landing at Vicksburg, in November of 1843, *en route* from Tennessee to New Orleans, I found Mr. Prentiss and Col. Forrester, an old friend and former colleague in Congress from Tennessee, looking out for me. They made so strong an appeal, that I was induced to leave the steamer and accompany them to Hillsborough, the county seat of Scott County, situated in the interior of Mississippi, where the Board of Commissioners appointed by the President to adjudicate the claim of the Choctaw Indians, was about to meet. A few days before my arrival, a most violent and calumnious article appeared in a newspaper published at Vicksburg, in which these claims were denounced as fraudulent and Col. Forrester and Mr. Prentiss held up in a most odious light before the public. The name of the author was demanded, and after some hesitation, rather than meet the consequences of a refusal, the editor agreed to place in the hands of Mr. Prentiss a sealed package containing full and undeniable evidence of the authorship, to be opened at Hillsborough, on condition that Mr. ——, one of the commissioners, should deny himself to be the author of the article.

"This expedition, partaking somewhat of both a civil and military character, afforded the best opportunity I ever had for appreciating the personal qualities and splendid abilities of Mr. Prentiss. Our journey led through Jackson, the capital of the State, where I heard him publicly denounce repudiation as a *crime*, as an act of *moral turpitude*, when surrounded by repudiators who had all 'been out,' and many of whom had shot their man with perfect impunity; but those who did not like him too well, dreaded him too much to make it a personal matter.

"After travelling several days over roads almost impassable, through a country thinly settled, chiefly by squatters, we arrived at Hillsborough. It was a small village, with the forest trees standing on the public square and in most of the streets. Here and there lay a fallen trunk, cut down for fire-wood; the limbs being lopped off as occasion required. The court-house, jail and private dwellings were built of trees, the former and some of the latter having two sides hewn. At this rude place were collected an immense number of Choctaw Indians and land speculators.

"The object of Mr. P.'s visit was to expose the commissioner, who had publicly denounced the claims he was about to adjudicate, drive him from the Board, or induce the other commissioners to refuse to sit with him, on the ground that he had disqualified himself, both as a judge and as a gentleman, to be associated with them in the decision of causes which he had prejudged; and also to demand personal satisfaction for the abusive article.

"This journey to Hillsborough, as I have said—the nature of the business which called him there—the crowd of men, savage, semi-savage, civilized and semi-civilized, amongst whom he was thrown, and to all of whom he was the chief object of attention; the philippics he hurled in the face of that commissioner, presented S. S. Prentiss in a great variety of scenes and in a more interesting point of view than I ever saw him or any other man.

"We arrived a day or two before the Board was convened for the transaction of business, and put up with an unlettered but well-meaning old gentleman, who filled a variety of public offices; being the town "squire," jailer and tavern-keeper, in which last vocation he had many competitors.

"When not otherwise employed, we amused ourselves in shooting squirrels, which proved to be no small accession to our bill-of-fare. Broiled grey squirrels are quite a delicacy when properly cooked, and this Mr. Prentiss superintended in person, calling loudly for butter with which to dress them.

"He was formally introduced to the chief, 'Captain

Post Oak,' a perfect model of the natural man, six feet six or eight inches in height; he joined, too, in the sports of the Indians, among other things shooting blow-guns, at which he soon became so expert that he beat the best of them. A blow-gun is formed of a reed or cane, from twelve to fifteen feet in length, bored through so as to admit the passage of a light arrow, which is ejected by the breath; hence the name. With this weapon the Indians are able to bring down birds and squirrels from the trees.

"In passing the jail one day, we caught a glimpse of a prisoner confined in the dungeon or lower story. He beckoned us to the grates, and then, through livid lips and chattering teeth, for it was frosty November weather, poured forth a touching appeal for protection, strongly protesting his innocence and declaring his ignorance of the charge against him. Additional interest was imparted to the situation of this man, on account of the fate of two who had been recently elected to the gallows by a public meeting of the sovereigns.

"Repairing forthwith to the tavern, we inquired of our landlord as to the charge against him and requested, as his counsel, to see the mittimus upon which he was committed. The "Squire" appeared to be somewhat embarrassed, and at length acknowledged that there had been no regular commitment, nor even any specific charge against him; but said the fellow was a doubtful character and had been imprisoned on suspicion. 'On suspicion of what?' asked Mr. Prentiss. "Has anybody been killed, or robbed, or lost a horse, a hog or a cow?' 'No, no,' said the Squire, 'nothing of that sort has hap pened, but then he is a kind of surplus character, circulating about, and not very agre'ble at that.'

"Mr. Prentiss declared that he should be set free; that if the Squire refused to turn him out, he should be discharged on *habeas corpus*, if he had to go to Jackson himself for the writ, and sue every man concerned in his detention, for false imprisonment. This startled the Squire, who had never seen nor had he any definite idea of a writ of *habeas corpus*, and entertaining a respect mingled with awe for Mr. Prentiss, he consented to discharge the prisoner. Unfortunately however, his son, who had that morning ridden twelve miles into the country in quest of butter wherewith to dress our squirrels, had carried the key of the jail with him; so that it could not be opened until he came back. Meanwhile, Mr. Prentiss, whose whole heart was now in the matter, and who felt like an ancient knight bent upon the rescue of an unfortunate captive from some feudal castle, returned to console the prisoner with the prospect of his early liberation. He, poor fellow, stood shivering, with sunken eyes and hollowed cheeks, looking the picture of despair. Mr. Prentiss inquired if he did not think a little brandy would help him! 'Mightily! but there is no chance to get it in to me.' Mr. Prentiss, however, set his fertile ingenuity to work, and succeeded, by introducing a blow-gun through the grates, one end of which the prisoner put to his mouth, while the brandy was poured into the other.

"Finally, the young man having returned with the key, he was brought to the tavern, ate a hearty meal, received a handsome purse, sufficient to supply his immediate wants, and went on his way rejoicing; looking upon his liberation as next to a miracle, and on the generous man who accomplished it, as his good angel.

"There was to me something inexpressibly interesting in this scene, as the poor fellow gazed in the face of his deliverer, and hung around him as though he felt secure in his newly-gained freedom, only in the presence of Mr. Prentiss. It called to mind the touching picture of Uncle Toby at the bedside of Lefevre, and the effect produced by his honest, benevolent face, in winning the heart of the little son of the dying officer, who was unconsciously drawn to his side and took hold of his hand.

"All that Sterne said of his hero, and more, might without exaggeration be said of Mr. Prentiss. 'There was a frankness in him which led you at once into his soul, and showed you his goodness of nature. There was something in his look, and voice, and manner, which internally beckoned to the unfortunate, inviting them to come and take shelter under him.' He was, indeed, a man whom, at first sight, the lowest would trust, the distressed appeal to and the brave confide in.

"But to return to our business at Hillsborough. When the Board met in the log cabin, the scene was picturesque in the extreme. There were the three commissioners, Mr. Graves, Mr. Tyler (a brother of the President of the United States) and Mr. ——, with their clerk, seated on one side of a table made of pine boards; on the other sat the counsel of the Indians, while the building was filled to overflowing with their clients, hundreds of whom, unable to find room inside, were crowded around the house, with their swarthy faces and dark eyes peering through the apertures between the logs.

"Mr. Prentiss rose to a preliminary question, and handing a newspaper containing the offensive article to Mr. ——, inquired whether he was or was not the author; to which he replied, with some hesitation and evident embarrassment, in the negative. Whereupon, Mr. Prentiss drew from his pocket and broke the seal of an envelope containing the papers which had been placed in his hands by the editor of the Vicksburg *Sentinel.* They proved to be the original manuscript from which the article was published, in the handwriting of Mr. ——, and also his letter to the editor which accompanied the same. In this letter he boldly assumed whatever responsibility might attach to him as author of the article, and in advance tendered personal satisfaction to the party aggrieved. As these documents were produced, and the truth flashed upon him, the commissioner made a lame effort to qualify his denial by saying, 'I was the writer, but not the author of the article, having copied it for a friend.'

"Mr. Prentiss proceeded to read the letter and manuscript article, in the latter of which 'one Forrester,' and certain 'influential men' acting with him, were denounced in unmeasured terms, the claims they advocated condemned, as 'the most stupendous fraud ever devised,' and the whole thing represented as a deeply-laid plot to swindle the United States and the good people of Mississippi.

"The commissioner was eulogized as if he were the only man in the commission who possessed the talents, honesty, independence and patriotism to throw himself in the breach and resist the peculators.

"Having read these documents with marked deliberation and emphasis, Mr. Prentiss threw down the papers and raised himself to his full height, his noble front erect and chest expanded by the tension of his soul; his countenance then glowed with the fire of intellect, and his eye consumed, with 'lightnings of scorn that laughed forth as he spoke,' the form of that base commissioner. Thus as he stood, the painter or the sculptor who should have mirrored his features on canvas, or graven them in marble, would have then and there won immortality.

"Ere he had uttered one word, his work was accomplished; the man was gone—the former judge was the convicted culprit. During the two hours in which that torrent of eloquence descended, I do not believe its effect at any moment exceeded what his look had realized. I never till then understood the force of an expression used by Disraeli, I believe in describing Voltaire, 'That he possessed in a remarkable degree, physiognomical eloquence.' If the philippic of Cicero which drove Catiline from Rome was as terrible, no wonder that traitor left the city.

"On this occasion, Mr. Prentiss, with an oppressed nation as his clients, had a noble theme for oratory, scarcely inferior in interest and variety to that of Sheridan in the trial of Hastings.

"He gave a most interesting history of the Choctaws as a nation, of their pacific character and uniform friendship for people of the United States; dwelling with great effect upon the oppression and injustice which they had already experienced. He described what a judge should be, investing him with almost divine attributes of virtue, and wisdom, and justice; and then contrasted such a pure and elevated character with the prejudiced partisan and unprincipled demagogue, who acting in the name, and clothed with the power of his government, was about to crush the last hope of an injured people, and filch from them the mite which that government, in the exercise of its resistless power, had seen fit to grant them. In alluding to the wrongs which the Choctaws had experienced in return for their good conduct, he melted the hearts of all—Indians and white men—and drew tears from eyes before which death had no terrors; groans and sobs burst from stoic bosoms, and cheeks were wet which had seldom or never been profaned by a tear.

"The Board adjourned to consider the motion to expel Mr. ——, and at its next sitting he read a protest against the power of his colleagues to deprive him of a commission he received from the President of the United States, which was the occasion of such another speech from Mr. Prentiss as I have just described. But the other commissioners refused to sit with him, referred the question to Washington for the decision of the President and adjourned *sine die.*

"The personal satisfaction which had been tendered in advance by Mr. ——, was refused by him, and having thus retreated beyond the pale of honor, he was dropped. The President afterward removed him."

Mr. Prentiss' power over juries is illustrated by the following incident which occurred in a piney-woods region, not far from Pearl River, Mississippi. He appeared for the defendant in a suit brought for damage, the panel, composed of wire-grass people, were thrilled by his marvellous eloquence, and despising the technical forms of the law; without retiring from the box, agreed upon their verdict, which was thus delivered viva voce by the foreman; "We finds for lawyer Prentiss, the plaintive to pay the costs."

He was the head and front of that party in the State, respectable for intelligence and position, but overweighed at the polls, which insisted upon the payment of the bonds due from Mississippi to her creditors. This party had been defeated in one popular election, but some of the leaders thought that success might yet be attained by nominating for the office of governor, Judge Sharkey, a man of irreproachable character and withal very popular in the State. Mr. P. felt that it would be hazarding too much to remove Judge S. from the place of Chief Justice on the Supreme Bench, and subject him to the chance of a popular election, he therefore induced the nominating Committee of the Whig Convention, assembled in Jackson in June, 1843, to alter their determination of proposing Judge Sharkey, and to substitute the name of another prominent member of the party. This created a perfect furor of dissatisfaction among the members of that body. Complaints and murmurs arose from all quarters of the hall. No one objected to the gentleman who was offered, but nearly everybody preferred Judge Sharkey.

During all this excitement, Mr. Prentiss, clad carelessly in a plain summer suit, his collar open and his fine flowing locks streaming unarranged and almost wildly, sat perfectly calm and silent. The time had not arrived at which he decided to mingle in the strife and assign the reasons for his conduct. At length a member addressed the president, and proposed to strike out the name of the person reported from the Committee as the candidate, and to insert that of Wm. L. Sharkey. The motion was not even seconded before Mr. Prentiss sprang, rather than rose, to his feet, threw his well-known stick in its accustomed place to support his infirm limb, and advancing energetically to the front of his desk, began to pour forth one of those powerful and overwhelming torrents of eloquence for which he has become so famed. The peculiar sound of his cane, as he limped along from his seat (a sound which is well remembered in Mississippi and which never failed to draw universal attention whenever, during his service in Congress, he entered the Hall of Representatives), at once stilled the audience into the most perfect silence. Every one could see that the mood was upon him, and that he had been touched by the magic wand of his ministering Genius. He assailed the motion, as striking a death-blow at the already crippled character of Mississippi. With more than usual skill, he drew a graphic picture of the whole array of repudiators, "with their ragged pirate flag, borne shamelessly in the midst of them, advancing in swarms to do their murderous, infamous work. He described them as "Huns," guided by leaders who owned all the atrocious principles of Attila, without possessing his courage or his talents." Alluding to the defeat which the bond-payers had sustained at the last elections, he spoke with power unsurpassed against that policy which dictated to us, "after having lost the main battle and been driven back from every post and routed at all points, to draw our greatest leader from the strong citadel of the Supreme Court to encounter an uncertain fate in a hazardous campaign." This citadel maintained, he declared that the "wild beast of Repudiation" was restrained from striking, at least, the last fatal and irrecoverable blow on the already prostrate name of Mississippi. "Here, after having scattered his vile foam and exhaled his pestilential breath in every other quarter, he could at last be muzzled and strangled." He then spoke with deep feeling of the purity, learning and spotless character of Judge Sharkey, and declared that "the honest men of Mississippi could not spare him from the bench at such a time." His court "was the last refuge left under the inflictions of this worse than Egyptian plague," and they would rise up in one solid mass to protest against his being surrendered—against the "letting go of our only hold, to flounder amidst the uncertainties of a political campaign." He said, with an expression of countenance that thrilled the audience, that "Judge Sharkey should not be forced to soil the pure ermine of judicial eminence by seeking an engagement with this unclean monster." Still, he continued, it was "essential to fight the beast, pestiferous as it was." He had read in Roman history that the march of a whole army had been once arrested by coming in contact with a huge serpent, whose very breath poisoned the entire atmosphere around them. Regulus halted his columns and decided that safety called for the destruction of the monster, even though many human lives should be the forfeit. If the serpent, as was naturally to be expected, should follow on their march, the whole army must inevitably be swept away by pestilence; and thus, day after day, were detachments drawn out, until the destroyer was in turn destroyed. "Our march," he continued, "to fame and to greatness as a State has been impeded by the intervention of this vile serpent, Repudiation." "Its hiss [illegible] which the [illegible] in question, if adopted, must [illegible] upon the [illegible]-paying party."

Col. Thorpe [illegible] a scene which occurred at New Orleans, in February, 1844, on occasion of Mr. Clay's visit: "The streets around the St. Charles Hotel presented a vast ocean of heads, and every building commanding a view was literally covered with human beings. The great statesman of the West presented himself to the multitude, between the tall columns of the finest portico in the country. The scene was beyond description. As the crowd swayed to and fro, a shout was raised for Mr. Clay to speak; he uttered a sentence or two, waved his hand in adieu, and escaped amidst the prevailing confusion. Prentiss meanwhile, evidently unconscious of being himself noticed, was at a side window, gazing upon what was passing with all the delight of the humblest spectator. Suddenly his name was announced. He attempted to withdraw from public gaze, but his friends pushed him forward. Again his name was shouted, hats and caps were thrown in the air and he was finally compelled to show himself on the portico. With remarkable delicacy, he chose a less prominent place than that previously occupied by Mr. Clay, although perfectly visible. He thanked his friends for their kindness by repeated bows and by such smiles as he alone could give. 'A speech! a speech!' thundered a thousand voices. He lifted his hand, in an instant everything was still—then pointing to the group that had surrounded Mr. Clay, he said, 'Fellow citizens, when the eagle is soaring in the sky, the owls and the bats retire to their holes.' And long before the shout that followed this remark ceased, Prentiss had disappeared amid the multitude."

The popular assembly was the place of his proudest exhibitions. To the multitude, he was as a trumpet. He said, "Fellow citizens!" and, *auribus erectis*, the people stood still, or swayed to and fro, or shouted, or were sad, smiled or frowned, at his magic will. He was invited just after the adjournment of Congress, in the summer of 1838, to address a mass meeting at Havre de Grace, Maryland, and thus made his bow to the audience: "Fellow citizens, by the Father of Waters at New Orleans, I have said Fellow citizens—on the banks of the beautiful Ohio, I have said Fellow citizens—here I say Fellow citizens—and a thousand miles beyond this, North, thanks be to God, I can still say, Fellow citizens!" Thus, in a single sentence, he saluted his audience, drew every man, woman and child near to him, made himself dear to them; by a word covered the continent—by a line mapped the United States from the Gulf to the Lakes—by a greeting warm from the heart, beaming from the countenance; depicted the whole country, its progress, development, grandeur, glory and union. Every hat was whirled in the air, every handkerchief was waving, the welkin rung with hurrahs, the multitude heaved up to the stand, stood on tip-toe and shouted cheer after cheer, as if wild with joy and mad with excitement.

While Mr. Prentiss was delivering a speech in Faneuil Hall, Boston, Edward Everett, unable to contain himself, turned to Mr. Webster and said, "Did you ever hear such astonishing eloquence?" "Never from any one, but Mr. Prentiss himself," was Mr. Webster's reply.

During the presidential canvass of 1844, he was making one of his great speeches before an immense audience in Nashville, Tennessee. Overcome by his exertions, he fell fainting into the arms of his friend,

Gov. Jones, who, frenzied with excitement, shouted at the top of his voice, over the unconscious form which he supported, "Die, Prentiss! die now, you will never have again an opportunity so glorious."

Having used his best exertions to convert the people of Mississippi from their disgraceful policy of Repudiation, and mortified beyond expression at the idea of remaining in a State which refused to pay its debts, he removed, in 1844, to New Orleans. It was in the bar-room of the St. Charles, in February, 1848, that I saw this extraordinary person for the first time. He died a little more than two years after, in his forty-second year. His death was hastened by the fearful drafts made upon his admirable constitution in his political career; and by the superhuman exertions he put forth in professional labors, to relieve himself from embarrassments which hedged him about, and were in great part the results of gaming. Few books of American biography reveal a character possessed of such sweet, beautiful and noble traits, adorned with the highest gifts of genius, and enriched by all the culture possible in his position, as the Memoirs of S. S. Prentiss; to which by the way, I am indebted for much of the material for this sketch. But few leave so painful and sad an impression. It is the story of a man who might have been the boast of his race—the glory of his nation;

who with talents and opportunities the greatest, died before his time, and now discrowned of his kingly power, with ghostly finger points the eyes of his countrymen to that solemn warning coupled with the imperishable truth, "Whatsoever a man soweth, that also shall he reap."

CHAPTER XVIII.

"GOING TO AND FRO IN THE EARTH, AND WALKING UP AND DOWN IN IT."

It had been my intention to winter in the South and bear warm weather company in its progress northward. Accordingly, after a sojourn of two or three weeks in that least American of our cities, New Orleans, I crossed the lake and gained the quiet town of Mobile. During my stay among kind friends in this place, I received a letter from the presiding elder of the Montgomery district, in which he stated that the church in Montgomery was without a preacher and that they would like to secure my services. The world was open to me where to choose a residence, my passion for travelling was sated for the present, I yearned for an opportunity to devote myself to study. I was charmed with the beautiful social life and warm-hearted hospitality of the South, and above all I longed for a home, and for the opportunity to keep up something like a personal acquaintance with my wife and child. These considerations, together with an inviting field of labor, decided me to accept the offer.

As we drew near the end of a pleasant steamboat sail of four hundred miles from Mobile, a company of passengers were seated on the boiler deck, enjoying the scenery of the beautiful Alabama. The boat swept around a bend of the river, disclosing the noble amphitheatre of hills on which Montgomery is built; a fine State-House stands on the left, and stretching away to the right, every eminence is crowned with handsome residences, surrounded by gardens and forest trees, forming an exquisite landscape. But our quiet enjoyment was suddenly broken upon by peals of laughter. The pilot, who had kept his steam-whistle for some time silent, sounded an unearthly scream, loud, long and piercing, from this favorite instrument. A distinguished foreign vocalist who had been seated with us, sprang to his feet, upsetting his chair as he did so, and fled with precipitation to the ladies' cabin, shouting as he went, at the top of his well-trained voice, "The boiler is bursted, we're all blown up! The Lord have mercy on my soul!"

Before taking leave of a section of my life devoted almost entirely to wandering, and entering upon one of comparative quiet and seclusion, it may be well for me to answer a query which I feel sure has risen more than once in the reader's mind. "How did you manage to travel alone?"

In common with all boys in this country, I had

rejoiced from early youth in stories of Indian and frontier life. What especially delighted me were the records of practised senses, sleepless vigilance, alert comprehensive observation, resources equal to any emergency, and in the midst of difficulty and peril, an unshaken self-reliance. Tales of the same purport floated from the desert of the Bedouin; I carefully read all books within reach which told of struggles with privation and hardship, especially the lives of men who had suffered from blindness. Edgar A. Poe's wonderful stories produced a profound impression on my boyish fancy; not so much by their ghastly horrors as by their power of analysis. I therefore set to work to educate my senses, thinking that if an Arab, an Indian, or a half-savage backwoodsman, could bring his perceptions to such precision, keenness, and delicacy, why might not I? It became a matter of pride to conceal my defective vision, to make up for the want of eyesight by the superior activity of the other faculties. The foot became almost as delicate as the hand, and the cheek well-nigh as sensitive to atmospheric impressions as the ear is to acoustic vibrations. By reason of the difficulties which encompassed it, travelling became an art, involving in its practice many elements of science. If I preserved the air and seeming of a man with two good eyes, my step had to be as cautious and well-considered as an Indian's on the war-path, and my dislike of being recognized by strangers, as partially blind, was almost as great as his dread of detection by an enemy. Self-dependence delighted in obstacles. There was a pleasure in scouring strange regions alone, and although I have often had my face severely cut by thorny branches while riding through the woods, and was frequently obliged to hold my right hand in front of my face, the elbow extended to the right and the riding whip to the left, for hours together, as a protection to the upper part of the person; fatigue and wounds were alike accepted as a part of the salutary discipline. Boarding a steamer in the middle of the river, after night, by means of a yawl, after having descended a steep, slippery bank, with no assistance but from a cane, gave me quiet satisfaction. To roam about a strange city, and make myself master of its sidewalks, gutters and crossings, and become familiar with all its localities, thus qualifying myself to become a guide to others, was a favorite pastime. There was hardly a large town of the country in which I did not know the shortest way between any two given points. Self-conceit was gratified when on being introduced to people who had heard of me, they exclaimed, "Why, I thought you could not see very well!" Mere walking was an intellectual exercise, and the mind found constant amusement in solving the physical problems which were ever do manding instant settlement; as, for example, given the sound of a footfall, to find the nature and distance of the object from which it is reverberated; or the space betwixt yourself and the gutter you are approaching; or, amid the Babel of a crowded thoroughfare, to ascertain by your ear when it will be safe for you to cross, and how long a time the rush of hurrying vehicles will allow you.

Many a man has found to his cost that necessity is a stern old pedagogue, intolerant of dullness and negligence, administering severe buffets to the slothful and the incorrigible. I bear about on my body many a mark of his heavy rod. My forehead still carries the trace of an iron pillar, standing at the corner of Gravier and St. Charles streets, in New Orleans, which laid me senseless on the sidewalk, for stupidly rushing against it, to avoid being run over by a drunken driver, the first night I spent in the Crescent City. My nose carries the remembrance of a huge ladder which careless workmen had allowed to remain standing over night across the pavement in St. Francis street, Mobile. An occasional twinge in my neck serves to remind me of a dive which I once made head foremost over an embankment into a trench ten feet deep, in Decatur street, Boston. I found it impossible to run away from my old preceptor, and thus, while almost every part of my person bears tokens of nearly every section of our widespread country, an enumeration of which might almost form a chronicle of my journey, they serve to remind me that the one lesson which my schoolmaster tried to teach me was, "Keep your wits about you."

I am sorry to confess, however, that I have sadly degenerated since the period which the narrative has now reached, namely, March, 1848. Wife, children, and an increasing number of friends, have combined to render me less self-helpful, and I am afraid that I should cut a sorry figure enough if I were now turned out into the Rocky Mountains, or on the western prairies and forced to shift for myself. Loneliness is the condition of self-reliance. Society weakens the instincts and the senses. Love softens while it blesses. The eagle's eye and wing are not found in the dovecot. Home enlarges the sphere of the sympathies, but limits the arena of self-trust. I have relinquished my pride about dependence, exchanged the delicacy of hand, foot, ear, and cheek, for the offices of those who love me, and move about the streets with scarce a pause to regret my privation, when my hand clasps the hand of either of my children, who are as watchful and tender toward me as if they were parent and I the child.

Once I would have scorned as unworthy my manhood any assistance in travelling unnecessary to a man complete in all his organs; later years, while relaxing this tension of the perceptive faculties, have shown me how full of genial sterling kindness is our human nature. I have rarely had occasion to appeal to a fellow-creature for aid without a prompt and hearty response. Only twice or three times have I ever been refused the help I asked, and only once have I been meanly imposed upon. A single day's journey in Ohio taught me more of such littleness than I had learned in all my life besides. It chanced that I reached Columbus from Cleveland, too late for the train for Cincinnati, so that I was obliged to lie over for several hours. At nine o'clock in the evening we left the door of Neil House in an omnibus for the railway station. The fare was a shilling, and as I handed the conductor a quarter of a dollar I said, "I don't see very well; won't you be good enough to assist me from the stage to the cars." In returning the change, he gave me a five and a three cent piece and two pennies. I said, supposing it a mistake, "Do you know that you have only given me ten cents when I am entitled to twelve?"

"Look here," he replied, "I thought you said you could not see," forgetting that a man can tell money as well by his fingers as his eyes. After the other passengers had entered the depot, I said to the worthy who was amusing himself by patting Juba upon his knees:

"Will you give me your arm to the train?"

"I'll be darn'd if I do," he rejoined. "If you can tell a three cent piece from a five, you can find your way to the cars."

After some trouble, I succeeded in gaining a seat, and soon discovered that I had a crowd of gamblers for fellow-passengers, who amused themselves with poker, seven-up and brag, throughout the journey. They partook largely of red-eye whisky, with which they were bountifully supplied, and a more profane, clamorous crew of blackguards I have never met. As the conductor passed through the train, I informed him of my condition, and asked if it would be convenient for him to assist me to a carriage at the end of the journey. He was too much absorbed in the players and their cards to heed my request. Presently the agent for the omnibus line came along, selling tickets which would entitle the passengers to a ride from the depot to his hotel. I asked him if he could help me to the stage, he said he would see about it when we got to town. At four A.M., we reached Cincinnati. The passengers rushed from the train and I could discover no one to appeal to but a brakeman. He replied that he could not leave his brake, but calling a person whom I took to be an employee of the company, said, "Here's a chap what seems a little blind, just lead him to the buss." Taking the man's arm I gave him my carpet-sack, and as we reached the door of the stage, I paused a moment, removing my hand from his arm to take out a piece of money to reward him, and said, "Here is a quarter for your trouble." There was no reply. "Where's the man that brought me here a moment ago?" I inquired of the agent who stood by. "How the d—— do you suppose I know! If you want to go to town, jump right in, we won't wait another minute for you, and don't be trying to come the d——d blind humbug over us." This witty observation was received with a shout of laughter by the stage full of passengers, and I had no resort, but minus my carpet-bag, to clamber to a standing-place inside, for not a man or woman offered to help me to a seat, and thus we rattled to the Burnet House. Do you wonder that I asked myself whether I had reach- Cincinnati or Pandemonium?

At another time, I was en route from New York to Charleston, and as we were approaching Baltimore, was engaged in conversation with a young man, who said that he was a merchant from one of the towns in Carolina. I informed him of my condition and suggested that as I was an experienced traveller, we might form an agreeable partnership for a day or two, by uniting his eyes with my knowledge of the world. He agreed rather coldly, but as we were obliged to hasten, in exchanging cars at Baltimore, he annulled the contract by running off precipitately, leaving me to pick myself up as best I might from a severe fall, received in jumping for the platform. My wife and I interpreted differently the doctrine of total depravity, and whenever I indulged in *couleur de rose* pictures of human nature, drawn from personal experience, she maintained that the kindness which I had invariably received was rendered not to humanity, as such, but to a person of interesting and gentlemanly appearance. Both our theories seemed at fault for once; I supposed that my young Carolinian was not guilty of brutish insensibility, but that he took me for a land shark that intended to devour him on the first occasion. I was so shocked by this, the first rebuff I had ever then experienced, that I could not bring myself to ask guidance of any of my other fellow-passengers, notwithstanding it was pitch dark when we reached the wharf at Washington, where lay the Potomac boat. The night was bitterly cold, there were no waiters at the pier, my comrades used great expedition in gaining the cabin, and I was soon left alone, to feel my way on board. As I went staggering along, I presently felt a strong hand laid upon my shoulder and a friendly Irish voice said: "Come, my darlint, what are you going to throw yourself into the dock for? I see how it is, you've been taking a dhrop too much, and you're not fit to be parading about alone. Come wid me, I've a carriage here, I'll drive you up to a hotel and have you put to bed, and in the morning you'll be all right." I thus found I had gained the side instead of the end of the pier, and a step or two further would have given me a cold bath. I replied, "No my friend, I am not drunk, but I am nearly blind; won't you give me your arm to the cabin of the boat." "Bless your dear little soul," exclaimed the hearty fellow, in a voice tremulous with emotion, "is that what's the matter? what did them brutes leave you here by yourself for? Give ye my arm, is it? I'll take ye in my arms if it will suit ye better," and lifting rather than leading me, he soon deposited me in the bright warm cabin, as tenderly as a mother would have placed her babe. "Look here," he almost shouted to one of the colored waiters: "Here's a gentleman that can't see; if ye don't take the best of care of him; when the boat comes back, I'll break your head, or my name is not Patrick O'Donahue." Extending my hand with a piece of money, I said: "I am much obliged to you, here is something for your trouble." "Something for my throuble, indade," he almost indignantly exclaimed, "Divel a bit of it will I take; do you're think I'd take money for helping a blind man? My old mother wouldn't spake to me, if she thought I would. God bless you, sir," he added, wringing my hand, "may the Vargin and Saints prasarve ye." I like to believe that human nature is represented by the kindness of the Irish hackman, and that the Carolina merchant is a rare exception in his own or any other country.

CHAPTER XIX.

A SOUTHERN HOME—HARD STUDY—CHAUNCEY HOBART—THOMAS CARLYLE.

Shortly after my arrival in Montgomery, I was joined by my wife, with our little daughter Fanny; and our kind-hearted parishioners soon made us feel as much at home as if we had been born and bred in the "Sunny South." The Sunny South indeed I have ever found it, full of generous, noble people, independent in thought and speech, tolerant of the opinions of others, as they are bold in the avowal of their own. I went among them a Northern man and comparatively a stranger; yet no questions were ever asked as to my views of "the peculiar institution," no pledges in regard to my conduct were either desired or given. I was taken at once to the homes and the hearts of the people, and during the six years of my sojourn in that land, I experienced nothing but kindness. Years have passed since I quitted it, not by my own wish, but sorely against my will, for Providence had said, Arise and go hence, for this is not thy rest; yet my feelings instinctively turn toward Alabama as a home, and toward the Southern people as my kindred.

In due time we were established in the parsonage, which stood in the rear of the church, and frequently, during our residence in Montgomery, I did not quit the premises for weeks together. The opportunity to study, so long postponed, had at length arrived, and I seized it with a mixture of desperation and delight. I now look back upon those two years with a feeling something between wonder and fright. The average time bestowed upon my intellectual labor was eleven hours per diem, it sometimes went up to fifteen; my wife has many a time read to me sixteen hours out of the twenty-four; I recollect that we went through the first two volumes of Macaulay's "England" at that rate. Nothing came amiss. Newspapers, reviews, history, voyages, travels, poetry, everything, but especially metaphysics. It was clear that I had been born to comprehend the incomprehensible. I greedily devoured the New York *Tribune* and the *National Era*, the Massachusetts "Quarterly" and the "Westminster," the "Essays of Emerson," "The Reports and Addresses of Wendell Phillips," "The Lectures and Sermons of Theodore Parker." It was the era of revolution. The millions of Europe, roused by the tocsin of liberty, February, 1848, were demanding their rights of the trembling monarchs, and the mind of the world glowed with enthusiasm for freedom. While the peoples on the other side of the deep, waged valiant war for civil enfranchisement, holding life cheap if only honor and independence could be won; it was no less the duty of those on this side the world, to free themselves from the bondage of tradition; to vindicate the claims of the present against the tyrannical despotism of the past; and to assert the indefeasible claims of the supreme private soul. Patriotic armies were tearing to shreds the fictions of kingcraft, and jubilant nations were exulting in their new-found "Liberty, Equality, and Fraternity." The heroic Ego must also acquit itself of *its* sublime trust, and, flinging the superstitions of antiquity to the winds, established in the impregnable citadel of consciousness, owning no light but intuition, using no weapon but abstraction, must wage puissant and victorious war, unfurling the banner of ideal perfection. Divine philosophy was the panacea for the wounds of humanity, and whoso would befriend his race must combine the lores of the East and of the West, must become the disciple at once of Confucius and of Schelling, and must, with open ear, attend to the utterances of all the oracles, between the Chinese seer and the German Professor.

Zoroaster and Aristotle, Plato and Bruno, Thomas Aquinas and Duns Scotus, Des Cartes and Leibnitz, Kant and Fichte were honored as the greater luminaries of my firmament. I adopted Germany as my Fatherland, discarded cigars, smoked a meerschaum, talked learnedly about Goethe, and became a thorough Teuton in everything but lager-bier. I was disposed to believe that, excepting Shakspeare and one or two other writers who had been favorably noticed by the German critics, the English language contained very little worth a scholar's regard—some of my illustrious contemporaries, of course, being regarded as "*present company.*" My reading in German theology began with Neander's "Life of Christ," and I was not long in reaching Strauss's "Life of Jesus." "Theodore, or the Skeptic's Conversion," by De Wette, fell in my way, and I was not long in discovering his Introduction and Commentaries. Openness of mind is the divinest gift of the Oversoul, while universality of inquiry and catholicity of taste are the invariable attributes of the true critic and scholar. I read a great deal about High Art, and thought that I understood it. I undertook Lessing, and in fine, I became a transcendentalist of the supra-nebulous order. And yet I was a Methodist preacher, whose one business it was, or should have been, to teach the people righteousness.

My many books, like Dante's one, made me lean. I restricted myself to a spare regimen. The intellect was to be regnant, the appetite to be controlled, and the spirit to become all in all. Eating was a vulgar necessity which had to be performed in common with the brutes; therefore, the less of it the better, the true element for humanity was thought. The thinker was the one person of consequence in the universe; all else were but as chaff, which the wind might blow whither it listed. I was a philosophical critic—or, which amounts to the same thing, fancied myself one—in sympathy with the Age, armed with a vocabulary of high-sounding words, and fortified with the largest candor. "Is not Protestantism the emphasis of the private judgment? Let us then be Protestants and carry our work to a logical and legitimate extremity. Reverence for anything but myself is an absurdity. Sit calmly upon the Olympian summit of your individuality, and all the divinities, major and minor, will hail you as their peer. Obey the law of your being. Sin, what is it? An incident which helps to higher perfection." I was as severe, as my candor would permit, upon priestcraft and hollow symbols, and waxed awfully eloquent upon cant and shams, but I was particularly profound when I reached the regions of the subjective and objective, the "me," and the "not me," and no doubt Sir William Hamilton would have been charmed could he have listened to my subtle distinctions between the reason and the understanding. I possessed vast hermeneutical skill, and was able to distinguish with the most exquisite accuracy between those parts of the Hebrew and Christian scriptures which were authentic, and those which were supposititious. I could indicate to you with the greatest nicety those parts of the Pentateuch which

Moses had composed, and those which he had copied from elder historians and lawgivers. I had great respect for the poetry of David, Job, and Isaiah; notwithstanding they might suffer somewhat by comparison with the Iliad, the Sagas of the Norsemen, and the Vedas of the Hindoos. There was one fact however that always stood in my way—the person and work of the Redeemer of the World. My powers of scientific analysis were never competent to dispose of that; true, I read Strauss and was familiar with the rules of exegetical criticism adopted by the Tübingen school, and I did venture to speculate somewhat upon the sacred and awful mystery, but I had to give it up. I suppose this must have been the result of weakness and superstition acquired from my mother and some of my other early friends; they were very plain people and did not know a thousandth part as much as myself and some of my later friends. Really, I fancy they must have been so ignorant as never to have heard of Baur and Zeller, and perhaps it went so far that they even did not know Goethe, that demi-god of the modern world. Yet I had seen them in the furnace of affliction heated seven times over, and there had walked with them one as it had been the Son of Man; and they came forth without the smell of fire upon their garments. I saw that by a simple faith of the heart in their dying and risen Lord, their passions were schooled, their tempers softened, their hope animated, so that they were like citizens of a better country—of a heavenly rather than of this lower world. I knew that, to them, Jesus Christ was a merciful and faithful high-priest, and at the same time, the nearest, dearest and most intimate of friends. I had been educated from infancy to hallow His name—to revere, love, and worship Him. I had been taught to look upon Him as a Comforter full of grace, truth and tenderness, from whom, and from whom alone, through the Father, I might receive mercy in time of need.

Despite the spirit of free inquiry, I was held fast by the feelings of earlier years. Prayers learned when a child—views informed from the heart and vital with its blood, rather than those statuesque idioms of thought chiselled by the pure intellect—had become a part of me, and I could not entirely free myself from their authority. As I sat in my study, communing with my oracles, bracing myself with their utterance for the sharp contest with prejudice and puerile misconception, a burst of triumphant song from my negro congregation would, at least for a moment, disarm the metaphysician of his power and bring back the childish weakness of tears. I was keenly alive to the discrepancy between the profession and practice of Christians. I was pained by the apparent absence of high ethical character, at once refined and stalwart, which one is justi fied to expect in the disciples of Jesus of Nazareth. I was morbidly sensitive to the frailties and infirmities of my brethren, and asked, if Christianity be indeed the spiritual and divine power which it is said to be, why are not the lives and characters of its professors spiritual and divine? I demanded of the church an ideal perfection, and shrunk back from it because it presented me flesh and blood. I was out of sympathy with my people. It was painful for me to visit them or receive their visits; they were interested in houses and lands, in buying, selling and getting gain, in betrothals and weddings, in christenings and funerals. They talked about the weather and crops, politics and the price of cotton, the size of the congregations that attended my ministry, and revivals of religion that were occurring in the conference. I was not interested in those things. I was clothed upon with Theological Methodology and encircled in the sinuous coil of the Mythical Theory. None of my people cared for Spinoza or Berkeley; how, then, could I care for my people? They were hospitable and kind as they could be, doing everything possible to promote the comfort and happiness of myself and family, yet they were not baptized with my "baphometic fire-baptism." My æsthetic judg ment could not elect them my peers, and it was impossible that we should have lot and part together. The kindred of the soul alone must be recognized; the tongue and ear are each other's complement. Most of what I spoke, my parishioners did not comprehend; most of what they said, I did not appreciate; therefore it was clear that God had not made of one blood all nations to dwell together upon the earth. They were of pipe clay and I of alabaster. Sympathy with any but those of your own kind is of course impossible. I lived in a world of ethereal abstraction. They plodded in a region of sublunary cares and anxieties, where almost their only lights were the fires blazing on the household hearth, and the lamp which glows upon the altar of religion. Our relations were antipodal, our planes infinitely removed. I claimed fellowship with Homer, Dante and Shakspeare, and became great by talking about their greatness. I studied books on architecture, painting and music, and dilated much upon æsthetics and the dynamic forces of the divine idea which reproduced themselves in the terrestrial forms of art. My poor parishioners loved their wives and children, their neighbors and friends, horses and cattle with a hearty and homely love, and thus our spheres were wide apart as the planets. Alas! alas! for the blatant, the worse than Pharisaic egotism of transcendental shallowness and sophistry. All this while, I thought myself an idealist, and folded the mantle of my superiority about me as I looked with ineffable indifference upon the mundane cares and joys of society; yet was I nothing better than a babbling fool, deluded with self-conceit and intoxicated with weak tea, made by steeping the leaves of a so-called œcumenical philosophy in the liquid of a high-sounding and oracular vocabulary. One comfort grows out of this "Phase of Faith"(?) to wit: "the burnt child dreads the fire."

When my appointment to the Winchester Circuit was announced by Bishop Andrew in the autumn of 1843, he at the same time read out the name of Chauncey Hobart, as preacher in charge of Jacksonville, the town in which my father lived.

I have before spoken of the stronger than Masonic bond uniting Methodist preachers, especially those living in the newer regions of the country, whose lives are exposed to privation and hardship. As I was accustomed to spend the few "rest days" which each round of the circuit allowed me under my father's roof, it is not to be wondered at that an affectionate intimacy quickly sprang up between Chauncey and myself, notwithstanding he was a dozen years my senior. Nearly all the waking hours of my visits at home, we spent together, and almost every month he would pass several days with me on my circuit, "taking a through," as it was called, wherein we preached and exhorted time about.

Chauncey was born in Vermont, but removed when a child, with his father, to the "Military Tract" lying between the Illinois and Mississippi Rivers, while this was yet almost an Indian country. Here he grew up a backwoods farmer, his only opportunity to get "a schooling" being an occasional "quarter" in the winter time. He was converted under the ministry of some of our pioneer preachers; joined the church, and soon became an itinerant. He was tall and large-limbed, with a noble head, fronted by a magnificent forehead, and a face beaming at once with intelligence and kindness. One day, finding his boots in a leaky condition, he stopped at the shop of a frontier cobbler to get them repaired. While the son of Crispin was at work with awl and hammer, another person entered, who gazing with fixed attention at the pedal extremities of my friend, exclaimed, with mingled astonishment and admiration:

"Well, I never! Stranger, I resign in your favor."

"I beg your pardon," said the *pro-tempore* bootless divine; "I don't comprehend you."

"Howsomdever notwithstanding," replied the other, "I resign to you. You see, I have always been called President of the Track Society in these parts, because the people said my feet was as large as good-sized spades; but I give in, for I swear I never see a man of such powerful understanding as you."

I mention this incident to illustrate at once the genial temper of my friend, for no man could more keenly appreciate the joke, and the well developed size of his *physique.* Within the bounds of one of his first circuits was a little village, into which had recently removed some people of the better class from New England. As he walked forth once at eventide to meditate, on the edge of the settlement, his ear was caught by a concord of sweet sounds, borne upon the breeze. He stopped to listen, and exclaimed with rapture: "Was ever such a set of sheep-bells heard!" He was listening to a pianoforte for the first time. A genuine child of the woods, he was truly a great man. Quick of observation, with a judgment calm and trustworthy; a courage characterized no less by modesty than intrepidity, a disposition frank and fearless, as it was generous, and a soul that felt the things invisible and eternal as if they had been tangible and palpable. He was one of the noblest men I have ever known. He had wrought faithfully, exercising the gift that was in him to approve himself a workman that needed not to be ashamed. By dint of indefatigable industry, he had gained not a little knowledge from books, which was seasoned to use by common sense and experience. All that he had was at the service of his friends, especially at mine, for I became to him as a son in the Gospel. He has ever loved the frontier, where the work was hardest, while the fare and pay are poorest. With gifts and graces that would render him eminent in a metropolitan pulpit, he has chosen to forego ease and wealth and fame, that he might be among the foremost to preach the glad tidings in the cabins of the wilderness. There was nothing morose or gloomy in his piety, for he was ever the most cheerful of companions; having learned, in whatever situation he was, therewith to be content. He was healthful in mind and body, and his soul was buoyant as a lark. It would have made all the blood in your body tingle to hear him shout, "Glory to God for the hope of everlasting life." The judgment-seat of Christ, Heaven and Hell, were not to him metaphors or myths; but awful realities, in whose light he walked by day and night. Self-depreciation was almost the only fault I ever detected in him. But his trust in the living God was invincible, and he seemed to enjoy the full assurance of faith. He was a thorough Methodist; and surely John Wesley never had a more worthy disciple. He believed the doctrines and obeyed the discipline of the church, from love of them. He revered the memory of the founder, honored his institutions, and fulfilled the duties of his place with unquestioning submission. His zeal was unquenchable; and his one hope was, that he might have souls for his hire, and at last hear the Master say, "Well done, good and faithful servant."

Such was the man who blessed the early years of my ministerial life with his confidence and affection; and never did David love Jonathan more warmly than I loved Chauncey Hobart. David owed Jonathan less, and I feel pretty sure that he was my "guide, philosopher, and friend." From him I received the first satisfactory instruction in the art of preaching; and I often said to him that if I ever became a preacher I would give him the credit due to his unfailing kindness. I sketch my friend not only as a grateful duty, thus recording some of the virtues of a man to whom I am under weighty and profound obligations, but as a representative of the best class of Methodist preachers, many of whom it has been my happiness to call friends. When I state, therefore, that I have been reared under the influences of such men, nurtured in their views, and habituated for years to an implicit acceptance of their doctrinal opinions, it can easily be seen from the first part of this chapter how far I had wandered from the paths of my youth.

Ah! Thomas Carlyle, you have much to answer for, in sending adrift upon the fog banks, such raw and inexperienced boys as I was when your mighty genius found me out. Many a day of miserable doubt, and night of morbid wretchedness have you caused me. Yet for all that, I owe you more and love you better than any author of the time. "Sartor Resartus" first fell in my way while I was living in Washington, and I much question if Christopher

Columbus was more transported by the discovery of America, than I was in entering the new realm which this book opened to me. Everything was novel, huge, grotesque, or sublime; I must have read it twenty times over until I had it all by heart. It became a sort of touch-stone with me. If a man had read Sartor and enjoyed it, I was his friend; if not, we were strangers. I was almost as absurd as a Kentucky girl, of whom it is stated, that on a gentleman's introduction to her, her first observation invariably was, "Have you read Moore's Melodies?" I had not been long in Montgomery before I had read every word that Mr. Carlyle had ever published. I was as familiar with the everlasting Nay, the Centre of Indifference, and the everlasting Yea, as with the side walk in front of my house. From Herr Teufelsdroeckh I took the Teutonic fever, which came nigh costing me so dear. It became incumbent on me to read what he had read, to admire what he admired, to scout what he scouted; I was a hero worshipper of the most approved sort, and hated cant and Sir Jabez Windbag with due intensity. What a witches' dance I had of it through those years; the wizards and Brocken never had a wilder. Mr. Carlyle's books had much the same power over me, that Mephistophiles exercised over Faust—I at least might have chanted the chorus to the ignis-fatuus:

"The limits of the sphere of dream,
The bounds of true and false are past;
Lead me on thou wandering gleam,
Lead me onward far and fast,
To the wide, the desert waste.
But see how swift advance and shift
Trees behind trees, row by row—
How cliff, by cliff, rocks bend and lift
Their frowning foreheads as we go,
The giant-snouted crags—ho; ho;
How they snort, and how they blow."

Scarcely less appropriate, as descriptive of the tumultuous state of my mind and its commotion, which almost threatened at times to end in hallucination, would be the description of the tempest, in Faust.

"A cloud thickens the night,
Hark! how the tempest crashes through the forest;
The owls fly out in strange affright,
The columns of the evergreen palaces
Are split and shattered.
The roots creak and stretch and groan,
And ruinously overthrown;
The trunks are crushed and shattered
By the fierce blast's unconquerable stress.
Over each other crack and crash they all
In terrible and intertangled fall,
And through the ruins of the shaken mountain
The airs hiss and howl—
It is not the voice of the fountain,
Nor the wolf in his midnight prowl.

Dost thou not hear?
  Strange accents are ringing
Aloft, afar, anear;
  The witches are singing!
The torrents of a raging wizard's song
Streams the whole mountain along."

A remarkable goblin crew, was that to which my new guide had introduced me. This is not the place to attempt a critical estimate of the genius of Mr. Carlyle; yet I could not forbear to mention one who had so much to do with my life and character. Years have passed since he led me forth to the dance of ghosts, and I have learned to read him with a less feverish enthusiasm, but I believe with a more genuine appreciation of his rare and extraordinary powers. He did me harm, but he has helped me to far more good. With all his defects, to me he stands first among the men of this generation. Honor, long life, health and peace to thee, Thomas Carlyle, is the message which a friend wafts from beyond the sea.

About a year and a half after my removal to Montgomery, it happened that I was invited to attend the funeral of a prominent citizen. A discourse was to be delivered by one of my brother ministers, whose name I had often heard, but with whom I had no acquaintance. He belonged to the Methodist Protestant Church, between which and our own, there was little or no intercourse. Besides performing the duties as pastor of a small congregation, he was the principal of a large female school. I had heard it incidentally said that he was a man of considerable cleverness, and withal of a poetical temperament. Nothing, however, that I had heard concerning him had excited the slightest interest, or awakened the desire to form his acquaintance. I therefore entered the church to attend the funeral service with no feeling save that of sympathy for the bereaved family. The minister announced his text and in a rather tremulous manner proceeded with his introduction. The language was accurate, the style chaste, the thought striking and profound. Borrowed! said I to myself, and no credit given; but he will find his own level presently. The critic sat intrenched in his indifference, awaiting the catastrophe which must terminate this Icarian flight. But the catastrophe did not come, and the critic was driven out of his strong position, and admiring wonder soon gave place to tears and a heart suffused with the glow of a religious emotion such as had not been experienced for many a month. As I left the church, I felt that I had never listened to so wonderful a preacher, and I think so still, after having heard most of the renowned pulpit orators in England and America. It was as if, upon the copious diction, the calm, elevated philosophic thought of Channing, had been ingrafted the vital energy and evangelical fervor of John Wesley.

Yet it is hard to say wherein his special power lies; there is such a harmonious blending of gifts and grace. Allowance must be made for a bad voice, the result of a diseased throat; and for a self-distrust which amounts to the shrinking timidity of a girl. His strength is in the tongue, for he speaks incomparably better than he writes—the magnetism of a listener is essential to his full inspiration. His intellect is athletic as it is subtile, delicate as it is strong. But for me the charm of the man lay in his genuine, unaffected piety, his rich experience of the deep things of God. In him reverence was profound as the source of life, yet without the slightest shadow of superstition. Faith seemed to have wrought its highest results in his character, and to have become the evidence of things not seen, the substance of things hoped for. His love toward God and man showed itself in unfaltering obedience to the divine law, and in a tender regard for his fellow-beings, which took all the shapes of compassion, forbearance, toleration, courtesy, sympathy, benignity, as personal relations required. But I am anticipating, for I did not come to all this knowledge of the man at once. After the discourse in question, I inquired of a number of persons if this was his usual style of preaching; for, notwithstanding that my doubts as to the genuineness of the production had been laid, my surprise could not but vent itself in an occasional query. I was answered that he always preached as well, and usually better. Thereupon I fell into a great disgust toward the people of Montgomery; for they did not appear to have discovered that they had one of the greatest living preachers among them. As I lay weltering in my chaos, it looked as if God had sent an angel to succor me. I therefore went to him at once, and said, "If thy heart is as my heart, give me thy hand." From that time until I quitted Montgomery, a part of almost every day was spent in his society. Such was the commencement of my acquaintance with Andrew A. Lipscomb, whose influence over me, together with that of Chauncey Hobart and Thomas Carlyle, forms the most significant and important chapter of my mental history during these ten years.

In Mr. Lipscomb there was not only a singular union of the old and of the new, the learning of the schools and the simplicity of the Gospel, but also of metaphysical acumen with spiritual insight. He seemed to breathe the atmosphere of prayer, and yet walked upon the firm ground of reason. His religion was devout, but without an accent of cant. His sensibilities stood him in the stead of a powerful imagination, enabling him to reproduce most perfectly my morbid consciousness, and thus did he minister to a mind diseased. I was fond of quoting, "Do the duty that is nearest thee; thy next duty will become plainer!"

But that nearest duty, alas, which is it? To reach truth, of course. But truth, what is it? and where? At the bottom of the well? I had very nearly broken my neck and got drowned besides, seeking it there. No. Truth is in your home, among your neighbors and in the fellowship of the church; and clear views of it can be acquired more easily and wisely by carrying the heart into practical life, than by stretching the neck and straining the eyes in gazing at the milky way, or at its reflection in a mud-puddle. Eat more, sleep more, and take tea with your parishioners; romp with the children, talk to the negroes, and believe that a man should read to live, not live to read. Go fishing, visit the sick, and become heartily interested in the poor and ignorant. Get the material for your sermons out of the lives of the people, rather than from speculations of the sages. Read John Bunyan for his English, and the Bible not only for its English, but because the entrance of "that Word giveth light: it giveth understanding to the simple." Cultivate the charities and sympathies of common life; apply yourself to the rhetoric of the market-place; be able to discuss the making of bread and darning of stockings with the good housewife, and relish that discussion too. Above all, as thou hast known the Scriptures from a child, cultivate a deep and reverent confidence in its holy teachings. "Remember the instructions of thy father and forsake not the law of thy mother," whose godly counsels nourish the highest instincts of our being;—

"Those first affections,
Those shadowy recollections,
Which, be they what they may,
Are yet the fountain light of all our day,
Are yet a master light of all our seeing;
Uphold us, cherish, and have power to make
Our noisy years seem moments in the being
Of the eternal Silence: truths that wake,
To perish never;
Which neither listlessness, nor mad endeavor,
Nor Man, nor Boy,
Nor all that is at enmity with joy,
Can utterly abolish or destroy!"

It is a difficult thing for the proud intellect, confident of its own resources, to appreciate the meaning of that prayer of our Saviour's, "I thank thee, O Father, Lord of heaven and earth, because thou hast hid these things from the wise and prudent, and hast revealed them unto babes. Even so, Father; for so it seemed good in thy sight." Nor is it easy for oracular self-conceit, to credit that He prescribed the one great condition of Christian discipleship when he took a little child and set him in the midst of his followers, and said: "Whosoever will not receive the kingdom of Heaven as a little child shall not enter therein." My passage through Rationalism was not easily or quickly accomplished. Two years after this date, I was arraigned before the Alabama Conference on complaint of heresy, but with no acrimonious or harsh intent. And I here must be allowed to bear witness to the uniform consideration and kindness which were extended to me by my brethren in the ministry. They treated me on the principle that time and experience would work the best cure, and I trust they have had no cause to regret their leniency. I have heard somewhere in the rural districts the following prescription for invalids: "Let the patient go to the 'bars' at milking time and stand so close to the cows that they can breathe in his face." I cannot tell how this may operate in chronic disorders of the body, but I know that a hearty interest in homely things and a genuine love of the common people are the best cure for neology, the chief element of which I take to be egotism, and the sublimest manifestation of which is doubtless somewhat dependent on dyspepsia, neuralgia, or the liver complaint. When the diagnosis of doubt is fully set forth, I fancy that physiology will have as much to do with it as psychology.

CHAPTER XX.

ON THE ROAD AGAIN.

It must not be supposed that because I had taken to hard study, or addicted myself to metaphysics, I had altogether abandoned the road. During my six years' residence in Alabama, I was accustomed to spend a good part of the summer and fall of every other year in extensive journeys through the State, generally preaching once or twice a day. The monotony of student life was thus relieved, and I had the fullest opportunity to become acquainted with the life and habits of the Southern people. I was once riding from Tuscaloosa to Greensborough, a day's journey, forty miles; the only passenger for the first two hours was a little music teacher from down East, who spent most of his time on the box with the driver. As I lay extended on the front seat, enjoying the fumes of my cigar, my head leaning out of one window and my feet protruding from the other, the stage suddenly stopped in front of a plantation gate, and I found that we were to have another passenger, whose air and tone bespoke him a man of the world. His good byes to friends were soon said, and as he mounted with some difficulty to his place, I discovered that he had the gout; he waved adieu, and the stage rolled off, but not until I had caught the words, "God bless you, Sam!" Every gentleman in the South is supposed to smoke, so pulling out my case, I offered him a cigar. He lit, the conversation commenced, and as a matter of course, politics was the first subject broached. He was a lawyer, had been an editor, and I was not long in ascertaining his identity. He was a New England man, born and bred, but had resided many years in the South. He had a brother in the Senate of the United States, who was as noted for his free-soil opinions, as my new companion was decided in his aversion to them. From politics we turned to books, then to men, and so on to matters and things in general. In due time, the hamper of good things with which I was provided was produced, and breaking bread together, we became confidential.

"I suppose," he said, "you're a brother of mine—a sprig of the law?"

"Not at all," I replied, indisposed to surrender my personality so easily.

"An editor, then?"

"No."

"What! is it possible that you give people calomel and jalap, and cut off arms and legs?"

"No indeed; I am not such a barbarian."

"You are not a planter?"

"No."

"In heaven's name then, what are you?"

"Nothing much," I replied, "but a poor scholar."

Just then we stopped at the half-way house in Havanna; slapping me on the knee, he said with great *bonhomie:*

"Whatever else you are, you're a thundering good fellow. There's a juicery here; let us get out and wet our whistles with some bald-faced whisky."

I declined his polite invitation, and he drank alone. We chatted along pleasantly through the afternoon, and he favored me with his views upon the deleterious influences of Puritanism, based upon his own experience of the tendency to reaction from early rigid restraint. He denounced Calvinism fiercely, and said that it was chargeable to a large extent for the infidelity and ultraism of his native land, and added that he had only found refuge from deism and atheism, in the teachings of Emanuel Swedenborg. The Swedish seer, it seemed, had been making not a few proselytes among the members of the bar upon his circuit. After he had descanted at length on the true Christian religion, in a style more emphatic than proper, for the leaven of mystical contemplation had not succeeded in purging his conversation from an occasional oath, I observed that I had read a number of the books of Swedenborg and of his principal disciples.

"What the dickens haven't you read, I should like to know?" he interrupted.

"But," I continued, "it is hardly to be expected that I should become a "receiver," and at the same time remain a Methodist preacher."

"A Methodist preacher!" he shouted. "You! If I had been out with a rifle to shoot parsons, I should never have pulled trigger at you." Then, recollecting himself, he said, "Is it possible that I have the pleasure of travelling with Mr. ——?" and pronounced my name.

I assured him that I was the person mentioned.

"What a fool I am!" he continued; "I might have known it, if I had the sense I was born with. I heard that you were coming down this road, and so laid over two days at the house of a friend, to avoid you. I don't like parsons as a general thing, but I confess that I am fairly caught, and moreover, I am not sorry for it."

He then apologized for swearing, saying that it was such a habit in his part of the country, that men were scarce conscious of it, unless they found themselves in the presence of women or of ministers. By this time we had reached our journey's end, and parted; but I have no recollection of a pleasanter stage ride than that.

At another time I was on my way from Montgomery to Tuscaloosa, a distance of one hundred and thirty or forty miles. We had ridden eighteen hours, and stopped at the town of Marion to dine. A number of the passengers left the stage at this place, and their seats were taken by others; among these were a gentleman and two ladies, who, of course, occupied the back seat. As I was immediately opposite, on the front seat, the elder of the ladies commenced a conversation with me. I was a stranger to every one of the party, and it must be premised that a leather cap, linen overcoat, a figure completely covered with dust (for the season was very dry), and withal an exceedingly youthful appearance, did not render my presence very imposing.

"Travelling, sir?" she began in a voice which at once revealed to me her New England origin.

"Yes, madam, as far as Tuscaloosa."

"Ah, I see; on your way to college."

"No."

"What! you are not going to take a course, then?"

"I left college some time since."

"You've been to college?"

"Yes, madam."

"What one?"

"Illinois College."

"Ah, I guess that don't amount to much. Where do you live, sir?"

"I can scarce be said to live anywhere; but I have been spending some time in Montgomery."

"Ah, in Montgomery—do you know the Rev. Mr. Milburn of that place?"

"Yes, ma'am, I have some acquaintance with him," I replied, with entire self-possession.

"I've had a great desire to hear him preach," she continued. "My husband, niece and myself stopped in Montgomery last Saturday, but unfortunately I was taken very ill in the night at the hotel, and was so sick all the next day, that none of us could get out to church. We were very much disappointed."

"I don't think you missed much."

"What do you mean, sir?" she said, rather tartly.

"Only that I heard him preach twice on Sunday, and I didn't think much of the sermons."

"You didn't think much of the sermons," she replied, with a sneer. "I think it perfectly disgusting to hear the young men of the present age talk about ministers; that's the regular cant; nothing is eloquent or great enough for our would-be smart young men. If an angel from heaven were to come down and preach, I suppose you would criticise him. Your mother ought to have taught you better, sir, than to speak slightingly of eminent divines; I'd have done it, if I had been your mother. Birch oil--birch oil, sir, is the thing that's wanted in the education of these times."

"Really, ma'am," I replied, with great humility; "I had no notion of disparaging Mr. Milburn, or of hinting the slightest disrespect toward the Christian ministry."

"Oh, no; of course you hadn't."

After a moment she resumed, "I suppose you mean to study law?"

"No."

"Medicine?"

"No."

"Ah, you're going to be a planter and not a professional man?"

"I am a sort of a professional man now."

"You a professional man—I should like to know what profession you belong to?"

"I am a preacher, ma'am."

"A preacher!" she exclaimed, with unfeigned surprise, "do you belong to any church?"

"Yes."

"To what church?"

"To the Methodist."

"Oh, I beg your pardon," she said; "I thought from your appearance you must be one of the Comeouters. We are just from Boston, where we've been visiting our friends, and they've a dreadful lot of people there that wear long hair, and look very frowzy, and are called Comeouters. I don't know where they came from, but I can guess where they're going to. I thought you must be one of them," then bethinking herself, she repeated. "To the Methodist church? I see how it is. Young man," she proceeded, with great solemnity, "envy and jealousy are the meanest passions that rankle in the human bosom, and I am afraid that nothing is more common than for young ministers to have such feelings toward their elders and their betters. Let me warn you against indulging that, for it looks to me very much as if you had such feelings toward the gentleman of whom we have been speaking. You are just beginning life—get rid of them or they will ruin you."

"I am very much obliged to you for your good advice, but really I am not aware that I am the victim of these bad passions, and Mr. Milburn is the last man in the world, of whom I would be jealous or envious."

"You may think so; but oh! the heart is deceitful and desperately wicked." She then went on in a more cheerful tone, "May I take the liberty of asking your name?"

"Certainly, madam; my name is Milburn."

"Ah!" she said, "any relation to the gentleman of whom we have been speaking?"

"To tell you the truth, I am not aware that there is any other person of that name in Montgomery."

"Are you the pastor of a Methodist church there?"

"I am; and you must allow me to thank you for the manner in which you have defended me from myself." Soon after, we reached Greensborough, where we went our several ways, and I saw them no more.

Early in the month of July, 1852, I was again on my way to Tuscaloosa, but this time from Mobile. I had stopped at various places to preach, and had become not a little exhausted by reason of the labor and the excessive heat. Nevertheless, as I had appointments for every day in the next four months, extending through a wide region of country, it was necessary to push on without regard to weakness. I had quitted the house of a friend in the canebrake early one morning, hoping to reach Greensborough, forty miles off, by night. My conveyance was a one-horse buggy; the driver a kind-hearted old negro. By eleven o'clock I found myself growing faint, and requested Uncle Sam to stop at the first house, that I might rest. A gate was soon reached, and lifting me from the carriage, Sam supported me to the door, in which stood a damsel, to whom I said, "May I have leave to rest here a little while? I don't feel very well." Perhaps my pallid, ghostly appearance scared her, for without a word she pointed to a room on the right, and then fled with precipitation.

Sam had hardly laid me upon the bed when I fell

into a deep swoon, from which I did not recover for an hour. As consciousness began to revive, I found the kind-hearted negro sedulously engaged in rubbing and fanning me.

"Can't you get something to strengthen me, Sam?" I feebly said.

"No, massa," he replied; "dey got nothin but whisky; and dere nothin but trash, poor, mean white folks; dey won't come a-near you, nor do a hand's turn for you, 'cause dey think you got de cholera, and dey catch it. Never mind, massa," he said in a cheery way, "I kin nuss you;" then adding with the finest scorn, "dey's nothin but nasty piney woods people, nohow."

His untiring exertions, together with a bucket of cool water which he brought from the well, restored me so far that in another hour I was ready for the road.

As we drove away, the indignant old fellow exclaimed: "I hope de Lord will strike dat house wid lightning, and kill all dem people's geese and chickens. Dey don't own no colored people, so dey ain't nobody."

We had not proceeded more than ten miles, when I again felt the need of rest, and desired him to draw rein at the first house. We entered a plantation, and stopped before the porch of a house, where an old, infirm man was seated. I stated my case to him, but had hardly done so, when he said in a most cordial manner: "Come in, come in, my dear sir, the house and all that it contains are at your service."

Sam helped me to the drawing-room, where I was no sooner placed upon the sofa, than I sank into another deep swoon. When I awoke and could look about me, it was so dark that I thought it must be night. The day had been brilliantly beautiful, scarce a cloud could be seen, except along the southwestern horizon, where piles of white vapor seemed reposing. But within an hour these had risen and overspread the firmament, and gave dark and threatening token of elemental war. I tottered to the porch to gaze at the coming storm, the air was close and sultry, an awful stillness reigned, broken only by a low, distant sigh, heard ever and anon, or a terrified bellow from the frightened cattle. Presently an alarming spectacle made its appearance in the sky, coming from south of west. It was a black, pear-shaped cloud, with its stem toward the earth, surcharged with lightning, thunder and tempest. Now it looked like an out-spread umbrella, with its handle near the ground, its bending top a sheet of vivid flame, ribbed with zig-zag flashes. Then it became compact, and resembled an inverted cone, and soon after it seemed a funnel through which the contents of some fearful caldron were pouring.

Lightnings of all colors streamed from it and in every direction, straight and zig-zag toward heaven and earth, and in transverse lines toward every point of the compass; the thunder, loud as a thousand pieces of artillery, seemed one prolonged concussion; but even over this din rose the roar of the wind. The rain fell in foaming sheets, and its white floods, all fire-wreathed, lent a spectral horror to the sepulchral gloom. Fortunately, our house was on the remotest verge of the tornado, which had here compressed itself within narrow limits, and swept along with astounding velocity, finding the fruitful bounty and joyous verdure of summer, but leaving desolation and ruin. My energies were prostrate, my nerves unstrung; and I believe that, overpowered by the electrical state of the air, I experienced, for the first time, physical terror in all its intensity. I crept to the door of one of the family rooms and tapped. It was opened by a matronly woman, who said in the gentlest tone:

"What will you have?"

"I am alarmed, may I come and sit with you?"

She took my hand, led me to a seat, and with the kindest assiduity sought to soothe my apprehensions and quiet my fears. She laid aside her own alarm that she might minister to a helpless and suffering stranger.

In another hour the sky was almost clear of clouds, and the sinking sun threw his farewell beams up the vault of heaven, which never seemed more beautifully blue. All around the east

> "Shone the million colored bow,
> The sphere fire above its soft colors wove,
> While the moist earth was laughing below."

As twilight was deepening into darkness, I entered the gate and bade my driver stop at the foot of a hill, on whose top, not many yards distant, stood the house of one of my Greensborough friends. The delicious coolness and balmy air of evening had invigorated me, and I was disposed to terminate this rather trying day with a little sport. It was too dark for persons in the house to recognize one at any distance, so putting my hand to my mouth to disguise the voice, I shouted, "Halloo the house."

"What do you want?"

"Some supper and a bed."

"Go to the hotel and get them."

"I had rather stay here."

"But we don't keep tavern."

"I can't help that, you'll have to keep me."

"Leave my yard at once," shouted my friend, fairly excited.

"Never a bit of it," I replied, and began to get out of the buggy. By this time, the entire household had collected at the front door, and lights had been brought, so that my movements were discovered. My friend, the Doctor, was a man of small stature, but high-spirited and bold as a lion.

"What do you mean, sir?" he cried, as he came bounding down the hill. "Leave these premises instantly, or I'll put you out, neck and heels."

"Doctor! Doctor!" shouted his wife, hardly able to speak for laughing (for woman's more delicate ear had detected the voice, notwithstanding its disguise) "Don't you know who it is? It is Brother ——."

I need hardly say I was not kicked out. Warm hearts and good cheer and the long talk about Europe, whither my friend had been since we last met, made a bright and happy night after a day of weakness and suffering. God bless thee, and all that are dear to thee, my noble hearted friend, Doctor Tom Webb.

In the morning I was up with the lark, and went on my way rejoicing, nor did I miss one of my appointments during the next four months.

CHAPTER XXI.

SOUTHERN CHARACTER.

According to the law of the Methodist Church, a preacher can only remain two years in charge of one society. At the expiration of my time in Montgomery, I was transferred to Mobile and appointed to the St. Francis street Church. That pleasant little city, by the by, was my home for four years. When my time in St. Francis street expired, the bishop made me city missionary, in which capacity it would have been possible for me to remain permanently; and I suppose that Mobile would then have been my home and my grave. It came near being the latter; but the former, it was not destined to be.

We bought a cottage on the edge of the town, and with about half an acre of ground, embarked in that most hazardous of all undertakings, making improvements. We laid out a garden and planted the different kinds of vegetables and flowers, but somehow or other they would not grow satisfactorily. Having a cow, we built a two-story stable, containing, besides a carriage house and stalls for several horses and cows, a loft for hay, corn, oats, etc., a neat room for servants. In one of my visits to the country, a friend, thinking that I needed exercise, presented me with a valuable saddle horse. By the way, I must here indulge in an episode illustrating a curious superstition of southwestern steamboat-men. In my endeavor to transport my quadruped to Mobile, I spent three days on a river bank, hailing every boat that passed, and desiring them to receive my steed and myself on board as passengers, but in vain. The captains all knew me, and would have been glad to serve me, but not at such a fearful risk of fire, explosion, collision, or snagging, as would have been involved in carrying a parson and a grey mare. They would take either separately, but not both; and after a number of fruitless attempts to keep together, we were obliged to divide, I going by one boat, leaving her to follow by the next.

A saddle horse is an expensive comfort in the city, and my wife averred that mine would eat her own head off in six months, that the idea of a Methodist preacher, on a narrow stipend, keeping a horse for an occasional ride, was preposterous and not to be tolerated. The wife of one of our neighbors had been delighting herself in a little speculation, to wit, driving a dray; that is to say, having a horse and a negro man, neither of whom had anything to do, she purchased a dray and set the man to driving it.

Glowing accounts of the profitable returns from this investment fired my wife's imagination, and we bought a dray; but neither of us could drive, nor were any of our children large enough to do so. We therefore did what was considered the next best thing—hired an Irishman. The Irish have one peculiarity, there is nothing they cannot do. My horse was a saddle-beast, and had never been broken to harness, but our man declared that he could break her just as easy as rolling off a log, that he had broken horses all his life. I do not believe that he had ever anything to do with a horse before. As I never had a knack for business, my wife agreed to engineer this project. The driver was to get twenty-five dollars a month and be found, the horse food was to be paid for, the cost of the dray and harness to be replaced in the family fund, and then all the profits were to inure to my spouse as pin money; but, alas, the profits never came, the horse stalled with her first load, which Patrick was to take seven miles, and for which he was to receive four dollars and a half. He worried the poor beast so much, and beat her so cruelly, that she was never fit for harness afterward. When we retired from the transportation and forwarding business, drays were not in demand; we did not even succeed in forcing a sale, and the vehicle stood in the yard until the sun and the rain took it to pieces.

About this time the chicken fever was prevailing

as an epidemic. Of course we took it. My brother, who was the first member of the family attacked by this disease, presented my wife with a pair of Shanghais, costing ten dollars. The possession of so remarkable a pair of fowls awakened in us a lively interest toward this branch of natural history. We obtained the various books which treated of it, and became exceeding learned in chicken lore. We added to our improvements, by the erection of a spacious hen-house, and by fencing a handsome inclosure for the benefit of the broods we were going to have. We did not mean to eat the monster birds, but desired to raise them for sale, that we might thereby turn an honest penny. But Shanghais soon became very common, and although our first pair had multiplied exceedingly, there was no demand for the article. Still our ardor was not cooled. We attended a chicken fair, and were ravished by the incredibly long legs appertaining to a magnificent pair of feathered bipeds, styled "Brama Pootras," for which the modest price of fifty dollars was asked. The chief trait of these remarkable birds, so far as I have been able to discover, was that they could stand on the floor and eat corn from a table, and enough of it in the course of a day to supply a good sized family with bread for the same length of time. Several of our neighbors told us that if we would buy the fowls, they would each take a dozen eggs, at the rate of twelve dollars a dozen. What a stroke of fortune; the goose that laid the golden egg had come to us at last. The Brama Pootras were ours. But where were they to be kept? Although the hen-house was padlocked at night; cunning thieves, used to robbing hen-roosts, could easily remove that obstacle. We were oppressed with all the weight of care which newly-found riches are wont to bring. After much deliberation, it was decided to give them the carriage-house, and it was a matter of no little moment to see them safely bestowed every evening and released in the morning. But when would the hen begin to lay? It became a subject of serious speculation to the neighborhood. Her aristocratic cackle was waited for with impatience. Friends inquired, day after day, if the important event had yet taken place; we were obliged to answer as cheerfully as we could, that it had not, then we moralized about "haste making waste," "Rome not being built in a day," etc., winding up by counselling patience. At length the cackle, so long waited for, was heard, and the entire family, white and black, old and young, hurried to look for the egg, and discovered to our horror that the barbarous chanticleer had with his beak pecked the precious deposit of his dame, and that the white and yolk were oozing from the fractured shell. I never heard that that hen laid another egg. Our fears that the hen-house might prove an unsafe asylum, were justified ere long, for one stormy night the door was forced, and of fifty Shanghais, not one was left. We began at once to recover from this attack of chicken fever, and our convalescence was soon pronounced complete. This disease is said to resemble the yellow fever in one respect—the patient never has it a second time; if he succeeds in living through it, he is supposed to be stronger for it ever after.

Since the failure of the dray and chicken business, we have not embarked in any mercantile operations.

In the matter of society, Mobile could safely challenge comparison with any city of the Union. Upon the Creole or native population had been ingrafted favorable specimens from almost every State in the Union, and from the principal nations of Europe. The circle was large enough to afford the richest variety, but not so large as to destroy unity. The leaven of the early French element had not ceased to work, but showed itself in the exquisite courtesy of the people's manners. Every city of the Republic has a topographical and no less a social physiognomy of its own. In Boston the test question as to a man is, What does he know? In New York, How much is he worth? In Philadelphia, Who are his relations? In Baltimore, Has he a good digestion? In Washington, How many votes can he command? In Charleston, Who was his grandfather? In Cincinnati, How many hogs does he kill? In Chicago, How many "corner lots" does he own? In St. Louis, Has he an interest in the Fur Company? In New Orleans, south of Canal street, How much cotten does he sell? North of Canal street, How does he dance and dress? In Mobile, Is he a man of good manners?

Throughout the South, whether in city or country, there is an attention paid to the proprieties and courtesies of life, which I have failed to observe in some other parts of the Union—a reverence for age, deference to childhood, a polite regard for equals, a kind tone to the poor, treatment of the negro as if he were one of the family, and a truly chivalric bearing toward women. I believe that it is a universal practice there for a man to uncover when saluting a lady—not simply to raise the hat from the head, but to let it fall as low as the knee, while she passes. Mr. Thackeray pays a deserved tribute to the men of our country, in his lecture on "Charity and Humor." "I will tell you when I have been put in mind of two of the finest gentlemen books bring us any mention of—I mean *our* books (not books of history, but books of humor). I will tell you when I have been put in mind of the courteous gallantry of the noble knight, Sir Roger de Coverley, of Coverley Manor, of the noble Hidalgo Don Quixote of La Mancha—here, in your own omnibus-carriages and railway cars, when I have seen a woman step in, handsome or not, well-dressed or not, and a workman in hob-nailed shoes, or a dandy in the height of the fashion, rise up and give her his place. I think, Mr. Spectator, with his short face, if he had seen such a deed of courtesy, would have smiled a sweet smile to the doer of that gentleman-like action, and have made him a low bow from under his great periwig, and have gone home and written a pretty paper about him. I am sure Dick Steele would have hailed him, were he dandy or mechanic, and asked him to share a bottle, or perhaps half a dozen." But nowhere have I seen the homage to woman, thus fitly commemorated, so fervent, refined, complete, as in the Southern States. Many a time, in that land, have I listened with wondering delight, as when under the spell of music, to the tones of a man's voice as he conversed with a lady. There was no trick of conventional affability, no conscious and voluntary deference put on for the occasion, no cockney lisp or stammer, or mannerism of honeyed condescension; but the thing signified by the symbol of an obeisance, wherein self-respect maintains its noblest attitude, by bending lowly in presence of something more beautiful and sacred. Manhood shows no symptom of reaction from the education of the fireside, and the reverent loyalty toward "mother," combined with a cherishing affection for sisters, is carried forth into society.

It is rare to hear a fine voice in the North. There must be a quality in the atmosphere which we breathe, to brace and stiffen the muscles of the throat, and to narrow the orifice of the mouth, so that a part of our vocal tone is obliged to escape through the nose. The unventilated state of our lungs, and the imperfect development of the chest, so dismally manifest in the prevalence of pulmonary diseases, conspire to bereave us of much that is sweetest and most beautiful in that finest organ of humanity, the voice. But it is not so in the full throat, the deep chest, of the South, where the lungs do not fear to welcome the profound inspiration of a genial, balmy ether. In the North, people seem to be fearful that the respectability of their position is not assured; and that they must therefore guard it, in chilly isolation, by a stiff reserve.

Our educated men, lured by the prospect of gain and distinction, are centralized in the great cities; while money is used for investment in stocks, for the purchase, in fashionable neighborhoods, of stately houses with brown stone fronts, and for maintaining a style of extravagant civic outlay. "Going to the country," for the most part, means the stay of a few weeks at a fashionable watering-place, where the routine and excitement of conventional life are aggravated. Over-work is charactered in lines of care on the face of almost every intellectual man you meet, and over-dressed is equally legible in the costly rustling costumes of the women. Men of fortune rarely seem desirous to become owners of large landed estates except for the purpose of speculation; they rarely hunt, and are as seldom good riders. Rural life has few charms for our educated women; social life is so badly organized that the present race of wives and mothers must expend their energies and achieve martyrdom in attempting to train raw Irish peasants to become serviceable domestics. And if they would fain reside among orchards and meadows, the chances are that they must perform their own household drudgery, at least a portion of the time, and be prepared for it on any emergency. Few of the sons of our farmers who acquire an education beyond what the common school affords, become farmers themselves, and few of the daughters of our wealthy and educated classes, but would think it beneath them to marry a farmer. The city, and the life of the city, have absorbing power and irresistible charm. The American citizen is apt to have no leisure, but leisure is necessary to society. North of the Potomac we have few country gentlemen, and yet country gentlemen and their families must ever constitute the nucleus of the best society.

It is not to be wondered at that there is an increasing attrition between those parts of our country styled Northern and Southern, for their directions and the types of their civilization are widely and growingly different; climate, the style of employment, the mode of life, the forms of society, the ideals of character are producing their definite and inevitable results.

If a Southern man makes a fortune by trade or in a profession, he at once invests in a plantation; if he reside in a city, it is an episode to afford the opportunity of good schools to his young children, or that he may attend to some pressing business; but his home and his heart are in the country, his estate is his pride, and in any event, several months of the year are sure to be passed there. Every gentleman keeps open house. In the coldest weather it is hardly allowable to close the front door, because it seems inhospitable. Friends in any number at a time, and even well-behaved strangers, are always welcome. The planter is an early riser, and his round of duties is usually completed by ten or eleven o'clock; thus he has the remainder of the day for literature and society. His first visit is to the hospital of the quarter, to care and prescribe for the sick; next to the nursery that he may look after the children, who are in charge of the old maumas; then to the fields, where the people are at work, or in the fall of the year to the gin-house, where the cotton is being cleaned and baled. He has labor enough to discipline his mind and exercise his body; imparting to both a manly energy and easy grace. He lives much in the society of women; thus his ways are softened and refined, and as the desire to be agreeable to those with whom they live, is an instinct with women; their constant and intimate association with husband, father, brothers, incites them to the study of graver topics, with an interest in higher themes than is customary in our crowded and hard-driven society.

It must not be supposed that the life of the mistress of a plantation is passed upon a bed of roses. Let me sketch one of these matrons, and she shall stand as a representative of her class; higher, it is true, than the average, but by no means a head and shoulders above them all.

Imagine a handsome and spacious mansion crowning a mound which lifts itself gently from a broad, alluvial plain. From the observatory on the roof, you may catch an occasional glimpse of the Black Warrior River on the east, and of the Tombigbee on the west, as their silvery currents shimmer through the funereal groves of cypress or fantastic groups of cotton-wood which line their banks. Belts of timber girdle the plain at intervals, marking the course of meandering creeks, while the landscape gains additional interest from the variety of orchards, fields of corn and cotton, and the long row of whitewashed cottages forming the village of the quarter, nestled under the leafy covert of the trees. That village is inhabited by several hundred negroes, big and little, all of whom look up to the mistress of this mansion as to a mother. She has a large family of boys and girls, whom she is rearing in the fear and love of God. She superintends the entire education of her daughters, and that of her sons as well, until they are prepared to enter college. The clothes for her people, as well as for her family, are all cut and made under her eye. Each negro on the place has, besides his patch of land for vegetables, a piece in which he can cultivate corn and cotton for himself, in his own time, for Wednesday and Saturday, from 12 M., are a holiday on every well ordered plantation. When the cotton is ginned and weighed, each person receives from the overseer a slip of paper, on which is written the quantity he has produced; this is carried to the mistress, who keeps a book in which each one is credited with his or her share. When the cotton is sold, the people receive their due in money or in such articles as they may have ordered, for the mistress attends to the purchases for them as carefully as for her own household. As colored people are very fond of barter, differences of opinion frequently arise, which, as among the more highly civilized portions of mankind, are apt to lead to wrangling and disputes. She has therefore caused the village to be erected into a municipal corporation, herself acting as recorder or as chief justice of the high court of errors. An election for sheriff, the only officer chosen by popular suffrage, is held once in six months. When a radical and irreconcilable difference of opinion arises between any two parties concerning their "perdjuce," poultry, or other rights and belongings, this magistrate is at once apprised; he then informs the mistress, who, causing the parties to be brought face to face in her presence, seeks to act as referee. If, however, the matter cannot thus be adjusted, the law of the commonwealth requires that the case shall proceed to trial. The sheriff summons a panel of six jurors, to whom the oath is administered that they will deal fairly and truly, without bias or prejudice. The chief justice is on the bench; plaintiff and defendant appear and have right of counsel; witnesses are examined, arguments are heard, the case summed up, the charge given, and the cause is submitted to the six men good and true; their decision is final. On Sunday, if there be no preacher at hand, she has religious service in the quarter, reading, then explaining and catechising, and joining devoutly with them in their hymns and prayers.

Thus it used to be at Rose Mount; but, alas! the people will look up to that mistress no more. I have never known a woman on whose tombstone the wise man's description could be more fitly graven:

"Who can find a virtuous woman? for her price is far above rubies.

"The heart of her husband doth safely trust in her, so that he shall have no need of spoil.

"She will do him good, and not evil, all the days of her life.

"She seeketh wool, and flax, and worketh willingly with her hands.

"She is like the merchant ships; she bringeth her food from afar.

"She riseth also while it is yet night, and giveth meat to her household, and a portion to her maidens.

"She considereth a field and buyeth it: with the fruit of her hands she planteth a vineyard.

"She girdeth her loins with strength, and strengtheneth her arms.

"She perceiveth that her merchandise is good: her candle goeth not out by night.

"She layeth her hands to the spindle, and her hands hold the distaff.

"She stretcheth out her hands to the poor; yea, she reacheth forth her hands to the needy.

"She is not afraid of the snow for her household; for all her household are clothed with scarlet.

"She maketh herself coverings of tapestry; her clothing is silk and purple.

"Her husband is known in the gates, when he sitteth among the elders of the land.

"She maketh fine linen and selleth it, and delivereth girdles unto the merchant.

"Strength and honor are her clothing; and she shall rejoice in time to come.

"She openeth her mouth with wisdom; and in her tongue is the law of kindness.

"She looketh well to the ways of her household, and eateth not the bread of idleness.

"Her children rise up and call her blessed; her husband, also, and he praiseth her.

"Many daughters have done virtuously, but thou excellest them all."

I may be allowed to sketch another Southern woman, the wife, not of a planter, but of a professional man. She is a person with the fine Grecian contour of whose head and face, and with whose stately figure you never associate the idea of age, but she must be approaching the forties. Her countenance, I should say, had never been beautiful, but it is more, for there reigns in it the expression of calm, benignant wisdom. There is nothing of studied elegance in her mien or of *statuesque hauteur* which often passes for repose of manner, but an indefinable blending of gracious kindness and simple dignity, which at once insures your confidence and awakens your reverence. She does not overawe you by her learning, although she has enough to qualify her for a professor's chair, nor fascinate you by her conversation, albeit few people talk as well; she is a finished woman of the world, and yet lives in a region high above the artifices of mere conventional life. In the longest acquaintance with her, you never hear her tongue debased to scandal or gossip, of which the well-bred are often as fond as the vulgar; yet is she mistress of all the lighter parts of conversation as well as of the graver. She never flatters you save with that most subtle and exquisite of all compliments, the interested and appreciative listening to your discourse, which inspires you to talk better with her than anywhere else. Servants, children and all simple folk revere and delight in her, while the wise and great find in her a companion fit for the fellowship of their selectest hours; yet she is not what is styled universally popular, for she has no magnetism with which to attract the frivolous, false and foolish. She is not a blue stocking, for there lives not a more thorough housekeeper or a more admirable cook. Her taste in dress is faultless, and she possesses an artist's eye for the harmony of colors. Plato, Bacon and Shakspeare are her handbooks, but she is not above darning stockings, teaching her negroes to read and write, and in an intimacy of years, I never saw her in other than an immaculate costume. With her I began the reading of Grote's "History of Greece," as the successive volumes made their appearance in England, and I am sure that Mr. Grote has never had a more appreciative reader on either side of the Atlantic. It was she that introduced me to Comte's "Positive Philosophy," while as yet it was almost unknown either in Great Britain or America (a capital prescription by the way for my then transcendental tendencies). Her reading has been wide, but more select than various, and she has studied more than read. With an intellect in which creative and reflective powers are singularly united to administrative faculty, her highest praise is that she is every inch a woman. On occasion, she could sail a ship, handle an army, or administer the affairs of the state or treasury departments, yet she is the ideal of a wife, mistress and friend. She will probably go down to the grave known only to that private circle, the measure of whose reverent love for her is gauged by the knowledge of her character and their own capacity to esteem the highest worth and loveliness; but if the juncture demanded, no woman of whom history tells us has played a nobler part than she is competent to do.

Next to the Bible, Shakspeare is more read in the South than any other book, and old books are usually preferred to new ones. The mind of the educated classes is occupied by affairs rather than by the production of literature. An instinct for politics, and a vivid interest in concerns of State, are well-nigh universal. Every gentleman is accustomed to administration, and the management of his plantation almost implies the capacity of a statesman. It is a national calamity, as well as a misfortune to personal character, in both ends of the Republic, that a question of such magnitude as that of American slavery should so far degenerate as to have become mere matter of partisan politics, a foot-ball for demagogues, a fertile field grown up in weeds, producing an exuberant annual harvest of paradoxes and platitudes, a theme the discussion of which involves acrid disputes and vituperative personal controversies. To deal with the fact, as justice demands it should be dealt with, requires candor, mutual forbearance, patience, courage, broad intelligence, and an enlightened Christian conscience; not the mind of a fanatic, or the temper of a desperado. All the men south of Mason's and Dixon's line are not thieves and robbers, any more than all north of it are fools and bigots. This is the one subject upon which Southern people are often unduly sensitive, compromising self-respect by inviting the views of strangers, or making a difference of opinion a personal affair. True, I have seen them display this weakness rather when in the free States than at home. I confess that I perceive no reason why people should not discuss the question of slavery as good-naturedly and reasonably as any other, and when this is introduced, if a man fly into a passion, or fall into a style of railing accusation, the conclusion is inevitable, that his cause is a bad one, or else that he is incompetent to deal with it. The people of the South have been grievously denounced, their conduct and character aspersed with the falsest and foulest of calumnies. I have myself read and heard hundreds of public statements concerning persons and events where I had been a witness of the transaction, or was acquainted with the parties, and perceived that either credulous ignorance or the spirit of gross perversion must have fathered such stories; more than this, I have known many a case where men and women entered Southern homes as guests, or stayed in them through the courtesy of the owners, receiving a bountiful hospitality and the most generous treatment, and yet have repaid all this by malevolent misrepresentations and slanderous falsehoods; nevertheless, I have to say, after a rather large acquaintance with men and manners in the South, that I never heard an uncivil word spoken to a stranger, whether in public conveyances or in private relations, and that I have never witnessed an act or look of rude suspicion or impertinent curiosity touching a man's views of the peculiar institution. On the contrary, if you bear about with you the tokens of a gentleman, I think you will agree with me that there is no country where a larger liberty of thought and expression is not only tolerated in the conversation of society, but solicited, and where the most decisive individuality is sacred from the attacks of inquisitorial impudence.

A tranquil self-respect, secure in the consciousness of its position, leisure attending upon labor that is not drudgery, and upon energies that are disciplined, not overwrought; an appreciative love of the best books, and a large experience of life; courtesy, not the result of conventional arrangements, but the outgrowth of a genial nature; an instinct educated within the hallowed circuit of the household, reverence for age, deference for woman and a full liquid voice are the constituents of the best society, such as is frequently found in the Southern States. All who have enjoyed its advantages and who have been capable of appreciating its excellence have borne delighted testimony to its wondrous magnetism, its unrivalled charm.

The first man who took me by the hand in Alabama, was Phillip P. Neely, as generous and noble-hearted a Methodist preacher as breathes. How well I remember our first dinner under the hospitable roof of our dear old Major Ryland; then there was Duke Goodman, with the soul of a prince and the guileless heart of a child; the refined and urbane James Sanders, the frank and genial Price Williams, and Col. Baker, who never heard a tale of distress but that his eyes overflowed with tears, and his hand gave more dollars than his eyes drops, with a host of others in Mobile who came to welcome me as unknown, and yet well known. When I went up the country, there was Colonel Joe Hutchinson, with a nature open and benign as the day, ever thenceforth my true yoke-fellow; the accomplished and scholarly Judge Ormond; Governor Collier, the consistent and upright; the jocund, steadfast Col. Garrit; the courtly and polished Wm. Henry Taylor; my neighbor Lewis Owen, unfailing in attentions, and unostentatious in his liberal providence; the impulsive and magnanimous Tom Brothers, Clayton C. Gillespie and Tom Foster, who became to me almost as sons in the Gospel; and best loved of all, my venerable friend, my second father, L. Q. C. de Yampert, whose house, heart, purse were always open to me. These and a thousand more from whom I received deeds and words of loving kindness were preachers or members of the church. When I turn from them to recall the names and forms of those, who though not bound to me by the ties of church-fellowship, nevertheless gave me confidence, cheer and love, and treated me as if I had been bone of their bone and flesh of their flesh, when I look back upon the six years of my residence in Alabama and remember how I received good and not evil at the hands of the people of Mobile, Montgomery and indeed the entire State, through all those days; I feel a new thrill as I read the words of the Psalmist, and believe that I understand them better than before: "If I forget thee, O Jerusalem, let my right hand forget her cunning. If I do not remember thee, let my tongue cleave to the roof of my mouth."

What man with a soul in him can wonder that I cherish the recollection of my life in the South, or that I love and honor the people there

CHAPTER XXII.

THE NEGRO.

EVERY stationed Methodist preacher in the South has the cure not only of the whites, but also of the colored people, and there are usually more of the latter in his parish than of the former. The galleries of the church are filled with negroes Sunday morning and evening, but the preacher is also expected to superintend the religious service sacred to themselves in the afternoon; preaching to them as often as his strength will allow, and administering the sacraments once a month. They have an official meeting of their own, composed of preachers, exhorters, stewards and leaders, for the transaction of their own business, of which he is the chairman, one of their own number acting as secretary. He sits as the presiding judge of their church trials, and if his character be such as to warrant the confidence, he is usually the umpire to whom is referred not only the minor difficulties of the church members, but of the colored people at large. He marries, baptizes and buries them; visits them in their houses, comforts them in their distresses, prays with them when on beds of sickness; is their counsellor, friend and spiritual guide. Singularly trustful and simple-hearted, for the most part, they admit him to their most sacred confidence. From him, they have scarce a secret. Few men, therefore, know the negro so well as the Methodist preacher, and no men are to-day exercising so powerful an influence over negro character in the South as the preachers of the Methodist and Baptist denominations. It cannot be denied that these are the only bodies of Christians that are doing much in that most important and desirable of all mission fields—the slave population of our southern States. Here and there, especially in the neighborhood of cities, you may see a colored Presbyterian or Episcopal church, but from Delaware to Texas, from Florida to Missouri, there is scarce a plantation which is not visited by a Baptist or Methodist missionary, and hardly a negro that does not hear the word of life from their lips. Of course I know more of the operations of my own, than of any other church, and shall therefore confine my remarks to it.

Whatever men may think or say as to the political, legal, constitutional, social, domestic or personal aspects of slavery, there can be no two opinions among those who profess and call themselves Christians, as to the duty of preaching the Gospel to the slave, and bringing him within the pale of the church. I am proud to say that Methodism has felt this claim from the beginning, and accepting this as its special field, and working with unwearied energy, has gathered therein its most precious harvest. From the sickly rice fields and deadly soil of the sea-island cotton on the coast of the Carolinas and Georgia, to the swamps of the Red and Ouachita rivers, over which malaria hangs as a canopy; along the banks of the Rio Grande and the Trinity; on the sugar estates of the Attakapas, and the cotton plantations of the Mississippi; wherever a negro quarter rises, and the people are toiling in furrow, brake or forest; there you will find my brethren, regardless of privation, hardship, cold, heat, hunger, pestilence and death; preaching the unsearchable riches of Christ, and in His name praying men to be reconciled to God. Our venerable bishops and junior preachers, editors and presiding elders, men of all ranks, ages and grades of culture, vie with each other in this, who shall be first and most efficient in planting the cross of Christ in the hearts of the children of Ethiopia. The saintly service is adorned with the names of such men as Capers, Andrew, Paine, Pierce and Early among the bishops; Wightman, Summers, McFerrin, Myers, McTyeire and Rosser among the editors; Keener, Jefferson Hamilton, Drake, Winans, Lovick Pierce, Crumley and Walker among the presiding elders. Through the devout and self-denying labors of these men and their fellows, hundreds of thousands of the sons of Ham have been turned from darkness to light—from the power of Satan unto God, and to-day have their faces Zionward; while myriads, ceasing at once to work and live, have died in sure hope of the inheritance which is incorruptible, undefiled, and that fadeth not away. All honor, say I, to these servants of the Master, who though poor are yet making many rich, and who esteem the reproach of Christ greater riches than the treasures of Egypt. "They are in their duty, be out of it who may."

You cannot live among the negroes without loving them; there is something so genuine, gentle and docile in their character. They overflow with sensibility, and refined feeling seems to be an instinct with them. They are the tenderest and most faithful nurses in the world, and they possess a knack for the management of children. There is something exquisite in an old "mauma's" manner of handling a babe. A Highlander was never more loyal to the head of his clan, than a family servant to a good master. The French have not a greater genius for cookery than the negroes.

Music seems their native element. I do not remember ever to have seen a negro that was not a sweet singer. Nothing can be finer than to hear a congregation of two or three thousand of them; as at a camp-meeting, with one heart and voice they pour forth in plaintive or triumphant strains of their own composition, hymns of praise to God. Never did the Girondists chant the Marseillaise with greater fervor than I have heard them sing the following:

"Jesus, my all, to heaven is gone,
And we shall gain the victory;
He whom I fix my hopes upon,
And we shall gain the victory;
His track I see, and I'll pursue
The narrow way, till him I view;
And we shall gain the victory!
March on, march on, and we shall gain the victory;
March on, and we shall gain the day."

Tears would come to the eyes as I listened to the plaintive sweetness of the music set to these simple words:

"There's a rest for the weary, there's a rest for the weary,
There's a rest for the weary, where they rest forevermore;

"In the fair fields of Eden, in the fair fields of Eden,
In the fair fields of Eden we'll rest forevermore.

"I've a Saviour over yonder, I've a Saviour over yonder,
In the fair fields of Eden we'll rest forevermore."

Or the following:

"Oh, brethren, will you meet me, oh, brethren, will you meet me,
Where sorrows never come?"

But the "Old Ship of Zion" is their greatest favorite:

"What ship is this that will take us all home?
Glory! hallelujah!
'Tis the old ship of Zion, oh, glory! hallelujah!
But are you sure she will be able to take us all home?
Yes, glory! hallelujah!
She's landed many a thousand, and she'll land as many more;
King Jesus is the captain! oh, glory! hallelujah!"

The unction with which the words, "King Jesus," are pronounced thrills you like an electric shock—for it is as a monarch, they most love to think of Him. Great tears are rolling down every sable cheek, while every eye is lit with joy, and you feel the sincerity of their rapturous shouts, "Oh, glory, hallelujah!"

I must be allowed to give some account of one of our dear old brethren, whom I shall call Uncle Nathan. He was a consistent and godly member of one of my societies, and being a good judge of human nature, chose my wife for his confidante. He was a venerable man, with a tall, erect figure, a dignified presence, a pleasing expression of countenance, his head crowned with hair white as wool. He completely won my wife's confidence and regard, and they were frequently closeted, discussing at length the matters which interested him. She ascertained from some quarter—not from himself, for he had never whispered it—that he was supplying two worthless scapegraces, sons of his former master, with money, which they spent in riotous living. She therefore admonished him on this point, saying:

"Uncle. Nathan, you have a wife and a large family dependent upon your exertions. You are wronging them by giving your hard-earned money to these wicked young men. It is only helping them in their evil courses."

"But, missis, they are the sons of my old master!"

"I can't help that, Nathan; it is wrong for you thus to squander your money. They are more able to work than you are, and you must leave them to themselves."

"Well, missis, if I must I must; so I'll tell you how it is. You see, my old master and me was married about the same time, and our first children was born purty near together; for my Sally and young master Jack is about of an age. My old master and me happened to be out in the field together just about that time, and he says to me, 'Nathan, we was children and boys together, and growed up side by side. Do you love me, Nathan?' He was always a good master to me, missis, and I always did love him, and so I told him yes. Then says he, 'Nathan, I want to make a compack with you. Your free papers, and your wife's, is lying in my drawer; they were made out the day your child was born, and you can have them whenever you please. Now, Nathan, I promise you most solemnly before God, that if I live longer than you do, I will look after your wife and child, and they shall never want for anything. And I want you to promise me that if you live longer than I do, you will do the same by mine.' So we took off our hats, missis, out there in the field, and took a hold of each other's hands, and promised each other solemnly before God and the holy angels. He was a rich man, and I was free; but I never left him. He lived a good while after that, and was always kind to me and mine. At last he died, and somehow or other the old missis and the boys got through with the property mighty fast, and so it was all clean gone. Now, missis, don't you think it is my duty to take care of them? They're poor, helpless things, and they haint no one else to look to." And the old man's voice was choked as big tears rolled from his eyes.

Sure enough, he did take care of them. Both those young men died drunkards, and their mother's grey hairs were brought down in sorrow to the grave. She would have died in the poor-house, and they would have been buried like paupers, but for Uncle Nathan, who fulfilled his word to the letter.

One of our old preachers had been a hereditary slaveholder in his early life. One of his servants was a zealous local preacher long before his conversion, and to the ministry of this man he owed his awakening. Some time after he joined the church, Jake said to him:

"Mass Kitty,* I think you's called to preach, and

* Kitty is the negro abbreviation of Christopher.

I'se gwine to give out an appintment for you at de old schoolhouse, to hole forf nex Sunday arternoon a week."

The master protested his inability to preach, and endeavored in every way to evade the responsibility; but Jake was inflexible.

"De Lord hears prayer: claim de promise, Mass Kitty," said he. "Don't be afeard; open your mout and de Lord 'll fill it. 'Out of de mout of babes and suckling he's ordained praise.'"

At length it was arranged that the master should make the effort; but Jake was to sit behind him in the pulpit, and in case the former broke down, the latter was to rise and finish the discourse. Nerved for the trial by their common devotional exercises, the master was succeeding very well with his sermon, when suddenly, self-consciousness obtruded itself, and as he thought where he was and what he was doing, his heart failed, he stammered and turned pale. Casting an imploring look at Jake, he said, in a tremulous voice:

"I must stop; do get up and conclude."

The servant had been listening with intense interest, breathing frequent and fervent prayers for his master's success, until now his sympathies were wrought up to the highest pitch. Springing to his feet, he slapped his master on the shoulder, exclaim-ng, at the top of his voice:

"Go on, Mass Kitty—go on. Ye preach right well, ye do, considering it's nobody but you!"

The master, feeling it to be his duty to preach, set his temporal affairs in order, manumitted his slaves, and entered the Itineracy. After an absence of two years, he returned to visit the neighborhood, and the first man he met on the road was Jake, who had remained on "the old stamping ground." The embraces of the old friends were hearty and affectionate. The bridle fell from the rider's hand, and he leaned forward on the horse's neck, while Jake's arm was about him, and his own around Jake, as they talked over the events that had occurred since they parted. Finally, the master said, his voice trembling with religious emotion:

"Well, Jake, my brother, how do you come on down at the old schoolhouse? You sing and pray as much as ever, and get happy in prospect of immortality and eternal life?"

This appeal touched the negro in his tenderest part. Straightening himself, while his face glowed with unspeakable delight, he cried with vehemence:

"Take care your horse, Mass Kitty—take care your horse, or he'll be skeert, for I feel the shout a coming." And having given this timely warning, he clapped his hands in a jubilant shout, "Glory to God—yes, I'm on my journey home."

Negroes are rather fond of litigation, and church

trials are frequent among them. I recollect one where I presided. A bright, strapping fellow, himself not a member of the church, had preferred charges of unchaste conduct against one of my members, a damsel, who had otherwise a good report. Charges and specifications were served in due form, the time fixed for the investigation, the colored officiary was summoned and the issue made. Jim, who was the dining-room servant of a distinguished lawyer, and had picked up some scraps of law, appeared himself as prosecutor; Aunt Nancy, the girl's mother, sat by the side of her child.

"Aunt Nancy," said I, "have you counsel, or do you wish for any?"

"No, sir," she replied; "I trust in de character of my child, and in King Jesus; I'm sure that he'll bring out all for de best."

It appeared, in evidence, that Jim, the plaintiff, had been a persistent suitor for the hand of Emily, the defendant; she had refused his presence, refused to hearken to his importunity, and he had vowed to ruin her character. Witnesses for the prosecution were skillfully examined by Jim, who ventilated rumors and hinted suspicions against the girl, but nothing more, and it became partly evident that the whole affair was instigated by malice and supported by falsehood; nevertheless, Jim's effrontery in the examination of witnesses and in his argument, would have done credit to a "New York Shyster." * It was now Nancy's turn.

"Have you anything to say?" I asked. "Not much," replied the infirm old woman, as she rose and stood, one hand leaning on her staff, the other on the shoulder of her child. "All you brevren know me, and have knowed me for many a year, and ye know that I would not lie. Now listen to what I'm gwine to say: Dis is my dorter, de only child left out ov ten; de rest, bless de Lord, is safe in de kingdom, whar dey shall go out no more forever. Most of you are fathers and you know what it is to love a child; that is, you know all that men can know. But you can't begin to know what a woman feels for her darling. This is my child, and she has slept in my bosom every night since she was born; she is eighteen now. She joined the church several years ago. She's a consistent Christian, and is walking hand in hand with me on the road that leads to the land of everlasting rest. I've watched her as an old hen, tied to a stake, watches her only chicken. I know her through and through, and I know that these things that Jim has brought against her are mean, dirty lies. Jim's smart, but not as smart as he thinks he is; for the liar will be caught in his own

* A class of ghouls, self-styled lawyers, haunting the "Tombs and practising in the Police Courts held in that great prison.

trap, and 'the wicked shall be turned into hell with all the nations that forget God.' Yes, Jim, you've lied, and done the dirtiest thing that ever a man could try to do: tried to take away the character of one that you knew was an innocent and virtuous girl. You haven't proved a single thing against my child, and you couldn't. The devil put you up to this revenge, and if you don't look out, he'll get you for your pains. But, Jim, I won't curse you, though you've tried to break my heart. I forgive you, you poor miserable sinner, because the Bible says: 'Be not overcome of evil, but overcome evil with good.' I'll pray for you, Jim; but I never want to see you again in this world, for you've done my child a great wrong. A lie travels faster and further than the truth, and many a one will hear of your charge that won't hear that it wasn't sustained. A good reputation is more precious to a woman than diamonds. Though I don't want to see you again in this world, Jim, I hope we'll meet in Heaven." Jim couldn't stand this; and, as the old woman sat down, burst into tears, fell upon his knees, and confessed that the whole story was an infamous slander, vowing that from that time forth, he would try to be a Christian, that he might at last meet her on Canaan's happy shore.

If I have succeeded in reproducing feebly the old woman's speech, the reader will observe the illustration of a remarkable fact: the power of deep, excited feeling to correct the language, elevate the style, and impart a force and vividness of expression otherwise impossible.

Whatever may be the issue of the slavery agitation, one thing is certain, and upon this I must be permitted to speak an earnest word. The duties of the white race toward the negro, are not duly recognized. It were a truism to affirm that he is a human being; but it would not be impertinent to ask if he is treated as one. The first and most imperative demand which justice makes of the people of the southern States is the passage of laws forbidding the separation of man and wife, of parents and children. Such rending asunder of the holiest bonds of our nature should not be allowed, cannot without incurring the dread anathema of a Christian civilization and the righteous indignation of God. Let no embittered sectional controversy, let no exciting political contest be used as an excuse to delay action, or hinder this consummation so devoutly to be wished. Loyalty to the South, to its sentiments, reason, conscience, demands the definite legal recognition of the negro as a human being, and of his family as sacred and inviolate. Worthy of immortal honor shall those men be that compass this end!

If I turn from the other end of the Union to this, I see the negro a Pariah, supine beneath the ban of caste, stricken by the contempt, or stolid from the indifference of the greater portion of the community. He is degraded by the vulgar and abominable appellation—"nigger." If he take a seat in a car or stage, his white fellow-passengers change their places with eager haste, avoiding contact with him as if his presence brought loathsome contagion.* He is shunned as a thing unclean. If a professed friend of his race summon sufficient moral courage to shake hands with him, there is apt to be a condescension in the act, which is in itself an insult; and if you watch the hand-shakers narrowly, you will probably observe the white man slily wiping his dextral extension as if the black man's had left a stain upon it. The negro is, as I have said, a being of peculiarly fine sensibilities; indeed, I presume I might say with justice, possessing the finest sensibilities of any race upon earth in its condition. Without *sympathy*, he is a cypher or worse; he must be educated through his genial and generous affections, his rights

One is always reminded upon such occasions of the justice of Sidney Smith's witty reply to Mr. Webster. "How is it, Mr. Webster," said the reverend philosopher, "that the Americans in the free States treat the negroes so badly?" Mr. Webster, willing to waive the discussion of the subject, answered jocosely, "The truth is, we can hardly do otherwise, they have such a bad smell." "A great people like yours," replied Smith, "should not be turned aside from justice and be led by the nose in that way."

must be guaranteed to him, not grudgingly or of necessity, but with hearty warmth and benignant kindness. It will be some time before he is raised to the level of a perfect human being—indeed, before any of us reach that enviable station.—Meanwhile let every man, whether Abolitionist, Conservative or Fire-eater, bear in mind that this nation owes an infinite debt to the negro, and that it is our solemn duty to do what in our power lies, not by idle boast or braggart vaunt, fierce tirade or empty profession, but by earnest, affectionate good will and effort to secure his temporal and eternal welfare.

CHAPTER XXIII.

FLIGHT FOR LIFE.

I WENT to the South in pursuit of health and strength, but it will not require much sagacity to perceive from the hints which have been given of my way of life, that I did not find them. It was necessary for me several times to quit home, that I might overcome languor and recruit my energies in the more bracing atmosphere of the North.

The approach of summer was always as the coming of a strong man armed, and frequently I was compelled to flee almost for life. Lassitude, which often amounted to utter prostration, prevented my enjoyment of that season so delicious on our gulf coast, which poets have ever been wont to sing, and which none of them have more happily described than Solomon:

"Lo, the winter is past, the rain is over and gone.

"The flowers appear on the earth; the time of the singing of birds is come, and the voice of the turtle is heard in our land.

"The fig-tree putteth forth her green figs, and the vines with the tender grape give a good smell."

In the course of one of my northward flights which occurred in the spring of 1850, I formed some acquaintances and revived some old associations, the reminiscence of which will ever be grateful. I made the voyage from New Orleans to St. Louis in company with a large number of the prominent ministers of our church, who were on their way to attend a session of the General Conference to assemble in the last named place. The man of the party in whom I felt the deepest interest, was the venerable Dr. William Winans, who joined us at Natchez.

An Englishman, accustomed to the trim white neck-tie, the cassock vest and shiny black suit of the professional costume at home, could scarce have guessed from his appearance, that the old man was a preacher. The commanding height of his large muscular figure, was surmounted by a broad-brimmed white beaver, and he was clad in brown jeans, while his throat had not the slightest covering except the collar of his shirt. You saw at a glance that he was a backwoodsman, but one of the finest type. His face was bronzed by exposure and withal seamed with countless wrinkles. As you looked at the lines about his mouth, you were in doubt whether iron resolution or genial kindness were the prevailing expression, but as you caught the warm sunny light, which beamed from his rather small grey eyes, you felt that the casting vote was given in favor of the latter. I at once devoted myself to this veteran, whose name had been familiar as a household word from infancy, and we were inseparable for the rest of the voyage. I have seldom enjoyed a week more than that, notwithstanding it was a cholera season on the Mississippi, and that the pestilence was daily numbering some of our fellow-passengers as its victims. Day by day the boat would lie to and be made fast to the shore, while one or more rude boxes, hastily constructed by the boat's carpenter, were carried to land, a pit hollowed out, the burial service read, and they were left to return to the dust from whence they were taken.

I suppose that I must have a constitutional insusceptibility to epidemic diseases; at all events, this close neighborhood of the plague did not affect my regained appetite, nor interfere with the delight I experienced in the society of the pioneer preacher. He had looked upon death so often and in so many awful forms, that he did not dread it now; our conversation, therefore, was scarce suspended except for visits to the sick or to attend the burials, or when the tolling bell announced that another spirit had departed. He had begun life as a blacksmith, in the Northwestern Territory, and in time became one of Bishop Asbury's preachers. There was hardly an inhabited nook or corner in the great valley of the

West, which he had not visited to proclaim the glad tidings; but his special work had lain in the newly opened plantations of the Southwest. His life had been a hard one, but his manners were quiet and refined, showing that labor and hardship had not crisped or soured his temper. His voice was peculiarly sweet and soft, and I shall never forget the way in which he would say, "My son." "Why do you not wear a neckerchief, doctor?" "Because it gave me the bronchitis; I wore one when I came as a young man into the settled and civilized parts of the country, but discovered before long, that it was a halter which was choking me; so I tore it off and threw it away. When I married, my wife thought that a man could hardly be a minister, unless he wore a neckerchief; to please her, I put it on again, but was not three months older, when I discovered that my throat was becoming seriously affected, and that I must either give up my voice or my cravat. It is my opinion that these starched, stiff choke-rags which clergymen call the badge of their profession, together with reading sermons, are the cause of the throat disease, styled the minister's complaint, and I am sure that if they would pitch them to the dogs, and preach off-hand, you would never hear of another case of bronchitis in the pulpit." He mentioned two instances which illustrate the impressible nature of young men, and indicate the origin of many of the bad habits of public speakers. One of his presiding elders, not knowing what to do with his right hand while preaching, was accustomed to place it behind him, and afford it occupation in twisting off the buttons from the back of his coat. Another of his seniors was a little hard of hearing, and to catch the sound of his own voice more distinctly, would put his right hand around his ear, thus forming a concave mirror to collect the reverberated sound.

Young Winans, from sheer admiration for these his elders and betters, quite unconsciously adopted these pleasing and graceful attitudes and occupations, and when admonished by some judicious friends, could scarcely believe that he had fallen into such practices it required the care of months to desist from.

As we sat upon the hurricane deck of our proud steamer at sunset, or deep in the night, talking of old times, of the hardships which our men endured, and of the labors which they performed, my breast glowed with pride at the thought that I was counted worthy to belong to an army which had numbered such heroes in its ranks. It is impossible to exaggerate either their toils, their sufferings, or their successes. I cannot state the case better than in using the language of a friend.* "When Methodism began to spread in America, converts rapidly multiplied under

* The Rev. J. B. Hagany, in his article on John Wesley, in "Harper's Magazine."

the missionaries sent out by Wesley, and the necessity for more preachers was greater than the supply. Almost anything that offered was accepted. Few had any acquaintance with English grammar, others could not write their names, and some could scarcely read. Good lungs, a loose tongue, personal piety, zeal that could dare the rigors of a northern winter, or the ardor of a southern sun, joined to about as much theological knowledge as that a man must mend, or the devil will away with him, made up the sum total necessary to a beginning. Thus equipped and mounted on horseback, these men penetrated every State and territory of the land, enduring the hardest fare, sleeping in the woods, chased by wolves, pounced on by panthers, laughed at, pelted with rotten eggs, stoned and beaten by the motley crews who composed their congregations. Yet they were successful in thousands of real conversions. Following the tide of emigration westward, their plain preaching kept the religious sentiment alive, and thus laid a sure foundation for civil government in the western mind, which otherwise had degenerated to the savage State. It is illustrative of the vital power of the Gospel, that its elementary truths, earnestly delivered by men who knew no more of general literature than the horses they rode, led the worst classes of society from the most dissolute to the most moral and orderly habits of life. Francis Asbury was the ruling spirit among the American Methodists; their first bishop, with a continent for a diocese, and, for labors, sufferings and success, unsurpassed by any name in modern Christianity. Washington was not better entitled to be called the father of his country than Francis Asbury its apostle."

Poor and unlearned as these men were, they were yet, according to their means, the munificent patrons of learning; for by their gifts and energy our schools and colleges were established. Many of them became themselves admirable scholars, and made an ample provision for the future, that their successors should not want the means of liberal education. They were generous with the little money which they received, as they were magnanimous in the use of health and life. Of them it might be said, what the great apostle spake of himself: "In all things they approved themselves the ministers of God; in much patience, in afflictions, in necessities, in distresses, in stripes, in imprisonments, in tumults, in labors, in watchings, in fastings; by pureness, by long suffering, by kindness, by the Holy Ghost, by love unfeigned, by the word of truth, by the power of God, by the armor of righteousness on the right hand, and, on the left, by honor and dishonor; by evil report and good report: as deceivers, and yet true; as unknown, and yet well known; as dying, and behold they live; as chastened, and not killed; as sorrowful, yet always rejoicing·

as poor, yet making many rich; as having nothing, and yet possessing all things."

As setting forth the more cheerful side of their character, I cannot resist the temptation to use the language of another of my friends, the Rev. Dr. Stevens, whose history of Methodism is probably the most brilliant production in literature to which the mind of our church has yet given birth. "Notwithstanding their many hardships, the early Methodist preachers were notable as a cheerful, if not, indeed, a humorous class of men. Their hopeful theology, their continual success, their conscious self-sacrifice for the good of others, the great variety of characters they met in their travels, and their habit of self-accommodation to all, gave them an ease, a *bonhomie*, which often took the form of jocose humor; and the occasional morbid minds among them could hardly resist the infectious example of their happier brethren. While they were as earnest as men about to meet death, and full of the tenderness which could 'weep with those who wept,' no men could better 'rejoice with those who rejoiced.' They were usually the best story-tellers on their long circuits, and of course had abundance of their own adventures to relate at the hearths and tables of their hosts. Not a few of them became noted as wits, in the best sense of the term, and were by their repartees, as well as their courage and religious earnestness, a terror to evil-doers. The American Methodist preachers were the greatest wits of the last century in the New World; the fact is historical, whether it be esteemed creditable or not; and, rightly considered, it is far from discreditable. If few men could better relish innocent humor, few were more devout, few greater laborers or greater sufferers."

It is not unusual for the polite literature of the time to sneer at, or to satirize and caricature the Christian ministry. I do not remember the worthy portraiture of a single preacher of righteousness in the writings of Mr. Thackeray, or Mr. Dickens, or in those of Mr. George W. Curtis, one of our own rising young authors. They have favored the world with pictures of the Stigginses, Chadbands, Honeymans, Creamcheeses, and Peewees of their acquaintance: perhaps they have been so unfortunate as to possess none other. If so, I am sorry for them. But let me assure them, and all who think as they seem to think, that while there may be unworthy members of the clerical profession; for patient toil and disinterested labor, for self-sacrifice extending through life, for brave and cheerful performance of duty, that profession stands unrivalled, unapproached in the annals of the world. I submit, if it be fair in art, to represent a class by an exception, or to stigmatize those, who, notwithstanding all that has been written against priestcraft, the tyranny and superstition of the clergy, have, nevertheless, been in every age the best friends of their kind, and in no age more truly than in our own.

Shall the hive be denounced because it contains solitary drones? or the entire literary profession held up to ridicule, because it may happen to have snobs or tuft-hunters, or rogues in its ranks? I claim for my brethren no exclusive sanctity; I ask no tribute for them which is not justified by their courage, honor, fidelity, their love of man, and fear of God; and the worst wish I cherish for those who have been, unconsciously or not, their detractors, is, that they may die as happily. "Our people die well," said Mr. Wesley. And his own last words, echoed by thousands of his sons in the Gospel on both sides of the Atlantic, in their final hour, were, "The best of all is, God is with us."

My venerable friend, Dr. Winans, closed his long and eventful career two years ago, while I was abroad. I have never learned the particulars of his death, only this, that his end was peace.

My various efforts to regain health while residing in the South were futile, and at length, toward the close of a six years' residence there, in the summer of 1853, the physicians assured me that I had no alternative but to leave the country or die. The climate had made fearful inroads upon my system, my physique was utterly prostrated, and my mind almost a wreck. I could barely drag one foot after the other, and it was with difficulty that I could remember my own name. With a sad and heavy heart I turned my back upon my adopted home, and by slow and easy stages, with my wife and three little children, reached New York.

September 26th, 1853.—This is the thirtieth anniversary of my birth-day, and it closes the first ten years of my life as a Methodist Preacher. The cry of a new-born babe, my fourth child, is heard in the house, and I feel myself almost as weak and helpless as that infant. In that sea of waters which threatens to ingulf me, there is nothing to which I can cling but the word of Him who hath said:

"Behold the fowls of the air: for they sow not, neither do they reap, nor gather into barns; yet your heavenly Father feedeth them. Are ye not much better than they? Consider the lilies of the field, how they grow; they toil not, neither do they spin: and yet I say unto you, that even Solomon in all his glory was not arrayed like one of these. Wherefore, if God so clothe the grass of the field, which to-day is, and to-morrow is cast into the oven, shall he not much more clothe you, O ye of little faith? Take therefore no thought for the morrow; for the morrow shall take thought for the things of itself Sufficient unto the day is the evil thereof."

THE END.

THE STANDARD FRENCH CLASSICS.

II.

Pascal's Provincial Letters.

This will be the finest edition of the PROVINCIALS ever published in English. It contains a very eloquent Life of Pascal; a fine Essay on his Genius as a Writer and Moralist, by Villemain; a copious historical Introduction, giving an account of the Port-Royal Controversy out of which the Letters sprang; a Bibliographical Notice of all books treating of Pascal's Life and Writings; and the Letters in the translation of Rev. Mr. M'Crie.

"Pascal has borne the Christian Religion the greatest of human testimonies."—VILLEMAIN.

"That miracle of universal genius."—SIR WM. HAMILTON.

III. IV. V. VI.

The Complete Works of Montaigne.

This edition of Montaigne's Works is a reproduction, with corrections and important additions, of Mr. Wm. Hazlitt's edition, published by Templeman in London. Hitherto, the edition of Mr. Hazlitt has been the best in the English language. Our edition will be incomparably superior to his in typography, besides being more complete and more correct. Our editor and the Cambridge printers have verified the classical quotations of Montaigne (nearly three thousand in number), new letters of Montaigne have been added, bibliographical and critical notices have been extended, and the fourth volume prefaced with a biography of Montaigne (200 pages long) abridged especially for this edition from the recent work of Mr. Bayle St. John. This edition will also contain a portrait and copious Index. For beauty of typography, convenience of form, correctness and completeness, the publishers can confidently promise an unequalled edition of the quaint old Gascon Essayist.

Price per Volume in Cloth,	. . . .	**$1 25**
" "	**Sheep, library style,** . . .	**1 50**
" "	**Half calf, gilt or antique,** .	**2 25**

THE STANDARD FRENCH CLASSICS.

X.

Voltaire's Henriade

AND SOME OTHER POEMS.

It is not necessary to say anything about the Henriade, which has been a text-book in half the schools of the land. We reproduce the once famous but almost forgotten translation by Lockman, and from the latest French editions an abundance of historical notes are added.

XI.

The Thoughts of Pascal.

This volume will be a new translation of the Thoughts, embracing all the discoveries recently made in France by an examination of Pascal's MSS.

XII.

The Martyrs of Chateaubriand.

In due time will follow the Works of Rabelais, Molière, Montesquieu, Massillon, Bossuet, Le Sage, Corneille, La Fontaine, Racine, St. Pierre, etc.

We would respectfully call attention to two points, in these editions of the French Classics:—The translations are either new or carefully revised according to the best French editions; and the first volume of each author's works contains a great abundance of introductory matter of the best quality.

We trust that in this great and expensive enterprise of reproducing in convenient and attractive form the classical literature of a great people, we shall meet with encouragement from American scholars and readers.

The whole Series will be uniform in price and style with our editions of the British Classics, viz.:

Price in Cloth,	$1 25
" Sheep, library style,	1 50
" Half calf, gilt or antique,	2 25

W. H. Tinson, Printer and Stereotyper 43 & 45 Centre St., N. Y.

THE

STANDARD FEMALE NOVELISTS.

THE WORKS OF JANE AUSTEN, Comprising "Pride and Prejudice," "Sense and Sensibility," "Mansfield Park," "Northanger Abbey," "Emma," and "Persuasion." First American edition. With steel vignettes. Complete in 4 vols., 12mo.

Price in Cloth, $4 00; *Sheep, library style*, $5 00; *Half calf, extra or antique*, $8 00.

THE WORKS OF HANNAH MORE, Comprising "Cœlebs in Search of a Wife," and her Tales and Allegories complete. With portrait on steel. 2 vols., 12mo.

Price, in Cloth, $2 00; *Sheep, library style*, $2 50; *Half calf, extra or antique*, $4 00.

THE WORKS OF JANE PORTER, Comprising "The Scottish Chiefs," and "Thaddeus of Warsaw." With steel portrait. 2 vols., 12mo.

Price in Cloth, $2 00; *Sheep, library style*, $2 50; *Half calf, extra or antique*, $4 00.

THE WORKS OF ANNE RADCLIFFE, Comprising "The Mysteries of Eudolpho," and "Romance of the Forest." With steel portrait. 2 vols., 12mo.

Price in Cloth, $2 00; *Sheep, library style*, $2 50; *Half calf, extra or antique*, $4 00.

THE WORKS OF CHARLOTTE BRONTE (Currer Bell), Comprising "Jane Eyre," "Shirley," and "Villette." Complete in 3 vols., 12mo.

Price in Cloth, $3 00; *Sheep, library style*, $3 75; *Half calf, extra or antique*, $6 00.

EVELINA; or, The History of a Young Lady's Introduction to the World. By Frances Burney (Mme. d'Arblay). With a Life of the Author by T. B. Macaulay. 12mo.

Price in Cloth, $1 00; *Sheep, library style*, $1 25; *Half calf, extra or antique*, $2 00.

CORINNE; or, Italy. By Madame de Stael. Translated by Isabel Hill, with Metrical Versions of the Odes by L. E. Landon 12mo.

Price in Cloth, $1 00; *Sheep, library style*, $1 25; *Half calf, extra or antique*, $2 00.

*** The above will be sent by mail, post-paid, on receipt of price

W. H. Tinson, Printer and Stereotyper, 43 & 45 Centre St., N. Y

W. H. Tinson Printer and Stereotyper, 43 & 45 Centre St. N. Y.

GOOD AND POPULAR BOOKS,

PUBLISHED BY DERBY & JACKSON.

TEN YEARS OF PREACHER LIFE. By Rev. W. H. MILBURN. 12mo.	$1 00
RIFLE, AXE AND SADDLEBAGS. " " " 12mo.	1 00
GREECE AND THE GOLDEN HORN. By Rev. STEPHEN OLIN. 12mo.	1 00
TRAVELS IN EGYPT AND THE HOLY LAND. By STEPHENS. 8vo.	2 00
CAPTAIN COOK'S VOYAGES ROUND THE WORLD. 12mo.......	1 00
PICTORIAL LIFE OF BENJAMIN FRANKLIN. 8vo.............	2 00
RANDALL'S LIFE OF THOMAS JEFFERSON. 3 vols. 8vo.	7 50
BUNYAN'S PILGRIM'S PROGRESS. 12mo........	1 00
BUNYAN'S HOLY WAR. 12mo..................................	1 00
FOX'S BOOK OF MARTYRS. 12mo........	1 00
DODDRIDGE'S RISE AND PROGRESS OF RELIGION. 12mo....	1 00
BAXTER'S SAINTS' REST. 12mo.	1 00
TAYLOR'S HOLY LIVING. 12mo.................................	[illegible]
THE SCOTTISH CHIEFS. By JANE PORTER. 12mo........	[illegible]
THADDEUS OF WARSAW. " " 12mo....................	1 00
ADVENTURES OF DON QUIXOTE. 12mo.........................	1 00
ARABIAN NIGHTS' ENTERTAINMENTS. 12mo.......	1 00
ADVENTURES OF ROBINSON CRUSOE. 12mo.....................	1 00
SWISS FAMILY ROBINSON. 12mo.	1 00
ÆSOP'S FABLES, with the Morals attached. 12mo.	1 00
VICAR OF WAKEFIELD and *RASSELAS.* (Two in one.)	1 00
PAUL AND VIRGINIA and *EXILES OF SIBERIA.* (Two in one.)..	1 00
RELIGIOUS COURTSHIP and *GREAT PLAGUE.* By DE FOE.	1 00
CŒLEBS IN SEARCH OF A WIFE. 12mo........................	1 00
HANNAH MORE'S TALES AND ALLEGORIES. 12mo............	1 00
THOUGHTS AND ESSAYS OF JOHN FORSTER. 12mo.	1 00
THE ESSAYS OF ELIA. By CHARLES LAMB. 12mo.	1 00
JOHNSON'S LIVES OF THE POETS. 2 vols. 12mo..................	2 50
THE SPECTATOR. By JOSEPH ADDISON. 2 vols. 12mo.	2 50
THE TATTLER AND GUARDIAN. By ADDISON and STEELE.....	2 00
WIRT'S LIFE OF PATRICK HENRY. 12mo......................	1 00
SIMMS' LIFE OF GENERAL MARION. 12mo........	1 00
WALKER'S LIFE OF GENERAL JACKSON. 12mo.....	1 00
LIFE AND CHOICE WORKS OF ISAAC WATTS. 12mo...........	1 25
LAYARD'S POPULAR DISCOVERIES AT NINEVEH. 12mo.......	1 00
FROST'S INDIAN BATTLES AND CAPTIVITIES. 12mo..........	1 00
WORKS OF OLIVER GOLDSMITH. 4 vols. 12mo.	5 00
WORKS OF CHARLES LAMB. 5 vols. 12mo.......................	6 25
BOSWELL'S LIFE OF DR. JOHNSON. 4 vols. 12mo.	5 00
ROLLIN'S ANCIENT HISTORY. 2 vols. 8vo..................	4 00
PLUTARCH'S LIVES OF THE ANCIENTS. 8vo....................	2 00

Either of the above sent by mail, post-paid, on receipt of Price. A liberal Discount to Preachers and Agents. Address

DERBY & JACKSON,

119 NASSAU STREET, NEW YORK.